"Trust me. I will not harm

Con stilled, praying Charlott

"Very well." Once again, s~~he seemed as i~~f she was working out her path as she spoke.

He threaded their way through the crowd to the French
windows closest to them. Turning right, they walked to the
end of the terrace, and there, in the shadows where no one
could see them, he placed his hands on her small waist. "I
want to kiss you. Like we did before."

She would not know that it had been years since he'd experienced such an innocent kiss, and the innocence had
been on his part.

Charlotte stared at him for a moment, as if she would
discover something she didn't know. "Yes."

He lowered his head, and their lips touched. He moved
his mouth over hers, waiting for her to return the caress,
then she placed her hands on his cheeks, raised up, and
kissed him back. The purity in her touch almost brought
him to his knees.

"Thank you." Con touched his forehead to hers.

Even in the dark, he could see her blush. "You're welcome."

He brushed his mouth across hers again. "We should go
back now."

Charlotte hadn't known what to expect, but it was not a
kiss as sweet as Kenilworth's. Once, she had seen Merton
kiss Dotty. That kiss had been demanding and full of
passion. If Kenilworth had attempted anything like that,
Charlotte would have hit him and run. Yet now, now that
she had felt his lips on hers again and his hands tightening
around her waist, she almost looked forward to the other
type of kiss . . .

Books by Ella Quinn

The Marriage Game

THE SEDUCTION OF LADY PHOEBE

THE SECRET LIFE OF MISS ANNA MARSH

THE TEMPTATION OF LADY SERENA

DESIRING LADY CARO

ENTICING MISS EUGENIE VILLARET

A KISS FOR LADY MARY

LADY BERESFORD'S LOVER

MISS FEATHERTON'S CHRISTMAS PRINCE

The Worthingtons

THREE WEEKS TO WED

WHEN A MARQUIS CHOOSES A BRIDE

IT STARTED WITH A KISS

THE MARQUIS AND I

Novellas

MADELEINE'S CHRISTMAS WISH

THE SECOND TIME AROUND

Published by Kensington Publishing Corporation

The MARQUIS And I

ELLA QUINN

ZEBRA BOOKS
KENSINGTON PUBLISHING CORP.
http://www.kensingtonbooks.com

ZEBRA BOOKS are published by

Kensington Publishing Corp.
119 West 40th Street
New York, NY 10018

All Kensington titles, imprints, and distributed lines are available at special quantity discounts for bulk purchases for sales promotion, premiums, fund-raising, educational, or institutional use.

Special book excerpts or customized printings can also be created to fit specific needs. For details, write or phone the office of the Kensington Sales Manager: Attn.: Sales Department. Kensington Publishing Corp., 119 West 40th Street, New York, NY 10018. Phone: 1-800-221-2647.

Zebra and the Z logo Reg. U.S. Pat. & TM Off.

First Printing: March 2018
ISBN-13: 978-1-4201-4516-8
ISBN-10: 1-4201-4516-9

eISBN-13: 978-1-4201-4517-5
eISBN-10: 1-4201-4517-7

10 9 8 7 6 5 4 3 2 1

Printed in the United States of America

For my granddaughters, Josephine and Vivienne.
You are the lights of my life.

And to my wonderful husband,
who puts up with living with an author.
Thank you, sweetheart.

ACKNOWLEDGMENTS

Anyone involved in publishing knows it takes a team effort to get a book from that inkling in an author's head to the printed or digital page. I'd like to thank my beta readers, Jenna, Doreen, and Margaret for their comments and suggestions. To my agents, Deidre Knight and Janna Bonikowski, for helping me think through parts of this book and for their advice for Charlotte not to give in too easily. I'm quite sure Kenilworth didn't like it, but oh, well.

To my wonderful editor, John Scognamiglio, who loves my books enough to contract them for Kensington. To the Kensington team, Vida, Jane, and Lauren who do such a tremendous job of publicity. And to the copy-editors who find all the niggling mistakes I never am able to see.

I'd also like to thank the lovely Tessa Dare for the ideas she gave me. Last, but certainly not least, to my readers. Without you, none of this would be worth it. Thank you from the bottom of my heart for loving my stories!

I love to hear from my readers, so feel free to contact me on my website or on Facebook if you have questions. Those links and my newsletter link can be found at www.ellaquinnauthor.com.

On to the next book!

Ella

Chapter One

Prickles of fear ran down Lady Charlotte Carpenter's spine, and she fought back the gorge rising in her throat. Inside her gloves her hands grew damp.

Not even as a child when she was afraid of thunder had she been so terrified. This must be what her sister Grace and her friend Dotty had felt when they were abducted. Charlotte drew a shaky breath. Well, they had survived and so would she.

She had been shoved roughly into the coach, hitting her knees on the door edge and almost falling to the floor. Fortunately, her basket had broken her descent before meaty hands had grabbed her, placing her none too gently on the forward-facing seat.

"Don't give us no trouble, and we won't hurt ye," the ruffian across from her had said.

Not looking up, she'd nodded.

After her sister had been kidnapped, Mattheus, the Earl of Worthington, her brother-in-law and guardian, had ensured that she, Louisa, her sister—actually her sister-in-law, yet Charlotte considered all her sisters-in-law sisters—who had just wed, and Augusta their sister who was three years younger than Charlotte and Louisa, had been given lessons on how to protect themselves and what to do if something like this happened to them.

All she could do was trust her lessons would stand in her good stead and remember all she had been taught. She should concentrate on that instead of panicking. Yet for what seemed like an eternity, her mind refused to cooperate. Closing her eyes, she focused on gathering her scattered wits.

Gradually, pieces of what she had learned began coming back to her. The first thing she had been taught was to let the curs believe she was under their control. That was supposed to lull them into thinking she would not try to escape. Under the circumstances, that wasn't very hard to do. She *was* under their control. Both the men were much stronger than her, making escape more difficult.

Second, she was to take inventory of what she had that could help her flee their control. That should make her feel better. She had a dagger strapped to her leg. Although she needed much more practice to be able to draw it out properly. Her basket held a pistol made just for her—loaded—and with extra bullets and powder. Unfortunately, her kitten, Collette, was in the basket as well. But she was in the harness and lead Charlotte had fashioned for the cat. Both items would serve her well if she had to abandon the basket. She tightened her hands on the wicker handle.

And the third part of the plan was to think of a way to escape. That might be a little more difficult. She had not intended to go farther than across the square to Worthington House; therefore, she had no money. Even if she did manage to get away from the brutes, she wouldn't get very far without funds. On the other hand, she knew how to tool a carriage, so she might be able to drive the coach if she could steal it.

Her breathing steadied and she began to feel a little more in control. As long as she ignored the brutes who had kidnapped her, that is.

A friend of Matt's had also taught her and her sister to pick a lock. It might take her a while, but she was sure she could do it if she had to.

She was wearing sensible leather half boots, and a twill walking gown, practical and sturdy enough not to fall apart if she had to go traipsing across the country.

There, already her heart had stopped beating as if it would fly out of her chest.

"Got any victuals in that basket of yourn?" the man across from her asked.

Oh, Lord, Collette! Who knew what they'd do to her kitten. Charlotte couldn't let them look in the basket. "No. I was going to fetch some things."

He leaned back against the worn cushions again, and she resisted the urge to breathe a sigh of relief.

Her abductors were dressed neatly, in a middling sort of way, even if they didn't speak like one would expect. They wore breeches instead of pantaloons, and Belcher scarves rather than cravats. At least they didn't smell or appear overly dirty. That was helpful as her stomach was still a mass of knots. It wouldn't take much to make her ill.

If she only knew in what direction they were traveling it might help her form a scheme to escape.

A few minutes later, a large estate situated on a hill caught her attention. "What is the building over there?"

The kidnapper across from her slammed the shade down. "None of yer business is what it is."

"Shut yer gob, Dan. We ain't supposed to talk to her." Next to her the other scoundrel shoved his chin forward as if daring Dan to defy him.

"An whatcha think the mort's goin' ta do? Jump out and

run for help?" The man called Dan sneered. "She'd haf ta get away from both of us. I only closed it so no one could see inside."

Charlotte's cheek felt as if it was burning, as if the black-guard next to her was staring at her face, but she did not dare return his gaze.

"We got our orders," the man next to her said. "I don't need you ta put us aground."

Dan shrugged, and the burning feeling went away.

She had no idea how long they had been traveling, but surely they would stop to change horses soon. Perhaps then she could find someone to help her. She wondered how her kitten was doing, but she didn't dare show any interest in the basket. The two villains would be bound to notice, then they would find the pistol and her cat.

The men had once more lapsed into silence. Dan's eyelids drifted shut, but she doubted the other man would be so lax. Not that she could have jumped out of the coach in any event. The traffic had finally lessened, and they were moving along at a faster, steadier pace.

Sometime later, Dan's foot pushed against her shoe. She moved her leg to give him more room, but the foot followed.

Suddenly, he yelped, and when she sneaked a look he was holding on to his knee. The other man must have kicked him. "What'd ye do that fer?"

"Leave the mort alone," the blackguard next to her growled. "No talking. No touching."

She should be relieved. Someone obviously wanted her unharmed. Yet that begged the question of who could have ordered her abduction? She was positive that she had not made any enemies. Matt kept such a careful eye on her, no fortune hunters had been allowed within several yards of her or Louisa.

She gave an imperceptible shudder. Going down that line of thought would not help her escape. All it would do was distract her. And possibly frighten her even more than she already was.

The coachman's horn sounded, and the carriage began to slow. They must be at a toll. But before she could think what to do, they sped up again. Well, drat! She'd have to be faster the next time. A short while later she noticed a pattern of speeding up then slowing down, but not for the tolls. The driver must be sparing the horses so that they would not have to be changed.

"I have ta go ta the bog house," Dan said in a sullen tone. "Surprised she ain't whined about wantin' ta go. Ye musta scared the piss outta her." He laughed at his own joke.

The man next to her grunted.

Well, if they were going to stop somewhere, perhaps she could relieve herself and find help. Thinking about it made the urge almost too strong to hold. "I must use the necessary very soon."

"Burt, ye can stop here. I'll watch the mort." Dan leered at her, turning Charlotte's stomach.

"We're almost to the inn," Burt said. "If ye say a word, or try to get anyone to help ye, yer ladyship, I'll bind and gag ye. Understand?"

Charlotte nodded. The last thing she wanted was to be constrained in any manner.

Several minutes later the coach came to a halt.

"See ta the horses," Burt barked, and Dan jumped down quick as a rabbit. An ostler came around and let down the steps. The boy helped her out, but Burt grabbed onto her elbow and guided her into the inn.

"Sir," the landlord said, hurrying up to them. "How can I help you?"

"I'm Smith. Ye have rooms fer us."

"Oh, yes. Yes, indeed I do." The innkeeper cast Charlotte a disapproving glance. "Right this way."

Bother. The landlord had probably been told some Banbury story just as the couple who'd held her friend Dotty had been told. Two days before her wedding, Dotty, now the Marchioness of Merton, had been abducted by a man who wished to stop her from marrying Merton. She'd been taken to a house in Richmond and the caretakers had been informed she was a runaway. By sheer luck, Matt and Merton had discovered where she was, and the men had ridden *ventre à terre* to her aid. By the time Merton arrived, Dotty had already found a way to escape.

If only Matt were not out of Town. But he was, as were Dotty and Merton. Charlotte did not even know if anyone had seen her abducted. If that were the case, there was only one thing to do. She would simply have to find a way to escape by herself.

"My lord, my lord!" Constantine, Marquis of Kenilworth, glanced at the crazed man in black waving to him whilst running down the street.

Good God! It was Thorton, his friend the Earl of Worthington's butler. What the devil was going on?

Drawing his phaeton to the pavement, Con slowed the horses, bringing them to a halt.

"My lord." With a shaking hand, the servant pointed at a black coach driving down the street. "You must go after them. They took Lady Charlotte."

"Lady Charlotte?" He could have sworn Worthington's wife's name was Grace.

"Lady Worthington's sister."

"Where's Worthington?" Somewhere close, Con hoped.

"His lordship is out of Town with her ladyship for a few days." The butler glanced worriedly at the coach. "Hurry, please, my lord. You must save her."

He glanced around, but for some reason, no one he knew was in the square.

Bloody hell!

This is not what he'd planned to do this afternoon.

"Tell me everything you know while I turn this rig around." The sooner Con took care of this problem, the faster he could get back to his own business . . . and his mistress.

"Lady Charlotte was crossing the square from Stanwood House, where his lord and ladyship's brothers and sisters live, to Worthington House, when two blackguards grabbed her. They threw her in that carriage and drove off." The butler wrung his hands.

"Did she not have a maid or footman with her?" He couldn't imagine Worthington being so careless with his charge.

"He did try to stop them, but it was too late." The butler frowned as if he was still trying to figure out how he had failed to protect the lady. "After Lady Worthington—" The lines bracketing his mouth deepened. "What I mean to say is that for the first few weeks after his lordship's wedding, there was more vigilance, but the children go back and forth so often, we didn't think . . ." The butler took out a handkerchief and mopped his brow. "There was no reason to believe she or the others would be in danger."

Con wanted to ask just how many children there were that Worthington would occupy two town houses, but that question would have to wait until later.

"Is it possible she eloped?" As scandalous as it was, the dash to Gretna Green wasn't that uncommon. Although, it generally did not involve bullies.

Con's only hope that this would be an easy task died a quick death when the servant's features froze. Definitely not a pretty sight. No wonder Worthington wanted the man to smile.

"Indeed not, my lord." The butler's lips barely moved. "Her ladyship would never disgrace her family in any way." The man glanced down the street in the direction of the carriage. "Please hurry, my lord. They are getting away."

Con gritted his teeth. "I am turning the horses as quickly as I am able." What a pity. That meant someone was intent on harming Worthington or his family. Then again, it could be an attempt to compromise the lady into marriage. "Inform Lord Worthington that I have gone to her rescue." Con almost cringed. Devil take it. He sounded like a character out of those romances his sister liked. "Better yet, tell him I have it all in hand."

"Yes, my lord. You might also wish to know that Jemmy, one of the younger boys, jumped onto the back of the coach."

How young? Con wondered. Still, it didn't matter. He hoped the lad would be helpful. If not, he would be rescuing a helpless lady and an equally useless boy.

Devil take it.

The Lords wasn't in session today. He had no real reason to be out and about. He should have just stayed at Aimée's house. If it had not been for a letter concerning a problem at his main estate—that still would not be taken care of—he would have been there, and not here chasing after some insipid young female.

Never mind that she was a friend's sister; he had yet to meet a young lady who wasn't too dull to bear. And this one would most likely be hysterical as well.

Con scowled. He had done nothing to deserve this inconvenience. He took care of his holdings and dependents, was active in the Lords, and he loved his mother and other family members, even if he did refuse to heed their exhortations to wed. He had plenty of time yet before he had to don a leg-shackle. His life was exactly as he wished it to be.

Until now.

An uneasy feeling like ants crawled up his neck. *What rot. Now is not the time to become fanciful.*

He'd rescue the girl, Worthington would owe Con a favor, and all would be well. With luck he'd be back in time for dinner with the lovely Aimée, and then the theater. Innocents held no interest for him at all. He didn't even like being around them. Still, he could not refuse to help a friend.

Glancing up the street, he saw the coach was still in sight. "I shall return her to you soon."

He gave his horses the office to start. Fortunately the pair was fresh and ready for some exercise.

Several minutes later, Con had time to take in the details of the vehicle he was following. Not so large, most likely it had once been a town coach. The boy—for the figure on the back was definitely a child, a small child—had a wide enough platform on which to stand. There were handles as well and no back window. The carriage had obviously belonged to someone who, while concerned for their servant's comfort, did not wish to see them or vice versa. And that worked out well for Con. By the time whoever was in charge of kidnapping the lady—damn, what had the butler said her name was? Lady Charlotte. That was it—knew Con was after them, it would be too late for the blackguards to escape him.

Better yet, he might be able to steal the lady away when the coach stopped to change horses or for a rest. Stealth in these matters was much better than declaring his rank and making a scene. It would help no one if the girl's reputation was ruined in the process.

Checking his pair, he stayed far enough back to blend in with the other traffic, but not so far away that there was a chance of losing them in the midday traffic. If he had brought his pistol, or there were not three of the black-guards, Con would have attempted to drive ahead of the coach and stop it. But there was too much traffic, and he did not have a death wish.

He transferred the ribbons to one hand, pulled out his pocket watch and flipped it open. Blast it all. It was almost four o'clock. That would teach him to laze about in the mornings.

Nevertheless, if the Fates were with him he'd be able to get the young lady back in good time to finish his business and attend the theater this evening.

An hour later, Con resigned himself to not only missing dinner but the theater as well. He had passed the southern outskirts of London into Surrey, heading toward the coast. That was not a good sign at all.

Chapter Two

Con drove into the yard of the Hare and Hound on the heels of the coach carrying Worthington's sister. Jumping down from his phaeton, he strode to the back of the coach and grabbed the boy, Jemmy, before anyone else saw him.

"Hey!" The lad wiggled, trying to get away. "Whatcha doin'?"

The boy couldn't be more than five or six. How in perdition had he been left unsupervised?

Before Jemmy could start yelling and draw unwanted attention to them, Con bent down and whispered into the boy's ear, "Worthington's butler sent me to help."

"Yer here to help Lady Charlotte?" the boy asked.

Con inclined his head. "Yes, indeed. I am Lord Kenilworth, a friend of your master's."

Talk about an old soul in a young body. Con was sure he had not been eyed that suspiciously since he'd been caught stealing a whole pie from his mother's cook and had lied about it.

Finally acceptance showed on Jemmy's face and he nodded. "How're we running this rig?"

Glancing up, Con saw the lady propelled into the inn by

a big brute. "I want you to pretend you're my groom. Do you understand?"

Jemmy's sharp eyes narrowed. "How's that going to get my lady out of here right and tight?"

He wasn't at all stupid. Con's first thoughts had been to see the child safe, but now he'd have to come up with a plan before he could see to Jemmy's well-being. "You help the ostler with my horses. At the same time, get a good look at the man with black hair who went into the stables. He's one of the rogues that abducted your lady. While you're doing that, I'm going to make myself the most pompous lord you've ever seen. All you have to do is get friendly with the inn's staff. Make up any story you want, but find out which room Lady Charlotte is in and whether or not she is alone."

Bouncing on the balls of his feet, Jemmy began to smile and he looked like a young child again. "Then we rescue her?"

"Then you tell her *I* shall rescue her." When the boy's face fell, Con held up his hand to stop the coming argument. "I'm sending you back to Worthington House to inform the others of her ladyship's whereabouts and that she will be safe. But first you must find her and tell her I'm here. I'll use the name Lord Braxton." That way if anyone came looking for Lady Charlotte, they'd be following the wrong man. It was a shame Con could not simply walk in and take her back, but the lady's reputation was at stake, and he still had to contend with the blackguards who had kidnapped her.

The inn was in a village off the main toll roads, but not by much. All he could do was hope that neither Braxton himself nor anyone who knew him would make an appearance. Con glanced at the inn once more. It didn't appear to be a place the *ton* would frequent, but one never knew.

Jemmy seemed to consider Con's orders before agreeing. *Perdition!* Did any of Worthington's servants behave as they should?

"I'll do it." He gave a sharp nod.

"Good." Not that the lad had had a real choice in the matter. "I'll hire a horse for you to ride back to London on."

The boy's brows lowered and he shook his head slowly back and forth. "Can't do it."

"What do you mean you cannot do it?" Raising a brow, Con gave the boy a look that struck fear in most who saw it. "Of course you can."

"Can't, not won't. I don't know how to ride yet."

Hell and the devil. He dragged a hand down his face. "Find out if a stagecoach goes through here, or the mail."

A grin appeared on Jemmy's face. "I ain't never been on a public coach before."

"I hope you enjoy the treat." And did not cause too many problems. "Hurry up. These horses must be rubbed down and settled. They can't wait until the other coach's horses are finished." Con started to walk away, then turned. "You do know how to do that?"

"I'm really good at taking care of horses. The riding's goin' to take a bit."

Why in God's name Worthington had a groom who couldn't ride was beyond Con. Then again, why a child was in the man's employ didn't make sense either. He felt like he'd been dropped into a madhouse.

He waited, perusing the outside of the building with his quizzing glass. The inn was at least two hundred years old. As with many of the older structures, the windows were not terribly large. A small person could climb out of them. But that was all one could do. No obliging trellis or ivy vines graced the outside walls of the inn.

One of the ostlers came out, and after having a word with Jemmy, took the horses into the stables. From the corner of his eye he saw Jemmy run around to the back of the building. It should not take him too long to discover where the lady was.

Several moments later, after scanning the area as if he were looking for something, Con quickened his pace, striding into the inn and bellowing, "Landlord, I must have the landlord now." Pitching his voice in a higher, more peevish tone, he continued. "Do you not know who I am?"

A man who looked to be in his twenties came running up, untying his apron from around his waist. "My pa will be back directly. May I help you, sir?"

Con leveled his quizzer at the man. "Your lordship—not sir, lordship. I am Lord Braxton. My valet was to have arrived over an hour ago, but I do not see my traveling coach. His orders were to bespeak a bedchamber and private parlor for my use, as well as rooms for him and my grooms and footmen."

"No—no, my lord. The only guests we have are a—a . . . another party that just arrived."

So, the landlord and his employees knew not to talk about Lady Charlotte. That was interesting. Were they also involved in the abduction?

Con puffed out his chest, and huffed. "Are you telling me you have no chambers?"

The innkeeper arrived, pushing the younger man out of the way. "My lord." The landlord bowed low. "We do indeed have a large chamber and a private parlor."

Con let the landlord soothe his supposedly ruffled feathers for several minutes before he agreed to the accommodations. "However, the fact remains that my valet is lost.

I shall need to send my groom back to London. Does a mail coach come through here?"

"Indeed, my lord." The innkeeper bowed again. "It should be here in two hours."

He kept the man busy discussing items of which he normally took no notice. After sufficient time had passed to assure Jemmy had been able to speak to Lady Charlotte, Con said in the tone of one who cannot be pleased, "That will do. As for now, I have waited here long enough. I wish to be shown to my chamber."

The landlord bowed once more. "Please follow me, my lord."

He strode off after the innkeeper, hoping he'd given Jemmy enough time to find the lady. Con wished to be on the road back to Town before much longer.

Charlotte had been given warm wash water and was promised her dinner would arrive shortly. Yet when she had tried to strike up a conversation with the maid who had brought the water and told her what she'd have to eat, the girl's lips clamped tightly together.

She sighed. "I take it you are not allowed to speak to me beyond what is required."

The maid nodded. Obviously, there would be no help from that quarter.

Drat. At the very least, she had hoped to discover more information about the inn and where exactly she was in relation to London. Yet, it would have been nice to enlist help in escaping.

After the girl left, Charlotte glanced out of the open windows. She might be able to climb out of them, but there did not seem to be any way to climb down. Aside from that, her chamber faced the street, where anyone would be able to see her.

If only she knew where the two dastards who had abducted her were, she was sure she could pick the lock on the door and sneak downstairs, safe in the knowledge they could not catch her. It would not do her any good at all to run smack into them when she was trying to escape. She was sure the one would make good on his threat to tie her up.

There must be some person in the village from whom she could seek help.

Charlotte peered out the window again. A church steeple rose not far away. Possibly the vicar? Surely a clergyman would consent to aid her and keep her confidence. After all, she did not want everyone and his dog to know she'd been kidnapped. Even if none of this was her fault, it would ruin her reputation if anyone discovered what had happened.

Then again, she did not wish to place anyone else in danger. And there was still the question of who had taken her.

A scratching came from the basket.

Before she did anything else, she had to take care of Collette.

Charlotte opened the basket lid, and the kitten popped up.

Picking the poor little thing up, she scratched her jowls until the cat began to purr. "I know, sweetheart. This has not been a wonderful day." Going to the space behind the dressing screen, she located the chamber pot, but not the lid. Finally, she found it in a corner. "We shall have to try something new." At home she and her sister Louisa had taught their kittens to use a board placed over the chamber pot. This would be messier, but at least the lid had leather hinges so that half of it could be folded over the other half, providing some stability for the cat. "Here we go."

Thankfully, Collette was either too happy to be able

to relieve herself or she was a much better traveler than Charlotte could have thought, for she did not complain at all but merely did her duty.

She had just put the kitten down when someone scratched at the door. Goodness, it couldn't be the maid again so soon. She'd have to hide Collette.

As she lifted the kitten, a childish voice whispered from the other side of the door, "My lady, it's Jemmy."

Jemmy? Did that mean some of the other servants had come as well? Was she saved?

Charlotte rushed to the door. "Jemmy, what are you doing here?"

"I remembered how you helped me, and when I saw those men, I jumped on the back of the coach so's I could help you."

She had rescued him from one of the criminal organizations that trained young children to pick pockets and other things.

Tears of gratitude pricked her eyes. "Did any of the footmen or grooms come with you?"

"No, my lady. Just me. None of them was fast enough." That was said with more than a little pride.

"Very good." He was being taught along with her younger brother and sisters, and she praised him for his progress. She wondered what he was doing outside by himself. That, however, would be a question for later. At the moment, Charlotte was glad to hear his voice, yet now she would have to find a way to get them both home safely. "Jemmy, you must not let them catch you."

"I won't, my lady. I come—came to tell you a friend of his lordship's is here. He's gonna rescue you. He told the innkeeper he was Lord Braxton and acted all pomp—pomp something so's I'd have time to find you. He's sending me back to London on a coach." His whispered voice became excited. "Won't that be a grand adventure?"

"Yes, it will." Charlotte leaned her head against the door as her anxiety flowed out of her.

Thank God *someone* had come after her. A burble of laughter almost burst forth.

And thank the Fates it was not the real Lord Braxton. The man had the biggest mouth in Town. Less than an hour after they returned, the whole *ton* would have heard about her misadventure, and she'd be ruined.

Still, the idea was brilliant, and Jemmy would be safe. "What is the gentleman's plan?"

"Don't rightly know—" Just then an aristocratic voice broke the relative silence of the inn. "That'd be him now. Said he was going to cause a bobbery."

When they got home, she would have to work with him some more on his language.

"Thank you for coming to me. Please tell him that I have a scheme to get out of my chamber and that if he would kindly be standing by with his conveyance . . ." She frowned. There was no knowing when the inn would quiet down and she could trust her abductors were asleep. "Well, he should know when it is safe."

"Someone's coming. I gotta go."

A few moments later a loud knock sounded on the door.

"Unless you want that maid to get hurt, and yourself tied up and gagged, don't try to talk to her no more," Burt growled from the corridor.

Well, drat. The girl must have told the innkeeper. She certainly did not wish to be responsible for the maid being harmed. "I promise I shall not do so again."

"See that ye don't."

Charlotte leaned her back against the door and listened

to his steps on the bare wooden floor as he strode down the corridor.

The loud, aristocratic voice had faded.

It was good of the gentleman to send Jemmy back to Town. If only she could go with him she would be happier. Although, he had said that the gentleman had a carriage. With luck she could be home before morning. She did not want to consider what would happen if she did not return by then. The stagecoach would have been much less trouble.

With her eldest sister, now the Countess of Worthington, and her brother-in-law gone away for a few days, and Lord Harrington, the only man currently courting her, attending his father, Charlotte had cried off her engagements rather than bother her cousin Jane to chaperone her. It was, there-fore, a possibility that no one would notice she was not present. If someone did—she grimaced—well, she would simply have to cross that bridge when she came to it. Surely, between her and her family, they could come up with some believable story.

Sometime later, the sound of a team of horses stamping and a coachman calling for passengers told Charlotte the stagecoach had arrived. She prayed Jemmy was on it when it left.

Lying down on the small bed, she tucked her cat next to her. It would behoove her to get as much rest as possible in preparation for a full night of travel, and a nap before dinner would be just the thing.

She was not a light sleeper, but if someone knocked or called her name she would wake immediately. That proba-bly came from being the second oldest of a large family.

Yet, before she could lull herself into unconsciousness, sharp steps struck the floor in the corridor, and a door near hers opened. "Here ye are, my lord. You'll find water waiting. Dinner will be ready in a half an hour."

There was a brief silence before the gentleman said, "Are you absolutely sure this is your *best* chamber?"

Charlotte stifled a giggle. Whoever was impersonating Lord Braxton must know him well.

"I am sorry, my lord, but this is the best I can do."

A loud sigh followed. "I do hope you set a better table than this room would indicate."

Slapping her hands over her mouth, she tried to hold back her laughter. The poor gentleman would be lucky if someone didn't spit in his food.

At the mention of food her stomach began to grumble. Fortunately, a knock sounded on the door and the maid entered with her dinner. She was pleased to find it more than sufficient as well as tasty. She ate the soup and vegetables, but shared the meat, fish, and cheese with Collette.

When Charlotte and the kitten had eaten their fill, she wrapped the remaining bread, cheese, and meat to sustain her on the journey to Town.

As she glanced out the window, several men strolled down the street toward the inn. It might be quite some time before the innkeeper and his workers settled down for the night.

Chapter Three

An hour later, the maid, accompanied by Burt, came to Charlotte's room for the dinner dishes.

As the girl quietly cleared the table, he glared at her. "She'll be back up later to help ye change." He shoved a large cotton garment at her. "The landlady offered you one of her nightgowns."

"Thank you." Charlotte wanted to groan. As luck would have it, she could not manage to put this particular gown back on without help. If forced to change, she'd be making her escape in the nightgown. That would not do at all. "Please convey my gratitude to her."

"There's a toff here ye don't want to meet if you're smart," Burt said. "So don't get any ideas about callin' fer help. Wouldn't want him getting hurt."

"Thank you for warning me." She kept her eyes demurely lowered, attempting to convince the blackguard that she was intimidated by him and his accomplice.

He held the door open for the maid, then closed and locked it. As soon as she heard them go down the stairs, she drew two pins from her hair.

Sleep would have to wait. It was time to practice unlocking the door.

After pulling a chair next to the door, she sat down and began to slide the pins into the lock. Fifteen minutes later, her neck was clammy and droplets of water slid down her face. A damp curl fell over her eyes and she tried to blow it out of her way.

Every time she expected to hear the snick of the lock opening, it slipped. "Drat it all." She stood and stretched. "I shall never get it open at this rate."

"My lady?" a man whispered through the door.

Thank God! With a voice that cultured, it must be the gentleman Jemmy told her about. No one else, other than the inn's staff and her abductors, knew she was here. "Yes?"

"I wanted to tell you that your groom is on the mail coach to Town. I instructed him to hire a hackney to take him to Mayfair and gave him the necessary funds." Now that he was not attempting to act like Lord Braxton, he had a deep and almost melodic voice. Who could he be? Charlotte was almost certain she had never met him. She would have remembered that voice.

"Thank you very much." She brushed more damp curls away from her face. "I was so worried he would be caught and injured. The blackguards who abducted me are dangerous."

"Have—have they harmed you at all?" There was an urgency in his tone that had not been there before.

"I have a few bruises on my wrists. That is all. I have been trying to pick the lock, but it's not working. Do you have any ideas as to how to get me out of this room?" She prayed no one heard them. She did not want the gentleman to be captured or hurt. Even if he had a pistol, that only gave them two shots between them.

"No," he replied flatly. "Unfortunately." Charlotte dropped her face into her hands. If neither of them could figure out a way to get this door open, how was she going to escape? "I *have* managed to reduce the number of scoundrels by one." He sounded a little more assured than before. "The black-haired one is too inebriated to stand."

That was good news. "Well done. What about the other man?"

"He's not downstairs. Does he always come with the maid?"

"No." Come to think of it, that was a little strange. "He only came one time to help her take my dinner remains away. Earlier he warned me that if I attempted to have a conversation with the girl, she would be injured, but he spoke through the door."

The gentleman made a harrumphing sound. "I doubt the young woman will be harmed. It is my belief that most of the staff here are related to the innkeeper. I also think the landlord is helping the scoundrels." Another reason to keep their voices down. "Will she return to you this evening?"

"Yes. In fact, she should be here soon." Charlotte straightened. She did not wish to hurt the maid, but she did have to escape.

"Don't worry. I'll think of something," the gentleman said confidently. Shortly thereafter the door across the corridor opened and closed.

Yet by the time he had reentered his bedchamber, an idea immediately came to her. She opened the basket, drew out her pistol, and made sure all was in order. Then she lay back down once again with her kitten curled up next to her, and waited.

Con gazed consideringly at the door behind which Lady Charlotte was imprisoned, and wondered how in perdition he was going to get her out of it. He thought about telling her to rip up the sheets, tie them together, secure them to something, and climb out of the window. But she had probably never climbed anything but stairs in her life. There was also the real possibility that the other miscreant would see her if his room was on the same side of the building as hers.

Fortunately, she was not the type of young lady he had expected to find. Even her voice was not that of a lady just coming out. It sounded more mature than seventeen or eighteen. He remembered Worthington saying it was her first Season—surely she was not older.

At least she had not seemed as if she was in a panic or about to swoon. He'd almost laughed when she'd told him she was trying to pick the lock. It would never have occurred to him she would be so inventive or intelligent.

Con wondered if she had the signature dark Vivers hair and blue eyes that Worthington had.

Not that it mattered. He was not looking for a wife. He and his mistress, Aimée, had excellent relations. He was fond of her and considered her a friend. At times he had the feeling Aimée was in love with him, yet she knew her place and would never enact him a scene, unlike other mistresses he'd had.

That, though, was the problem with women. They fell in love too easily. It was the reason he had stopped dallying with widows and married women. Come to think of it, he hoped Lady Charlotte would have the good sense not to fancy herself in love with him.

Con trusted Aimée was not overly concerned about his failure to take her to the theater this evening. He'd have to remember to purchase a trinket to make it up to her.

The sound of heavy boots, most likely the other villain, walking down the corridor and stopping at Lady Charlotte's door, brought his attention back to his immediate dilemma: how to release her from the bedchamber.

He could probably overpower the one brute who was left, but with the landlord in an alliance with the scoundrels, Con might find himself beaten and locked up, not to mention the scandal it would cause if Lady Charlotte were found here in the company of ruffians.

He had taken a good look at where the keys were stored, yet he doubted the key to her room was there. One would have to be extremely sloppy to lock a woman up and leave a key where it could be found.

No sound came from Lady Charlotte's room and soon he heard the man walking down the corridor to his chamber. It was a shame the villain was not as fond of gin as his companion.

Con smiled to himself. Jemmy had done an excellent job of ensuring the black-haired man had sufficient funds to make the man as drunk as David's sow.

There was also the problem of harnessing his pair to the phaeton so Con and Lady Charlotte could leave in an expeditious manner. Chances were he would have to do it himself and be very quiet about it so that anyone sleeping in the stables wouldn't waken.

He scraped his hand down his face. Dear God, what had he got himself into?

The whole thing would have been much more straightforward if she had eloped. He could have returned to Town immediately. It was none of his bread and butter who eloped with whom. Yet, this did not have any of the hallmarks of an elopement or an abduction for marriage. The problem was that he didn't know what the deuce it did seem like.

The only thing he was sure of was that he must rescue

her ladyship and return her to her family before word of the kidnapping got out and her reputation was destroyed.

But first he had to get her out of the blasted room.

"My lady?" Charlotte's eyes shot open.

She had not remembered falling asleep, but she must have. The room was dark except for the one candle she had left burning, and the inn was quiet. "Enter."

The lock clicked open, and the maid walked into the chamber. "I come to help you undress."

"Thank you." Rubbing her eyes, Charlotte smiled warmly. "I am absolutely unable to remove my gown without help." She paused, assuming a rueful look. "I do not suppose you would be able to bring me some bread and cheese? Dinner was excellent, but I am still extremely peckish, and I shall not be able to sleep if I'm hungry."

"I suppose so," the girl said with reluctance. "I'll go ask my ma."

A few moments after the maid left, the gentleman was back at the door whispering, "My lady, I have an idea."

"As do I." She waited to see if he would actually listen to her scheme. Some gentlemen—Lord Harrington, the man who had been courting her, came to mind—would not.

"Ladies first." His voice was so rich and expressive she could almost see his hand gesture. How nice of him.

"I have a pistol. I shall point it at her while you tie her up. She must be gagged as well."

"Much neater than my idea." She could hear him shifting. "I believe she is returning."

Charlotte removed her pistol from the bedside table and placed Collette back in the basket. "Stay here, sweetheart. We will be departing soon, and I will not have time to crawl under the bed after you."

As the door swung open, Charlotte hid the weapon in her skirts. "My ma was in bed, so I just brought it up. I don't suppose your husband and Miss Betsy want to starve you."

Charlotte was about to utter her thanks again when what the girl had said struck her, and her mouth went dry. *Husband?* Her whole being filled with dread. This was much, much worse than she had imagined.

Her voice came out in a hoarse whisper as she gripped the chair with her free hand to stop her knees from buckling. "Miss Betsy?"

"Your husband hired her to find you," the girl said as she set out the bread, cheese, and fruit on the table. "My ma and pa don't hold with wives running away, so they help her."

Charlotte tried to swallow, but was unable to get any moisture past the knot in her throat. "Does she—she . . . retrieve only wives?"

"There's no one to hear me now, so I can tell you," the girl said as she set out the silver. "Children get lost and sometimes young ladies run away. She makes sure they all get back home."

Home, hell.

Charlotte's hand began to shake and she tightened her grip on the pistol. To a brothel, more likely.

She had to get out of here and warn her family and Dotty that Miss Betsy had changed from drugging the wives of soldiers stationed overseas and making them work as prostitutes, to a much wider range of victims.

Charlotte forced a smile to her face. As long as the girl was being chatty, she might as well obtain as much information as possible. "How long has she been doing this type of work?"

"I dunno. We've been helping her for about two months, I think. You're the fourth or fifth one."

Somehow, Charlotte vowed, she would find a way to rescue the women and children that woman had abducted. "Do you know where she takes them from here?"

The girl's eyes widened. "To their families. Where else?"

Where else, indeed. Well, now was not the time to fight this battle. Once she was home she would work to stop the former madam.

When the maid placed the large cotton nightgown Charlotte had left hanging over a chair on the bed, she leveled the pistol at the girl. "I am terribly sorry, but I must ask you to sit on that chair." The girl's mouth dropped open. "Please do not scream. I will shoot if I have to."

Not that she thought she could kill the maid, but she had to make the threat.

The girl's throat worked, and she nodded a few times, then sat on the chair.

"Good, I'm just in time." The gentleman who had been speaking with her through the door strode into the room. He had on a greatcoat and his hat was pulled down, shading his face.

Even if the room had had more than one candle, it would have been hard to get a good look at him. All she could make out was that he was tall and at least as broad in the shoulders as her brother-in-law, and he had an almost square jaw with a dimple. She wondered what the color of his eyes was and if he was as handsome as she thought he might be.

The pounding in her chest increased. Really, this was *not* the time to be having any sort of reaction to a man.

He quickly tied the maid's hands and feet. "If I may make a suggestion?"

Charlotte blinked, bringing her attention to the matter at hand. "Of course."

The corners of his lips tipped up. "She can make a great deal of noise in this chair. I suggest we tie her to the bed."

"Very well." She helped him move the girl and secure her to the small bed.

When that was done, Charlotte put her bonnet on and tied the ribbons, then gathered the food in a napkin before placing it in the basket.

"I do apologize," she said to the girl. "But I do not wish to go where Miss Betsy would take me. Despite what you may believe, she is not a good person." She tied a gag around the girl's mouth. "I am sorry about this as well."

The gentleman slid a sharp glance at Charlotte, but said nothing. She retrieved the keys, locking the door behind them. "Is your carriage ready?"

"Yes. That's the reason I was a little late. I went to the stables and harnessed them myself." He held out his arm and whispered, "My lady?"

She placed her hand on his arm, and they quietly made their way down the front stairs and out into the yard. A pair of neatish bays were harnessed to a very dashing phaeton.

"They are lovely," she said, keeping her voice as low as possible. At the same time, her heart was pounding so hard she thought it might burst from her chest. At the rate she was going, she'd have apoplexy before she was twenty.

"Come, we must hurry. We only have a few hours before it is light. I would like to have you back at your own home before then."

"What time is it?" She hadn't bothered looking at her watch before they left the bedchamber, and, even with the moonlight, it was too dark to see it now. Still, it could not be past midnight.

"Almost two o'clock." Oh, dear. She must have slept much longer than she'd thought. "Why would she have come to me so late?"

"She was working in the common room. Their last customer left about a half hour ago."

"That makes sense, then." She wondered what the maid and her parents would think if they knew what Miss Betsy truly did with the people she kidnapped. Perhaps Charlotte should have told the girl everything she knew, but if the innkeeper confronted the woman, Miss Betsy would merely change where she took her captives. As soon as Charlotte arrived home, she must write Dotty.

Once they were in the carriage, he clicked softly and the pair began to walk. For the next several minutes Charlotte's skin prickled with fear that someone in the inn would discover they had gone and come looking for them. She wished he would go faster, but she knew that making as little noise as possible would help them get away.

Finally, he urged the horses to a trot, and she relaxed a little.

Neither of them spoke, not, she thought, because they had nothing to say, but due to the fact that sound seemed to carry more at night. Charlotte wondered how long they had before the maid's disappearance was noted, and prayed it was not until after the sun had risen.

Still, she would not get the problem off her mind. How much sleep was the girl allowed after working until two in the morning? Her sister insisted that the staff be well rested, and Charlotte made sure that May, her dresser, napped if Charlotte was coming in late. Yet she did not think the innkeeper and his wife would be so kind, even to their own daughter.

She and her rescuer passed an open field and Charlotte could see the horizon lightening. How long would it be before the sun rose?

The road in front of them appeared almost white, and she murmured to herself, "It seems too light."

"The moon has not yet set."

Charlotte jumped. Really, she had to stop talking to herself, particularly when she wasn't alone. Or be prepared to receive an answer.

She glanced at the sky, which was a strange thing to do when the gentleman had already told her that the moon was still up. But people did that type of thing all the time. It could not be because they did not believe the other person, it just seemed to be a natural, albeit unnecessary, reaction. "So I see." She could also see his lordship's white teeth flash in a grin. "I have never been awake at this time of day. Do you know how many hours there are until dawn?"

"We have at least another two hours or more."

With luck, that would be enough time for them to be too far for her abductors to catch them, even if they did give chase.

"Here." He passed her a metal object. "When I tell you to, blow into the small end."

She turned the thing over. It had a large open part at one end and it narrowed to a tiny hole at the other end. "What is it?"

"You'll know when you blow on it. Now."

Chapter Four

Taking a deep breath, Lady Charlotte blew through the small end. "This is what our coachman uses." She sounded astonished at the discovery. "And to think I had never even seen one before."

"It's called a horn," he added.

"Yes, I know." She studied the horn some more. "What is it made of?"

"Mostly tin."

He had slowed the pair, and waited as the toll keeper, dressed in breeches, nightshirt, and night cap came out of a small house. Con tossed him a coin, and started the horses again.

"How did you know how much the toll was?" Lady Charlotte asked.

"There is a fee schedule," he explained. "Once one has traveled outside of Town often enough, one learns it."

"I have not traveled much at all. Only from home to Town once. Although, I would like to travel much more."

Despite himself and his expectations, Con was having a pleasant time. Lady Charlotte really was a remarkable young lady. Even after all she had been through, she hadn't given a hint that she would dissolve into vapors. In fact, the only sign of tension she had exhibited was the grip of her hand on the basket in her lap.

He let the conversation lag until they had traveled another mile or so before asking, "You mentioned Miss Betsy. I have not heard that name in a few months. I thought she was in Newgate."

"You know about Miss Betsy?" Lady Charlotte turned to face him, her eyes widening.

"Er, yes. Some of what happened got around." He should not have asked at all. He wouldn't have, except she seemed to know about the bawd.

"From what Worthington told me, she escaped," Charlotte said. "However, I know he never expected her to attempt revenge on him. That is all this could be."

Con knew of the former brothel owner from snippets of conversation he'd overheard from his mistress and a few of her friends. "She is not a woman to cross."

"So I have been told. However, I do not have any personal knowledge of her. My brother, cousin, and friend helped in destroying her." The lady pulled a face, causing her nose, which turned up a bit at the end, to wrinkle. "At least, that is what I was told. She would have been more sensible to leave the country. However, it appears that she is still causing problems."

With her golden beauty and innocence, Lady Charlotte would have made Miss Betsy a great deal of money in an auction. If that was her intent, she'd probably not try to abduct her ladyship again. But if Lady Charlotte was correct and the woman wanted revenge or ransom, Worthington would be better off removing his family from Town at once.

For some reason Con wanted to know more about his charge. "Do you always carry a pistol with you?"

"No." Her voice was full of suppressed laughter. "I was going to Worthington House to practice shooting and have another session of teaching my kitten to walk on a lead. She has been doing quite well, but she can become distracted."

Con had been going to ask what Worthington's neighbors thought of the noise, but . . . No, it wasn't possible. "Don't tell me you have a cat in that basket as well."

Now Lady Charlotte did laugh. The sound was light, and tinkling, and completely enthralling. "I do, indeed."

"Every cat I know would have been screeching by now."

She opened the lid of the basket and stuck her hand inside. "She is a silent cat. The only noise she makes is a chirp." Turning her head slightly toward him, she grimaced. "It is not a very pretty sound."

"You said something about a breed." Con wanted to encourage the lady to continue talking. Not only did he like the sound of her voice, but sooner or later, despite the courage she had displayed thus far, shock could set in, and talking might keep her from thinking about all that had occurred and could have occurred.

"She is a Chartreux. They are an old French breed. My friend Lady Merton rescued them from some boys who were trying to drown the litter. I was fortunate enough to be given one. Collette doesn't like strangers. I think that is the reason she has not even tried to climb out of the basket." They fell quiet, and a few minutes later she covered her mouth and yawned. "Thank you for all your trouble."

"It was my pleasure to be able to assist you." He turned his head toward her, bending it, and her lips touched his.

Lady Charlotte had probably only meant to change positions or to make another comment. Yet once their mouths met, he could not seem to stop himself from moving his lips over her soft plump ones. He quickly trailed his tongue over the seam of her mouth, tasting what little of her he dared. Still pursed together, her lips softened, and he moved to encourage her to open to him.

The ribbons jerked, causing him to break the kiss.
Damnation!

When he glanced at her she was gazing at him as if confused. A few moments later she yawned again. Her long, dark blond lashes lowered and she slumped against him, her soft breast brushing his arm.

Immediately, his body hardened as if it had received an invitation to play.

Bloody hell!

This was not happening to him. It was simply that he had missed last evening with his mistress, and he was used to having conjugal relations whenever he desired them. He had heard that many men sought conjugal relief after a battle. He had had a battle of sorts. Those were the only possible explanations for his sudden lust. Innocents did not arouse him in the least. Not mentally or physically. He applied his attention to the road, willing his cock to stand down.

Sometime later, Con's stomach growled. He'd not eaten much of his dinner last night as he'd had the distinct impression someone had spit in the soup.

He remembered Lady Charlotte wrapping cheese and bread into a napkin and putting it into the basket. Not wishing to wake her, he stretched his arm across her body, carefully opened the basket lid, and stuck his hand in.

"*Ow!* What the devil!" He snatched his hand back. Blood welled on one of his fingers.

Lady Charlotte jerked up with a start. "What happened? Have they caught us?"

"No, your cat scratched me."

"I'm sorry." Blinking, she looked down at his finger. "I did tell you she does not like strangers."

"That doesn't mean she had to attack me." He glared at the basket.

"Of course, it was very bad of her. Generally, she just hides. I must say that I dreamed she had left the basket, and we had to chase after her."

"She did not," he grumbled. A good thing too, as he was not stopping for a cat. "I reached in for the foodstuffs you packed."

"That accounts for it then." Lady Charlotte stuck her hand into the basket and pulled out the small bundle of food. Next she withdrew a handkerchief. "I'll bind your wound so that you do not bleed all over everything." Before he could protest, she had torn a strip off the handkerchief and tied it round his finger. "There." She patted it. "It will be better soon."

"Thank you." He hadn't meant to apologize, but she had behaved so sensibly that he . . . had to get away from her as soon as possible. "I should not have made such a fuss."

"I am sure it was a shock." She placed a hunk of cheese in a piece of bread and folded it over. "I hope it tastes as good as it smells. The cheese that is."

Not as good as her lips had, but he would not be tasting them again. Ever.

Con devoured the sandwich as she neatly broke off another piece of cheese and held it down into the basket. A few moments later, she handed him another piece of bread and cheese and took some for herself.

She swallowed. "It is good. I wish I could ask where the cook got it."

He turned to her and smiled. "I do not think we shall be returning."

"Nor do I wish to. Once was quite enough, thank you." Her tone, as dry as dust, surprised him.

Remarkable. He'd never met a young lady or many older

ones with such sangfroid. She hadn't even mentioned the kiss. "Is this your first Season?"

"It is." He could almost feel her smiling. "Until yesterday, I had been having such a good time."

"Truly?" Even though she would not be able to see his expression, he had raised a brow.

"Yes, truly. I do not understand why ladies, especially those just out, pretend to be bored. It's ridiculous."

"What a refreshing point of view." Some gentleman was going to be lucky enough to marry her. When that happened, Con hoped her husband did not try to snuff out Lady Charlotte's sense of joy. "I think I agree with you."

"You mean you do not know if you agree?" An inflection of incredulity colored her voice. "I thought all men knew exactly what they wanted and did not want."

Ahh. She was dangerous. He had no doubt she could quickly wrap any man she chose around her little finger. It was a good thing he was not in the market for a wife and didn't like innocents. "I suppose you are looking for a husband."

"Only if I meet a gentleman who believes in the same things I do and whom I can love."

"If you do so, would you always agree with your husband?" He found he enjoyed prodding her.

"I? Not unless he was right."

Perhaps not any gentleman. The man would have to like being managed at times, and challenged. She should not be allowed to wed anyone who would ignore her or make her unhappy.

"We have not met, have we?" she asked.

He glanced at Lady Charlotte; her brow was slightly pleated, as if she were trying to place him.

Con was not going to explain to her that there was another part of London society that she knew nothing about. "No."

"I didn't think we had." Her brow cleared and her tone was lighter. "I would have recognized your voice. Are you not in Town for the Season?"

"I have been busy with other ventures." It wasn't much of an answer, but it would have to satisfy her.

The path ahead of them darkened and he glanced at the sky. The moon had set and in the distance the sky was the color of sapphires. Dawn was coming before he thought it would. They had an hour at the most. Con wished he could urge his team a bit faster, but without the light he had to slow them to a walk.

It must have taken longer than he'd thought to take care of the maid and leave the inn. And the one thing he did not want to have happen was for him to be seen with Lady Charlotte. That would be disastrous for them both.

God's teeth! Without more light, he'd never get her to Town in time. If only he was familiar with this road he could travel faster.

Thinking back to yesterday's journey, he realized that the scoundrels had taken several back roads which had the effect of avoiding the larger posting inns. Clearly he had somehow missed one and got lost. Now, what the devil was he going to do?

They passed a road sign to a village only a mile from the estate where his mother lived. How had he not realized how close he was to Hillstone Manor? Well, that settled his problem. He'd take Lady Charlotte to his mother. After which, Con would continue his journey to Town.

And have Mama planning my wedding.

Perdition! That is exactly what his mother would do. She'd been after him for the past few years to take a wife.

The sky was becoming lighter. Even if he did take Lady Charlotte to Hillstone, they would not arrive for another hour or two at the earliest.

"No," she said to the basket as she closed the lid.

"The kitten?"

"Yes." She smiled.

He looked at Lady Charlotte for a moment. Her eyes the color of the now lightened sky grew wide, and her lush rose lips formed a perfect O.

"I have never seen such green eyes."

He had heard the same thing all his life, but coming from her it seemed . . . special. "My father's family is littered with eyes this color."

Pulling her full lower lip between her teeth, she suddenly lapsed into thought. A few moments later, she said, "Is it proper for you to know my name when I do not know yours?" Her cheeks flushed with color. "I mean, I know we should be properly introduced, but"—she held her palms up and glanced around—"I do not see anyone who could perform the duty."

He grinned. "Kenilworth, at your service, my lady."

"*Kenilworth?*" Her lovely smile was suddenly replaced by a scowl, and her light tone became as cold as his ice house in the dead of winter. "*You* are *the Marquis of Kenilworth?*"

"I am indeed." Con wondered what he had done to deserve such a negative reaction.

A golden blond curl slipped loose, and she tucked it back under the bonnet, muttering something about courtesans and poor women. Something he was not going to ask her to repeat.

But when had she seen him? The only public place he'd been to recently was . . . Damnation. The theater. That hair.

How could he have forgotten? She was the young lady in Worthington's box who had been glaring at him when he had attended with Aimée and one of her friends. The lights in the Worthington box had been raised, as most were. Yet, Con had lowered the lights in his box because his mistress did not like to call attention to herself. Her friend, however, had practically hung over the rail, gathering all the notice she could. The woman had even had the temerity to ask to be escorted to Worthington's box because the Duke of Rothwell—now married to another of Worthington's sisters—was there.

Yet, surely Lady Charlotte did not know . . . Young, unmarried, gently born ladies did not know of mistresses. On the other hand, she knew of Miss Betsy and had mentioned courtesans—but even if she had been told, why would she care? It was no bread and butter of Lady Charlotte's if he had a mistress. Most men did.

"I appreciate you going to such lengths to rescue me," Lady Charlotte said in a tight voice. "However, I would prefer that we find an inn where I may take the mail coach back to Town."

The devil she would. Worthington would kill him if Con put his sister on a common stage. He would take her home. She was, after all, wearing a carriage gown. It was a bit wrinkled, but no one would know that they had not been out for an early ride. As long as he got her back without anyone seeing them before they reached the Park, all would be well.

Rot. He, of all people, knew better than to believe such a faradiddle. If anyone saw them he was done for.

Hours had passed since they had left the inn. The sun was rising in the sky more quickly with each minute. If only he had not got misdirected they could have been in Town long before now.

They entered what appeared to be a market town. Shopkeepers were sweeping their walks, and women, old and young, dashed about with large baskets hanging on their arms. Fortunately, he did not see any carriages or people he recognized, and drove straight through. So far, so good.

"Why did you not stop there?"

"It is not serviced by a mail coach," he lied. No doubt she would jump out of his carriage if she knew it was most likely a primary stop. Market towns were.

"Oh." She lapsed into a tense silence again.

A purring sound emanated from the basket. At least the cat was having a good time.

Chapter Five

A half hour later, the only thing about Con's situation that had improved was that he had seen another sign to the market town near his mother's estate. At least now he knew where he was. Holding his breath as they passed through a village, he prayed no one would notice them.

Since learning his name, Lady Charlotte had moved as far away as possible from him—which was not that far considering her skirts still brushed his thigh—and refused to even glance in his direction. "Please halt the carriage."

Without thinking Con pulled the horses up. Before he could ask what she needed or grab her arm, the woman had climbed down from the phaeton and started off down the road toward the village.

Aggravating chit. "Just where do you think you are going, my lady?"

"Back to Town," she threw over her shoulder. "We should have been there long before now."

Bloody, bloody, hell. "I got . . . misdirected. We will be at my mother's house soon." She mumbled something he could not make out. "Do you even know the way?"

"No." She raised the nicely rounded chin he had admired earlier. "But there was an inn about a mile or so back. They might not be serviced by a mail coach, but I am sure they will help me arrange transportation to Mayfair."

Make that *ignorant, aggravating* chit. Leave it to Worthington to keep his sister so close she did not even suspect the scandal she was courting.

He jumped down from his carriage, turned the rig around, and followed her as she marched her way toward the village, inn, and certain ruin. "Do you have any money?"

"Of course not," she shot back in an irritated tone. "Why, pray tell, would I need my reticule to walk across the square to Worthington House?"

Con wanted to turn her over his knee. "Then please explain to me," he said with excruciating calm, "how you plan to pay for your passage to Town."

This time she stopped, her back as straight as a poker. "I do not know how that is any business of yours, my lord." He could practically hear her teeth grinding. "I shall merely hand them my card, and explain that I have been stranded. Surely they will understand that my family will reimburse them for any of my expenses. If they will not assist me, I shall apply to the local vicar."

"Why me?" He covered his eyes with one hand, and mumbled to himself, "Why was I the only one riding by when this termagant was abducted?"

"Did you say something?" Her tone was as haughty as his eldest sister's.

This did not bode well for him. "No."

"Good." She swept him a curtsey worthy of a ballroom. "In that case, I shall wish you a good day, my lord. I do not wish to be seen with you. It might ruin my reputation."

What had he ever done for fate to hand him such a yoke? Merely entering an inn without her maid, luggage, or a visible form of transportation would ruin her.

Perdition. This was the first time he had ever wished for

a younger sister. At least then he might know how to talk sense into Lady Charlotte.

What was it his German tutor had always said when Kenilworth was having difficulty? Ah, yes, *Schritt für Schritt.* Step by step. Somehow, he would have to lead Lady Charlotte to understand the danger in which she was placing herself. "You do know that a well-bred lady does not wander around by herself, do you not?"

"Yes, of course I do. That is the reason I normally have a footman with me. However, the curs failed to abduct him when they abducted me."

Con was certain his elder sister would not approve of sarcasm. "Do you have any idea what the landlord will think of a young lady appearing at his inn with no luggage or maid? Hmm?"

Her step faltered for a moment. When she continued, her tone was not nearly as confident as before. "Mr. Brown was very kind to my sister when she was stranded by the weather, and she did not have her maid with her."

Con's back teeth began to hurt. "And did the estimable Mr. Brown happen to *know* your sister previously?"

"Naturally. My family has known him for years."

"I can guarantee you that whoever this innkeeper is, he will not be as welcoming."

Pivoting on her heel, she glared at him. "And why should he not be?" The hand that was not holding her basket went to her hips, and he was able to see how small her waist really was.

Not only that, but her breasts were heaving up and down, and the memory of their softness played havoc with his cock.

"What do you think you are looking at?" Her blue eyes reminded him of ice chips.

At least she forgot to add *my lord* this time. "Nothing."

Turning back, she strode off. "I do not know why I must explain anything to you. You are a rake after all. How would you know anything about how a respectable lady should be treated?"

"First of all, I do have sisters and a mother. And secondly, I am not a rake."

"Really?" she said, drawing the word out in the most derisive voice he had heard lately.

This was the reason a man had a mistress. A mistress never spoke to him in such a tone. A mistress never defied him. A mistress did exactly as she was told.

"Yes, really." If only he had some way of tying Lady Charlotte up and taking her back to Town. "A rake preys on innocents. I most assuredly do not." Mainly because they bored him to death—or had. No one could accuse Lady Charlotte of being boring—and he valued his life.

"Harrumph."

She fell silent, and he thought he'd give the voice of reason another try. "What will you do on the off chance the landlord does not believe you?"

"As I previously mentioned, I shall seek out the vicar and have him send a letter to Worthington."

Dratted female. She had an answer for everything, except how to get out of the bumble broth into which they had both been catapulted. If he could catch Miss Betsy, he'd strangle the blasted bawd's scrawny neck and damn the consequences. He was tempted to throttle Lady Charlotte as well, but she truly did not realize how tenuous her position was. As if the *ton* or even the landlord would not immediately think the worst of a young lady wandering around the countryside by herself.

The inn came into sight, and her sigh of relief was so loud, he could hear from where he stood several feet away.

"Now you shall see that I am right," she said, lengthening

her stride as much as she could, given her narrow skirts. Clearly she had spent most of her life in the country.

Another carriage drove into the yard at the same time they had reached the door. Damnation! It was Braxton. The biggest gossip in town, and Lord Gerald with him.

Somehow Con had to get control of this situation. He tossed his ribbons to a stable boy, and rushed to the door of the Green Man, opening it before she could do it herself. Head held high, she entered the building like a ship under sail.

Lord save them both. He strode in after her, ready to pick up the pieces. Not that she'd thank him for it.

Standing before the startled innkeeper, she announced, "I am Lady Charlotte Carpenter—"

"And I am Lord Kenilworth. My betrothed and I are visiting my mother and we had an accident with our carriage." He resisted the urge to blow out a breath as Braxton strolled through the entrance.

Betrothed? Charlotte whirled around to protest when she saw Lord Braxton and quickly schooled her expression to one of calm.

For the love of God! Could nothing go right? After everything she had said to Lord Kenilworth, not to mention his smug replies, she could not bear the humiliation, or his self-satisfaction.

She had allowed her normally slow-to-rise temper— and, to be honest, her fear of what a man who bought women for pleasure would do to her—get the better of her. He was right, of course. Young ladies did not simply stride into an inn and demand a room.

Perhaps it was even that kiss. It had been so soft and sweet—better than she'd ever thought a kiss could be, yet exactly how Dotty and Louisa described it—and for the first time in hours, Charlotte had felt so safe, and she had thought that . . . well, she refused to think about that now. The kiss would never be repeated. Once she was home, she would never see him again.

"Kenilworth," Braxton called out. "I thought that was you. Did you say you are betrothed?"

"Indeed we are. Lady Charlotte and I are visiting my mother." Lord Kenilworth raised his quizzing glass, focusing it on the other man. "Although, I cannot imagine what your interest might be."

She stifled a groan. Why her? What had she ever done to deserve to be in this situation? She had always tried to be kind to others and help those who needed it. Yet now, Matt was going to murder her, and Grace would not be able to stop him. At least Lord Kenilworth had ceased smirking. If only Charlotte could think of something to say. Something to stop this madness.

Down the short corridor behind her, a door opened. *Please let it not be another gentleman of Lord Braxton's ilk.*

"Lady Charlotte—"

Letting go of her breath at the familiar voice, she could not resist giving Lord Kenilworth a small triumphant smile before sending up a prayer of gratitude.

"—I wondered what was taking you so long to arrive."

A wave of relief swept over Charlotte as she curtseyed to the grand dame who had been instrumental in Dotty and Dom's marriage. "Lady Bellamny, I am sorry to have kept you waiting." Charlotte bussed the older lady's cheek and whispered, "I am desperate to return home. How did you find me?"

And get as far away from Lord Kenilworth as she could. She would deal with his unwanted, though most likely necessary, announcement later.

"Pure serendipity, my dear. I am glad to see you safe," her ladyship said in a hushed tone before patting Charlotte's cheek and stepping back. "Yes, yes, I can imagine, but all in good time, my dear. All in good time," her ladyship said with infuriating calm. "Come with me." Lady Bellamny's gaze seemed to sweep the hall as she beckoned Charlotte to follow.

Her ladyship glanced over her shoulder. "You too, Kenilworth. I am looking forward to seeing your mother again. It was kind of you to meet me here. Mrs. Watson"— Lady Bellamny beckoned the landlady—"we shall require tea and something to eat." When Lord Braxton started forward, her ladyship fixed him with her basilisk stare. "Not you, my lord."

Sweeping through the door to a good-sized parlor, her ladyship waved Charlotte to one of the chairs at a square oak table. Lord Kenilworth followed, taking up a position against the fireplace.

Fortunately, they did not have long to wait before Mrs. Watson and a servant carried in two pots of tea, bread, cheeses, meats, and fruit. After arranging the repast on the table, the women left the room, closing the door behind them.

Neither her ladyship nor his lordship had said a word. However, he had lost the humorous look he'd been wearing earlier. It served him right for being so pleased with himself. Now that Lady Bellamny was here, Charlotte could be home by tea.

Glancing between the two of them, she twisted the pearl ring on her right hand. Briefly, she considered breaking the silence, but decided against it. Something seemed to be going on. She just did not know what it could be.

"I heard you state that you and Lady Charlotte are betrothed." Lady Bellamny took the chair across from Charlotte and began to pour tea.

Lord Kenilworth's jaw moved slightly, as if he was

grinding his teeth, before replying with bad grace. "Under the circumstances, there was little else I could do."

Her ladyship raised one imperious brow. "Do not look so down in the mouth. Lady Charlotte will make you a perfectly lovely wife. Your mother will be thrilled that you have finally decided to wed."

Wife? Wed? No, no, no! Being betrothed was bad enough. But she could get out of that. But married! Lord Kenilworth was the last man in the world she would wed. Just the idea that he would touch her with the same hands he used to mistreat other women made her stomach lurch.

Charlotte quickly shoved the memory of his kiss aside. If she had known who he was, she would never have kissed him.

Taking a deep breath, she said with as firm a voice as she could muster, "Despite what his lordship said, I do not wish to marry him. There must be a way to—"

"That is neither here nor there, my dear." Lady Bellamny waved away Charlotte's complaint in a voice so composed it made her want to slaughter someone. Preferably Lord Kenilworth. "I stopped by Stanwood House to inform your sister I intended to be out of Town for a few days. Instead, I found your cousin Jane, Mrs. Addison. Knowing that I am a trustworthy friend of the family, she told me what had occurred. Unless I am mistaken, you were with Lord Kenilworth at least overnight, and you were seen entering the inn with him." She raised a brow. "In a rather disheveled state."

Charlotte decided to ignore her creased, dusty gown, and address the most important issue. "I did not exactly spend the night with him." Not all night and, technically, she had entered the inn first. "He followed me into the inn. I—"

"Close enough, my lady." His tone was as dry as sand. "We were seen together walking toward this place, and I held the door open for you."

"Charlotte, my dear." Lady Bellamny's hard tone took Charlotte aback. She had never before been on the receiving end of her ladyship's bite. "I do hope you were not going to tell me that you spent the night in the company of those ruffians who abducted you." Her other brow rose as she finished the sentence.

"No, my lady." She barely got the words out as the ramifications of *that* getting out slammed into her consciousness.

Unfortunately, in the eyes of the *ton*, being with those blackguards would be even worse than spending the time with his lordship. No one would believe she had not been violated. The fact that he had helped her get away early this morning would not mean anything to a scandal-monger such as Lord Braxton.

To make matters worse, Lord Kenilworth had been right. She had been naïve and stupid. Although, she still did not trust him. Any man who would use women the way he did was a cur.

"Excellent." Her ladyship took a sip of tea and focused an innocuous gaze on Charlotte. "Then what objection do you have to Kenilworth? He is good looking—"

She felt her eyes widening.

"Heavens, girl. I may be old but I'm not blind."

His lordship inclined his head slightly—the hint of a smile quivering at the corners of his lips—as her ladyship raised her cup of tea to him. "Now, as I was saying, he is not hard on one's eyes, wealthy, and a marquis. Most young ladies would be overjoyed to be making such a match."

Most perhaps, but not her. "But—but I had never met him before last evening." She sat straighter in her chair. "I cannot possibly marry a man on so small an acquaintance."

Surely the fact that they were strangers would hold some

sway. She had sworn never to wed a man who engaged in buying a female for his own gratification, and that is exactly what keeping a mistress was. Not to mention, two of them at the same time. No, she must hold fast to her principles.

"Under the circumstances, you have no choice." Lady Bellamny calmly sipped her tea.

"He is a rake." Charlotte raised her chin, daring either of them to tell her she was wrong. "I will not wed a man who abuses women."

"Abuse a woman?" Lord Kenilworth's green eyes darkened as his gaze pierced through her. His voice was dangerously quiet, and a shiver chilled her spine. "I have never in my life harmed a female."

How dare he lie? The mere fact that he paid to use a woman's body was more than she could tolerate. Dotty had told her how demeaned the women she had rescued were. They had been forced to submit to rape, or drugged with opium until they would do anything for the drug. Only a very few of the women at Miss Betsy's had said they had chosen that life. The rest did it because they had been forced into it by someone else or because it was either that or die of starvation.

"Indeed, my lord." Charlotte narrowed her eyes at him. "What do you call it when you pay to use a woman's body?"

"A business arrangement," he shot back as if he had done nothing wrong.

"*That* is *quite* enough from both of you." Lady Bellamny rang a small handbell. "Lady Charlotte, you should know better than to discuss topics you should know nothing about. As for you, Kenilworth, remember you are a gentleman speaking to a young lady. Obviously, the two of you have some differences to work out." Lady Bellamny rang the bell again. "Lady Charlotte, you shall retire to a chamber. After you have washed and broken your fast—for it is clear something is making you out of sorts—I shall accompany you and Kenilworth to his mother's estate. You will remain there until Worthington is able to take you back to Town. I'll write Grace, informing her that you are safe. Kenilworth, I suggest you write Worthington." Mrs. Watson entered the parlor. "Please take Lady Charlotte to a room where she can wash. The small repast you provided was very good. However, I shall also want a complete breakfast for three served here as soon as her ladyship returns."

Chapter Six

Charlotte was more than grateful to be able to leave the parlor.

It was fortunate that Lady Bellamny had been here for her—the Fates must have had a hand in bringing that about. Still, the idea that she would be forced to marry a man who used prostitutes, the type of man she had vowed never to wed, made her stomach ache. If only she had the funds to return to Town, she would leave and refuse to see him again. She could tell anyone who asked that they'd had an argument and she had changed her mind about the marriage. Now she must remain in the same house with him for at least a day or so.

They reached a door near the top of the stairs. "I'll send my eldest daughter up to assist you, my lady."

"Thank you."

After the door closed behind Charlotte, she removed her bonnet and the pins from her hair, running her fingers through her long tresses to untangle the snarls. What she would not give for a full bath. Since she did not have the wherewithal to go home, hopefully she could have one once she was with Lord Kenilworth's mother.

Oh, God. Her heart contracted painfully as if it had been

squeezed by an invisible hand. She could not accept that her situation was impossible. That she would be forced to marry him.

The worst part of it all was that before she knew who he was, she had begun to like him. After his kiss, she had thought she might have found the right gentleman for her. Yet she could not, would not marry him.

Surely Grace would be able to help her get out of it. Although she had not been able to assist Dotty. Still, Dotty's marriage had turned out much better than anyone could have expected. Merton doted on Dotty and she on him.

Charlotte could not even think of a way she could be happy with a man who thought of a female's body as a business arrangement. He must know the damage he was doing to the women he used.

She had begun pacing the chamber, and halted. Or perhaps he did not know how harmful his behavior was. Dotty had said many men did not think of the consequences of their actions. Even Grace had agreed that men could be blind when it came to fulfilling their needs.

Charlotte was not willing to wed Kenilworth, still, she would do her best to convince him that he should help women in trouble, and not use them as he was used to doing.

A knock came on the door, and a woman who looked to be about Charlotte's age entered the room. "I'm Sally. My ma sent me, my lady."

"Thank you. I was attempting to comb my hair."

"If you'd like me to help you undress so you can wash, I'll do your hair too."

"Yes, please." Charlotte turned her back to the girl. "I would greatly appreciate your help."

A half hour later, she felt much cleaner and more able to

meet the challenge she had set for herself. She would take
her stand against the marriage and not be swayed.

"I shall require paper and pen," Con said when the innkeeper's wife returned. "I also wish to send a messenger to
Hillstone Manor."

"Yes, my lord." The woman bobbed a curtsey.

Once he had been shown to a small room with a desk,
he settled down on a hard wooden chair and began to write.

My dear Worthington,
*   You will know by now that your sister is safe. I*
shall escort her to my mother's house, Hillstone
Manor, in Kingsbrook. Lady Bellamny had the good
sense and excellent timing to be visiting the area—
apparently there is a rock formation her husband
wished to view—and will travel to my mother's
with us.
*   I would like to assure you that all is well.*
However, your sister and I were seen by Certain
Persons as we drove into the yard. Naturally, I put
it about that we are betrothed and are visiting my
mother.
*   I shall be prepared to discuss the settlement*
agreements when you arrive.
*   Yr. Servant,*
*   C. Kenilworth*

Next he wrote a missive to his mother warning her she
was about to have guests, but not giving her any idea as to
what sort of visitors to expect. That was probably not well
done of him, but he must explain how his betrothal came
about and the reason his betrothed—if one could call a lady

who refused to wed one a betrothed—was not happy about it. And that must be accomplished in person. Although he never thought to be happy about Lady Bellamny's presence, he'd most likely need her help.

He also penned a note to his valet, Cunningham, directing the man to travel immediately to Hillstone Manor with whatever clothing and other items Con would need for at least a week. Upon reflection, he instructed his valet to contact Lady Charlotte's maid and tell her she was to accompany Cunningham to Hillstone Manor.

Con placed the pen down, replaced the cork in the standish, and sanded the letters before dripping wax on the folded papers and pressing his signet ring into the red blobs.

He leaned back in the hard wooden chair. If only Braxton—of all the care-for-nobody slibberslabbers—had not seen Con and Charlotte come into the inn yard after having traveled most of the night. If Con were a superstitious man, he'd think that his pretending to be Braxton the previous evening had conjured up the popinjay.

Con rubbed his chin. There was nothing for it now. The die was cast and all of that. At least he would make his mother and sisters happy.

He strode to the front of the inn and found the landlord. "I must have these missives sent out by messenger immediately. Please have the man wait for a reply. I shall also require a chamber and some wash water."

"Very good, my lord." Mr. Watson pulled his forelock. "I'll have a room made up straightaway."

Con wandered into the common room that stood off to the side of the hall, preparing to partake in the house's ale while he waited for his chamber to be readied.

"Kenilworth." Lord Gerald Heathcote gave Con a toothy

smile. "The ale here is excellent." The man shoved a chair out from the table with his foot. "Join me."

"So I have heard." He glanced around and not seeing Braxton, joined Lord Gerald. "I believe I will. It's been an interesting morning." And evening, yet what else was he to say? "What brings you to the country?"

"Boxing match, don't you know." He held up two fingers to the barkeeper. "Decided to come down early. Inns fill up quickly for that type of thing. Braxton heard me tell another fellow and said he'd come as well."

How could Con have been such a dunderhead? Despite what he said earlier, he had been planning to attend the match himself. "I'd forgotten."

"Uh, about that." Lord Gerald lowered his voice to a whisper. "What *is* Lady Charlotte doing here? Braxton thinks you must be eloping, but I told him you was going the wrong way to Gretna Green." Lord Gerald frowned. "Can't think why you'd have to elope in the first place. You're eligible enough for any lady." Two mugs were set before them. Lord Gerald took a long draw on his. "Didn't know you was looking for a wife. Would have suggested my sister. The eldest one. The other one's not out yet. Come to think of it, don't remember seeing you at any of the balls and such this Season."

Because I haven't been at any of the entertainments, and I have been actively not looking for a wife. The Fates have a strange way of interfering with one's plans.

He would have to remember to tell Charlotte—he supposed he no longer needed to use her title—the bouncer he was about to tell his acquaintance. "Lady Charlotte and I recently formed an understanding. I decided it was as good a time as any for her to meet my mother. During the journey down we had a slight accident with the phaeton. No one was harmed. However, she and I became a bit rumpled. Naturally, Lady Bellamny was accompanying us in her coach." He had to think back to what had been said when Lady Bellamny appeared. Thank the Lord, Braxton had not heard Con and Charlotte bickering.

"Never thought I'd see you leg-shackled so soon." A large smile spread over Lord Gerald's face. "Nevertheless, I'm happy to wish you happy. But why the rush down, when you could have attended the match?"

"We wanted to inform my mother of our decision to wed." Con had no doubt that once Mama and Worthington heard that Con and Charlotte had been seen by Braxton, Charlotte would be made to go through with the wedding.

"Thought Worthington was out of Town?" Lord Gerald asked, confused. Then again, he had always been a bit buffle-headed.

"I spoke with him just before he left. However, as I said, my mother needed to be informed before an announcement was made."

"Well, then." Lord Gerald finished off his ale and rose. "I'll just toddle off and tell Braxton he was out." The man gave Con a jaunty bow. "Very glad we had this talk. Braxton owes me a pony now. Told him Lady Charlotte wouldn't have just run off. Not the type, if you know what I mean." Lord Gerald suddenly looked anxious, and his mouth started to open and close. "My apologies. Not what I meant to say a'tall. Naturally, you'd know she isn't that type. Wouldn't be marrying her if she was."

"Naturally." Con's hand clenched. Given any reason at all, he'd gladly plant Braxton a facer. Unfortunately, that wouldn't help the situation. The man was as poisonous as a viper. He would ruin Charlotte and Con simply for his own amusement.

"I'll just be off."

Con stifled a sigh of relief. At least Lord Gerald had swallowed the story.

A few moments after Con finished his ale, the landlord appeared to take him to his chamber.

He stripped and poured warm water into a bowl, then washed as best he could before shaving. There was nothing to be done about his crushed cravat or shirt points, but Cunningham would be at the manor by this evening.

Con wondered if Charlotte had written to her maid, and if he should tell her he took care of the matter for her. Or perhaps, considering she didn't seem to wish to have anything to do with him, he would be better off keeping his own counsel.

Until she understood how precarious both their positions were, that was going to be a problem. He had never wanted a reluctant bride. One of the reasons he eschewed balls and other *tonish* events where young ladies would be present was to avoid just this type of situation, betrothed to a lady due to forces beyond his control.

Good God. What a muddle. Wellington had married from a sense of obligation, and look how badly that had turned out. Con had even less of a choice in the matter than the general. If only he had not got lost. If only he'd been able to get her back to Town before dawn, this problem could have been avoided. Or if she had not formed a completely unreasonable opinion of him that was as ridiculous as it was insulting.

What was the world coming to when the mere possession of a mistress caused a man to be accused of abuse? Not only that, but it was not true. He always treated his ladybirds with generosity and kindness. None of them had ever complained. It was the nature of the business that, eventually, one moved on.

What manifest nonsense to think badly of him for doing what all men did.

Charlotte must be made to understand that Cyprians were in a different class than the poor women at Miss Betsy's or some of the other brothels. He agreed that some of those women were badly treated, even if they chose to be there. His mistress, however, and others saw the advantages in entertaining gentlemen, and enjoyed their work. There was nothing unsavory about it, and the women were well compensated.

Someone had to make Charlotte see sense. Although, it would not be him. She wouldn't listen to him if he was fool enough to make the attempt. Hopefully, Lady Bellamny would have a talk with Charlotte and explain the ways of the world. Then again, she might come around when she understood her option was to wed him or be cast out of Polite Society and never marry.

If she did not wed him, no one would believe the story that they'd been traveling with Lady Bellamny. If anyone actually looked into the matter, that clanker wouldn't hold water, and her reputation would not be the only one at risk: Her sisters would be harmed.

He groaned. Not to mention *his* sisters. He could hear them haranguing and condemning him for an unthinking here-and-therian without the intelligence to convince an innocent young lady to marry him.

Damn if he'd let Charlotte make him look like a veritable coxcomb. There was no choice. She must wed him.

Con rubbed his cheek as he remembered her soft curves. His earlier reaction to her—before she'd begun harping about him keeping a mistress—had been strong enough that he thought he might enjoy teaching her about the sensual arts.

She was beautiful, well dowered, passionate, and intelligent. Other than her unfortunate tendency to champion impures, she was exactly the type of woman he had planned to wed . . . one day.

He stared at himself in the small shaving mirror. Whether he wanted it or not, that day was here.

He would simply have to channel Charlotte's passions away from what he had done with his mistress to what he would be doing with her. What could be easier than seducing one's own betrothed? An innocent who had probably not even been properly kissed—or kissed at all, if he knew her brother—before him.

Con made his way to the stables, where his leader had been tended. "I'll need to hire another pair. My stable master will make arrangements for these two to be taken to Hillstone Manor."

"Aye, my lord," an older groom responded. "We'll take good care of them. I got that pair of grays. Good goers, if ye ask me."

He looked over the horses' points. Satisfied, Con replied, "Have them ready in a half hour. Lady Bellamny's coach will be required as well."

He'd be damned if he was going to wait all day for the ladies, and he had to arrive at his mother's house with an attendant for Charlotte.

"I'll call fer her ladyship's coachman."

"Good man." Con strode back to the inn and went directly to Lady Bellamny's parlor, where he found her and Charlotte drinking tea. Two plates with leftover food were on the table, but there was enough on the tray for him to break his fast.

An almost empty bowl of milk sat on a table next to Charlotte. Collette was on the sofa, curled next to her mistress, who was absently stroking the feline. The homely, domestic scene belied their current circumstances.

"I ordered our carriages to be ready in half an hour, if that suits you."

"Excellent," Lady Bellamny replied. "I took it upon myself to write Lady Charlotte's cousin, asking for her maid to attend her. I also wrote to Lady Worthington. Worthington can be a bit of a hothead where his sisters are concerned. She will be able to exert a calming influence."

That was probably the best idea anyone had had all day. "Very well." Con lowered himself onto a chair next to Charlotte. "Is there any tea left?"

"I shall order a new pot." Lady Bellamny tugged the bell pull.

"Please." He glanced at Charlotte. She had not even looked up from gazing at the cat.

The blasted chit probably thought that if she ignored him he would go away.

Con opened his mouth to address her when Lady Bellamny caught his eye and shook her head. Very well. He'd leave well enough alone for the time being. She had not been at all ill-mannered or petulant before she had discovered his identity. Perhaps the events of the past day were catching up to her, and she would be better behaved when she was at his mother's home and had an opportunity to recover.

He had rank, wealth, and had been told by more women than he could count that he was handsome. Con did not believe he was being immodest in thinking that she could really not do much better than him. Unless, that is, she was after a duke, and young dukes were thin on the ground. Sooner or later Charlotte would come around.

He filled his plate with slices of rare roast beef and bread.

If the Fates were with him, he'd have enough time before Worthington arrived to persuade her she wished to spend her life with him.

Chapter Seven

Elizabeth Bell, Miss Betsy to most people and Mrs. E. Bottoms to others, arrived at the Hare and Hound shortly after ten in the morning to find the place in an uproar. "Burt"—she grabbed the man's arm as he rushed by—"what is going on?"

"My girl, my poor Annabelle, has gone missing," Mrs. Wick, the landlord's wife cried into a large handkerchief. "It was that man who was here, claiming he was lord, as took her." She wrung her hands in her apron. "I know he made my poor girl go with him."

Betsy immediately clasped her hands together, holding them to her chest. "My dear Mrs. Wick, surely she would not have run off. Annabelle is such a good girl."

"She is at that." The older woman wiped her eyes and nodded. "He must have knocked her out and took her." Betsy could see when the idea entered the woman's head. "Can ye help, miss? I know yer used to working for folks richer than us. We don't have a lot, but we'll give ye what we got to get our dear girl back."

"You do not even need to ask." She wrapped her arms gently around Mrs. Wick. "You and your family have been such good friends to me, I will do it without compensation."

"Oh, thank ye, thank ye. I don't know what we'd do without ye!" She straightened her apron. Pulling out a fresh handkerchief, she blew her nose. "Will ye go right away?"

"Of course. If you will tell me the name of the man who took her and anything you can remember about him, I shall begin the search as soon as I have delivered the lady the Smiths brought in yesterday." Betsy glanced at Burt. "We'll leave within the hour." Turning back to Mrs. Wick, Betsy asked, "Do you think you are well enough to prepare something for the young lady upstairs to eat, and help her clean up?"

"Oh, goodness." The woman jumped. "I'd forgot all about her. I'll have her ready directly after I bring you a cup of tea in the parlor. Won't do for a lady such as yerself to be in the common room. Not even this early in the morn."

"You are so kind, Mrs. Wick. I thank you." Betsy smiled at the lady before making her way to the only room in the inn that could pass for a parlor.

It was because the place did not generally cater to gentry that she'd chosen it. What she really wanted to know now was who the gentleman was who took Annabelle and how much he'd pay Betsy to keep the chit. It stood to reason that by the time she found the girl she'd no longer be a virgin.

Several moments later, an ear-piercing scream stabbed the air.

"I've found her, I've found her!" Mrs. Wick's shouting could have been heard in the next village.

Well, that was a short-lived deal, Betsy thought sourly.

The landlady ran into the room. "Oh, Miss Betsy, you won't believe what happened. That wicked young lady, although I don't know as I should use that term for her after what she did, had a gun and tied my Annabelle up. That Lord Braxton helped her." Mrs. Wick was wringing her apron again. "He must have been the reason she ran away from her lawful husband."

Betsy bit down on her lip hard to keep from saying things she shouldn't. Burt and Dan would have a lot to answer for. Bloody fools letting Lady Charlotte get away after all the planning that had gone into capturing her. And how the devil had she got ahold of a pistol? They'd answer for that as well.

"Please tell both Mr. Smiths I would like to see them."

"Yes, Miss Betsy. I'll get them right away."

She had just drained the cup when Burt knocked on the door and opened it, dragging Dan by the sleeve. For several long moments, she remained where she was, allowing the silence to weigh heavily while the two men fidgeted. Finally, she asked, "How did she get a pistol?"

Burt looked at Dan, then back to her. "She must a had it in her basket."

Betsy's back teeth clenched as she tried to control her temper. Losing it here where everyone thought she was a lady would not help. "A basket." She bit off the end of the word. "Is there a reason you did not look in this basket?"

"I asked," Dan said, glaring up at Burt. "Asked if she had any food in it." Dan shrugged off Burt's hand. "She said she was going to fetch somethin'."

Betsy focused on Burt. "And it did not occur to you to think she was lying?"

"No, miss. I was busy keeping Dan from trying to get to know her, if you know what I mean." He glowered at Dan. "I never thought a young lady would have a gun. She was just walking to the other house."

Well that, she had to admit, made sense. Betsy didn't think she would have thought of it either. Although, if she were a man, she'd plant both of her employees facers just for losing the chit. And Dan. *Bloody hell!* Just what she needed, a man who couldn't keep his hands to himself.

Reaching into her reticule, she pulled out a sack. "Dan, here is your payment. I will not need you again for a while."

His jaw dropped, but he grabbed the money and dashed out of the parlor.

"Burt, how do you plan to remedy this problem?" Because she would get Lady Charlotte back. The amount that lord was willing to pay for her made the gentry-mort worth more than Betsy's last three packages all together.

The early morning dew had dried when Lord Kenilworth handed Lady Bellamny and Charlotte into her ladyship's large traveling coach. She could barely stand to have him touch her and was glad for her gloves.

Thinking he would travel with them, she had sat next to Lady Bellamny. Thankfully, his lordship had opted to drive his phaeton instead of riding in the carriage with the ladies.

"I shall put your lack of manners, which I know you possess," Lady Bellamny said in a caustic tone, "to the horrible experiences of the past day." Her ladyship looked at Charlotte, making her feel as if she were six again instead of eighteen. "I will expect you to behave correctly to Lady Kenilworth."

"Yes, ma'am." After all, *his* mother had nothing to do with the way *he* behaved. Not that Charlotte would disobey Lady Bellamny in any event. She had been a friend to Charlotte's mother and now to Grace and the rest of the family.

"Neither will I have you showing that Friday face to her ladyship. It is her son to whom you are betrothed." Charlotte tried to paste a polite smile on her lips and failed miserably. "It is my experience that everything always turns out the way it is meant to be." Lady Bellamny lapsed into silence for a few minutes, but Charlotte did not expect it to last, and she was right. A few moments later, her ladyship continued. "You could do much worse than Kenilworth. He does not gamble or, as far as I know, drink to excess. He has an excellent reputation in the Lords. As a matter of fact, he has worked with Worthington to pass some important bills. I am positive that when you have had an opportunity to rest and reflect on your situation, you will come to the conclusion that you could have done much worse. It is a good match."

Not if he bought women, it was not. Lady Bellamny's sharp gaze focused on Charlotte, and she felt compelled to respond. "Yes, my lady."

Satisfied, Lady Bellamny closed her eyes and dozed, leaving Charlotte to her thoughts.

Mostly she just wanted to go home. She wanted to be with her sister and the children and not have to think about what had happened, or what could have happened, or what might happen.

If only she had not sent her footman, Frank, back to the house for her shooting gloves, he might have been able to fight off the miscreants until other help had arrived. With him there, and if she had practiced with her dagger more diligently, she could have stabbed one of the men and got away.

Tears pricked the back of Charlotte's eyes, and she gave herself a shake. There was no point in crying over what was already done. She would find a way forward. A way that did not include marrying a man she had detested long before she'd made his acquaintance.

At least Jemmy would have arrived in Berkeley Square by now with the message that she would be rescued. That was a happy thought. Although, she wished her champion had been someone else. That situation, though, was beyond her control . . . for the moment.

She could not stop her mind from wandering back over the past day. At first, Lord Kenilworth had seemed so nice, and she could not deny he was handsome, and there had been that kiss. Still, handsome is as handsome does and . . . She really had to stop thinking about Kenilworth.

Matt and Grace wouldn't be home yet, but Cousin Jane would come as soon as she received the letter giving her the direction of Lady Kenilworth's house. Perhaps her cousin would have some ideas Charlotte could not think of. After all, Jane had successfully managed not to marry the man her father chose for her.

Charlotte would write to Dotty as well. Her friend had always helped her find the best solutions to the problems Charlotte faced. And Dotty would understand why it was impossible for Charlotte to wed Lord Kenilworth. After all, she was the one who had discovered Miss Betsy's brothel and what she had done to the poor ladies there.

In the meantime, Charlotte would stay out of his lordship's way. After Charlotte's ordeal, perhaps his mother would expect her to be ill or out of sorts for a few days, and allow her to take her meals in her chamber. Normally, she would scoff at such mawkish behavior, but in this case she'd make an exception.

In a day or two, Jane would have arrived to take Charlotte home. And maybe her sister would already be waiting for her. And, if she wrote to Dotty right away, she might be in Town as well. Charlotte started to feel better, more hopeful. She wished Louisa could come, yet she was newly married and it would not be fair to drag her back to Town.

If only Lord Braxton and Lord Gerald had not been there, none of this would be necessary. Still, they had been, and Charlotte must think of a way out of this tangle.

She nodded to herself. She would write to her oldest sister and to her friend and tell them everything that had occurred—well, maybe not about the kiss—and among them, they would figure out a way for her to jilt Lord Kenilworth. He shouldn't even care if she ended the engagement. He did not want to marry her in any event.

Lady Bellamny was right. Everything would be as it should be, just not as her ladyship expected.

Less than thirty minutes later, Con turned down the familiar drive lined with linden trees. Leaning forward slightly, he waited until the Elizabethan manor house came into view. Even the horses seemed to sense his excitement and sped up a little.

As he approached, the windows sparkled as if diamonds had been set in the glass panes. Wooden beams crossed not only the cream-colored wattle and daub but the red brick as well. Although hidden from the front, the gardens in back had been restored to their original splendor, and he could not wait to see them once more. The manor house was easily the favorite of all his properties.

And even though Charlotte had given him nothing but trouble, he wondered if she would be as impressed by the manor as he always was.

He slowed the pair to a stop, jumped out of the phaeton, and threw the ribbons to a groom who had run up.

When Lady Bellamny's traveling coach stopped, Con opened the door and let the steps down.

"My ladies, welcome," he said, offering his hand. Once Lady Bellamny was out of the carriage, he turned to assist Charlotte down, almost expecting her to refuse his offer. Instead, she was standing in the door gazing in what appeared to be awe at the house's façade.

"It is lovely," he murmured, praying this new side of her would last.

"Yes. It is beautiful." Her expressive blue eyes sparkled. "I love the wattle and daub, and the windows. Is it in an E shape?"

"It is indeed. You know your architecture." He had never before met a young lady interested in old buildings, and his appreciation of her grew. Had Lady Bellamny said something to Charlotte to make her change her mind about him? He had never before been rejected by a woman, and it pricked his pride that the lady he must marry did not want him.

"Did one of your ancestors build it?" She scanned the front of the building as if she was attempting to take in everything about the structure before entering.

"It has been in my family for only about one hundred years." Con offered her his hand again. "There are knot gardens in the back as well as a maze."

The massive double doors to the house opened, and a butler emerged. "My lord, welcome. Her ladyship shall be here directly."

A bevy of footmen swarmed the carriages, then fell back looking confused. Good God. How had he forgotten how singular it would appear for two ladies to arrive with no luggage?

"There is no baggage, Dalton." Con held out one arm to Lady Bellamny and the other to Charlotte, and he almost sighed with relief when she placed her slender fingers on his jacket. "It will be here later along with my valet and Lady Charlotte's maid."

For a scant moment, the butler's lips pursed as if he had tasted a particularly sour lemon. The man needed to work on keeping his thoughts to himself. "Very good, my lord."

He escorted Lady Bellamny and Charlotte as they made their way into a grand hall. Removing her hand from his arm, Charlotte stared up at the carved wooden beams darkened by age, then looked down, taking in the checkerboard pattern of the marble tiles in dark blue and white.

Before his mother had moved in, old weapons adorned the walls. They had been replaced by old paintings and even older tapestries.

"One could easily spend a lifetime exploring this house and the grounds," she said, strolling around as she gazed up at the walls.

"Almost." Was that a pang of regret in her voice? He hoped it was. "I certainly have not been able to explore it all, and it was not from lack of trying."

He was congratulating himself at how well things were going, when his mother, a tall woman with russet-colored hair, descended the stairs. Her skin was still flawless. It was as if she had not aged a day since the last time he had visited. Mama glanced from Con to Charlotte, then to her ladyship.

No one could accuse her of being stupid. In the brief time she'd traversed the stairs, he could tell she had apprehended most of the situation. Finally, she was going to get her wish that he wed.

Slowly, Mama's lips formed a wide smile. "Almeria, I am overjoyed to see you. What have you brought me?"

"As I am to see you." Lady Bellamny touched Lady Kenilworth's outstretched hand and bussed her cheek. "You must come up to Town more often."

The older ladies embraced before his mother turned to him, raising a brow as she did. "Constantine?"

Immediately, he bowed and made a nod in Charlotte's direction. "Mama, this is Lady Charlotte Vivers—"

"Carpenter," Charlotte corrected him in a firm but cordial tone as she made an elegant curtsey. "Vivers is my brother-in-law, the Earl of Worthington's, family name."

And guardian. Con finally remembered that Worthington was raising his wife's sisters and brothers along with

Worthington's own sisters. Con tried to keep his back teeth from grinding. At the rate he was going, he'd wear them down before he was much older. "My mistake."

Perdition. How in hell could he have forgot the name she had given the landlord? Not only that, but she didn't have the Vivers' dark hair and lapis eyes. Carpenter? Stanstead? *Hell.* She must be the old Earl of Stanstead's daughter and the new earl's sister. Nothing like feeling a fool.

Not only that, his fumble put paid to the story he'd planned to tell his mother; that he and Charlotte had known each other before.

"Lady Charlotte, my mother, the Marchioness of Kenilworth."

"A pleasure to meet you, my lady."

Not batting an eye, his mother held out her hand in welcome. One would almost think he was in the habit of bringing home disheveled young ladies whose names he did not know. "I believe we shall take tea in the morning room, and you may tell me what this is all about." Lady Kenilworth's eyes narrowed slightly as she gazed at Charlotte and her son. "However, that can wait. Lady Charlotte shall have a chance to rest. You look as if you have not slept well, my dear."

Although Charlotte's back was still erect, she seemed to droop, and there was a twinge of something in the region of Con's heart. She *had* been through a great deal lately.

"Thank you. I am rather fatigued," Charlotte replied.

As if she had been waiting to be summoned, Mrs. Moore, his mother's housekeeper, came up next to Charlotte, curtseyed, then looked to his mother.

"Here you are, my dear." His mother maintained her smile and the light tone with which she had greeted them. "Mrs. Moore will be happy to escort you to your chamber."

"If you will come with me, my lady, I have a room ready."

"Thank you." She smiled gratefully.

That was the first time Con had seen her smile since . . . well, since she discovered his name. He didn't know what had caused this complete turnabout in her attitude, but he was grateful for it.

Once Charlotte and the housekeeper had ascended the stairs and turned into the east wing, Mama flew into action. "Dalton. We shall want tea and whatever else Cook has on hand at this hour of the day."

In an attempt to escape, Con bowed. "Lady Bellamny, thank you for your help. Mama, I shall see you after I have rested."

She glanced at him, both eyebrows climbing toward her hairline. "Not so fast, my boy. Before you do anything else, I shall have this story from you."

Without waiting for him to reply, she took Lady Bellamny's arm and turned on her heel, leading the way to the back of the house.

He followed the ladies down the corridor. At least he'd get to tell his story without Charlotte interrupting, and enlist his mother to his cause.

Chapter Eight

Charlotte followed Mrs. Moore up the grand staircase to a large, pleasant room overlooking a rose garden edged by what looked to be boxwood.

A tub and screen stood before the fireplace, which had been lit and was already warming the bedchamber.

"I'll send her ladyship's dresser to you."

"Thank you."

The door closed behind the housekeeper, and Charlotte rubbed her arms, more to stay awake than for warmth.

A few moments later, a light rap sounded on the door before it opened and a woman carrying a linen nightgown entered the chamber. "Good morning, my lady, I am Gray." She looked around the room, then, seemingly satisfied, asked, "Shall I help you undress?"

"Yes, please," Charlotte repeated. Unlike last night at the inn, she longed to change into nightclothes, sink into a soft bed, and sleep.

Despite Lord Kenilworth being in the house, she felt as if she was safe. Even a rogue such as he would not accost her in his mother's house.

"I shall clean and brush your garments while you sleep."

The dresser's voice was soothing, easing her into a feeling of contentment. "I understand your maid will arrive later today."

"She will." Thankfully, Lady Bellamny had taken care of that.

Charlotte turned, allowing the maid to unfasten the back of her carriage gown, when she remembered the dagger. "If you will give me a moment, I must go behind the screen."

Gray pointed to a door nestled between two bookcases. "You will find the garderobe through that door."

"I shall be just a moment." Charlotte strode into the small room. There were shelves with folded cloths to one side. She removed the dagger and holder, placing them behind the cloths, then returned to the main chamber.

While Gray was undressing Charlotte, she had the opportunity to think back. She had been surprised to see how young Lady Kenilworth appeared. Even as she had come to greet them, Charlotte could see her ladyship's flawless skin. Other than some small lines radiating from Lady Kenilworth's eyes, there was hardly a wrinkle to be seen.

She had not appeared old enough to be his lordship's mother, and Charlotte thought the lady could be a stepmother like Lady Worthington, now Lady Wolverton, was Matt's step-mother. Yet, her ladyship's eyes were the same beautiful leaf green of Kenilworth's, so they must be related.

It had not been until Lady Kenilworth had mentioned resting that Charlotte had allowed herself to flag, and suddenly the hours of travel and very little sleep had caught up with her all at once.

Charlotte raised her arms, and the dresser slipped the nightgown over her head. Charlotte covered her mouth, hiding a yawn.

Gray ran a warming pan under the top bedcovers. "Well, now. Let's get you into bed, my lady."

A moment later Charlotte was tucked under the bedcovers,

the door had closed on the maid, and nothing short of another abduction could have stopped her from succumbing to Morpheus . . . except—a plaintive chirp sounded from the basket—Collette.

Charlotte threw the covers back. How could she have forgotten her kitten?

She must be much more tired than even she had thought. After opening the basket and seeing to the poor kitty's needs, she set Collette on the bed and climbed back in, snuggling the kitten next to her. "Now we shall have a nice nap. Once I'm rested I shall find a way out of this ludicrous betrothal."

The bed was soft, the curtains closed, but still sleep didn't come. Lord Kenilworth could not wish to wed Charlotte. Indeed, earlier at the inn he had not even cared enough about her to notice she was ignoring him. Then when he had given his mother her wrong last name, he had not appeared at all contrite for the mistake he had made. He clearly possessed no proper feelings. Yet another reason not to marry him.

Well, what more could she expect from the man—she would not call him a gentleman even though that was his rank—who bought a woman's body? Women's bodies.

Most likely, he merely did not wish to face Lady Bellamny's ire by refusing the betrothal. That must be it. Even Matt and Merton did not like to get on the wrong side of her ladyship. The more Charlotte considered it, the more convinced she became that Lord Kenilworth would be happy to be rid of her.

That settled, she began to feel sleepy again. There was nothing to worry about. If all went well, she would be home tomorrow evening at the latest.

* * *

Con followed Lady Bellamny and his mother down the corridor to a light-filled morning room in the back of the house.

The parlor—filled with old furniture—was comfortable rather than formal. The lower walls were painted a muted shade of apple green. The curtains and upper walls were of a large floral pattern. Paintings, mostly portraits of children, pets, and other people, covered almost every surface running up two of the walls. The French windows his mother had had installed led out to her favorite part of the garden.

"Constantine," Mama said, motioning him to one of two chairs near the sofa next to which she stood. "Please sit where I can easily see you."

That never boded well for him. Instead of complying, he took up a position next to the fireplace. "I believe I would rather stand."

"As you will." Her eyes narrowed at him as she gracefully sank onto the sofa, settling her skirts as she did.

When the butler entered bearing a large tea tray, Con was glad to see his favorite lemon tarts covering one plate. *Were they Cook's idea or Mama's?*

Lady Bellamny chose an old French cane-backed chair to Mama's right.

Once he received a cup of tea from her, Con decided to begin with the most relevant piece of news first. "Lady Charlotte and I are betrothed."

"Betrothed!" His mother opened and closed her mouth as if she would say more but did not know quite what. Unfortunately, that did not last nearly long enough. She had been waiting for this day since he went on the Town. "You did not even know her surname. How can you be engaged to the lady?"

Devil take it. Why did she have to focus on that slight mistake?

His back teeth started grinding again. "Mother, if you would allow me to continue."

Raising one brow, he waited. A few moments later, she inclined her head. "Very well. You may go on."

If only he could think of a better, more amenable way to put this. But he couldn't. "It appears I compromised Lady Charlotte—"

"*You did what?*" His mother's face flushed with anger. "Kenilworth, how could you do such a thing? And how could it *appear* that you compromised her? Either you did or you did not."

Thankfully, Lady Bellamny cleared her throat . . . loudly. "If I may?" She paused for the briefest second, then carried on without anyone's permission. "Kenilworth was passing Worthington House yesterday when he was called upon to aid Lady Charlotte, who had been abducted."

His mother gasped, holding her hand to her bosom. "Oh, the poor dear."

"Precisely." Lady Bellamny nodded. "He followed her to an inn where she was being held captive and rescued her."

Mama smiled. "That was extremely clever of you, Constantine."

He gave a shallow bow, and waited for her ladyship to continue.

"He was unable to return her to Town before this morning, and they were seen by two worthless fribbles, entering an inn." His mother looked as if she would interrupt once more but held her peace. "One of whom would not hesitate to blacken both Lady Charlotte's and Kenilworth's names. Naturally, as a gentleman and a peer, Kenilworth is prepared to do his duty."

"I think both you and Lady Charlotte were extremely brave," his mother said. "It is a wonder she was not suffering from strong hysterics when she arrived." Mama took another sip of tea, all the while gazing at him with a calculating look in her eyes. "As you know, I wished for a love match for you. However, there is no reason why you cannot *make* her fall in love with you. You are very charming when you wish to be."

Except for the fact that she doesn't want to have anything to do with me.

"I am well pleased that you have behaved as a gentleman should—not that I would have expected anything less—and, as you know, I shall be happy to finally have grandchildren."

How his mother could completely ignore that his sisters had given her four grandchildren she doted on, was beyond him. She probably meant an heir but did not want to say it.

"What I would like to know is, how do you feel about this?"

Mama's question shook him out of his thoughts. How did he feel?

At first, infuriated that he was being put upon. Then he'd seen how truly distraught Charlotte was, and lost much of his ire. As wrongheaded as she was, at least she believed passionately about the rightness of her cause. And where there was such passion, there was an opportunity to direct it into more appropriate avenues. She was not afraid to express her mind. That, though, was a double-edged sword that was currently being held to his neck.

Her innocence was refreshing, as was her honesty. He could do much worse and most likely not a great deal better. The only real problem was that she could not stand to be around him.

"She is beautiful, intelligent, and will make me a fine wife and marchioness."

His mother nodded.

Now was the time to tell her Lady Charlotte was not as sanguine about this situation as he was. "However, I am afraid she is not as pleased about our betrothal as I am."

Mama's eyes hardened into emerald shards, and he hoped it was in defense of him. He was her only son after all. "Does she think she can do better than Kenilworth?"

"*I* think she could do better," he retorted, attempting to lighten Mama's mood. "That, however, is not her complaint. She objects to my keeping a mistress."

"For Heaven's sake, Constantine!" Mama threw up her hands. "What on earth were you thinking of to mention your mistress to her? Have you been avoiding Polite Society for so long that you have forgotten how to behave? Unmarried young ladies should not know—"

"I was not the one who brought up the subject."

"Then how did she know?" She asked as if she did not believe him.

Con swiped a hand down his face. "She saw me at the theater."

"Well"—his mother blinked a few times, as if digesting this information—"That is of no consequence. You will simply assure Lady Charlotte that you shall give up your ladybird, and indeed, have already done so in your mind."

He wished to God it were that simple. "She has stated she will not wed a man who has kept a mistress."

"How absurd." His mother waved her hand dismissively. "It is the way of our world for gentlemen to keep mistresses. Even your father had one"—Mama's face and lips lowered into a frown—"before he met me, of course. After that . . . there was no need."

Mama glanced at Lady Bellamny, who shook her head.

Good, at least someone knew Charlotte was not going to be so easily reassured. "Unfortunately," he said, "Lady Charlotte was made aware of the deplorable conditions in which some unfortunates are kept. Eventually, she will come around." Lord, he hoped so.

"I suggest waiting until her sister and Worthington arrive to broach the subject. In the meantime"—Lady Bellamny rose—"I must return to the inn. Even though I left him a note, my husband will be wondering where I've got to. He left shortly before Kenilworth and Lady Charlotte arrived to view some rock formation or another."

"And I," Con said, straightening, "am for my couch. Lady Charlotte is not the only one who was deprived of a night's sleep." He dropped a kiss on his mother's head. "Lady Bellamny, allow me to escort you to the hall."

They were halfway down the corridor when her ladyship said, "I wish you luck. I have a feeling you are going to need it. From what I have seen, Lady Charlotte is quite loyal, to her family, her friends, and her beliefs."

"I have no doubt you are correct."

"As there appears to be a boxing match in the village, I shall inform my husband we are returning to Town today." She sighed. "Although, I wouldn't be surprised if he decided to return home. He only came to Town to present a paper and has remained much longer than I expected. Be that as it may, I shall do my best to make your road easier."

"Thank you." It would not suit Con to have his wife hie off to Town if he wished to remain in the country, but the Bellamnys obviously had an arrangement that suited both of them.

After seeing her ladyship off, Con made his way to his bedchambers. Yet, rather than falling into peaceful slumber, he tossed and turned, punching the pillows more than once.

Visions of Charlotte attempting to make her own way

back to Mayfair from here kept intruding into his more delightful dreams of making her his. It was, after all, inevitable. Therefore, he might as well enjoy it.

Logically, he thought she was too intelligent to do anything that stupid. She must know that bawd and the blackguards who had abducted her would be searching for her. From what he'd heard of Miss Betsy, she would be extremely unhappy that her tool for avenging herself on Worthington had got away.

Giving up on sleep, Con tried to remember what exactly he had heard about the procuress. He'd been at one of the French-style drawing rooms his mistress, Aimée, liked to hold. It must have been shortly after the destruction of Miss Betsy's brothel. One of the other Cyprians knew one of the prostitutes who had worked there. It appeared that even the women who went voluntarily were being held against their will. More by the supposed debts they owed to Miss Betsy than anything else. That type of arrangement was, unfortunately, not unusual. Or so he had been told.

What had been disturbing were the claims of innocents and ladies being forced to work at the bawdy house, as well as the use of opiates to subdue them. This last bit he did not believe at all.

He punched his pillow again. Naturally, everyone had heard of country girls coming to Town and being lured into prostitution. He had even met a few, but once settled they were perfectly happy in their profession.

All of which begged the question of why Worthington had put Miss Betsy out of business. Or the reason Charlotte would have been told anything at all. What had possessed him to do something so ill advised as to mention a brothel to an innocent young lady?

That was something Con would not discover until his friend came to fetch Charlotte, which brought his overactive mind back to the problem at hand, keeping the lady safe and, more importantly, here where he could not only look after her, but convince her to wed him.

For despite the circumstances surrounding his betrothal, and for reasons he did not fully understand, he found himself looking forward to having Charlotte in his life and in his bed.

Chapter Nine

"Do you want me to wake her up, ma'am?" May's whisper pierced Charlotte's sleep.

"No, I shall sit with her until she wakens." That sounded like Jane.

Charlotte heard a rustle of skirts and a soft whoosh as her cousin sat in a chair next to the bed. She should really tell them she was awake, but try as she might, her eyes wouldn't open. How strange.

Sometime later, someone was gently shaking her. "Charlotte, sweetheart."

Goodness, it *was* Jane.

"You must awaken, or you'll not be able to sleep tonight."

Opening her eyes, Charlotte rubbed the sleep from them. The curtains had been pulled back and sunlight poured into the bedchamber. "How long have you been here?"

"About two hours. It is well past noon." Even though Jane smiled, a worry line had formed between her brows. "I shall call for May, and she can order a nuncheon to be brought for you."

Just then, Charlotte's stomach growled. This morning,

her stomach had been so tied in knots she had only eaten a piece of toast. Now she was famished. "A large nuncheon, please. I am quite peckish."

Her cousin's smile grew and the worry line disappeared. "I'm glad to hear it."

Swinging her legs over the bed, she picked up Collette. "Is Hector here?"

"No, he wanted to come with me, but I thought it might be better if he remained with the children." Jane took the kitten from Charlotte while she went into the garderobe. "Worthington's butler sent for us shortly after . . . yesterday afternoon. As soon as we knew where you were, I wrote to Grace suggesting she and Matt come directly here. But in the event they do not receive my missive in time, Hector will be able to tell them where we are."

That meant at least another day or two with Lord Kenilworth and his mother. Charlotte bit her lip to keep from saying anything and went behind the screen, pleased to see that her soap and toothbrush were there.

A few minutes later, May scratched on the door and entered, scanning Charlotte before holding out her robe. "I'm so glad to see you, my lady. I've got your pale green gown ready after you finish eating. Let's do your hair while we're waiting."

That was surprising. She had expected May, if not Jane, to mention the abduction. Apparently, neither of them wished to mention the event.

Sitting at the dressing table, Charlotte watched as her maid twisted her hair into a neat knot high on her head.

"Do you still have your gold earbobs?"

"They are on the nightstand. I took them off before going to bed."

"Ah, I see them." As soon as Charlotte had donned the

jewelry, a knock came on the door, and May gave her another big smile, much as Jane had earlier. "That'll be your nuncheon, my lady."

Charlotte stood at the window taking in the view of the garden while her maid arranged the dishes.

"Doesn't all this look good," May said, and for the first time Charlotte heard the forced cheerfulness in her maid's voice.

She could almost see the worry in May's eyes, much as Charlotte had seen the line between her cousin's brows. Something was going on, but what? They were both treating her as if she were a fragile porcelain figurine and would fall apart at any moment.

The door closed, and she ambled toward the table where Jane had already taken a seat and tucked into the food. Charlotte was halfway finished eating, when it occurred to her that neither her maid nor her cousin were going to bring up what had happened. It was up to her to allay their concerns.

"I am fine, Jane. I really am. Lord Kenilworth helped me escape before anyone could harm me."

Jane set down the cup of tea she'd been drinking. "Charlotte, on our way here we stopped at an inn for directions. While the coachman was getting them, I heard two gentlemen discussing your betrothal to Lord Kenilworth. Are you truly betrothed? Neither Lady Bellamny nor Lady Kenilworth told me you had got engaged, but what brought about the talk?"

Charlotte twisted the napkin in her hands. "Lord Braxton and another man saw us enter the inn. Lord Kenilworth told the landlord we were betrothed. Then Lady Bellamny appeared and she asked him if he was going to do his duty and marry me." The concern in Jane's eyes had not lessened. "I do not wish to wed him, and I do not believe he wants to marry me. While I slept, a plan came to me. I will simply remain betrothed until sometime in the summer, after any talk dies down. Just like Dotty was going to do before she fell in love with Merton." Jane's countenance became graver than Charlotte had ever seen it. "It will be fine. You'll see."

Yet, from the look on her cousin's face, she was beginning to think all might not work out as she wished.

Reaching over, Jane patted Charlotte's shoulder. "Let us not make any plans now. Grace will be here soon."

A chill ran down Charlotte's spine. "What are you not telling me?"

Several moments passed before her cousin replied, "Due to the nature of your clothing"—last night it had looked as if she had slept in it, which she had—"there is a rumor that you and his lordship were trysting this morning."

No doubt started by Lord Braxton, yet Jane might not know the source. "But Lady Bellamny—"

"Oh, yes. The gentlemen accepted that her ladyship was with you, but they are under the impression the two of you stole away to be alone."

Blast, blast, and blast! Now what am I going to do?

Denying the rumor would be useless. Charlotte was well aware of what her sister and her friend had done with their husbands before their vows. Lady Bellamny had told Charlotte what Lord Kenilworth had said to Lord Gerald about having an accident with the phaeton. Obviously, despite what Lord Kenilworth thought, Lord Gerald or, more likely, Lord Braxton hadn't believed the story.

"We did not," she objected as strongly as possible. "We had been traveling and before that, I'd been thrown into a coach. He only said we were betrothed to save my reputation."

"Yes, my dear." Jane patted Charlotte's hand. "I believe you, and Matt and Grace will believe you as well. The problem is that once gossip such as this starts, it is almost impossible to stop it." Her cousin pursed her lips together. "And he did say you were to marry. That would give rise to speculation that something was going on as well."

"This is so unfair." Charlotte wanted to wail, but she refused to give in to such childish behavior.

"I understand." Jane was quiet for a few moments as she sipped her tea. "I do not know Lord Kenilworth, but Lady Bellamny thinks well of him. I know you want a love match, but are you sure you cannot wed him?"

Oh, God! Not Jane too! "I cannot." Charlotte wondered how much to tell her cousin, and decided if she wanted help, she'd have to tell the whole truth. "He abuses women."

Tea spewed from Jane's mouth before she could grab her napkin. "What?" Her shocked expression was everything Charlotte could have asked for. "Charlotte, how on earth do you know that?"

"Before Louisa married, we attended the theater with her and Rothwell. Kenilworth was there with not one but two courtesans."

Jane's brows rose. "That does seem a bit excessive."

That was not exactly the response Charlotte expected. "Do you know about the brothel that Dotty Merton found?" Jane shook her head. "Well let me tell you what Grace and Dotty told Louisa and me."

She related how ladies had been abducted to work in prostitution and when they refused had been made to take opium. "All because men wanted to buy their bodies and use them." Charlotte's voice shook with rage. Then she added her *pièce de résistance*. "And do you know what Lord Kenilworth said when I chastised him for keeping a mistress?"

"No," her cousin said slowly.

"He said it was a business arrangement." She hiccupped and blinked the moisture from her eyes. Still, everything was blurry. "Those poor women. A business arrangement."

She had barely got out the last word when she burst into tears.

Jane wrapped her arms around Charlotte and patted her back. "We will think of something. I promise you." Her cousin helped her up and back to the bed. "It would be best if you lie down for a while longer."

"You may be right." She hardly ever cried. Not since her mother had died and she discovered it did no good. "Perhaps I am more tired than I thought."

Charlotte woke a few hours later feeling much calmer, the bout of tears having worked to rid her of her excess emotions. She rang for her maid, who arrived several minutes later.

"We didn't know if you'd be up or sleep through the night."

"Have I missed dinner?"

"No, my lady. You have enough time to dress."

While her maid worked, she made a few decisions.

First of all, she must behave like the lady she was. Her sister Grace would have been mortified at her conduct toward Lady Bellamny and even Lord Kenilworth. No matter the provocation, Charlotte vowed she would remember her manners.

Secondly, she would not discuss the betrothal at all, with anyone, including his lordship. Make that especially his lordship. Men could be a strange species, finding challenges in almost anything, and she was not going to be a challenge.

Lastly, she was going to find a way to have Miss Betsy arrested and save as many of the odious woman's victims as possible.

"The pearls, my lady?" May asked.

"Yes. They will be perfect."

Charlotte attached the earbobs while her maid clasped the necklace. A silk ribbon with small pearls attached had been threaded through her hair.

Once May handed Charlotte her reticule and draped a Norwich shawl over her shoulders, she looked in the mirror and nodded. She was ready to face Lord Kenilworth and his mother.

As soon as she figured out where the drawing room was. Old houses were always difficult to navigate.

A knock came on the door and Jane poked her head in. "I thought you and I might go down together."

"Do you know the way?" Charlotte asked hopefully.

"No." Jane laughed. "I hoped to find a footman or maid."

Charlotte opened the door wider. "The worst that can happen is they'll have to send out a search party."

"No need for that." Lord Kenilworth stood in the corridor, smiling at her and Jane. "I have come to escort you. Lady Charlotte?" He held out one arm. "Mrs. Addison?"

They each placed a hand on an arm. She did not want him there, but this was her first opportunity to behave as she ought. "Lead on, my lord."

"The house is not as much a rabbit warren as some, but there are a number of rooms."

"I would love to tour it someday," Charlotte said. Although she doubted she would be there long enough.

Without question, his lordship and his mother had a great deal to keep them busy.

"I'd be happy to show you the house and gardens to-morrow."

Now she'd stepped into it. "I would love to."

"If you do not mind," Jane said, "I would like to see the house and gardens as well."

Charlotte sent up a prayer of thanks for helpful cousins.

"Not at all, ma'am. It is my pleasure." He sounded as if he really meant it, which surprised her.

Perhaps she had been right after all, and he would be glad to be free of her.

Then again, her sister always said that one caught more flies with a spoonful of honey than a gallon of vinegar. Not that she wanted him to catch her, nor did she wish to be drawing caps at every turn, and there was his mother to consider.

After descending the grand staircase, turning right, then strolling down another corridor, they finally reached the drawing room. It was just as light and lovely as the other rooms.

Lady Kenilworth was already sitting next to the fire-place with a glass of wine in her hand. "Welcome, Mrs. Addison." Lady Kenilworth set her drink on a small marble-topped table and rose. "My dear Lady Charlotte, how wonderful to see you so well rested." Her ladyship held out her hands to Jane and Charlotte. "Will you have wine or sherry?"

"Sherry, if you please," Charlotte replied.

"I as well," Jane agreed.

Lord Kenilworth poured, handing them their glasses.

"Kenilworth has told me about your betrothal. I cannot tell you how happy I am. A toast." Her ladyship smiled beatifically. "To your betrothal. You do not know how long I have waited to have a daughter."

Even though she had not said a word, Charlotte felt like the worst sort of impostor.

Charlotte had just taken a sip of sherry when Kenilworth retorted drily, "I am only two and thirty." Though at the moment he sounded more like thirteen. "And you already have three daughters. Surely you have not forgotten them."

Despite her vow to behave perfectly, she could not stop herself. "How dare you speak to your mother in such a way?" Her grip tightened on the stem of the glass as she fought to keep some control over herself. "You ought to be ashamed of yourself, my lord, and thank your good fortune that you still have a mother." Kenilworth and the marchioness turned their startled gazes to her. Oh, Lord. What had she done? "Forgive me," Charlotte said, vastly more contrite than she expected to be. Her nerves must be more frayed than she thought. "I should not have spoken. My mother died several years ago, and I miss her every day."

"I know exactly how you feel, my dear." Lady Kenilworth hurried to Charlotte, giving her such a sympathetic look that she had to force herself not to burst into tears again. "I too lost my mother when I was young. I do not believe one ever forgets. Constantine"—the marchioness's chin rose—"I approve of your choice of wife and as far as I am concerned, nothing else matters."

Oh no! She had not defended Lady Kenilworth to gain the woman's approval in a marriage Charlotte had no intention of making.

Yet, now what was she to do? She could not allow her ladyship to continue under the misapprehension that she would marry her son. She would have to explain that she did not truly have to wed his lordship.

She tried to ignore what her cousin had said. "It is a temporary engagement only. I am sure that under the circumstances, his lordship would agree that ending our betrothal in late summer or autumn is in both of our interests." She forced herself to smile at the others. "By then the events will all be forgotten."

"I disagree," Kenilworth said in what she was recognizing as his normal highhanded tone. "I have no faith that Braxton will not tell everyone and his dog that you and I were seen early in the morning appearing disheveled." Lord Kenilworth glanced at his mother. "The fact that neither of us were at the inn last evening is easily proven."

That was tricky of him. Worse, he might be right.

Although, why he would want to marry her, Charlotte could not even guess. "I am sure that once my sister and brother-in-law have returned to Town, they will post here immediately. I suggest that we wait for them to finish this discussion."

"I agree. We shall leave it up to Worthington and your sister." He took a sip of wine and smiled at her.

It was almost as if he knew something she did not. Yet, neither Matt nor Grace would ever make Charlotte marry where she did not wish. Of that she was certain.

Chapter Ten

Burt spent most of the morning and afternoon following any trail he could find of Lady Charlotte and Lord Braxton. Unfortunately, it was not until he was backtracking through a tollgate that he had any luck. The man collecting tolls was not the same one Burt had seen that morning.

Taking out the coins, he asked, "Don't suppose you seen a lady and a gentleman come through before dawn?"

The older man took the money. "That I did. Thought it was strange seeing them so early. This ain't London."

"Any idea where they went?"

"Only one town of any size round here, that'd be Black-well."

Burt tipped his hat to the toll keeper. "Thanks for the information."

It took him another two hours before he reached the town. The streets were lined with more sporting vehicles than he'd ever seen in one place.

Tables were set up outside two inns, and young men and boys ran in and out carrying pints of ale.

He grabbed one of the boys. "What's goin' on?"

"Boxing match. Finished not long ago."

Bugger it. That wouldn't make his life easier. How the

hell was he to find a gentry-mort and a gent with all these toffs around? "Been here all day?"

"Na." The boy's eyes didn't stay still as he scanned the crowd. "Only here to help serve. I work with the horses."

Damn, he might catch a break after all. "Ever heard of a Lord Braxton?"

"Wish I'd never heared his name." The boy spit on the ground. "Didn't even give me a ha'penny for takin' good care of his horses."

Burt fished a guinea from his pocket, handing it to the lad. "He here now?"

"Na." The coin disappeared. "Had a pint an' left for London."

Which is exactly where Burt would go. Finding a toff in Mayfair wasn't nearly as hard as finding one roaming around the country. The mort'd be there too. Probably where he snatched her in the first place. This time she wouldn't get away.

"Get me a pint and some food."

Grinning, the boy ran off. Morning would be time enough to find Lady Charlotte and take her to Miss Betsy.

Late the following morning, Con was in the library when his mother's butler scratched on the open door. "My lord, Lord and Lady Worthington have arrived. I have taken the liberty of ordering tea. Would you like me to inform her ladyship that Lady Charlotte's family is here?"

"Not yet, Dalton. I wish to speak with Lord and Lady Worthington first."

"As you wish, my lord. I shall show them in."

A few moments later, the Worthingtons were announced. For a moment, Con was shocked to see how much Charlotte's sister looked like her. Would her ladyship have the same aversion to him as Charlotte did? He found himself holding his shoulders more stiffly.

"Kenilworth, thank you." Worthington turned to the lady next to him. "My dear, may I introduce you to the Marquis of Kenilworth? Kenilworth, my wife."

"Yes, indeed." Lady Worthington smiled warmly. "I cannot thank you enough for rescuing my sister."

"There is no need to thank me, my lady. I assure you, any gentleman would have done the same."

"By God, man." Worthington held out his hand and Con clasped it. "I'm not sure anyone would."

Lady Worthington took a seat on the sofa, and Worthington took the place next to her. Although her face was drawn, she sat calmly with one hand in her lap and the other held by Worthington. When the tea tray arrived, she poured. "Cream or milk, my lord?"

"Milk and a lump of sugar."

While she prepared her husband's cup, he said, "I received the letter from you, and my wife received letters from Lady Bellamny and Charlotte." Con nodded. "When we arrived back in Town yesterday, Mr. Addison informed us that his wife was here with our sister. Naturally, I went to Brooks's to discover if any gossip had made it back to Town." Worthington grimaced. "It had."

"Braxton?" Con pressed his lips together. "That was to be expected."

"How is Charlotte doing?" Lady Worthington asked with a concerned look.

"As well as can be expected. I believe Mrs. Addison's presence is helping."

"I would like to see my sister now." Her ladyship finished her tea and rose. "I will leave this discussion to you gentlemen."

Con rang a crystal bell, and the door opened.

"My lord?"

"Please escort Lady Worthington to Lady Charlotte's chamber. After that, inform my mother that we have additional guests."

After the door closed, Worthington said, "In her letter, my Charlotte said she would not wed you. Although she did not mention the reason. Have you been able to convince her otherwise?"

"No." Con held up a decanter of brandy and Worthington inclined his head. "She still maintains that any man who keeps a mistress is abusing women, and she will not marry such a man."

"Hell and damnation." Worthington rubbed his face with his hands. "If only there had been a way to keep the stories about the brothel from her, she wouldn't have even known about demireps. She is—" He paused for a moment. "I cannot say she is impressionable, but she tends to still view the world in terms of good and bad."

Con had most definitely fallen into the "bad" category. He handed his friend a glass and took a sip of his own. "I do not suppose anyone would have mentioned to her that not all ladybirds are unhappy." Worthington raised a brow. "No, of course not." Con took a breath. "If you have any ideas how to change her mind, I'd be happy for a hint."

"Unfortunately, I will have to leave that up to you." Worthington held up his glass, looking at the amber wine. "I am told you have a great deal of charm. Surely you can find a way to make yourself acceptable to her."

"I'm glad you have confidence in me." Con wanted to groan. "At present, I can't even get her alone. She is clinging to her cousin like a limpet." He took another drink. "She also thinks you will support her desire not to wed me."

Shaking his head, Worthington replied, "That is not an option she has open to her."

"No, I didn't think it would be. There is something you should know. Miss Betsy was behind the abduction."

"Blast the woman!" Worthington raked his fingers through his hair. "I would have thought she'd have fled to the Continent. One would think she'd have learned her lesson."

"Apparently not." What Con had to say next would disturb his friend even more. "She's back to her old tricks, abducting children and young women."

"Does Charlotte know?"

"She was there. I should also add that the innkeeper who was helping Miss Betsy, and his family, think she is rescuing runaways and returning them to their families."

"I must notify my cousin. He was part of bringing her bawdy house down." Worthington was quiet for a moment, then grimaced. "Please tell me that Charlotte has not expressed an interest in helping save the latest victims."

For the love of Heaven. That is something of which she was eminently capable. And Con had been worried she would try to make it back to Town on her own. What a fool he was. "Not to me, but she did send a letter to Lady Merton."

Worthington took a large drink of brandy. "I hope you don't mind more guests. The minute Dotty Merton discovers Charlotte is not in Town she will insist on posting here."

"Not at all. In fact, I think my mother will enjoy it a great deal."

"I would like Charlotte to remain here. She will be safer. Grace and I will have to return. We have the other children to care for." Suddenly he grinned. "We'll take Cousin Jane with us. Perhaps seeing Dotty and Merton together will make Charlotte think again about refusing your offer." Worthington played with the cup in his hands, rotating it slowly. "We have all been concerned about Charlotte's feelings, but how do you feel about this betrothal? You were not in the market for a wife. In fact, as her brother and guardian, I must insist you cease to continue keeping the type of company you have been."

Con had known his life would change, yet he hadn't given it much thought. Not that he expected to continue to keep a mistress or attend the types of entertainments he had frequented. Still, to hear it from his friend brought the transformation he'd have to make crashing down on him. The strange thing was that he was not concerned about it. It was what he had expected to do when he married, in any event. "I am not unhappy about the betrothal." He might not have wanted to marry yet, but he was not going to allow Charlotte to jilt him. No woman had ever left him and she was not going to be the first. "As a matter of fact, I look forward to it and my reentry into Polite Society."

"Good. Then I hope to welcome you to the family."

The question was, would Con be able to court Charlotte with her friend about? Or would she use Lady Merton as a shield?

Just as Charlotte had returned from a stroll in the old Elizabethan knot garden, a knock sounded on her bedchamber door and her sister strode in, holding out her arms.

Without a thought, Charlotte ran into them. "Oh, Grace, I have made such a mess of things."

Stroking Charlotte's hair, her sister murmured, "How like you to take responsibility for events over which you had no control."

"No, but I made everything much worse." She sniffed. "If I had not got down from the carriage and insisted on walking back to the inn, no one would have seen me or Lord Kenilworth. Then there would be no issue of a betrothal.

But I could not trust him enough to remain with him. At the time, all I could think of was getting away." She backed up a step and gazed into her sister's eyes. "I cannot marry a man like him."

"Hmm." Grace's lips pursed. "He would seem to have a great deal to recommend him. May I ask the reason?"

"He has a mistress." Most likely more than one at a time, and who knew how many women he had used.

"Ah. I see." She stared at Charlotte for a few moments, concern writ on her face.

At least her sister understood. In fact, she was the only one who seemed to comprehend how she felt. "I thought"— she left Grace's embrace and began to pace—"that if I simply waited, any talk would die down. That would work, would it not? I mean, scandals do go away."

"Some do. It depends entirely upon the circumstances."

Her sister's tone was thoughtful, and for that Charlotte was grateful. At least Grace had not dismissed her idea out of hand, as Kenilworth had done.

Grace continued. "I must tell you that Matt heard some talk at his club, but, naturally, we shall not know exactly how far the rumors have spread until we return to Town."

Charlotte did not want to be the subject of gossip. Dotty had had to go through that and it was not pleasant. "Perhaps if we went straight to the country—"

"No." Grace's tone was so firm, Charlotte did not even consider arguing. "Fleeing will only spur the rumors on. The sooner we face what awaits us, the better. We shall leave here tomorrow."

"I think," Matt said, strolling through the open door, "Charlotte should remain here where she will be safe. We can send Dotty and Merton down as soon as they arrive in Town."

Grace seemed to consider his suggestion, then shook her head. "I am afraid that would appear strange. If Charlotte and Lord Kenilworth were truly betrothed, our visit would not appear out of the way. However, for us to return to May-fair without her would be seen as odd."

"But—"

Grace cut him off. "She should do what any young lady who has just contracted a betrothal would do."

"And that is?" he asked slowly, in a wary voice.

"Go shopping," Grace pronounced emphatically.

"Shopping?"

Charlotte couldn't tell if it was dread or doubt in Matt's tone.

"Indeed." Grace's eyes began to sparkle. "Although Louisa, Dotty, and I all wed so quickly, there was not a great deal we could do—"

"That was not how it seemed to me," her husband muttered.

Her hand fluttered, dismissing his statement. "Never-theless"—she speared him with a look—"while we are still in Town, and since the purpose is *not* to have a quick ceremony, she must be seen to be putting together her trousseau."

"What about Kenilworth?" Matt asked. "We cannot simply leave him here."

Quite frankly, Charlotte thought that was an excellent idea.

"No, my love, you are correct. I am sorry, Charlotte." Her sister gave her a sympathetic look. "You must be seen with him."

That was not what Charlotte wanted to hear. Then again, it was not surprising. She had seen how much time Dotty and Louisa had spent with their husbands before they married.

Charlotte had only one stipulation. "I will not be alone with him."

"As you wish, my dear." Grace smiled warmly as Matt's jaw began to twitch. "It is only for another few weeks."

"Then we may go home?" Charlotte asked, praying the answer was yes.

"Then we may go home." Grace put her arm around Charlotte's shoulders. "Try not to look so down in the mouth. I have found that things always seem to work out the way they are supposed to."

That was what Lady Bellamny had said as well. Perhaps they were right. Despite what he said, Kenilworth did not truly wish to wed her, and she would never agree to marry him. He could go back to his debauched life, and she would find a man she could love and respect. Perhaps even Lord Harrington, if he could prove he truly cared for her.

The following morning, Charlotte, Grace, Jane, Matt, and Kenilworth were not the only ones to depart. Lady Kenilworth had decided she should make the journey to Town as well. And ride in the Worthington coach.

At first, Charlotte had not minded the change in plans. Unfortunately, the moment the doors were closed, her ladyship could speak of nothing but wedding plans.

"Naturally, now that Kenilworth and your brother have spoken, the wedding announcement may be sent to the paper." Lady Kenilworth smiled beatifically at Charlotte as if making a formal announcement of a betrothal she did not want was the best news in the world.

Biting her tongue, Charlotte decided not to remind the lady that she had no intention of going through with the marriage. It would only make the ride back to Town even more disagreeable than it was turning out to be. She wished she could have ridden or taken another vehicle. But riding a horse was out of the question and the only other conveyance was Kenilworth's phaeton. "Naturally."

"I suppose you will wish to wed at St. George's." Her ladyship inclined her head toward Jane. "I understand all your recent family weddings have taken place there."

"I do not yet know where I wish to be married," Charlotte replied before that idea could grow in her ladyship's mind. Wherever her wedding took place, it would not be with Lord Kenilworth.

"I suppose we must discuss a date." Lady Kenilworth gave Charlotte a look filled with such hope that she felt horrible for disappointing the lady.

"Um, yes. However, there is no rush. Sometime in autumn would give his lordship and me time to come to know each other better." If she did not turn this conversation soon, she would go mad. "Where will you stay while you are in Town?"

"I wrote the Pulteney Hotel. I will remain there for a few nights while chambers at Kenilworth House can be made ready for me. I have not visited since my husband died, and it would not do for me to use my former apartments." Her ladyship gave Charlotte a significant look while she tried not to think of the marchioness's chambers. "I hope to host a dinner in honor of your betrothal."

Her own polite smile tightened. "You are very kind."

By the time they stopped to change horses, her head had begun to ache. If it was this difficult to maintain her countenance with a woman who knew her feelings on the betrothal, even if her ladyship did choose to ignore Charlotte's objections, how much more difficult would it be to

Chapter Eleven

The previous day, when it had become clear the scheme Con and Worthington had formed had fallen through, Con offered his friend a neatish bay mare.

From his gray gelding, he surveyed the coaches in the front of his mother's house. "Better to ride than be stuck in a coach."

Glancing at the carriage in question, Worthington nodded. "Much better."

They moved to the front of the conveyance carrying his mother, Lady Worthington, Mrs. Addison, and Charlotte. A second carriage holding their dressers, and the third vehicle transporting his and Worthington's valets had departed earlier to arrive in Town before their mistresses and masters as had his groom, who was driving Con's curricle.

The coach was flanked by two outriders. Con didn't believe anyone would attempt to attack them, but there was no point in tempting fate. It had not been kind to him recently.

He was about to give the order to start when his mother decided she needed an item her maid had packed, but soon they were on their way.

Yesterday afternoon when Worthington had spoken to

his wife and Lady Charlotte, the conversation had not gone as he and Con planned. Shortly thereafter, Worthington had informed Con that despite their best efforts to keep Charlotte in the country, his wife had insisted it would be better to return to Town, especially as there was already talk.

If he ever saw Braxton again, Con was going to plant the man a facer.

Later, when their little group had met in the drawing room before dinner, Con's mother had emphatically agreed. "Fight fire with fire, my son. If you and Charlotte are present, all gossip will soon fade."

As he and Worthington cantered in front of the coach, a problem came to Con that none of the others had considered. "You do realize I have not been invited to any of the events Lady Charlotte will attend."

"That is the least of your worries," Worthington retorted. "News of the engagement will prompt many ladies to send you a card. Not to mention your mother, my wife, and Lady Bellamny will be spreading their version of the story during morning visits."

No doubt dragging Charlotte around with them. Con might end up with a resigned wife, although *trapped* was likely a better word, and that was not good enough. Not for him.

He wanted to see the look she had given him when he'd rescued her. He wanted to sup on her soft lips and have them open to him willingly, and he damn sure did not wish to be berated for having had a mistress—an arrangement he must end at the earliest possible moment.

Blast it all to hell!

He hadn't wanted to wed yet, but now that it was inevitable he wanted Charlotte to wish to marry him. He didn't know another female who would have refused him. That the one lady who did was his betrothed was completely unacceptable.

He would make her understand that she was mistaken in his character, and his first step would be to convince her that high-flyers enjoyed their trade. It would, naturally, be a shock to Charlotte. After all, gently bred young ladies had been raised—for good reason—to believe conjugal relations between a man and a woman were proper only in marriage.

The primary difficulty was her knowledge of Miss Betsy's house. He was certain Charlotte had overreacted to what she had heard. "Do you happen to know what Lady Charlotte was told about the women at Miss Betsy's brothel?"

"Knowing Dotty Merton, more than she should have been told." Worthington's lips flattened into a tight line. "The situation was horrific. *Ladies* had been abducted and forced into prostitution either by threats of multiple rapes or drugged with opium. Their children were either murdered or sold into kid kens."

Bloody hell! "Ladies? Are you sure?"

"Yes, ladies." Worthington's gaze was hard and steady. "I am only telling you this because you need help with Charlotte, and you will soon be part of the family. It must go no further." He waited until Con nodded, still unable to understand how women of his own social status could have been in a brothel. "We found them through a woman who ran a boarding house for the families of military officers who could not take their families with them overseas and whose families had nowhere else to go. The ladies who were with child were given a drink made to abort the child. Some of the women died. Their children, usually ones too young to go to school, were sold to criminal gangs."

"Good God." Con felt as if his breath had been sucked out of him. As if Jackson himself had landed a punch in his stomach. Of course he knew not all women in the profession wanted to be there. Still, that was better than being on the streets. Yet for *ladies* to have suffered in such a way was unbelievable. That Charlotte, a complete innocent, knew about it made him feel slightly ill. "I don't understand why anyone would have . . ."

"My wife thinks it is better for ladies to know of the dangers that could befall them and others." Worthington shrugged. "I don't disagree. Yet I do think some of the more lurid details could have been left out of the telling."

Con was still having difficulty understanding how gently bred women could have been used so horribly. "What happened to the ladies?"

"My cousin Merton and his wife are caring for them." Worthington's brows drew together. "We are still waiting for most of their husbands to return."

"And the children?"

"Merton has hired men to find them. There's been some success. Jemmy, for example, though we haven't found his family yet."

"Wait a moment." Jemmy had said Charlotte had found him. "Why was Charlotte involved with that?"

"Dotty and Charlotte have been best friends since they were in leading strings. When Dotty decided the process was taking too long, she decided to oversee one of the raids. Naturally, Charlotte accompanied her."

Con opened his mouth to speak, but shut it again.

Worthington's eyes began to twinkle with mirth. "When Dotty told Merton what she was going to do, he was speechless as well. Short of locking her in her room, there was no way he could stop her. He was in the coach and they were well guarded."

"I still do not understand how Charlotte saved the boy."

"From what I understand, Jemmy was being taken away by one of the villains, and Charlotte shoved open the coach door into his face. He dropped Jemmy and Charlotte snatched him up. If you want more details, you'll have to apply to her."

That explained why she was not in a panic when Con rescued her. In fact, the only thing that seemed to overset her was him.

Still, the stuff about Miss Betsy was far and away worse than Con had thought it could be. It was no wonder Charlotte deplored men who frequented brothels. Although, the Covent Garden abbesses got the majority of the blame, and rightfully so: Without customers, those types of houses would not exist. Nevertheless, and this was a point that must be made, those poor women were not the same as the Cyprians he hired. All of his mistresses had come to him willingly. In fact, high-flyers chose their protectors more frequently than the gentleman chose the mistress. It was as different as night and day from the horrors she had been told about. That was what Charlotte must be made to understand. Con keeping a mistress was not at all the same as a man hiring a woman who had no choice.

About two hours later their cavalcade stopped to rest the horses and to partake in a light nuncheon. Con assisted his mother, then Charlotte, down the coach steps. Her countenance might well have been a mask for all the emotion she showed. And, although she didn't shrink from his touch, she was as cold and stiff as a block of ice. To make matters worse, if that was even possible, his mother spoke of nothing but how happy she was to be welcoming Charlotte into their family and the ball she would plan in their honor. He would have to talk to his mother. There was no reason to make his betrothed more recalcitrant than she was already.

Once in the private parlor he had hired, the cat resided in Charlotte's lap, eagerly lapping up pieces of meat and cheese. After the animal's hunger had been satisfied, the little beast emitted a large rumbling sound as Charlotte stroked the thing and effectively withdrew from the conversation. Con wondered if he'd ever receive as much attention from her as the damned cat did.

Unable to talk to Mama about mentioning her plans, he attempted to turn the conversation whenever she opened her mouth. By the time he was back on his horse, he had the beginnings of a headache. In the past, the only time his head had hurt was from overindulgence, and his valet had a remedy that cleared his head in short order. He had a feeling this ache would not be so easily cured.

Thank God she was finally home!

Charlotte had just set her feet on the pavement when Jemmy collided with her, his thin arms wrapping around her waist. "They told me you was safe, but I had to see fer meself."

"I am safe and well." She patted the child on his head. "And I'm very happy to see that you arrived home unhurt. You were quite brave climbing on the coach as you did. Thank you."

His face reddened as he looked up at her. "Weren't nothin'." He peered around her as if searching for something or someone. "Did the gent bring you back?"

"Ah, yes. He came back to Town with us but went to his own home." She had never been so glad to get rid of two people in her life.

"I knew he was a good'un. Gave me more than the coach fare and hackney." He lowered his voice. "Should I give him back the rest?"

"I don't think that's necessary. In fact, I am positive he would want you to keep it." She couldn't imagine even a man such as Kenilworth would quibble over a few pennies.

Jemmy's wide smile showed another missing tooth. Charlotte would make sure the stable master had noticed it and given the child *tand-fé*. After all, just because he still insisted on sleeping in the stables there was no reason he should not receive money for his tooth. They would have to move him permanently into the house soon.

"Do you think I'll have a chance to thank him for the extra?"

"Yes, indeed." And much too soon for her comfort. She ruffled the boy's hair and placed a kiss on the top of his head.

The next thing she knew, Jemmy was joined by her sister, Mary, her best friend and Matt's sister Theo, and the rest of the children. The noise level rose until Matt ordered them all inside. "You may ask your questions in the house. Go on, all of you."

The two youngest pulled her up the steps and down the corridor into the morning room, demanding to know everything that had occurred. Trays of tea and food arrived as the children settled themselves to hear the story. Phillip, eight years old and her youngest brother, sat with Theodora, also eight, and Mary, five. Matt's sister Madeline, age twelve, was in between the twins, Alice and Eleanor, also twelve years of age. His second eldest sister, Augusta, who was fifteen and Charlotte's brother Walter, fourteen, took chairs on either side of Charlotte. The only one missing was their brother Charlie, Earl of Stanwood, who was attending Eton.

After a brief moment of silence the questions started, and Charlotte held up her hand to quiet them. "This will be much easier if you will allow me to tell you what happened. After that, if you have questions, you may ask them."

Several minutes later, Augusta's brows drew together. "I

really did not think the lessons we received would be of much use. Now I shall have to start practicing in earnest."

"What lessons?" Alice, Eleanor, and Madeline asked as one.

"Ones you will receive before you come out." Charlotte glanced at the others. "Are there any other questions?"

Mary, sitting at Charlotte's feet, tugged her gown. "I was scared."

As she pulled Mary into her lap, tears filled her eyes for the second time that day.

"Me too," Theo said, making room for herself on Charlotte's lap.

"Me three." Phillip stood next to Charlotte, placing his arm around her shoulders.

"I was, as well, but everything is fine now." She gave them each a kiss, then set Mary and Theo down and stood. "Let me wash the dust off me and see to Collette. We will speak again later."

As Charlotte left the room, Walter strode with her down the corridor. "I'm glad you're safe. We were very worried about you."

She would have drawn him into an embrace, but lately he had been eschewing them as too babyish. "Don't tell the others, but I was terrified."

"I won't."

Charlotte thought his posture became a little straighter. "I'm glad you confided in me."

She was too. He was on his way to becoming a good man. She'd miss him when he joined Charlie at school in the autumn.

A few minutes later, she set the basket down on the floor of her bedchamber, before removing her bonnet and throwing it on the dressing table. Collette poked her head up and, after realizing she was finally home, hopped out of the basket and went behind the screen.

Finally with her family again, it was the first time Charlotte had felt completely safe in days. The thought stopped her. It was not the truth. Before she had known who Kenilworth was, she had felt safe with him. Safe enough to fall asleep against him and let him kiss her.

She yanked off her gloves, throwing them on the table. All that proved was that she had been tired and was a much worse judge of character than she'd previously thought. If only she had waited for her footman to catch up with her, or not gone at all . . . Charlotte took a large breath. There was nothing to be gained by rethinking over and over again what had happened or what she could have done to change the results. The only thing she might have any control over at all was marrying Kenilworth.

She turned her mind to the plans Lady Kenilworth and Grace had made on the way to Town. Grace's "at home" was in three days. Between now and then, Lady Kenilworth, Grace, and Charlotte would spend the days making morning visits, presenting what her sister called a united front. By the time she and Kenilworth made their first formal appearance together, no one could possibly think anything about Charlotte's betrothal was unusual, especially with her ladyship so ecstatic about the engagement.

That, though, had brought up the question of how they had met. Naturally, the truth would not do. After much discussion, it was decided they would say Matt had introduced them. Considering her sister Louisa and Louisa's new husband, Gideon, had met in Matt's study, that was the simplest solution.

Next was the problem of the gentleman himself. Somehow, Charlotte must find a way to make him understand that she had no intention of marrying him and that having a mistress, a woman he bought for her body, was morally depraved. Regrettably, he appeared to be convinced he was doing nothing wrong.

Charlotte glanced at the clock on the mantel. There was plenty of time for her to practice the piano before tea. Playing would help clear her thoughts. She might even come up with a persuasive argument to make his lordship change his hardheaded mind and agree with her.

May entered Charlotte's bedchamber from the dressing room, carrying her favorite Pomona-green day dress. "Pardon for being so long, my lady. I wanted to get everything put away. Let's get you out of your carriage gown."

After changing one garment for the other, she opened the door. "If anyone wants me, I'll be in the music room."

"Yes, my lady."

"Charlotte."

"Dotty!" Thank God. Just the person Charlotte wanted to see. "I am so glad you are here. How did you know I had returned, and when did you arrive in Town?"

Laughing, her best friend in the world took Charlotte's hands and squeezed them. "Let us go into the parlor, and I shall tell you."

"Would you like a cup of tea?"

"Very much, and if your cook has any of his biscuits, they would be welcome as well. I cannot stay long, but I will see you at dinner this evening."

She nodded to May, who rushed out the door as Dotty and Charlotte strolled into the Young Ladies' Parlor.

"Are you happy?" Charlotte searched her friend's face, pleased with what she saw. "You look to be."

"It is hard for even me to believe, but I have never been happier." Dotty's smile seemed to light the room. "Dominic is everything I could have asked for in a husband and partner."

Dominic, Marquis of Merton, was a cousin on Matt's

side of Charlotte's family. Before he'd fallen in love with Dotty he was so stuffy and puffed up in his own consequence that no one in the family liked him. "That is only because you changed him."

She gave a light shrug. "I merely encouraged him to be himself and not what his uncle had taught him to be."

The tea arrived and Charlotte poured.

Once they had each taken a sip of the strong gunpowder tea, and Dotty had had a bite of the lemon biscuits she liked so much, she said, "I received your letter, but I'd rather hear from you exactly what occurred."

Charlotte told her about the abduction, the kiss, finding Lady Bellamny at the inn, and the betrothal. "I have decided to wait until sometime late in the summer or autumn to break the engagement. Even after what Lord Braxton put around, I should still be able to call off the wedding." When her friend's brows lowered, she rushed on, "I am quite sure Lord Kenilworth will not mind"—even though that was not what he had said. She was positive he would change his mind—"and, after what I know about the poor ladies at the brothel, I cannot wed a man who hires women for . . . well, you know."

Dotty nodded thoughtfully. "Dominic tells me he is rather famous for his mistresses, but that he has never been known to frequent brothels."

"What does it matter?" Dotty's answer took Charlotte by surprise. And why was her friend not agreeing with her? "As far as I see, one is much the same as the other."

"Are you concerned he will continue to keep a mistress after he marries?"

The question stopped Charlotte mid-sip. "I have given it no consideration at all."

A few moments passed in silence, then Dotty set her cup down. "Do you remember our discussions about Dominic?

How his political views and his votes in the Lords were causing much suffering among the poor?"

"Yes, and you said you could never marry a man who believed as he did."

"Precisely. Then he began to realize the misery he caused others." Reaching out, Dotty took Charlotte's hands again. "Do you not think Lord Kenilworth could change his views as well? Perhaps he could be made to see how wrong his thinking is?" Her friend gave a sly smile. "You did enjoy the kiss, and from what I hear he is quite handsome and eligible."

She had and he was. *Maybe* if he could admit he was wrong she could reconsider him, but Kenilworth was so sure of himself. He was worse than Merton had been. "I have tried. He will admit that there might be some women who do not like their trade, but only in brothels. He is totally convinced that courtesans enjoy what they do, and nothing I have said thus far has changed his mind. In fact, he thinks I am being naïve in my beliefs and they have no merit."

"In that case, you must find a way to change his point of view. Show him, as I showed Dominic, the harm he is causing."

"But how?" Charlotte wanted to wail. Talking to him was like banging her head against a stone wall.

"You'll think of a way." Dotty grinned. "There are few ladies more clever than you." She tilted her head toward the door. "I shall leave you before Dominic invades."

"I'll see you out."

After saying farewell to Dotty, Charlotte finally made her way to the music room.

The moment she set her hands on the keys, the strain she had been under seemed to melt away. As she expected, her mind was able to open, ideas flew around her head, and she found the perfect solution to her most pressing problem.

Chapter Twelve

An hour later, Charlotte lifted her hands after the final notes of a divertimento by Johann Baptist Cramer. For a brief moment there was silence, then a slow clapping began.

"Excellent, my lady."

She had not expected to hear that voice for another day at least. She rose from the piano bench and curtseyed as he bowed. "Lord Kenilworth, what a surprise."

"Ah, and, from the look on your face, not a pleasant one. I do apologize for interrupting you."

"I had just finished the piece." She tried to retain the sense of calm she'd had while playing, as she sat back down on the bench and indicated he should take a nearby chair.

It was unfair and unwanted that his mere presence seemed to provoke such a strong response in her. He sauntered forward and Charlotte could not help but notice how well he looked in his dark blue jacket and biscuit-colored pantaloons. His dark hair, fashionably cut, curled slightly. Everything about him gave the impression of a wealthy, important peer. Only the slight shadow in his eyes, as if he was uncertain around her, belied his confidence.

Well, good. Let him be wary of her. "Did my brother invite you to join us for tea?"

"No." Lord Kenilworth stared at her for a few moments before finally lowering his long, elegant frame onto the chair. "I thought we might speak about a topic of interest to both of us. A subject about which we must come to an agreement and the sooner the better."

"If you have come to discuss our so-called betrothal, I wish you would not," Charlotte said, returning his steady gaze. "I will do what is expected of me for the rest of the Season. That must be good enough."

"I am sure you will. Yet, I have not come about our betrothal, but about your reason for not wishing to wed me."

For the love of God! The man was impossible. "We have been over this before, my lord. Until you can admit you are mistaken about how any woman feels about selling her body, we can have nothing further to discuss."

Charlotte's bountiful breasts rose as she took a deep breath. Her hands clenched. Her face was a portrait of outrage. This was a woman no one could dismiss. In short, she was magnificent, and—he vowed—she would be his.

Regrettably, she was also the most stubborn woman Con had ever had the misfortune to meet. "Some might consider marriage to be a form of prostitution."

He heard the crack of her palm against his cheek before he felt the pain radiating through his face.

Apparently, she did not agree.

"That"—her face was flushed, once again her breasts heaved in indignation, and he didn't think she had ever looked more beautiful—"was one of the stupidest things I have ever heard. A married woman has a position in society. Her children are legally born and can inherit lands, other property, and titles. She has settlement agreements to protect her rights. If her husband predeceases her"— Charlotte's eyes narrowed and Con thought she might be envisioning his death—"she may remain a widow or marry again. She is not in the position where she must seek another protector. She is not in danger, or in as much danger, of contracting some dreadful disease."

How the hell does she know about that? Con wondered.

"If her husband mistreats her, she has the protection of her family and possibly the law, as Lady Byron and others have shown."

He was not going to even try to inform Charlotte that many women could not take advantage of the law or that their families would not support them either financially or emotionally. All that mattered was that Charlotte's family would, and would make the courts do so as well.

She glared at him for several more moments, and he wondered if she was finished. Then she pointed a long, elegant finger at him. "You are so sure of yourself, my lord. Well, I dare you—no, I challenge you—to ask your mistress how much she likes living the life she is leading. Whether she would rather have had a different life than the one with which she is now stuck."

His cheek still burning, Con managed a half smile. "What are the odds?"

Startled, Charlotte gaped at him. "I do not understand."

Now was the time to make her promise to marry him. "What do I receive if I'm right and you are wrong?"

"The satisfaction that you were right, and I was wrong." Her chin rose. "More I will not promise."

Con considered attempting to convince her to wager with him; instead he stood and bowed. "Very well, my lady. I shall ask her. After which, I will faithfully report my conversation, and then we will have another sort of discussion."

"One where you will be forced to eat toads." She crossed her arms beneath her breasts, plumping them up nicely.

He'd wager that her nipples were the color of light pink

roses and tasted like honey. Marriage to her was enticing him more and more. Or rather having her in his bed was, but one came with the other. "Someone will be tasting something, in any event."

Con kept his smirk to himself as he rose—there was no point in tempting her to slap him again—and strode out of the room.

Less than fifteen minutes later, he knocked on the door of a house on a quiet street at the edge of Mayfair. He had bought the town house for Aimée about a month after he had hired her. The place she had been living in was too far away for his taste.

Con waited until the elderly butler opened the door and stood aside.

"Good afternoon, Clark."

"My lord." He bowed. "The mistress is in the morning room."

"Thank you." Con strode down the corridor to the open door at the end. "Aimée."

She rose slowly and as fluidly as flowing water. "Kenilworth." Her regular smile of welcome was absent and she did not move toward him. "I hear you are to wed."

Well, damn. It had not occurred to him that Braxton's talk would have spread to her, but that was the only way she could have found out. Con should have written to her so that she would have been prepared for the news. "Yes. I wish I had been the one to have told you. I returned to Town only an hour or so ago."

"It is not widely known in my world." She gave a slight Gallic shrug. "Lord Braxton thought I would be looking for another protector and offered himself."

Bugger the man! "Is that what you want?"

"Do you mean to say that you would keep me as your mistress after you married?" Aimée's eyes shimmered with tears. "I have known you to be selfish, *mon ami*, but never cruel."

Devil take it. This was not going at all as he'd expected it would. Did all the females in his life believe he was a cur? He'd thought Aimée knew him better than to ask such a question.

Charlotte was insistent that he discover how his mistress had become a courtesan, and he had agreed. Secure in his belief that the beautiful, talented, and intelligent Aimée had chosen this life. But now . . . now he was suddenly not so sure of himself. "I'm making a muddle of this. Please, may we sit down? I have a question to ask you."

"*Naturellement*." She glided to the bell pull. "I shall order tea."

After no more than a minute or two, her butler carried in a tray with tea, brandy, and wine, as well as small cakes and sandwiches. She must leave standing orders for the repast to be readied when he arrived.

A small smile wobbled on her lips. "I know how hungry you always are."

"Thank you." Food was the last thing he wanted right now, and he did not dare resort to the brandy. "I'll have a cup of tea."

Once she'd handed the tea to him and poured a cup for herself, she folded her hands in her lap. He supposed this was to create a feeling of calm, but her fingers had tightened to the point where her knuckles turned white.

"What is it you wish to ask me?"

"Aimée, why did you choose this life?"

For a moment she stared at him, a polite smile frozen on her lips. Then her top lip curled into a sneer. "I did not *choose* this life." Her voice was low, and brittle, and pain echoed through her words. "It was chosen for me."

Con's first reaction was to reach out to her, hold her

hands or take her into his arms. Yet he wasn't sure she would accept his comfort or that he had the right to offer it.

His second response was chagrin. Charlotte had been right and he, in his arrogance, had been absolutely wrong. "I would like to hear your story, if you will tell me."

Blinking rapidly, Aimée poured a glass of the claret he provided for her cellars and took a long swallow. "I do not think you truly wish to know. This is merely some fancy you have developed."

Then he did reach out, covering her hands with his. "Please. I need to understand."

Shaking his hands off as if they were dirt, she brushed at a tear. "I come from a good family. My father was a wealthy wine merchant, and my mother was the daughter of a baron." She pronounced the rank in the French manner. "They were very much in love, but they would not have been allowed to wed if it had not been for *la Terreur*. My grandfather did not cover his head. You would say ignore the facts. The noble he had wished my *maman* to marry had been murdered, and he thought she would be safer with my papa." Taking out a lace-edged handkerchief, she dabbed her eyes. "For many years we were happy. Then my parents died from *la grippe*. I was fourteen, *dévastée*. A man my father knew, a colonel, offered to take me to my aunt and uncle in Lyon." She took a larger drink of wine, almost emptying the glass. "Instead he made me his mistress." Her eyes had a dull, hopeless look and her tone was flat. "Some months later he was given a command in the south and left me with a well-known courtesan in Paris. She taught me everything she knew. Art, music, clever conversation. The last thing she did for me was to send me here, to England. I heard that she has since died."

Con poured her another glass of wine. *Fourteen!* He did not even know how to respond. How could anyone take the innocence of a child? Although, he knew it happened. He never expected to be on familiar terms with and care for someone it had happened to. But Charlotte, if she had not actually known, had suspected what had occurred. He almost wished she was here to tell him what to do.

He drank his now cold tea without tasting it. "Do you know if your aunt and uncle are still in Lyon?"

"They are. We write to each other. They think I am married to an English merchant."

Even in France, being a courtesan is not respectable. To keep up such a façade Aimée must want desperately to be respectable again.

He wondered if that was even her real name and thought it was probably not. "What if you had the funds to go to your family in France, with enough money to live on as if your 'husband' had died and left you a widow? Would you like that?"

She looked at him for the first time since she had begun her story, and stared. The soft ticking of the gilded clock on the mantel filled the silence. Still, it was several moments before she replied, "More than anything in my life I want a real husband and children. Very few women want to have the life I'm leading."

The last part of what she said answered another question. Most of them? How could he have been so wrong?

"You are shocked, *mon ami*."

Con could only nod.

"How much would you pay for a woman who showed her distaste?" Aimée asked.

Not much, he answered, but only to himself.

He sucked in a deep breath. He might not be able to repair all the damage he and other men had done, but he could help her have what she wanted and deserved. "Then you shall have it. Or at least as much of that life as I can give you." His stomach twisted. The part he played in Aimée's life made him almost physically ill. "I will transfer this house to you. It is your decision whether to sell it or lease it. I will also set up an account that will be sufficient for you to maintain the fiction you told your family." The sick knot that had developed in his stomach began to unwind as he mentally reviewed the steps needed to accomplish his goal, and he smiled. "I'm afraid you will have to arrange the husband and children on your own."

For the first time since he'd entered the house, the smile Aimée gave him was genuine. This time, he hoped the tears shimmering in her eyes were ones of happiness. "*Merci beaucoup, mon ami*. I do not know how to thank you."

"It is I who should thank you." Con thought of the stories Charlotte had told him and how he had scoffed and not believed her. "You have given me a chance to begin making amends."

His former mistress moved to a small escritoire. Drawing out a piece of paper, Aimée made a notation. "This is the name I use for my family."

Folding the foolscap, he tucked it into the pocket in his waistcoat. "I promise you I shall never reveal to anyone your connection to this name."

"Thank you, again." She held out her hands. "I wish you much happiness with your fiancée. She must be *très spéciale*."

Taking her fingers, he kissed them for the last time. "She is more than that."

Much more than he had ever suspected.

Yet now, he would have to confess to Charlotte that she had been right all along. As he left Aimée's house, he wondered ruefully if his male pride could take the blow she was bound to land, and prayed she would be kinder to him than he had been to her.

Chances were he'd be eating real toads before this was over. But would even that be enough to convince Charlotte to marry him?

Con turned on Saint James Street toward his club. He'd never been at such a loss in his life. Fortunately, she didn't expect him until tomorrow. For the rest of the day, he'd simply forget about it and enjoy convivial companionship and a bottle of Brooks's excellent brandy.

Not long afterward, he opened the door to his club and handed his hat and cane to a footman. The club's master bowed. "Good day, my lord. May I felicitate you on your betrothal?"

Hell! Rumors be damned. The news was all over Town. "Thank you, Smithers. Perhaps a bottle of brandy to celebrate."

"As you wish, my lord." He bowed again before snapping his fingers at a footman.

Con had no sooner sat down with his glass of brandy when a friend of his, Lord Endicott, strolled up. "You're a sly dog, Kenilworth, snatching up Lady Charlotte when Harrington is still in the country."

What the devil did that pup Harrington have to do with Charlotte? "I beg your pardon?"

Endicott's brows rose at the same time his jaw dropped. "You mean you didn't know? He's been sniffing around her all Season. He had to get his father's agreement to the match. That is the reason he's out of Town now."

Was that why she was so hesitant to marry Con? She had said it was because of his mistress, but did she wish to wed Harrington? Was she in love with the man? "His name has not come up."

"How did you meet her in the first place?" Endicott settled on a leather chair next to Con's.

Now that was a question he *could* answer. "Worthington introduced us. Went to visit him and stayed for tea."

"If Worthington had any other sisters out this year," Endicott said with feeling, "I'd cultivate a closer acquaintance with him. That's how Rothwell met Lady Louisa, you know."

Lady Louisa? Oh, that's right. Worthington's other sister. He'd mentioned that she had got married not long ago. "Yes, of course. I'm fortunate to be a friend of his."

It began to occur to Con that coming to Brooks's was not one of his better ideas. At least until his life was more settled.

"Demmed fine ladies, Worthington's sisters." Endicott glanced at the bottle of brandy and frowned. "Come now, Kenilworth, you don't want to be drinking that stuff. A celebration is called for." Endicott turned his head and called out, "You there, bring us a few bottles of your best champagne. We have a betrothal to celebrate. Lord Kenilworth here has stolen the march on the rest of us and convinced Lady Charlotte Carpenter to marry him. Must wish him happy!"

Perdition. He couldn't let Charlotte jilt him now, even if she did prefer that pup Harrington. Con would never live it down.

Chapter Thirteen

The morning after Burt had left the Green Man, he found Lord Braxton's house in Mayfair and discovered the man'd left Town with a blond woman.

Miss Betsy wasn't going to be happy her chicken had flown the coop. After returning to his rooms, he wrote to her, and for the past two days he'd been at a tavern waiting to hear from her.

"Be there a Mr. Smith here?" a young boy dressed in little more than rags asked.

The lad reminded him of himself when he was a kid. "I'm Smith."

"Got this fer ye." The boy held up a letter and Burt flipped him a penny.

He swallowed the last of his ale, then went to his room to open the note.

Please continue to follow his lordship and recover the package from him.

B.

In his opinion, it were a waste of time. Likely the mort weren't still a virgin and the gent wouldn't want her no more. Not that anyone asked him. He shrugged. It was all the same to him as long as Miss Betsy was payin' for it.

Burt opened his watch. Still enough time ta try ta catch the nob's trail before dark. If he was lucky, that fancy coach'd be easy enough to find.

He packed up his sack and paid his shot at the tavern. It didn't take him nearly as long as he'd thought to get to the Great North Road.

Burt pulled up at the first tollbooth, and the toll keeper came out. "Have ya seen a flash cove with a fancy black carriage and a yaller-headed mort come by a day or so ago?"

"See a lot of fancy coaches this close to Lunden." Burt tossed a coin up and the lad caught it. "Two days ago, ye said? Reckon I did. Bought a ticket all the way to the next county. The coachman said they was goin' to somewhere called Biggleswade. Ain't never heard of it meself. Said it was in Bedford."

Burt gave the man another coin. The information would save him a lot of time. All he had to do was find Biggleswade somewhere in Bedford.

He traveled until dark, then found a room at a posting inn. The next day, shortly after noon, he arrived in the market town of Biggleswade. The first tavern he came to was the Dog in a Doublet, on the High Street.

No ostler ran out to help him with the horses, but there was an iron ring on the side of the building. After tying his leader to an iron ring, he entered the inn and headed for the bar. "I'm lookin' for a room and board for a day or two."

"Yer in luck," the innkeeper said. "I got one chamber left. Tomorrow's market day and the whole town'll be full up."

"Looks like I got here in good time."

The man signaled to a younger man to take his place. "I'll show ye up."

"I got a coach and pair too," Burt said.

"My son'll take care of them. That'll be extra for the carriage and horses."

He nodded, not minding the expense. Miss Betsy was good about paying him back.

The room was small but clean. There were two windows; one overlooked the street, which suited him just fine. "Thank ye."

"Dinner's at five. Anything else I can do fer ye?"

"I was told to look for a gentleman with a shiny black coach. Have ye seen him?"

"We got a lot of them coaches going through here. His lordship at the big house is having one of his house parties. Ye might find yer man tomorrow. He likes to bring his guests to the market." The innkeeper pulled a disapproving face. "By the way some of them London women acted, ye'd think they'd never seen a market town."

That didn't make a lot of sense to Burt. Even he knew most ladies lived in the country a lot of the year. But the landlord had said *women*, not *ladies*. Before he could think of a way to ask about it, the man went on, "Last time his lordship was here, my wife and most of the other women in town went to the rector about the gentlemen who were visiting. His lordship's got to bring his own maids with him now when he has one of his parties. None of us will let our daughters go."

Burt gave up trying to understand Quality. It didn't make sense that Lady Charlotte would be allowed to go to such a thing.

"They even stop at the White Hart and have ale!" the innkeeper said, clearly scandalized.

Well, if that's where they went, that's where he'd be. What Miss Betsy wanted she got.

* * *

Not long after Lord Kenilworth had left, Charlotte made her way to the morning room for tea. The house had been unusually quiet, which meant Matt had most likely taken the children to the Park and they had not yet returned.

Just then, the sound of the front door bursting open, the tromping of feet, and Daisy's bark, sounded down the corridor.

A moment later, Mary and Theo appeared in the doorway.

"Daisy and Duke are getting married," Mary called to Charlotte.

She shook her head, trying to clear it. "I beg your pardon?"

"We're going to have the wedding tomorrow," Theo confirmed as she and Mary held hands and danced around the room.

"We're going to make Daisy the most beautiful bonnet ever." Alice grinned while Eleanor and Madeline nodded excitedly.

"I have a feeling I've missed something," Charlotte said more to herself than anyone else.

Augusta came up beside her and whispered, "Daisy has gained weight in her stomach. Theo and Mary noticed it when we were at the Park."

The mystery cleared. "Puppies."

"That's what Matt thinks." The corner of Augusta's lips curled up. "Hence the wedding. He did explain to the children that we would not be going to church for the ceremony."

"Thank the Lord for that." With five weddings in half as many months, their family had given Mr. Peterson, the young clergyman at St. George's, a good deal of business this Season, and the *ton* a great deal of entertainment.

It occurred to Charlotte that the coming out party Grace had started planning for her, Louisa, and Dotty had never taken place. The weddings kept interfering.

Daisy ambled into the parlor, her tail wagging. She really

was increasing. It seemed as if everyone Charlotte knew was expecting, except Dotty, and that was only a matter of time.

If only Harrington had proposed before leaving town, Charlotte might be looking forward to a Happy Event sometime in the not-so-distant future as well. If she had accepted him, that is, and she was not sure she would have. There just seemed to be a quality of feeling or something missing whenever they were together. She had experienced more of a reaction to Kenilworth, before she knew who he was, of course, than she ever had to Harrington. Not to mention Harrington took her for granted, and as Louisa had said, that would not do.

Charlotte gave herself a shake. She was being a goose. If she had been betrothed to Harrington when she was abducted, then she would be in the position of being seen with Kenilworth while engaged to another man, which would have made all of this vastly worse than it already was. Maybe she should just stop thinking about any of it.

Then again, that was hard to do when it—and he— seemed to be controlling her life at the moment, and Charlotte did not like the situation one little bit. In her wildest dreams she never thought she would be betrothed to a gentleman she did not wish to marry.

She thought about her agreement with Kenilworth and what Dotty had said. He'd promised to tell Charlotte the truth about his conversation with his mistress, but even if she was right, would he really change his mind and his behavior?

Matt, Phillip, and Walter piled into the room followed by Duke, who went immediately to Daisy. Did he know that he was going to be a father? She turned her head toward the dogs and smiled.

The noise level rose with plans, sometimes shouted to be heard over the clatter.

Grace strolled in, next followed by their butler and four

footmen carrying trays. She elegantly sank onto a sofa. "As soon as you have quieted and taken your seats, you may have your tea."

Phillip and Walter sat quickly, and Phillip shouted over the rest of them, "Hurry up. I'm hungry."

Seconds later, Charlotte was helping Grace hand out cups of tea and plates filled with jam tarts, biscuits, and small slices of sandwiches.

Finally, Charlotte fixed her own cup and plate, carrying them to the window seat. Once the children's hunger had been satisfied, the wedding talk began again. Naturally, Grace had to be told of the coming event. Her eyes sparkled with laughter as Matt put a finger between his neck and cravat as if to loosen it.

Charlotte imagined herself as the mother of a brood of children with a husband who was as caring as her brother-in-law, yet as much as she tried to shove away the image of laughing green eyes, the picture would not leave.

I am not going to wed Kenilworth.

Even if he could admit he was wrong, he would probably never *do* anything to help women trapped in prostitution. And what did she know of him after all? Yes, he was handsome, and titled, and wealthy, but what did all that matter if he refused to help the poor and needy of their world?

"Charlotte, you looked to be deep in thought. Do you mind if I join you?" Matt stood before her, a dark brow cocked.

"Not at all." She made to move over, giving him room to sit beside her, but he picked up a nearby chair and set it down.

"You seem to be handling everything that has happened exceedingly well," he commented, taking a seat.

She shrugged lightly. There was no point in going into hysterics over what could not be changed.

"I haven't had a chance to speak with you about the abduction and . . ."

"Betrothal?" She dearly hoped he was not going to try to talk her around. If she changed her mind it would be because of Lord Kenilworth's actions, not the words of another, even a much loved brother.

"Indeed." His brows lowered for a moment. "I understand you do not have a good opinion of Kenilworth."

"You are correct. I do not." The image of him at the theater with not one but two Cyprians emerged. "I am not impressed with what I do know about him."

"Yes, well, of late, his personal life has not been pristine." Glancing at her, Matt pulled a face. "Based upon what you have seen, I cannot blame you."

She fought to keep from pressing her lips together. "But?"

A small smile appeared on his face. "I have known him for a long time, and can vouch for his general temperament. He does not fly into rages or abuse others—"

"With the exception of certain women."

Matt rubbed his hand over his jaw. "That is, unfortunately, a failing that society in general encourages."

It was time to bring this discussion to an end. "It is, nevertheless, a failing I abhor. You would not wish me to wed a man I cannot like or respect, would you?"

"No." His brows drew together and he shifted on the chair. "Allow me to just say that at first Grace did not think I could be trusted with the children, and none of us thought Merton could or would change." Charlotte nodded, accepting the truth of both statements. "I flatter myself that Grace is now happier than she has been in a very long time."

Charlotte could not argue with his statement. She had not seen her sister as contented and joyful since before their parents died. "Go on."

"Kenilworth might not be as bad as you think. At least politically he is much more liberal than Merton is even now." Matt rose, replacing the chair against the wall. "When you come to know him, if you still are of the opinion you cannot marry the man, I will stand by you."

"Thank you." That was much more than she had expected. Then again, she should not have been surprised. Unlike many fathers or guardians, he wanted all of them to marry for love. "I shall try to be fair-minded."

"That, my dear sister, is all I ask."

Three hours later, well before the family would gather in the drawing room before dinner, Charlotte was once again sitting at the piano.

She finished the movement and looked up to find Dotty sitting quietly not far from her. "I did not wish to interrupt you. From your choice in music, I take it you are still quite aggravated."

Only Dotty would know that Charlotte's favorite piece to play when she was upset was Mozart's *Piano Sonata No. 12*, even if her friend never could remember the name of it. "Lord Kenilworth came by after you left."

"Aha. Did he upset you?"

Charlotte couldn't stop from frowning. "We argued again, and this time I told him to ask his mistress if she liked being a courtesan."

"Oh my!" Covering her lips with her hands, Dotty started to laugh. "I do so wish I could have been listening at the keyhole. What did he say?"

"That I was wrong, naturally." Charlotte rolled her eyes, glad her older sister wasn't there to see her. "He said he would ask his mistress, just to prove to me I am wrong."

"He must really think he's right."

"Exactly." Charlotte grinned. "I told him he'd be eating toads."

Her friend went off into another peal of laughter. After a few seconds she took out a handkerchief and blotted her eyes. "I imagine he shall have to. You have not heard from him since he left?"

"No. He said he would come here tomorrow and tell me the result of his conversation."

Cocking her head to one side, Dotty asked, "Do you know that never once have you doubted he would tell you the truth?"

She was right. He had never struck Charlotte as being untruthful. "He is so blunt I never considered he would *not* be honest with me."

"Well, that is one thing in his favor," her friend prodded gently.

"I suppose it is." She could begin keeping a list of his good and bad points. If only it was that simple. "My doubt is that anything can change his mind. Even so, he has a long way to go before I could look favorably upon his suit."

"I cannot blame you for your scruples or caution. Marriage is, after all, forever." Suddenly, her friend's face seemed to light up. "I wanted to tell you first. Dom and I are expecting a baby sometime in late January or February."

"Oh, Dotty!" Charlotte jumped up from the bench, almost knocking it over to embrace her friend. "I am so happy for you!"

"It is early days," Dotty said, returning Charlotte's hug. "But I have no reason to think the pregnancy will not be successful. However, we have decided to tell only our particular friends and close family until I am further along."

"I am surprised Merton is not hovering over you."

"He would be if I let him." Grinning, she shook her

head. "As it is, I have had to promise not to tire myself, not to ride horseback, not to go anywhere without two footmen in attendance, and to only dance with him."

"Only dance with him?" Charlotte whooped with laughter. "The poor man. He would probably carry you everywhere if he could."

"I absolutely forbid you to give him any ideas," Dotty said sternly. "He is quite capable of doing that himself."

Still laughing, Charlotte glanced at the mantel clock. "We had better join the others, or he will come looking for you."

"You're most likely right." Dotty rose, a smile tilting her lips. "He is carrying this a bit too far, but I love him for it."

Linking arms, they left the music room. "I think he was extraordinarily lucky to have found you."

"And I him." Dotty squeezed Charlotte's arm. "I have faith you will find the love of your life as well."

"I hope you are right."

When they arrived in the drawing room, Matt was already pouring glasses of champagne and lemonade and handing them around. "There you are. We were about to come find you." He gave goblets to her and Dotty as Merton slid his arm around his wife. Matt held up his glass. "To our family and the next generation."

Charlotte held up her goblet as well. She could not be more pleased for her friend, but at the same time, wondered when she'd be able to celebrate her pregnancy. Yet first, she needed a husband. The right husband, which was turning out to be more problematic than she had thought it would be at the beginning of the Season.

Chapter Fourteen

Con arrived at Stanwood House at ten o'clock the next morning. He was not looking forward to the drubbing he was certain to receive from Charlotte, and slowed his steps going up the stairs to the front door.

He was a little surprised when the door was not immediately opened, as it had been previously, and he'd had to ply the knocker. He was also not pleased that a younger footman was in charge of taking his hat, gloves, and cane. Where the devil was the butler?

"I have come to see Lady Charlotte."

"Follow me, my lord. The family is in the garden for the wedding."

Wedding?

To the best of his knowledge, Charlotte was the only young lady of marriageable age not already wed. Had Harrington returned with a special license? He could go to the devil if he had. He could not have her. Charlotte was Con's, and it was about time she knew it. "I can find my way."

"As you wish, my lord. Go straight down the corridor."

"Thank you."

He must put an end to this wedding before it was too late. Rushing down the corridor, he looked to his right, and spied open French windows in a parlor. A large group of people were gathered just beyond the terrace.

Con prayed he was in time to stop her. Halt the wedding. Hell, what sort of man asks permission of his father to marry someone like Charlotte? Not one she needs.

The Fates had given her to him and no one was going to take her away. Even if the time to object had passed, he would make himself known. She was his.

Dashing through the room, he arrived in the garden in time to hear Worthington say, "If there is anyone who objects to this wedding, speak now or forever hold your peace."

Worthington? Con almost skidded to a stop.

A ringing of high pitched, childish giggles answered. Charlotte stood off to the side next to her elder sister and another lady with black hair. A smile was on her lovely face as she gazed forward.

What looked to be all of the servants were gathered as well. A long table was set up with an assortment of food and lemonade.

What the devil was going on?

"Very well. I now pronounce you . . ." Worthington glanced down. "Husband and wife."

"Matt," a young girl in an outrageous hat said, "do they not have to say their vows?"

This was greeted by more giggles and some laughter.

Worthington blinked once, slowly. "Madeline, they are dogs. They do not know how to say the vows."

Con edged around the crowd to see exactly who or what was in front of Worthington and, to Con's amazement, the two Great Danes, dressed in what could only be described as wedding finery, stood before his friend. Although, the smaller Dane appeared to be trying to eat her bonnet.

Lady Worthington whispered something to Charlotte

and her eyes began to twinkle as she nodded at whatever was said.

He, on the other hand, felt like a fool, even if he was the only one who'd thought a real wedding was taking place.

"Can we eat now?" the smaller of two boys asked.

"*May* we and, yes, we may," Lady Worthington said. "Mind you don't give the dogs too many treats. It will make them sick."

The children were the first to move en masse to the table. The servants melted back into the house, and a tall man escorting Mrs. Addison approached him.

"Good day, my lord. I am Mr. Addison. I've heard a great deal about you from my wife."

Con bowed. "A pleasure to see you again, Mrs. Addison, and to meet you, Mr. Addison."

She curtseyed. "I take it you have come to see Lady Charlotte. I shall fetch her for you."

"Thank you." Turning to the lady's husband, Con said, "I hope what you have heard does me—" Something pulled on Con's jacket, and he looked down at two pairs of blue eyes, one summer-sky blue, the same color as Charlotte's, and the other pair, more of a cobalt, were identical to Worthington's. "I do not believe I've had the pleasure of an introduction."

The girls glanced at Mr. Addison, who said, "Ah, Lady Theodora"—the dark haired girl curtseyed—"and Lady Mary"—the younger girl curtseyed as well—"allow me to introduce the Marquis of Kenilworth."

The one identified as Lady Theodora peered up at him as if trying to decide if he was welcome. "What are you doing here?"

"He has come to see me." Charlotte arrived just in time to stop what promised to be a budding interrogation.

"Er, yes. Excuse me for interrupting a family event, but I thought we might have a small discussion."

She glanced down at the younger girls, then to where the rest of the family and guests were gathered. "I cannot at the moment. However, you may join us if you wish, and we shall speak later."

He summoned a smile. "I would be delighted." A few of the other children began to notice him, and he thought about changing his mind. Still, if he wanted her to wed him . . . How bad could it be? They were only children, after all.

He held his arm out, waiting for Charlotte to place her hand on it. Instead a much smaller, younger hand gripped his sleeve. "Thank you." Lady Mary gave him a brilliant smile. "Are you here to court Charlotte?"

Before he could fashion an answer, his other arm was appropriated by Lady Theodora. "She is the last one left to get married this Season. So we thought you might be."

He heard a choking sound, and Charlotte's face took on a rosy hue.

"I, er, I, well as a matter of fact, I am indeed." That wasn't as bad as he'd thought it would be. "I understand that your dogs just wed." Lady Mary nodded her head several times. "May I ask why?"

"So they can have puppies," Lady Theodora answered.

He glanced at the "bride" and was able for the first time to see her slightly rounded stomach. "Yes, of course. Very understandable."

Con slid a look at Charlotte. She'd worn a pale yellow gown that reminded him of the early daffodils at his estate. Her golden hair was done in a knot fastened just above her neck. Spiraling curls framed her face, and at the mention of puppies the rosy color in her face deepened. He could easily, almost too easily, imagine her with a swollen stomach, carrying his child.

He had agreed to marry her. Indeed, he would demand she wed him. Out of duty at first, but his feelings for her seemed to be growing. At least his regard for her was increasing. That was an unlooked-for pleasure.

He had arrived at the refreshment table, the two girls still with him. They released his arms and took plates from a stack at one end of the table.

"Grace said this would be like a picnic, so we have to pick our own food," Theodora informed him.

Taking a plate for himself, he bent slightly and addressed both girls. "Perhaps you can advise me."

"The lemon cakes and cheese," Mary responded firmly.

"I like the cream tarts and the cheese," Theodora said.

"Hmm, is there something special about the cheese?"

"Yes." Mary grinned. "We make it at our home in the country. It's the best cheese in the world."

"In that case, I must try a taste." He bit off a piece. It was, indeed, one of the best cheeses he had tasted in a while, rich and sharp with a crumbly texture. "Excellent."

"We told you it would be." Theodora guided him to a selection of meats.

Pleased to have made it this far, he searched for Charlotte and found her at the end of the table. However, before he could move to join her, three girls, somewhat older than Mary and Theodora, with the extraordinary hats, joined him.

"What lovely bonnets. I do not believe I've seen anything like them before."

The girls preened. "Thank you," they said in unison. "We made them ourselves."

He looked around again in a vain hope that another adult

would be nearby, but they were all gathered near the table. Well, as they say, in for a penny, in for a pound. "Forgive my boldness, my ladies, but I do not see anyone who can perform an introduction. I am Lord Kenilworth."

The girls curtseyed.

"I am Lady Alice Carpenter." She pointed to the girl next to her. Another one with dark hair and the Worthington eyes. "This is my sister Lady Madeline Vivers, and this"—indicating the third girl with blond hair and Charlotte's eyes—"is my twin sister, Lady Eleanor Carpenter. We are twelve and when we are eighteen, we shall make our come out."

Lady Madeline and Lady Eleanor nodded in confirmation, and Con made a decision to keep Charlotte in the country that year. On the other hand, Worthington might insist everyone be in Town to help keep an eye on them. "A pleasure to meet you, ladies."

Dotty took Charlotte's arm as she ambled after her sisters and Lord Kenilworth.

"I see he is well in hand."

"Theo and Mary will take good care of him. The fun will begin when the twins and Madeline decide it's their turn to meet the visitor."

"I think you're about to see what will happen."

Charlotte glanced in the direction her friend was gazing to see the girls had taken over from Theo and Mary and wondered what the result of his conversation with his mistress was. Yet she was equally curious as to how he would handle being around the children. Her family meant everything to her, and whoever she married must love them as well.

She chewed her bottom lip. "He wishes to speak with me."

"Of course he does." Dotty pulled Charlotte to a halt. "Do not tell me you are concerned about what he may say?"

"Partly." She tugged her friend's arm and began walking again. "Truth be told, I do not wish to have been wrong."

"No," Dotty murmured. "Though, I shall own myself surprised if you are." They hung back from the table, allowing everyone else to make their selections. "It is more than that, isn't it?"

"I don't understand," Charlotte said, wondering what her friend was getting at.

"The way his gaze travels to you and the way you continue to glance at him . . . *Do* you like him, Char? Perhaps more than you are willing to admit at present?"

Maybe she did. Yet, he still had to prove himself before she would allow this to go any further. "Do you remember the night you and Merton became betrothed?"

"I could hardly forget it." Dotty laughed lightly.

"You were not really happy about it. Then you and he went off together and—"

"And he kissed me." A dreamy look appeared on her face. "After that, I did not mind at all being betrothed to him. I had not realized how much I truly liked him until that kiss."

"I don't want that to happen to me." They'd taken a few sweets and some cheese from the table and strolled back to the arbor against the wall at the back of the garden. "You had already begun to show him how wrongheaded he was. If I am to fall in love with Lord Kenilworth, I must have some assurances that he is able to change his behavior as well." She rubbed her right temple, trying to forestall the ache threatening to come on. If only he had not turned out to be the gentleman at the theater, she would have fewer doubts. She might even be happy about the engagement.

Still, she must deal with what she had. "Do you understand?"

"Completely," Dotty assured her. "And I agree. If he is not all you want, then you should not marry him. Provided you can think of a way to jilt him without creating a scandal."

That is what it all came down to. A scandal. Although neither Matt nor Grace had said anything, they did not seem to think much about Charlotte's idea to forestall the wedding indefinitely. "Thank you. It's good to know that my family and my friends will accept my decision."

Dotty grinned, and they started walking back to the festivities. "That is what friends and family are for. Now, fortify yourself with some of your cook's excellent lemon cake, then talk to Lord Kenilworth. I am certain everything will be fine."

"I shall." Charlotte prayed her friend was right. She could not put off the conversation much longer.

When they returned, his lordship was surrounded by the rest of her brothers and sisters. There was nothing unusual about that. They were curious children and the twins and Madeline would try to extract as much information as possible from him.

Her brothers would care for nothing more than what types of horses and carriages Lord Kenilworth owned and if he was a member of the Four Horse Club. Being admitted to that famous driving club was now both Phillip's and Walter's primary goal. Augusta would want to know if he had traveled to Europe and, if so, what he had seen.

As if he could sense her presence, Lord Kenilworth swiveled his head toward her. His green eyes seemed lighter than the last time she had seen them. Today they were the color of newly furled beech leaves. Did they only resemble grass when he was angry?

"Do you see what I mean?" Dotty asked. "Even surrounded by the children, he sees you."

Charlotte quickened her step. "I must have some more lemon cake and a cup of tea."

"Of course you must." Her friend gave her an enigmatic smile. "Yet, you cannot continue to put off the discussion indefinitely."

In fact, not more than a half hour later, he managed to escape her brothers and sisters, approaching her as she was removing Daisy's finery. "I would have thought she'd had eaten all of the flowers by now."

"She only sampled them. Apparently they do not taste as good as they smell." Daisy sniffed at a rose and sneezed. "Thankfully. Otherwise she would have an upset stomach."

"Your brothers and sisters are delightful."

"I agree." Charlotte pulled the last of the lace from around the Dane's neck. "We have been very fortunate that everyone gets along."

"Your twin sisters and the other girl seem to have formed a unique bond." He stroked Daisy's head and she leaned against him.

At least he liked dogs. "They have. It is not surprising. They are all very close in age. Madeline's birthday is only a week away from the twins', and they have a great deal in common."

"Such as bonnets?" He grinned.

"Yes, and fashion in general." Charlotte gave him a slight smile. "They can be very silly at times, but they are good girls and will grow out of it."

"Tell me about the others."

Charlotte wondered if he was truly interested or if his query was simply a way to make conversation that did not touch on their differences. "Walter, the oldest boy present, has formed a friendship with Augusta. It appears they both love maps and languages. I'm afraid Augusta will be a bit lost when Walter goes away to school."

"I understand he is to join your other brother Stanwood at Eton."

Charlotte wondered if Lord Kenilworth had asked or if one of the children had told him. "Yes, this autumn. The younger ones, Mary, Theo, and Phillip, spend a great deal of time together. The girls are almost inseparable. Phillip divides his time between them and doing things boys enjoy with Walter and Matt."

"How much longer will he be at home?"

"Only another year. Grace doesn't think the boys should be sent away at too early an age, but Matt says it is helpful for a boy to have a brother at school as well, so she agreed."

"An older brother was not something either Worthington or I had," Kenilworth noted, sounding a bit sad about it.

Family seemed to be a safe subject at the moment. "Do you have brothers and sisters?"

"I have three sisters. All of whom are several years older than I." Lord Kenilworth grimaced. "I'm sorry to say I do not have much experience with a large family. By the time I was ready to attend school, my youngest sister was having her first Season. I do remember the attendant drama," he added drily.

Charlotte couldn't help but to laugh. "I think there is always some of that."

"Your brothers and sisters are charming." His mien became sober and he raised a brow that she supposed was meant to intimidate. "However, they do not appear to know about our betrothal."

That was direct. Yet, based on her short history with him, she should have expected him to get straight to the point. "No. They do not. Matt and Grace have left it up to me when to tell them."

"And when exactly will that be?" His tone became tighter, almost irritated.

Charlotte straightened to her full height. Even though her head still did not reach his chin, it made her feel more in charge. "When *I* am convinced that a marriage *will* follow."

"Ah." Instead of arguing, as she had expected, he became quiet. "Is there a place we can speak where we will not be interrupted?"

She glanced around and saw Grace shooing the younger children into the house. "Here will do."

"Here?" he asked, looking none too pleased. "Is there not somewhere more private?"

After everything they had been through, how could he think Charlotte would agree to be alone with him? The man was delusional.

She moved the short distance to one of the several wooden benches scattered around the garden and sat. "No. We shall remain in full view of my sister."

Chapter Fifteen

This was a fine state of affairs. Not only would Charlotte not acknowledge their betrothal to her family, but she was forcing Con to discuss the subject of his mistress in a garden with her family looking on.

He was still having trouble with the concept of having this conversation with a lady, particularly a young, unmarried lady. He had taken himself to task for allowing her to goad him into mentioning demireps previously. Of course, if he had his way, she would not be unmarried much longer. The more he discovered about Charlotte, the more convinced he became that she was exactly the lady he wanted to wed. And bed.

He glanced back at the house. Worthington and his wife were sitting at a table on the terrace. Not the whole family, but Charlotte and Con were to be well chaperoned. As if they were not already betrothed.

Damn.

He may as well get this over with. "I did what I said I would do and spoke to my former mistress." He hoped she would notice his use of *former.*

Her hands rested in her lap as she gazed up at him. Her blue eyes were so unguarded Con thought he might be able to see her soul. How unusual for a lady of the *ton*. A feeling or emotion tugged in his chest, but he didn't have time to study it now.

"I have never impugned your honesty, my lord. To be frank, you have been extremely truthful in your dealings with me."

Too truthful, mayhap. A little roundaboutation would have held him in good stead. "I would hope that all of our dealings are honest."

She inclined her head rather regally.

"Well, as I was about to say. I did what we agreed and asked my—" Drat it. He couldn't keep using the term *mistress*. "The woman I have been dealing with if she"—suddenly there was a blockage in his throat that needed to be cleared and he coughed—"had chosen her profession." This was a damn sight harder than he thought it would be. Wishing he had a glass of brandy, he took a breath. "She had not. As a matter of fact, I—I was wro—wro . . ." He took a breath and tried again. "You were-were ri-correct."

Charlotte's lush lips pressed together and seemed to twitch a little for just a moment. The vein at the base of her lovely throat began to throb, and he thought her heart had started beating faster. He'd had no idea she would be so affected. "Do you plan to do anything to help her?"

Finally, he could give her an answer she would like. "Yes, indeed. I am in the process of doing so." His eyes were drawn to her neck again. The throbbing had slowed. "She told me she is in touch with her family, who do not know what she has been doing. I offered to settle an amount on her that will enable her to regain the life she should have lived."

Still clasped, Charlotte's hands moved to her breasts. She blinked rapidly, her lips formed a perfect O, then she said, "That is . . . that is most kind of you. I did not expect . . . I mean for you to—"

For him to do anything to help his mistress was what Charlotte meant. It pleased him that she seemed to realize she had been about to offend him and stopped. "I can understand how you might believe me to be less than sympathetic. I find I owe you an abject apology, my lady. For the most part, I have not exhibited my best side to you. Nor have I always behaved as a gentleman should."

"Nor I to you, my lord." Her tone was firm, but, as if suddenly shy, she did not look at him when she spoke.

"In any event, I ask your forgiveness. I was wrong." It wasn't nearly as hard to say the second time.

"You are forgiven." Her lips pressed together once again, but more in consternation. "I too have failed to always be at my best with you. I would like to apologize for my ill temper."

"There is nothing to forgive." As the words left his mouth, Con knew it was the truth. Any lady, especially an innocent one, would have been shocked at the idea of prostitution. For him to have baited her and engage in scandalous arguments with her had not been well done of him. "I would wish we could"—he glanced up at the sky, hoping for inspiration and found none—"for lack of a better way of saying it, begin again."

She pulled her bottom lip between her pearl-like teeth. "I do not wish to offend you, my lord, yet I am afraid that—" Charlotte covered her face for a moment. "Oh, this is so awkward. I vowed to myself never to wed a man who had engaged in purchasing a woman. Yet, my brother tells me that gentlemen are encouraged to-to—"

"There is no need to explain. I comprehend your meaning. He is correct." Con raked his fingers through his hair. He must convince her to accept him. The thought of being jilted was too much to stomach. Hell, he'd almost made a fool of himself trying to stop what he'd thought was her wedding. "Perhaps if I were to court you, and we came to know each other, you might look upon me more kindly."

Her hands were still, but her dark blond brows drew together, causing a fine line to form. The thought came to him that he would always know where he stood with her.

She stared at her tightly clasped hands before gazing up at him. "Very well. You may court me. However, I have one request. If we decide we do not suit, you will release me from our betrothal."

Never. The more he was around her, the greater his conviction that she would make him a perfect wife, marchioness, and mother to his children. Not to mention the damage to his pride if she rejected him. "Of course."

For the first time since she had discovered who he was, she gave him a real smile, and it was just as beautiful as the one he remembered. "In that case, I shall save you a dance at Lady Pennington's ball."

"Two dances." He could not stop himself from asking for more. "Both waltzes and one of them the supper dance."

Her steady blue eyes regarded him for several moments, and his cravat seemed to grow tighter. "As you wish, my lord."

As pleased as he was with her decision, he resisted the smug smile trying to form on his mouth. And two days was too long to go without seeing her. "Until then?"

Tilting her head to one side, she again drew her well-shaped brows together. "I shall have to think of something."

No. *He'd* think of something and damned fast too. He must strike while she was being so amenable. "Would you like to join me for a carriage ride in the Park this afternoon?"

"Lord Harrington to see Lady Charlotte," a sonorous voice announced.

Con glanced at the terrace and almost swore. What in the name of all that was holy was that pup doing here now? Just as he was making progress with Charlotte. Well, he wasn't going to lose this game to that young fribble.

Worthington and her sister were conversing with Harrington. "A ride this afternoon."

Con held his breath waiting for her answer.

Charlotte tore her gaze from the terrace back to Lord Kenilworth. His request had startled Charlotte as much as Lord Harrington's arrival. For some reason, she had not thought Lord Kenilworth would press his case so soon. If he thought she would simply fall into his arms, he was vastly mistaken. Still, she had made a bargain.

Yet what was she to do about Lord Harrington? Had he heard the talk, or did he expect to propose to her? This certainly made a bad state of affairs worse.

"My lady?" Lord Kenilworth said, his voice much calmer than the throb in his jaw indicated he was.

First things first. She would deal with the gentleman in front of her now and the other one later. "I would like that, thank you."

She had almost said she'd be delighted, but they were being scrupulously honest with each other and it would not have rung true.

"It is entirely my pleasure." His lips tilted in a strange, lopsided smile, and she wondered what it meant.

Despite her brother stating that he would leave the final decision of marriage to her, she knew he would be satisfied with her choice. After all Grace had done, and now Matt too, to keep her brothers and sisters together, she did wish her family to be happy with her.

A ride with Kenilworth would also allow her to come to know him better. That was all her brother-in-law had asked of her, to give the man a chance to prove himself.

She thought back to his confession and could not help but smile. It had taken a great deal for him to admit he'd been mistaken. For a few moments Charlotte had wondered if he'd be able to get the words out. Yet, it was what he had told her he'd done for his former mistress that had truly impressed her. How many men would try to make amends by attempting to give the woman back some of that which had been taken? Not many, she would wager.

Wealthy, handsome, and titled. Could she now add compassionate to his list of positive features? The last would mean more to her than the first three qualities together. Much more.

Well, time and a better acquaintance with him would tell.

He held out his arm and Charlotte placed her hand on it before strolling to the terrace with him. Dotty and Merton were gone and the children as well. Only Matt, Grace, and Harrington remained.

He rose as soon as she approached. "Lady Charlotte, I came to tell you I have just arrived back in Town." Ignoring Lord Kenilworth, Harrington bowed, and for a moment she thought he would try to take her hand. "I have excellent news. I should, though, have written your brother so that you would be expecting me."

She cut a look at Lord Kenilworth, but a mask had slid over his features. "Well, you are here now. What is it you wished to tell me?"

Harrington scowled slightly at Lord Kenilworth. "That will have to wait. Do you have a waltz free for me at Lady Hereford's ball?"

She quickly brought the dance card to mind. There were three waltzes that evening. "Yes. The second one is free."

He gave Lord Kenilworth, whose countenance showed nothing but well bred boredom, another angry look, as if he knew who had requested the other two waltzes. Not knowing what else to do, she gave her other suitor a polite smile.

Kenilworth took her hand and bowed over it. "Until this afternoon, my lady."

"Until then, my lord." She curtseyed.

Grace glanced from Charlotte to Harrington as Matt escorted Kenilworth to the front door, leaving them with Lord Harrington.

She took the chair on the other side of the small table, and her sister poured them both cups of tea. "I trust your father is in good health, my lord?"

"Yes . . . yes, indeed." He took a sip of tea, then placed the cup down. "He has arranged a position for me with the Foreign Office."

"How wonderful for you," Charlotte said. "Will you be in London?"

"I shall be with Sir Charles Stuart on the Continent." He grinned like a little boy. "I will join him as soon as I have matters here settled."

She hoped for his sake that Napoleon would soon be sent back to an island. "That sounds very exciting."

"I'm glad you think so," he said, looking contented with her answer.

He remained for another ten minutes as they discussed what had been going on while he'd been in the country. Their talk did not, however, touch on Charlotte's betrothal. Was he purposely avoiding the subject or had he not heard? She debated saying something, but decided that as she had not made a decision, it was too soon. Aside from that, she had been interested in him. If he could show her that he was willing to try to win her affections . . . well, who knew what the future might bring.

"Lady Charlotte," Lord Harrington said. "Will you walk with me in the Park tomorrow afternoon?"

From the corner of her eye, she saw her sister incline her head. "Thank you. I would be delighted."

Shortly after Grace's butler, Royston, escorted Harrington out, Grace said, "I take it your conversation with Kenilworth went well."

"I believe it did." Charlotte remembered that her sister didn't know the task she had set for the man. She began to explain what had occurred the previous day.

Her sister's brows rose. "My dear, that was quite bold of you."

"Mayhap." She smoothed down her skirts nervously. "But do you not agree that it was necessary? Especially after everything he had said?"

"I suppose." The brows dropped and Grace's forehead wrinkled as it did when she was in thought. "Under the circumstances, you made the right decision."

Charlotte let out the breath she'd been holding. "Thank you." Then she giggled. "You should have seen him trying to tell me he was wrong. I thought he would choke on the words. And you will never guess what else he has done."

"What?" Grace asked, sitting forward on her chair.

"He is giving her the funds to start her life anew."

"And that," she said sagely, "is what made you decide to give him a chance to prove himself."

"Yes." Charlotte was glad her sister understood and agreed with her. "Now we shall see about the rest. Because nothing is settled with Lord Kenilworth, I have decided to see if Lord Harrington is truly interested in me."

"An excellent idea." Matt stepped onto the terrace and stood behind Grace, placing his hands on her shoulders. "It never hurts for a man to have a rival."

Charlotte stared at him for a moment. "I do not understand."

"You still have not decided for Kenilworth, is that

correct?" She nodded slowly, noting the sly gleam in her brother's eyes. "Harrington has received permission from his father to marry you, and asked to speak with me." That his lordship would require permission from his father rankled her slightly. "Allow them both to court you."

"I had decided to do that, but I have a feeling you have something else in mind."

"A little competition can do wonders to focus a man's mind."

"A competition over me?" Charlotte asked. "I do not know how that will help me decide."

Her brother grinned. "You will."

Before she could ask for clarification, Grace looked at her watch. "The rest of this conversation will have to wait. Charlotte and I must change. Lady Kenilworth is coming to fetch us in less than an hour."

Rising, Charlotte followed her sister into the house. "What do you think about what Matt said?"

"That my husband can be extremely astute about other gentlemen, particularly when one of his sisters or charges is involved. Take his advice, and we shall see what happens."

It never occurred to her that two gentlemen might be interested in courting her. The thought that they would vie over her was a bit unsettling. On the other hand, it could be interesting as well. "I shall do as he suggests."

Chapter Sixteen

An hour later, Charlotte, Grace, and Lady Kenilworth were ensconced in Lady Bellamny's drawing room. It was the first time Charlotte had seen her ladyship since the day Lady Bellamny had declared Charlotte and Kenilworth must wed, and she still felt bad about her behavior that day.

After greetings had been exchanged and her ladyship had congratulated Charlotte on her betrothal, Charlotte went to the window seat, her favorite place in the drawing room. It seemed strange though, not to be sharing it with Louisa or Dotty.

Just then, Miss Turley entered with her aunt, Lady Bristow. After making her curtsey to Lady Bellamny, Elizabeth hurried to Charlotte. "I heard from my brother you and the Marquis of Kenilworth are betrothed. Is it true?"

She had been dreading this moment, but confirming the information was easier than she'd thought. "We are."

"Gavin said your brother introduced you?" When Charlotte nodded, Elizabeth sighed. "I do wish my brother would have the sense to be acquainted with eligible gentlemen who have not been around all Season. And so I told him when he asked why I had not found a husband as easily as you, Louisa, and Dotty had done."

Charlotte laughed lightly. "Matt is a few years older than your brother. Still I must say I agree with you. He should cultivate friends that are also eligible partis for you."

"Exactly." Elizabeth gave a sharp nod. "But, Charlotte, what of Lord Harrington? Did you not have an understanding?"

"Not really." Charlotte wondered how much to tell Elizabeth. She had been a good friend, but Charlotte had only really confided in Dotty and Louisa. Now that she thought of it, Kenilworth had done more to fix her interest than Harrington had done since the beginning of the Season. He'd probably had a mistress as well. She wondered if he would have been as kind as Kenilworth had been, and decided not. "I had not heard from him since he left Town to visit his father—until today, when he stopped by to tell me he had returned." Despite what Grace had said, Charlotte was a little surprised that Elizabeth had known about the betrothal. "Did your brother say where he heard the news?"

"Oh"—Elizabeth fluttered her fingers—"at his club last evening. Apparently, Lord Endicott was calling for champagne to celebrate your betrothal."

"Lord Endicott?" What had he to do with anything, and what business had Kenilworth spreading around word of their betrothal?

"Yes," Elizabeth said excitedly. "From what I was told, Kenilworth entered Brooks's and was congratulated by the master of the club. He ordered brandy and sat by himself, but upon seeing him, Lord Endicott got him to confirm the rumors were true and called for champagne. My brother said Kenilworth did not appear pleased with the interruption and tried to leave, but by then too many gentlemen were trying to wish him happy."

"I see." And a great deal more than Elizabeth understood. Lord Kenilworth would have already known his mistress's story and was most likely wishing for some quiet that he would not find at home.

His mother had taken one look at the Pulteney, one of the best hotels in Town, and declared she would rather stay at Kenilworth House, so there would have been little peace there. Charlotte almost felt sorry for him.

"Gavin said Kenilworth also refused to go with several of them when they left Brooks's to find other entertainment." Elizabeth cast her gaze to the ceiling. "Whatever that means. He will never tell me. However, he most likely means gambling hells and other forms of low entertainment."

Charlotte had a very good idea what that meant, and her esteem for his lordship grew a little more. "I am not sure I would wish to know."

"Very true," Elizabeth remarked unconvincingly. "You said Lord Harrington has returned?"

"He has." Charlotte studied her friend for a moment. "He has asked to speak with Worthington."

"Oh." Her friend's face drooped.

"Are you interested in him?"

"I might be." Elizabeth's tone was evasive. "Are you?"

This was a pickle. Charlotte wanted her friend to find a husband, but was it Harrington? She did not wish to stand in the way of Elizabeth's happiness. "I am not sure." Elizabeth gave Charlotte a sharp glance. "It is complicated."

"We are about to be descended upon. If you like, we shall discuss it later."

"I would like that." She smiled as if relieved. "Thank you."

She and Elizabeth smiled politely as a group of ladies surrounded them, and Charlotte was besieged by well-wishers with questions for which she did not have convincing answers.

Fortunately, a few minutes later Grace beckoned, and Charlotte was able to excuse herself.

When they arrived in the hall, Lady Kenilworth was smiling contentedly. "I have not had so much fun in a long time. Almeria was correct. I should spend more time in Town." Their carriage arrived and the ladies were handed in. "Charlotte, my dear, did you hear that news of your betrothal is all anyone is speaking of? It has even eclipsed Lady Jane Summers's marriage to Mr. Garvey. The Garveys are an old and well-respected family, but to allow Lady Jane to throw herself away on such a fellow . . . well, I do not know what her mother was thinking. She could have done much better."

"Their grandparents' estates run together, and they have known each other for years." Charlotte saw no reason to inform Lady Kenilworth that Jane's parents hadn't had a choice in the matter. Everyone had thought she had set her cap for Merton, but he was merely a diversion until she confirmed she was breeding and could wed the man she loved. "I received a letter from her when I returned. She is extremely happy being married to Mr. Garvey."

"She had better be," her ladyship responded laconically. "There is no changing her mind now."

That was true. Marriage was forever, or until one person died. Which was a very good reason for Charlotte to be as sure as she could be of Kenilworth and her feelings for him, as well as his for her. She should also discover if she had feelings, other than friendship, for Harrington. At this point, she wasn't sure how she felt about either man. It was as if Harrington had appeared merely to muddy the water. On the other hand, perhaps it would help her make the right decision. Then again, once he heard about her betrothal, he would most likely turn to another lady. Mayhap she could help Elizabeth.

Charlotte sighed to herself. Even in *Pride and Prejudice*, the book she had just finished reading, the hero and heroine did not get on immediately.

That thought made her feel better. Her mother used to say things always worked out for the best. *I hope so, Mama.*

Con lightly drummed his fingers on his desk. He had summoned his man of business and was growing impatient with the man's questions. "Suffice it to say it is a debt of honor. If you cannot see to it, I shall find someone who will."

"No, no, my lord." For the first time Sutton appeared ill at ease. "I was merely attempting to convey . . . I mean . . . but a debt of honor. I understand."

Sutton had originally been hired by Con's father because Sutton did not defer to every demand without ensuring a scheme was in the best interests of the marquisate. However, Con's promise to Aimée, at least as he saw it, meant that his man of business must be kept ignorant of some of the details.

"I shall see to the accounts immediately. Where do you wish me to send the documents?" Sutton asked.

"To me. Draw up papers to convey the house on North Row as well."

Sutton sat up straighter. "That is a fine property, my lord, even if you will not be using it as you have been."

"Now that I am betrothed, I would rather see it gone."

Con had stilled his fingers, but impatience continued to flow through him.

He wanted this business completed as rapidly as possible, and not just for his former mistress's sake. Charlotte had warmed considerably after he had told her what he'd done. Her brother had said the family would leave in less than two weeks, and he was determined that Charlotte would be his wife by then. This idea she had of pushing their wedding off, or not having it at all, was intolerable. He wasn't going to be jilted by the first lady to whom he was betrothed.

It was clear Charlotte had something of a romantic nature. Why else would she not care about more than his rank and wealth? He would spend as much time with her as possible, getting to know her, and charming her. Before long, she'd fancy herself in love with him and he would get her to church before she had time to change her mind.

As far as Con knew, none of the other gentlemen, aside from Harrington, had succeeded in courting her. If only that dammed cawker had not shown up, Con's way would be much simpler. Damn the pup for thrusting a spoke in his wheel. He'd just have to find a way to cut the man out.

"Very good, my lord," Sutton responded, apparently having given up the argument. "I shall have everything to you in the morning."

"Excellent." Con straightened the documents on his desk as his butler opened the door and Sutton took his leave. "Webster."

"My lord?"

"Have my phaeton brought around in twenty minutes."

"Yes, my lord."

Con leaned back against the soft leather squabs of his chair. Today would be the first time he and Charlotte had been alone since the morning he rescued her. Although to be fair, he'd merely given her a method of escaping. She had managed to foil the procuress's plans without his assistance.

He admired her independence, except, he thought ruefully, when she was challenging him. Well, if he wanted her, and he did, he'd have to become used to her strong will.

A half hour later, he strode up the steps of Stanwood House.

The butler opened the door and bowed. "I shall inform Lady Charlotte that you have arrived. Would you like to step into the front parlor?"

And be out of sight and, possibly, out of mind? "No, thank you. I shall wait here."

"As you wish, my lord."

Several minutes later, Charlotte stood at the top of the stairs, a vision in a turquoise carriage gown of grosgrain silk trimmed with yellow ribbon. Pearls dangled from her shell shaped ears. "I apologize for taking so long. I was having difficulty—" A gray streak raced down the stairs and sat at the door. Her eyes narrowed. "Collette, who let you out?"

"We're sorry, Charlotte." Lady Theodora leaned over the rail.

Charlotte came down the stairs, scooped up the cat, and handed it to the butler. "Please see that she is put back in my parlor." Only then did she turn to him. "We may leave."

Con glanced at the small feline who seemed to always be around. "Does she usually go everywhere you do?"

"I take her when I drive my carriage. She does not seem to understand that she may not accompany me today."

Something was wrong . . . not quite right with what she'd said. He mulled over her statement. "I would imagine there are many times when she is not allowed to go with you."

"Not really." The words came out in more of a mutter. "What I mean is that early in the Season, Matt decided we, Louisa and I, would be better served to drive ourselves. This is only the second time I have ridden in a gentleman's carriage. I believe you will remember the first time."

Interesting. "And you always bring the cat . . . Collette? She doesn't attempt to escape?"

"Yes, Collette. All the kittens have names beginning with C. And no, she is almost always with me. The breed travels quite well. Lord Merton has her brother, Cyrille, and he frequently rides with him."

Con had heard of dogs in carriages, the most famous being "Poodle" Byng's dog. But a cat? Then again . . . "I have no objection to Collette coming with us."

Charlotte's countenance brightened as she took her kitten from the butler. "Please send for her harness." She looked at him with what he hoped was new interest. "Thank you, my lord. I assure you she will be perfectly behaved."

He had his misgivings, but remembered how well the kitten had traveled in the basket. Until he'd stuck his hand inside—he still had some faint scars from that encounter— he had barely known she was present. "I have no doubt she will be showing off her best manners."

The harness arrived, and they were shortly on their way, the cat sitting snugly between him and his betrothed.

He feathered the turn from Berkeley Square onto Mount Street.

"Do you have pets?" Charlotte asked.

She had been stroking the cat and occasionally one of her fingers would lightly touch his thigh. At this rate, he'd be lucky if he survived the ride around the Park with his sanity intact.

"Hunting dogs." His voice sounded rusty as Con tried to rein in his rapidly rising lust. "I attempted bringing one into the house when I was around six years of age, but my mother wouldn't have it."

"Oh, dear."

From the corner of his eye, he saw her lips pitch downward and sought to reassure her. "You need not be concerned. If we marry, you will be mistress of all my properties . . . our properties." She still seemed unconvinced. "My mother does not live at my principle estate, and if she wishes to visit Town, she can stay elsewhere if she does not like house animals. I intend to ask Worthington if I may have one of the puppies."

That did the trick. Charlotte's smile returned and she glanced at him. "I am sure he will be glad of your offer. As much as we all love Duke and Daisy, we will have to find homes for their progeny." They rode in silence for a few moments before Charlotte commented, "It is a shame you are not closer to your sisters."

As close to her brothers and sisters, even her sisters by marriage, as she was, Con knew she would eventually bring up the subject of his sisters. She might even be concerned that he would not wish her to maintain close ties to her family. "My youngest sister, Annis, Lady Kendrick, and I write, but she is still five years older than I am and her family takes up much of her time."

"Do you have nieces and nephews?"

"Yes. Five nieces and six nephews." Thinking of them made him smile. Annis's children were much nicer than the children of his other sisters. Not that he knew the others nearly as well. "The ones I know the best are Annis's. The oldest, a boy, is fourteen. Then there is a girl, thirteen. Another boy, eleven, a girl, nine, and the youngest boy is seven. They live about a half day's travel from my mother. I usually make a point of visiting either before or after I see Mama."

Charlotte had turned in the seat so that she was facing him. "What of your other sisters?"

"Cornelia, Marchioness of Westborough, is eight years my elder and Sapphira, Duchess of Stafford, is ten years older than I. We are not close."

"I think I understand." Charlotte's lips formed a moue. "I have met both of your elder sisters. They are not particularly friendly."

"That is putting it nicely." He commended Charlotte's kindness. His older sisters were shrews of the first order. "In my considered opinion they are both puffed up in their own consequence. You should have seen the fit they threw when Annis was allowed to marry a mere baron. They had got together and decided she should marry one of the royal princes."

Charlotte wrinkled her nose. She, Louisa, and Dotty had all been presented to Queen Charlotte earlier in the Season. Two of the royal princes had been present and Charlotte had not been impressed by either of them. "Were they any better when they were younger?"

"In a word, no. She would have been made miserable. Fortunately, my mother's good sense prevailed."

When she had first met Lady Kenilworth, good sense was not a term Charlotte would have used. However, after having spent the early afternoon answering questions about Kenilworth, Charlotte had a new appreciation for the torture the lady had put her through during the journey back to Town. And no one who spoke to Lady Kenilworth today would doubt that her son and Charlotte had a love match, thus stopping the small bit of harmful gossip that had been bruited about and saving her reputation.

Yet, that brought her around to Kenilworth. He was turning out to be a much better gentleman than she had originally thought he was. Earlier, when he had told her about what he was doing for his mistress, she had been almost speechless at his generosity.

But could she love him? That is what she must discover before she kissed him again. "I am glad she was able to marry the man she wished to wed."

"So was she." He grinned. "Unfortunately, the decision caused a rift that has still not fully healed."

"That is sad." Although, she had still not completely forgiven her uncles for trying to stop Grace from gaining custody of her and the younger children. "I do not think something like that would ever occur with my brothers and sisters. We are already so close and there are so many of us."

"I find your family truly enjoyable," he said, trying to reassure her. "That type of affection is what I wish for in my future family."

One more of her concerns dissolved. Blowing away like dandelion seeds in the wind. "Thank you. They are very important to me."

And, equally important, could he love her? At the moment, she had a foreboding that he was insisting on this marriage because he said he would wed her, and not out of any true feeling toward her. Would a kiss show her how he felt? Dotty said it had with her, but for Charlotte it was much too soon. And there was Harrington to consider. She felt duty bound to give him a chance.

They were on the carriage track in the Park, and his

attention was taken by the various vehicles, horses, and people strolling along the verge.

"Lady Charlotte."

"Lady Jersey." Charlotte acknowledged the Almack's patroness's greeting. "How nice to see you."

"And Lord Kenilworth." Her ladyship looked like a cat lapping cream. "I am thrilled to learn the gossip was correct. May I wish you happy?"

"Thank you," Charlotte and Kenilworth said at the same time.

"I shall visit your sister 'at home' and congratulate her as well. It is not often one manages to marry off three young ladies in their first Season, and such good matches as well. Though, I suppose she has Worthington to thank for the last two." Her ladyship gave her coachman the office to go. "I look forward to seeing you at Lady Hereford's ball."

Charlotte noticed that Lady Jersey had not added Grace's wedding. "Yes, indeed."

"If the ball will be too much of an ordeal for you . . ." he whispered, his low tone causing pleasurable shivers to caress her neck. That had never happened before.

"No. Your mother is correct. We must attend." Charlotte studied him for a moment. "Unless it is you who does not wish to attend. In fact, I do not remember having seen you at any of the events this Season."

"This cannot be as bad as the last one," he groused, making her smile again.

"How so?"

"I shall have you to protect me."

"Ah, from all the marriageable young ladies." Matt had friends who attended only the entertainments they must. Even then they left early and did their best to avoid the more forward of the young ladies. In fact, her cousin Merton had almost fallen into a lady's trap.

"And marriage-minded widows. You can't forget them. They can be more ferocious than the matchmaking mamas."

She wanted to let out a peal of laughter, but contained her mirth to a light giggle. "I shall make sure to keep you safe."

He gave her a considering look, and she wondered if she had been too rash. "I shall hold you to your word."

Chapter Seventeen

Burt had had to wait three days in Biggleswade for the London guests to show up at the White Hart where his landlord said the nob in the big house took his guests. For the past two days, he'd watched the group of toffs swill ale, but there was no sign of Lady Charlotte or the gent. Where the devil could they have gone?

Two yallow-haired whores went around behind the inn, and one of the gents called out, "Braxton, I'll trade you for a day."

The game pullet sittin' next to the man punched his arm. "Don't think you can share me. I stick with the gent I come with."

"I'm satisfied with what I have," the man called Braxton said.

Braxton. That was the name of the gent who took off with Lady Charlotte, but the one here didn't look like the nob at the inn.

Bloody hell! Burt swore under his breath. He'd been gammoned. And he didn't have a clue where to find her ladyship. Miss Betsy weren't going to be happy about that.

"Did you hear Kenilworth is getting leg-shackled?" a toff with red hair asked.

The rest of the gents perked their ears up.

"Thought it would be years before he became a tenant for life. Who's the female?"

Red called for another round of ale. "Lady Charlotte Carpenter. Worthington's sister-in-law. It's her first Season."

"I could have told you that," Braxton groused. "I saw them the morning of the fight I attended before I came here. Looked smoky to me, then I saw Lady Bellamny was there too."

Fight? Bloody hell. He'd been that close to catching her in the village he'd passed through.

"Well, if she was around, it's all right and tight," another gent said.

"Wonder how Lady Charlotte snared him." A man with a purple coat tossed coins at the serving maid. "He always said he didn't like them young. Maybe I should have taken a look this year."

"I wonder if his mistress is looking for someone new," a tall man said.

The gent called Braxton scowled. "Not yet, she isn't."

"Asked her, did you?"

Braxton turned red and the rest of the crowd laughed at his expense.

Days wasted following around the wrong man. Burt didn't even know where she'd be. He waited, hoping he'd hear something useful, but someone started talking about horse racing and they lost interest in Lady Charlotte.

Bugger all. Burt was tired of listening to them. He finished his beer and stood. There had to be some way to get to the lady.

He walked back to the tavern he'd been staying at. By the time he returned to London, Miss Betsy would know how bad he'd cocked up. He was on Queer Street now.

He should have listened to himself when he'd thought no

gentry mort would be at a party like this one. What was worse, Miss Betsy'd know it too.

Burt paid his shot at the inn and started back to London. He'd have that square watched for a day or so. If he couldn't find Lady Charlotte there was nothing for it but to write to Miss Betsy and tell her what happened.

It did not take long for Con to discover Charlotte had gone walking with Harrington during the Grand Strut. Fury was not an emotion Con was used to, but it was all he could do to keep himself from flying into the boughs now.

He had arrived at Stanwood House certain he would find his betrothed at home. Instead he was met with the information that she had gone out. Royston, the Carpenter butler, stood impassively waiting for Con to hand over his card. Yet, the sound of children began to fill the silence, and an idea came to him. "Whose permission must I have to take the children to Gunter's for ices?"

For the briefest moment, he thought he saw a canny look enter the butler's eyes. "Lady Worthington, my lord." The servant stepped aside, allowing him to enter the hall. "If you give me a moment, I shall see if she is at home."

"Certainly."

A few moments later Royston returned. "She will see you, my lord."

Con was escorted to a room on the opposite side of the house from the morning room and announced. Sitting behind a large desk covered with documents and ledgers, Lady Worthington waved him to a straight wooden chair with a leather seat, in front of the desk. His father's study had a chair like this, and he had never enjoyed sitting in it.

Once he'd taken a seat, she folded her hands on the desk. "I understand you wish to speak with me."

Resisting the urge to fidget, he nodded. "I would like to take the children to Gunter's for ices."

Her eyes widened. "All of the children?"

"Yes." Con started feeling more confident. "I thought they might like a treat. I shall require a few footmen."

"Very well." She reached behind her and tugged a thick braided-silk rope. A moment later, the butler appeared. "Prepare the children for an outing to Gunter's. His lordship has very kindly offered to take them."

This time he was positive he saw Royston's lips twitch. "Yes, my lady. I shall notify his lordship when they are ready."

The door closed, and he glanced at Lady Worthington. "How long do you think it will take?"

"Not long at all." She tilted her head slightly to one side. "I take it you know Charlotte is walking with Lord Harrington?"

Nothing like a full frontal attack, as his army friends would say. It must run in the family. "So I was informed."

"Why do you wish to marry my sister?" His mind emptied of all thought, and she smiled at him. "Be assured, by paying attention to the children you are going about it the right way. However, I would like an answer."

"We must wed." The moment he said the words, he wanted to call them back. "I mean everyone knows . . ." That wasn't much better.

"I agree. The circumstances are not good." That was putting it mildly. "However, I tend to be of the same mind with Charlotte. A long engagement, a falling out, and a decision that you do not suit might work as well." She raised one expressive brow. "If you do not wish to wed her—"

"No." He'd leaned forward in the chair and sat back again. "I do want to marry Charlotte. I am not able to put my reasons into words"—none that Lady Worthington would find acceptable—"but I am determined."

"I will not have her made unhappy."

"Nor will I." Con's back teeth began to throb again. He had thought a great deal about how he felt. Not that it had helped. He had, however, considered Charlotte's feelings. He was going to make her fall in love with him.

A knock came on the door and it opened. "The children are in the hall."

Rising from his seat, he bowed. "Thank you."

Her ladyship inclined her head and went back to her books. Con followed the butler into the hall now teaming with children already in a line with the footmen.

He could barely hear himself think over the din. "Shall we depart?"

Somehow he'd been heard, evidenced by the children lining up in pairs flanked by footmen. Royston opened the door, Con stepped out, the children following along behind him, and almost ran straight into Charlotte and Harrington.

At first she appeared shocked, then a twinkle of laughter entered her bright blue eyes. "Are you going into the square?"

"In a manner of speaking. I am taking the children to Gunter's." Con met Harrington's glower by raising his quizzing glass and directing it at the popinjay. "Would you like to join us?"

"I would love to." She grinned at Con before turning to his nemesis. "My lord?"

"No. I have another appointment." Harrington gave a stiff bow. "I look forward to seeing you this evening, my lady."

Ha! Routed him. That was easy. The idiot clearly did not know the first thing about winning a female. Never let another man walk off with her.

"As do I, my lord."

He enjoyed the sight of Harrington stomping down the steps. Charlotte gave Con a graceful curtsey, then took his arm. They crossed the street and made their way up Berkeley Square toward the famous tea shop. He enjoyed the way she seemed to lean a bit near him as they walked.

"What possessed you to offer to take them all for ices?" Her gaze was still full of mirth.

He thought about shamming it, but they had agreed to be honest. "You."

"Thank you."

Thank you? Thank you for what? Being truthful? Asking the children? What the devil did she mean, and how was he to find out? "You are welcome."

This last was said so tersely, Charlotte glanced up at Kenilworth. A look of consternation had settled on his strong, lean face, making his brow furrow slightly, and his well-molded lips flatten. Men were such strange creatures. He had been almost playful before. What had happened?

"What is wrong? Are you regretting your largess?"

He whipped his head around. "Not at all. I like children." His dark brows lowered. "I did not understand what you meant by thank you."

"I am pleased that you would take my brothers and sisters out because you thought it would make me happy, and it does." He grunted, which she supposed indicated satisfaction with her answer. "How do you plan to order the ices?"

"Youngest first." Looking at her, he grinned. "Ladies Theo and Mary terrify me. They are already forces to be reckoned with."

They had reached Gunter's and he took charge, leaving Charlotte to compare Kenilworth and Harrington. During their stroll, she had asked Harrington if he had heard of her betrothal. It had seemed strange to her that he would ask her to go to the Park with him if he had.

"You cannot really be thinking of marrying the fellow?" His astonished look had surprised her. "I've spent the entire Season fixing my attentions with you, and my father has approved the match."

"I beg your pardon?" For a moment, she was too shocked to say more. After the first few weeks, he had acted as if he did not need to do anything more. Not only had he never danced with her more than once at a ball, he had only once sent her flowers. "After the first two weeks of the Season, I only saw you at balls and other entertainments. And you have spent the last few weeks in the country. That is hardly what I could consider fixing my attention."

"There is no reason to become upset. I was busy. You must have known I planned to offer for you." Harrington blew out a breath. "I even wrote to your brother, informing him I would do myself the honor of calling on him when I returned."

Actually, it was more like a huff, and Charlotte's temper rose. "Yes, you did. You did not, however, arrange to write to me."

"That would not have been proper before I had my father's permission." She had never before known how much he relied on his father's approval. "With the position with Sir Charles under discussion, I dared not make any mistakes."

"Sir Charles?" What had Sir Charles to do with Harrington's behavior toward her?

"Yes." Glancing down at her, he gave a patronizing look. "I suppose you do not know. He is the ambassador to France and The Hague."

Of course she knew, and he should know she knew from their conversation the other day.

"Naturally, as my wife, you will have to make a point to learn the people and politics involved—"

"I am well aware of who Sir Charles is. Why did you not mention it as a possibility before you left?"

"As I said, nothing had been decided, and I did not wish to get your hopes up."

Her hopes? Charlotte was so angry she could happily kick Harrington. Unfortunately, that was not a possibility. They had reached the Park and it seemed as if everyone was staring at them. She pasted a smile on her lips. Apparently, she had been right about him not really caring about her. He merely wanted a wife. It was fortunate that she did not have to marry this Season.

"Come, come," he said in a tone one might use with a child. "I will speak with Worthington and set it all straight."

Providentially, Lady Bellamny pulled up on the verge to speak with them. She was followed by several other ladies Charlotte knew, and by the time she and Harrington had arrived back at the gate, she was in charity with, if not him, the rest of the world.

"I should return home."

"If you wish."

It was during that part of the walk she noticed he never used an endearment when speaking with her, or told her how he felt about her. He also minced, making her slow to his step as if he thought she was walking too quickly, and the muscles in his arms were not as hard as Kenilworth's muscles. That thought startled her. Charlotte had never noticed a man's muscles before. Why would she care about them now?

She wondered if Harrington would have come to the house when the children were ill, as Rothwell, Louisa's husband, had, but Bentley, Harrington's friend who had thought himself in love with her, had not. "My youngest brother and sisters contracted the measles while you were gone."

"How horrible." His words were correct, but his tone indicated that he did not care.

"I helped nurse them," she added to see his reaction.

"Rest assured when we have children you will do no such thing."

She knew many mothers relied on their nurses and nursemaids, but Charlotte could not imagine not being with her children when they were ill.

They strolled up the steps to her house and the door opened, causing her to almost walk into Lord Kenilworth . . . with the children lined up behind him. Once again, Harrington was pouting like a small child and had refused to accompany them to Gunter's.

Charlotte savored the taste of the lavender ice. On the way here, Kenilworth's arm had flexed under her fingers, and she'd enjoyed the feel of his strength. Then he had said he had done this for her. It was time to discover if he was the one.

She handed her dish to Hal, one of their footmen. Kenilworth was wiping Mary's hands with a piece of linen.

"I like him," Theo said. "You can marry him if you'd like."

"Thank you." Charlotte held back the giggle burbling up. "I do not yet know if that is what I want to do."

He handed the cloth to one of the footmen, who returned it to the tea shop, then strolled over to them. "That was the last of them." He grinned at her and she smiled back. "I hope I haven't ruined their dinner."

Theo ran back to her footman, and Kenilworth held out his arm to Charlotte.

"I think they will be fine," she replied, taking his arm.

When she returned, she would ask Grace to invite him to dinner before the next ball.

Chapter Eighteen

The next morning, Charlotte and her sister visited Madam Lisette the modiste to whom they had been giving their custom.

"I wish you happy," Madam said as she spread out drawings over a long table. "I 'ave 'eard of your engagement."

As had everyone else in the *ton*. "Thank you, Madam."

Sleep had not come easily last night. Every time Charlotte thought she would surrender to Morpheus, another thought invaded her mind. Lord Harrington had shown himself to be someone other than what he had pretended to be when they had first met. Apparently, the attentions he had paid to her early on—pretending interest in her brothers and sisters—were not how he intended to behave as a husband. If he actually got around to proposing, she would reject him. Although, he would most likely not take no for an answer. That would be awkward.

Yet, were Kenilworth's attentions real? If they were, could she love him, and could he love her? Why did he wish to wed her in the first place? Perhaps, for her, there was another gentleman entirely.

She gave herself a shake. No matter what happened or

failed to happen, she was getting a new wardrobe. That was something to be happy about.

"What do you think of these?" Grace asked.

Charlotte looked at a carriage gown in Spanish brown—a color that looked well on her—and a walking gown in damascene, a deep plum. They would be perfect for autumn. Although, whether she would be allowed to wear them if she did not wed was another question. "They are lovely."

Madam showed her several other designs, including evening gowns, ball gowns, and day dresses. By the time she and her sister left, the order exceeded what had been purchased for the Season.

Deciding to simply enjoy the excess, Charlotte took out her list as Grace gathered up swatches. "The milliner next, then the shoemaker."

Later that morning when they returned home, Charlotte's spirits were much restored. She walked into the hall and stopped. Flowers filled the round walnut table, and both front parlors. "Where did these come from?"

Royston held out a silver salver with two cards, one from Lord Kenilworth and the other from Lord Harrington. The butler cleared his throat. "Lord Kenilworth arrived shortly after you left this morning. There is a note on the back of his card."

Picking it up, she turned it over.

Will you do me the honor of saving me two waltzes at Lady Pennington's ball, to include the supper dance? Please.

C.

She would send him her response later. "What does this have to do with the bouquets?"

"Lord Kenilworth brought the first bouquet." He pointed to a lovely arrangement of Provence moss-roses, which were her favorites, mixed with nigella and ivy. "Lord Harrington arrived before his lordship departed." She took the other card.

> *I would like to stand up with you for the supper dance at Lady Pennington's ball tomorrow.*
> G. Earl of Harrington

This was an easy decision to make. Kenilworth had asked first, and more politely. "Let me guess, Lord Harrington sent a bouquet as well."

"Indeed, my lady. The red roses are from him."

"Well, that accounts for two of the arrangements, but there must be at least ten of them." As well as the marigolds, delphiniums, and lupus. He was obviously guessing as to what she liked, yet how had Kenilworth known . . . Of course, the children had told him. More importantly, he had obviously inquired. "Fifteen, my lady. Thus far, Lord Kenilworth has the advantage by one. They have been arriving every hour. Mrs. Pennymore has run out of vases."

"Poor Pennymore. What a position for a housekeeper to be in." Grace collapsed onto one of the chairs, and began to laugh. A few moments later, she took out her handkerchief and mopped her eyes. "The flower war," she gasped before another peal of laughter erupted. "Matt was right. They are vying for you."

"Yes." Charlotte dropped into the other chair, unable to believe a rivalry was occurring over her. "But what are we going to do with all these bouquets?"

* * *

Other than their ride in the Park, this evening would be the first time Con and Charlotte would appear together in public. During the past few years he'd shunned these types of events—where young ladies and gentlemen expected to find matches—but now found himself looking forward to the evening.

He looked once again at the reply to his request to stand up with her tomorrow evening. It would be the second time, tonight being the first, that he would have two dances with her.

> *Dear Lord Kenilworth,*
>   *I would be pleased to grant you the supper dance and one other waltz.*
>   *Regards,*
>   *Lady Charlotte Carpenter*

Or, perhaps, he was merely looking forward to having Charlotte in his arms during the waltz, and on his arm for as much of the rest of the evening as he was able. A thought that pleased him more than it would have a few days ago.

What would please him even more was to have her in his home and in his bed. In some ways it was a pity that she was not a more biddable lady. It would save him from the worry that she might still actually jilt him.

Then again, he would probably not like and admire her as well. Hadn't that been his complaint against every year's crop of ladies who were just out? That they were all insipid and boring?

He looked in the mirror one last time as Cunningham made some last-minute adjustments.

"Very fine, my lord."

"I believe you are right. I expect to return before one o'clock."

"Yes, my lord."

Con went down to the drawing room and poured himself a brandy. A few moments later, he heard the rustling of his mother's silk skirts in the corridor and stood as the door opened.

She glanced at his goblet.

"Would you like a sherry?" He held up the decanter.

"If you please." He gave her a glass of the wine, and she took a sip. Her forehead pleated softly.

Had the sherry gone off? "Is anything wrong?"

"Not at all, dear." She smiled. "My, you look handsome. I wanted to remind you that as a betrothed gentleman you may dance more than twice with Charlotte." Mama tapped her finger against the glass. "In fact, you may live in her pocket this evening if you like and no one will think you rude for not dancing with the other young ladies."

"Ah. Thank you." He was pleased to learn this bit of information. Perhaps he had been away from Polite Society too long. "I was unaware that the proprieties had changed."

"They have not," his mother replied acerbically. "Your status has." Webster appeared to announce dinner, and she placed her hand on his arm as they made their way to the dining room.

He held the chair for her at the foot of the table that had been shortened to accommodate the two of them, and considered what she'd said. He might indeed be allowed to keep Charlotte by his side, but he had the distinct feeling that would raise her ire enough to defy him. And that was not what he wanted. It would not only fail to advance his cause, but it would make him a laughing stock. It was much better to take his lead from her and not expect *her* to run in *his* harness.

He would like to see her refuse Harrington. For some reason, Con could not like the younger man. Charlotte had been clearly upset when she returned from her walk with the coxcomb. Had Harrington tried to press her to marry him? Or worse, berated her for being betrothed to Con? He wished he could ask her to confide in him, but it was too soon for that.

Con had taken his seat, and his mother had signaled the footmen to serve. She would never become used to the plates being set on the table. He wondered how Charlotte would keep the table once this house was hers.

Two hours later, he entered Lady Hereford's ballroom. The woman was a friend of his mother's, thus enabling him to discover that she loved the new German dance. News that did not make him happy. There were to be three waltzes, and he had Charlotte for only two of them. That meant some other gentleman, probably Harrington, would have his arms around her.

He spotted her halfway down the room, not far from Worthington and her sister, surrounded by her court. Several of them were much younger than he and obviously new on the Town. Endicott was there, as were Harrington and two other gentlemen with whom he was not acquainted. One of the men caused his brow to rise. Con was surprised that Worthington would allow Lord Ruffington within a yard of Charlotte. However, the man stood back and did not engage in the banter.

Unfortunately, it took Con several minutes to reach his betrothed's side. It was amazing how many of his colleagues in the Lords had wives and eligible young daughters who must meet him. He managed to slide in between Charlotte and a young swain whose shirt points threatened to poke out one of the man's eyes.

She had been laughing at a remark and, when she

looked up at him, her eyes still sparkled with jollity. "Good evening, my lord."

He bowed slightly. "My lady." Other than Harrington, the other gentlemen seemed to step back a fraction. "I trust you are having an enjoyable evening."

If Con was waiting for her to announce that his presence was all that was needed to make the night perfect, he would have been disappointed.

"I am. Lord Endicott has told me a very funny story about the two of you as children."

Con cut his friend a look. "Not the bull."

Charlotte's laughter sounded like the tinkling of bells. "Exactly the one. Is it true you jumped down and distracted the bull so that his lordship could get away, and then had to hide behind a cow?"

"Cows." He was sure he should not mention that several of them had been ready for the bull's attentions. "One of them took pity on me and helped me get to the fence."

"How clever of you." She placed her fingers on his arm when she gazed up at him. "I hope you rewarded her later."

That he wanted to carry her off and make her his did not surprise him. What shocked him was that his yearning had nothing to do with his pride. "Cows are much harder to please than horses, but I believe treacle was involved."

The prelude to the first waltz began and he said, "My dance, I believe."

She made a point of glancing at the dance card hanging on a silken ribbon from her wrist. Every line was filled. "It is, my lord."

Harrington scowled and Con wanted to laugh.

Con and Charlotte took their places on the dance floor. When she placed her hand on his shoulder, he wished she would step closer to him. He put his hand on her waist, and her eyes widened for a moment before she lowered her thick, dark blond lashes. When they began to dance it was as if they moved as one. No other woman felt as if she were part of him like she did.

There *was* an attraction. He had not been mistaken when he'd felt it in the carriage as they'd fled from the inn. Yet how was he to convince her? She was likely too innocent to recognize the feelings she no doubt had when they touched.

He caught a glimpse of her brother-in-law as they circled the floor. Worthington was watching her like a hawk. There would be no help from that quarter.

Charlotte smiled at another couple.

"Who are they?" Con asked.

"One of my cousins, Miss Blackacre, and Lord Bentley. They recently became betrothed. They will marry in the country at his father's estate." Her voice softened when she mentioned the country.

"Will you be glad when the Season is over?"

Charlotte met his gaze with a serious one of her own. It occurred to him that she did not merely make polite responses, but honest ones.

"I think I shall. I have had a wonderful time in Town, but I miss the relative quiet of the country."

"I know what you mean." London was almost unbearable during the summer. He usually made a point to visit his estates, but also escaped to Brighton for a few weeks. Afterward, there were house parties to which his mistress would also be invited. It occurred to him that he did not have many friends to whom he would introduce Charlotte. He would remedy that as soon as possible.

"Will you travel to Belgium?" she asked.

"Many people are, but I cannot help but think that visiting the site of a probable battle is not the best idea."

She grinned. "That is what my brother says."

"I would imagine he has much more to say on the

subject than that." In fact, he knew Worthington's thoughts on the matter.

"I have no doubt you are right," she said, relaxing into his arms.

Con held her closer in a turn.

"I would like to visit Europe, but only after the war has ended," she added.

Harrington's father had arranged for the man to work with Sir Charles, Britain's ambassador to France, and would be gone for a few years. "Have you ever thought about living on the Continent?" Con asked.

She seemed surprised. "In truth, no. I would not like to be that far from my family for so long."

Lord Kenilworth's question reminded Charlotte that Harrington would soon leave for France. She wished him well, but had no desire to be with him. Even if she had fancied herself in love with him, she would not have wanted to leave her family and friends for years at a time.

Her breath hitched as Kenilworth held her a little closer than he had before. Not inappropriately close, of course. Neither of them wanted to court any more gossip. Yet his hand lay hot and heavy on her waist, sending shivers up her back and warming her body. She had never had that feeling before and did not know what to think of it. Lately, it seemed as if any touch of his caused some reaction. A prickling of awareness she had never experienced before.

Charlotte had lost count of how many times she had danced this Season. With some partners—fortunately not many—she'd had to watch her toes. Silk or even kidskin slippers were no match for a gentleman's evening pumps. Many times the man had danced extremely well, yet she had never before felt as if she was floating around the dance floor. Never had the waltz seemed so effortless, and she was sorry when the set came to an end.

As they strolled back to where her brother and sister would return and where her circle usually stood, Lord Kenilworth took two small bowls of ices from a footman, handing her one. "This is an inspired idea for a warm night."

"It is." She took a taste. Lemon. "How refreshing the ice is."

One day when she had a home of her own, she would do the same. Matt and Grace arrived at the same time Charlotte and Lord Kenilworth did. Soon Dotty and Merton, Lord Endicott, Bentley, her cousin Oriana Blackacre, Elizabeth Turley, Harrington, and some of the younger gentlemen joined them.

Charlotte glanced at Elizabeth and found her sliding a quick look at Harrington. She had said she might be interested in him. And if they had not previously met . . . "Miss Turley, have you been introduced to Lord Harrington?"

Elizabeth's eyes widened a bit, and the corners of her lips curled up. "No, I have not."

Harrington frowned, although Charlotte did not know if it was his usual expression these days or he was unhappy about something else. "In that case, may I make you known to Lord Harrington. My lord, Miss Turley."

Elizabeth curtseyed, and he took her outstretched hand when he bowed. "A pleasure to meet you, Miss Turley."

"I am delighted to meet you, my lord."

Lady Hereford was bearing down on them, ready to make the gentlemen dance with ladies who did not have partners for the next set. "Miss Turley," Harrington said quickly, "please tell me you will do me the honor of standing up with me."

"You are in luck, my lord. This is the last set I have available."

Charlotte was glad to see that Elizabeth's smile and tone

were nothing more than polite. If she was interested in Harrington, she should not let him think she was too eager.

"Thank you." He bowed again as Lady Hereford sailed up to them.

"My lords and gentlemen, I have several young ladies who require partners. I shall be happy to make the introductions."

The younger men muttered under their breaths, but the older ones bowed to their fate without complaint. Dotty whispered something in Elizabeth's ear before she went off to the dance floor, then turned to speak to Grace, and Merton had moved to speak with Matt. In a few moments, the only gentleman left next to Charlotte was Lord Kenilworth, who had only slightly acknowledged Lady Hereford's summons and had not followed her at all.

Charlotte would have to give him a hint. "Should you not have gone to dance with someone else?"

"But you promised to protect me." He raised a brow. "Did you not?"

Suddenly, the vow she'd made during their carriage ride came rushing back to her. She could not believe he had been serious. "I thought you were joking."

"Oh, no." He shook his head slowly. "I never joke about my safety."

Charlotte was torn between laughter and exasperation. He could not remain by her side all evening. "You should ask Lady Merton or Miss Turley to stand up with you. You will be safe with them."

"Miss Turley's last set has been taken, and Merton doesn't look as if he will willingly give up his wife." He lifted her hand to his lips. "You, my lady, are my only hope."

Incorrigible man. "I trust you do not think I shall remain here all evening."

"Not at all." He acted surprised. "Your dance card is full. I shall hide behind the potted plants until you have finished your sets."

How ridiculous he was. He reminded her of a cat who insisted on remaining on one's lap after having been made to get down. Charlotte took a deep breath. "Very well. Have it your way."

"Thank you." His lips touched her knuckles and a frisson of awareness slid up her arm. Now what was she going to do?

Chapter Nineteen

A few evenings later, Con caught himself from scowling as that popinjay Harrington led Charlotte to the floor. It was only a country dance and should not matter to Con. Endicott had managed to snag one of her waltzes, and a young Lord Henry, who considered himself a poet, had got the other. There were two more after supper, but they didn't count. Worthington never remained past supper. That, Con had discovered, made standing up with Charlotte more of a prize to the other gentlemen.

Even though he had managed to remain by her side most of the evening, the fact that her former suitor would not bow out gracefully and admit defeat irritated him to no end. The man had even attempted to insinuate himself on her other side and place her hand on his arm. As luck would have it, another set had started and she went off with her partner. That was the only thing that had stopped him from doing something he would most likely be sorry for later.

"You put me forcibly in mind of a caged lion," Endicott said. "For a moment, I thought you were going to plant Harrington a facer."

Close, it had been very close, and would have been extremely stupid. "He should find another lady."

"I imagine he was nonplussed when he got back and discovered you were engaged to Lady Charlotte."

"In that case, he should not have left Town," Con replied loftily. "Ladies do not like to be ignored."

"True, very true." Endicott smirked before ambling off.

Con was sure that Charlotte was merely being polite to the worthless fribble. But the fact that she had still not agreed to marry him—not that he had asked; he knew better than to press a reluctant lady—rankled. The only thing in his favor at the moment was that she did not appear to prefer any other gentleman.

If only he could think of something that would focus her attention on him as the gentleman she wished to wed. Thus far, carriage rides in the Park, visiting at her sister's home, and dancing with her in the evenings had not done the trick. And as far as he was concerned, time was not on his side. If he allowed her to return to the country without a firm commitment of marriage, he'd have lost his chance.

Then again, he had received an invitation to dine with them before tomorrow evening's ball. Yesterday's ride in the Park must have done some good after all. It might also mean that she did not care about Harrington. That, though, might be wishful thinking. The puppy would not go away, and Con was still not happy about Worthington's refusal to allow the engagement to be announced in the paper. Not that it truly mattered. Everyone knew they were betrothed.

The dance ended and Con pushed himself off the pillar he'd been leaning against. "It is time for the supper dance."

After which he and Charlotte would join her family and they would leave. Once again not allowing him any time in private with her. Somehow, he had to get her alone. He knew one way he could convince her to marry him.

* * *

The next night, his mother caught up with him in the corridor. "I am dining with Lady Bellamny and shall see you at the ball."

"Have a good time." He handed his mother into her town coach, then tapped on the roof and stood back.

"I shall, my dear. You as well."

He planned to do just that. This was the evening he would find a way to be alone with Charlotte.

A footman lowered the steps to his carriage. "When we arrive, ask the Worthington coachman when you should return to collect me."

Several minutes later Con jumped down from the coach and strode up the steps to Stanwood House. As expected, the door opened. Once the butler had taken his hat, he was escorted to a drawing room where Charlotte, Worthington and his wife, and Lord and Lady Merton were drinking sherry.

"I trust I am not late?" Con said as he entered the room.

"Not at all," Charlotte answered. His chest tightened when she came forward and held out her hands to him. "Dotty and Merton arrived a few minutes ago."

Con lifted first one of her ungloved hands to his lips, then the other. "You look enchanting."

A faint pink hue, the color of her favorite roses, caressed Charlotte's cheeks. "Thank you. You are very dashing as well."

He captured her gaze, searching their blue depths for a sign that she felt something for him other than their newly formed friendship, but instead of awareness, he saw confusion.

Before he could figure out the reason, a woman coughed and Charlotte glanced at her sister. "Would you like sherry or wine, my lord?"

Devil it. He must find a place to be alone with her.

"Sherry, please." While Worthington poured, he greeted Lady Worthington. "Thank you for inviting me to dine with you."

"You are welcome." She smiled and glanced at Charlotte. "However, it was my sister's idea."

That was a welcome surprise. "Was it?"

Charlotte blushed again. "It made more sense . . ."

"I can see that." But he'd be damned if he knew what it meant. Seeking to turn the subject, he said, "The house is much quieter than before."

"That's because the children are in bed," Worthington replied. "They do not do well with Town hours."

Con had the feeling his friend had wanted to say more but stopped himself. "I understand how."

"Normally we dine much earlier and *en famille*," Charlotte added.

Except this evening, when he, who was not a member of the family, joined them. And that did not make him happy. "Even when you are attending a ball?"

"Indeed. There is always something to fill the time before we go out."

"Cards and games, generally," Lady Merton added. "Have you ever played dominoes?"

He had not. "I don't believe I've ever heard of the game."

In short order, he was made to understand that his education, not to mention pleasure, was severely lacking. Naturally, the conversation turned to the game's rules and who of the present company generally beat the flinders out of everyone else. Charlotte was held to be a very good player, but Lady Worthington was the expert.

"Only because I have been playing so much longer," the lady demurred.

Before he knew it, the butler announced dinner. A short

glance around informed him that he was free to escort his
betrothed to the dining room. His mood improved when he
discovered he could sit next to her as well.

The conversation quickly turned from games to politics,
and Con was not surprised that Charlotte was well read and
well informed. That they agreed on most of the problems
plaguing the country didn't surprise him. He was, after all,
one of Worthington's allies in the Lords. Despite their conversation, which he thought was going extremely well, she
seemed skittish, something was not quite right, and Con
didn't know what to do about it.

It was fortunate that earlier Charlotte had eaten a light
dinner with the children, because her stomach was too tied
up in knots to do more than pick at her food. She had expected Lord Kenilworth to sit next to her. What she had not
expected was the impact his nearness had on her senses.

Throughout the meal, she'd had to force herself not to
fidget. At times, when he leaned closer to her to make a
comment, her breath shortened as if she had been running.
Even taking his arm earlier had caused a shiver of excitement, and when he had kissed her hands she had wanted to
fan herself. She did not know what to do with her reactions
to him. Harrington had never caused her to be so unsettled
or breathless.

Finally, just as she thought she would jump out of her
skin, Grace rose. "Ladies, let us leave the gentlemen."

Thank God! It was all Charlotte could do not to dash out
of the room.

Kenilworth assisted her to rise and his bare hand on her
equally bare elbow almost singed her.

"My lady?" His brows had drawn together slightly, his
emerald eyes appeared confused.

She ignored his inquiry and curtseyed. "Thank you, my lord."

Once she was with Grace and Dotty in the drawing room, Charlotte went immediately to the piano and began to play. The music flowed from her fingers as the keys responded to her hectic nerves, allowing her to calm.

A few minutes later, she closed the lid and stood. "I do not know how I will make it through the rest of the evening."

Dotty handed Charlotte a glass of wine. "Drink some."

Grace patted the seat next to her. "What exactly is the problem?"

"I don't know." Charlotte sank onto the sofa, wineglass firmly in hand. "It is Lord Kenilworth. When he touches me even in the most formal way, I *feel* it. This—these sensations started a few days ago, and I do not know what to do about them."

Dotty tilted her head first right then left, as if studying Charlotte from both angles would enlighten her. "Did you have the same reaction to him when he took you for the carriage rides?"

Charlotte thought about it for a moment. "Yes and no. At first his touch just warmed me, but it did not make me uncomfortable, but lately . . ."

Grace moved to face her. "Uncomfortable in what way?"

"I do not know how to explain it." She covered her face with her hands for a moment.

"Let me try." Dotty took Charlotte's hands. "You feel a tingle or a shiver when he is near."

"Yes." Thank the Fates someone understood. "And tonight it was more intense than before. I thought his fingers would burn me."

Her friend leaned back in her chair. "I think you need to kiss him."

"But I don't want to." Dotty raised her brows. Charlotte never had been able to lie to her dearest friend. Since Lord Kenilworth had arrived, she'd had a difficult time keeping her eyes from his lips. Still, that was the very reason she should not kiss him. "Not yet. Not when I do not know what I feel for him."

"It sounds to me as if you desire him and, for some reason, you are fighting your emotions."

That was not what Charlotte wanted to hear. "Grace?"

"I think Dotty has a point." Charlotte opened her mouth to protest, and her sister held up her hand. "But only you can decide if you are ready to take that step. *I* am certainly not going to tell you to kiss him if you are not ready."

She jumped up and started toward the piano again. "This would have been much easier if I had met him in the normal course of the Season. Or if I had not seen him at the theater with his mistress—"

"Or," Dotty said, "if I had not told you about the poor women Miss Betsy had abducted and used so badly."

Charlotte rushed back to her friend. "Please do not blame yourself. Even Grace said we should know."

"If only his courtship was not playing out in full view of the *ton*," Grace mused. "I know that is how it is normally done, but I think you would be better served if it was otherwise."

"Particularly as it is so late in the Season and there isn't anyone else to provide entertainment at the moment," Dotty added.

"Yes." Charlotte sighed. "And Harrington's behavior is not helping."

"This is most likely not the time to tell you"—Dotty grimaced—"but Dom and I are going to a property he has in Surrey for a few days."

That was not what Charlotte wanted to hear. "When do you plan to depart?"

"Late tomorrow morning. We will only be gone for a few days."

Other than wish her cousins a good trip, there was nothing she could say that would not sound selfish.

A few moments later, Royston entered with the tea tray and the gentlemen followed on his heels. Grace poured, and Charlotte handed out the cups. She moved to the window seat, allowing her sister to speak with Matt privately.

Kenilworth followed, taking a chair near where she sat. "I cannot believe the change that has been wrought in Merton. He seems almost like a different man."

Had Kenilworth not noticed her unease? No, at most he might think something was wrong but preferred not to address it. "Matt says he is much more like his father now."

"I am too young to have known the old marquis, but my father liked him a great deal." He took a sip of tea. "He seems greatly attached to Lady Merton."

Charlotte slid a look to where Dotty and Merton stood talking to Matt and Grace. For the first time she noticed the small touches and looks they gave each other. Matt and Grace engaged in the same silent communication. "Yes. They are very much in love."

"I hear your sister and Rothwell formed a love match as well."

"They did. My parents also had a love match. It is a tradition in both the Carpenter and Vivers families." Except for poor Patience, Matt's step-mother, but she was now happily in love and married as well.

"I see." His words were thoughtful, but he did not expound upon them.

But what did he see? Would it change what was going on between them?

Matt rose. "We must depart."

Well, of all the bad timing. Yet, by the time their party arrived at the ball, the first set was underway.

"I believe the next dance is a waltz," Kenilworth whispered, his lips so close to her ear she once again fought off the shivers his breath caused. She wanted to lean closer, but held herself rigid, fighting her reaction, just as Dotty had observed.

She and Kenilworth fell back from the rest of their group as friends she had not seen recently stopped them to wish them happy. This evening, she felt less like a fraud and wondered if it was because some part of her was growing to care for him.

"What I want to know, Kenilworth," one of the gentlemen said, "is how you managed to escape most of the events of the Season and still end up with one of the Graces."

"The Graces?" Turning to Charlotte he raised a dark sable brow.

Of course he would not know. Dotty, Louisa, and Charlotte were thrilled when they had first heard the sobriquet. "It was an appellation given to Lady Merton, my sister Louisa, and me."

"Then it is only right that since the other two Graces are wed, the last should be as well." He grinned, lightening his visage and making him even more handsome. There was not a lady here who would understand her hesitation in marrying him. "The Fates were with me."

"They must have been," another gentleman grumbled.

"Don't mind Ruffington," Lord Endicott said. "He is having a run of bad luck. Lady Charlotte"—he bowed—

"may I steal you away from your betrothed for this next waltz?"

Kenilworth's arm tightened, and he placed his fingers over her hand. "No, you may not."

He had been acting like a dog with a bone for days now, but this was the first time he had actually said anything. Yet she did not dislike his possessiveness. He sounded so much like Merton when he and Dotty were newly engaged, that Charlotte had to put her hand over her mouth to stop from laughing. "This set is spoken for. Perhaps the next country dance, my lord."

"Only if Kenilworth stops looking as if he'd like to run me through." Endicott bowed and strolled toward a group of young ladies.

By the time Charlotte and Kenilworth had reached her sister, the violins were beginning to play the first strands of the waltz. Dotty and Merton were already making their way to the dance floor.

Matt looked at Grace. "Come, my love."

"I would be delighted." She smiled at him, love shining in her eyes. "It is so much nicer dancing with you when you have only Charlotte to watch out for."

Kenilworth raised Charlotte's hand to his lips, and the sensations began again. "Shall we?"

Were her friend and sister correct? Did this mean she liked him more than she let on, even to herself? "Indeed."

The moment he took her in his arms, her world tilted. She felt as if her slippers had left the ground, and she was twirling on air. "I have meant to tell you that you dance well."

"It is easy when one has a partner who responds as if she knows my every move." He searched her eyes as if they could read her thoughts. "What confuses you so?"

Apparently he did know what was in her mind. That was a relief. "You. My reaction to you."

"We will figure it out." His tone was deep and firm. As if he knew what to do, how to help her.

If only she trusted he was right. But how could she trust him when she did not even know her own feelings?

Chapter Twenty

This was Con and Charlotte's second waltz of the evening. Some of the other guests slid looks at them telling Con they were the subject of speculation and gossip. He had done his utmost to ensure the *ton* knew Charlotte was his. All that was needed was a formal announcement.

Most importantly, Charlotte was finally beginning to soften in his arms, slowly trust him like a nervous filly. He was now certain he would have her as his wife. He'd have to make sure he brought her along gradually, something he'd never had to do with a female before. All his women had been experienced.

He cringed at the thought of Aimée. How many of his other mistresses had been forced into the same life and pretended to like it? Not all of them, he supposed, but too many.

Merton had mentioned the charities he and his wife had established for ladies and other women and children who had been preyed upon by brothel owners and procurers. According to Worthington, Charlotte already contributed far more of her pin money to those causes than she should.

That, Con was discovering, was exactly what he would expect from her. He would take up the cause as well. It would give them one more thing in common, and it was the honorable choice.

He gave her a reassuring smile and tightened his hold on her waist. She wasn't at all sure about his courting her, but she was giving him a chance to redeem himself in her eyes. And he had been doing his best.

A strange flutter caused his chest to tighten, and he knew his earlier possessiveness would last the rest of his life, as would his desire to protect her.

"You look very severe all of a sudden." She smiled, and the tightness in his chest increased. "What are you thinking about?"

"You. Us." His voice sounded as if he had not been speaking all evening—or perhaps talking too much.

A crease formed between her brows, marring the smooth beauty of her skin. "Do you wish you had not agreed—"

"No. The furthest thing from it. I wish there was more I could do to make you feel better about my courting you." One day in the very near future he would have to figure out just what his feelings for her were. Sometime this evening, they had grown beyond merely wanting her to something else. Something deeper. An answer to Lady Worthington's question the day he took the children for ices.

The corners of her lips tipped up. "It has not all been bad."

"We do seem to agree on many issues, and enjoy spending time together." At least he enjoyed being with her.

"Yes, we do." She said the words slowly, as if she had not thought about it before.

The set ended. She curtseyed, he bowed, and he made a decision. Taking her hand, he placed it on his arm. "Will you come with me?"

A slight look of hesitation formed on her countenance. "To where?"

"Trust me. I will not harm you, or worsen our situation."
Con stilled, praying Charlotte would go with him.

"Very well." Once again, she seemed to be working out
her path as she spoke.

He threaded their way through the crowd to the French
windows closest to them. Turning right, they strolled to the
end of the terrace, and there, in the shadows where no one
could see them, he placed his hands on her small waist. "I
want to kiss you. Like we did before."

She could not know that it had been years since he'd experienced such an innocent kiss. Back then the innocence
had been on his part.

Charlotte stared at him, as if she would discover something she didn't know. Finally, she nodded. "Yes."

He lowered his head, and their lips touched. He moved
his mouth over hers, waiting for her to return the caress,
then she placed her hands on his cheeks, raised up, and
kissed him back. The purity in her touch almost brought
him to his knees.

"Thank you." Con touched his forehead to hers.

Even in the dark, he could see her blush. "You are welcome."

He brushed his mouth across hers again. "We should go
back now."

Charlotte hadn't known what to expect, but she had not
expected a kiss as sweet as Kenilworth's. Once, she had
seen Merton kiss Dotty. That kiss had been demanding and
full of passion. If Kenilworth had attempted anything like
that, Charlotte would have hit him hard and run. Yet now,
now that she had felt his lips on hers again and his hands
tightening around her waist, she almost looked forward to
the other type of kiss.

But not tonight. Not when her comfort with him was
still growing and fragile.

Reaching up, she brushed her mouth against his as he'd done to her. "Yes. We should return."

His body tensed. Even the muscles in his lean face seemed like steel. "You will be the death of me."

She couldn't help but grin. "No one has ever said that to me before, my lord."

Kenilworth groaned, and she laughed lightly.

"I would like it if you called me Con or Constantine."

She had insisted on being more formal than most betrothed couples only because she was not sure they were truly engaged. Yet now, mayhap, it was time to move forward.

They did have a great deal in common. She had been surprised when he told her that he insisted all his dependents, not just the children, learn the rudiments of reading, writing, and arithmetic. She had heard him talking with Merton about the charities in which he, Dotty, and Charlotte were involved, and he seemed interested in them. Kenilworth was turning out to be a much better man than she had thought possible. And there was the physical connection she had with him that she had not experienced with another gentleman.

She did not know if she was in love, but she would give herself permission to discover what she felt. "Constantine, if you wish. It is a strong name. You may call me Charlotte."

He drew her gently into his arms and they kissed again. "Charlotte, we must go back now. Before anyone comes looking for us."

After the next waltz, they joined her family for supper. Matt found a table, and, as usual, he took Constantine and Merton off to select food for the ladies.

Ever since she and Constantine—she really did like his name—had reentered the ballroom, Dotty had been shooting Charlotte questioning looks.

Now her friend leaned close and asked, "Well?"

Her sister was studiously ignoring them as if she did not wish to overhear the conversation. Charlotte held her hand to the side of her mouth just the same and said, "I kissed him."

Dotty's smile grew. "And?"

"I liked it. I was very apprehensive at first and almost refused to go outside with him, but he did not attempt to go too far, and—and I liked kissing him."

"Charlotte, I'm so happy for you." Dotty's eyes misted a bit. "I want you to find love, and I think you have, or will do soon." She blew her nose. "If you have any questions, just ask. Or if anything he does frightens you, tell me."

"I shall." Charlotte did not think Constantine would harm her or even scare her, but she was grateful for the offers of aid and advice.

The gentlemen returned and Constantine sat next to her, serving her lobster patties, small mushroom tarts, asparagus wrapped in wafer-thin slices of ham, and ices. This time when he brushed against her, or spoke, his breath caressing her ear, she could allow herself to enjoy the pleasurable sensations he caused, and not run from them.

It was truly amazing what a kiss could do.

Charlotte woke early the next morning. She had dreamed about more of Constantine's kisses, even the ones she had not experienced yet.

Her door flew open, and Mary landed on the bed followed by Theo, who'd had the good sense to close the door behind her. "Good morning."

"Good morning," the girls chorused, scrambling up and hugging Charlotte.

She put her arms around both children. "To what do I owe this visit?"

Mary snuggled tighter. "We hardly see you anymore."

It was true that Charlotte had been spending much more time away from home.

Theo wrapped her fingers around one of the ribbons on Charlotte's nightgown. "Matt said that if you were awake and wanted to, we could go to the square and play."

"Well, I'm awake, so ring the bell pull and as soon as I have washed, dressed, and broken my fast, we will be off to the square."

"We love you," the girls cried, smacking kisses on each of her cheeks before jumping off the bed and running out of the room.

"I love you too," she whispered. When she finally did marry, leaving her brothers and sisters would be the hardest part of her new life.

She was glad that she had not fixed her attentions on Harrington. Being in another part of England would be bad enough. She could never have lived overseas for years.

By the time she arrived in the breakfast room, the children were tucking into their meal.

"Good morning." The low, now familiar voice took her by surprise. Constantine sat next to Charlotte's regular place at the table.

"Good morning." She smiled at him before going to the sideboard. When she brought her plate back, he held out her chair. "I did not expect to see you so early."

Still, she was happy he was here. All the gentlemen who had recently joined her family had taken breakfast with them.

"Your brother suggested I join you." After piling his own plate full of food, Constantine returned to the seat next to hers.

The twins and Madeline glanced up, exchanged looks, and giggled.

"At least they are not asking embarrassing questions," Constantine remarked in a whisper.

"That makes me wonder what they're planning," Charlotte shot back.

"Char, did you see the prime goers he has?" Walter asked.

"I did. They have very sweet mouths as well." She glanced at Constantine. "If you are extremely good, he might show them to you."

Walter's and Phillip's faces lit up. "Oh, would you, sir?"

"Yes, of course. They will be brought around when I leave. You may assess their points then." Constantine turned his attention back to Charlotte. "I understand there is an outing planned in the square before lessons begin this morning."

"There is." She slid him a look. He seemed almost nervous. "Would you like to join us?"

"I'd love to." He grinned at her before digging into his food.

She began to eat her breakfast also. This morning was going exceedingly well so far. She'd have to thank Matt for inviting Constantine. "Where are Matt and Grace?"

"Inspecting the renovations," Augusta replied. "I'm not sure they will ever be done."

"That is what Grace thought about changes she made to this house." Charlotte glanced at the younger children. "When you've finished eating, go get ready for the Park."

The sounds of chairs being pushed back and children rushing from the room filled the air.

"I hope I'm not being rude when I say that they sound like elephants going up the stairs."

She placed an elbow on the table and rested her cheek against the palm of her hand. "Have you actually heard elephants?"

"Yes. I was not allowed a Grand Tour, but I was allowed to travel to India for a short time. Although, I spent more time on the passages than in the country."

"You must tell me about all of it." She let out a sigh. "I would love to travel."

"Once Wellington has dealt with the Corsican, Europe will be safe again."

"So everyone says. My sister Louisa believes Napoleon will give him more trouble than many think he will."

"I tend to agree." Constantine blotted his lips with the napkin, reminding Charlotte how his lips felt on hers. "How long do we have before the children arrive?"

"A few minutes. I must fetch my bonnet."

He walked with her into the corridor. "Before you do."

Cupping her cheek in his hand, he kissed her. It was every bit as sweet as his kisses had been the night before. She sighed softly. Perhaps soon there would be more.

"I shall be back in a few minutes." She reached up, drawing her thumb along his bottom lip. He sucked in a breath.

Smiling to herself, she made her way to her bedchamber. Her life finally seemed right. As if everything she wanted— love, a home, and children—might be within reach.

Chapter Twenty-One

Con wanted to catch Charlotte's thumb between his teeth, and pull her to him. Instead, he let her go and enjoyed the view of her lush bottom swaying as she climbed the stairs. He was delighted she had accepted his kiss and returned it so easily today. Each day, his future with her was looking more and more certain.

Worthington was right. If Con wanted her, he must become part of the family. Today was the second time he'd be able to show her he had the makings of a good husband and father.

The Great Danes arrived first with their footmen. The children could be heard again coming down the stairs, and once they were assembled, more footmen appeared.

Finally, Charlotte walked down the stairs, stopping on the last tread to survey the hall. She smiled at him, and he held out his arm. Together they strolled through the front door and across the street to Berkeley Square.

They were not the only ones taking their leisure in the Park. Mary and Theo joined another girl who looked to be about the same age. The child was accompanied by a woman he supposed to be about Charlotte's age, and an older woman who had charge of a baby in an elaborately painted and gilded baby carriage.

"It is for Lord Wharton's son and heir." Her breath caressed his ear and he wanted to be able to slip his arms around her.

"How did you know what I was looking at?" he teased.

"How could you not notice it?" She looked as if she was about to go into whoops. "Grace said we had plain wicker baskets set on a frame with wheels."

"I have no idea what I had. I'll have to ask my mother." He glanced at it again. "I am quite sure it was not that elaborate."

Charlotte tucked her hand in his arm, and they strolled a little away from the others, albeit still keeping an eye on the children and dogs. Daisy lay on the grass and Duke stood next to her, nosing her every once in a while. "They paint a domestic scene."

"Only because she is *enceinte*. Otherwise she would be romping all over the Park."

"Maybe she will calm down after the puppies are born." That had occurred to several of his hunters after they gave birth.

"One can only hope. Grace and I came to Town ahead of the children. On their way here Daisy tried to make friends with a pair of horses." Charlotte grimaced. "Suffice it to say it did not turn out the way she wished."

He could imagine what his horses would do, but he asked anyway. "What happened?"

"They bolted. The gentleman who owned the carriage and the pair started to yell. Fortunately, the team for our coach had been changed, so Mr. Winter, the children's tutor, got them all back in the coach and didn't stop until he arrived here."

Con couldn't help but to bark a laugh. "I may have to reconsider a puppy."

"Oh, no." Charlotte leaned more heavily against him. "They are the sweetest beasts in nature. She is much better since Matt has been training her."

Con enjoyed the early morning as he rarely had before he'd met Charlotte. Not that he'd seen much of it. The air seemed fresher. The grass was still slightly damp. Other nurses and their charges began to enter the square.

"Lady Charlotte, good morning." Harrington bowed to her, once again ignoring Con.

"My lord." She curtseyed. "I am surprised to see you here at this hour."

"I thought I would see if you were in." The puppy's head seemed to twitch even further away from Con.

"I have been extremely busy of late."

Going for rides and walks with me. Con almost smirked.

Suddenly a scream rent the peace of the Park, followed by male voices shouting and dogs growling and barking. Con pushed Charlotte behind him, but the commotion was taking place near the old lady with the baby carriage. Mary and Theo—safe, thank God—were trying to calm the other girl, and the young woman who had accompanied the older woman was gone. Three footmen surrounded Duke, who was snarling at something on the ground.

Charlotte grabbed Con's hand. "Come. We must find out what has happened."

A moment later, he slid in between two of the footmen to find the Dane had caught and was standing on a man.

"Get him off me," the man cried. "I didn't do nothin'."

"Don't lie to his lordship," one of the footmen ordered. "You helped grab that woman."

Next to Con, Charlotte stared at the villain on the ground. "You!"

Con looked at the miscreant again. It was the blackguard he'd got drunk the night he'd rescued Charlotte. "Remove the dog. I'll take care of him."

The moment Duke stepped off, the scoundrel tried to bolt. Con caught him by the scruff of his neck, swung him around, and punched him in the stomach. The scoundrel dropped to his knees, heaving as if he'd throw up. "Now, unless you want a little more home brew, you'd better tell me where your accomplice took that young woman."

"I ain't telling you nothin'." The scoundrel spat, the glob just missing Con's boots.

"You think not? Well, you've got a choice: You can hang or you can be transported. If anything happens to that female, you'll hang, and I'll make sure the rope is nice and new."

"Takes a long time to die with a new rope," one of the footmen commented.

"He's takin' her to the Dove, on the other side of Richmond."

"One of you," Con ordered, "call the watch."

The rest of Charlotte's brothers and sisters had gathered next to her.

"What happened?" Walter asked.

"Hal, take Ben and lock this rascal in the cellar at Worthington House," Charlotte said. "The rest of you take the children back to the house."

Con looked around to see a large traveling coach stop in front of Stanwood House. The Mertons hurried over.

"What is going on?" Merton held his wife close to him.

"Miss Betsy kidnapped one of Lord Wharton's servants." Con looked down to see Theo tugging on his jacket. "What is it, sweetheart?"

"She isn't a servant. She's the housekeeper's niece, and she's getting married soon."

"Was she visiting her aunt?" Charlotte asked.

Theo nodded as Mary said, "Her name is Miss Cloverly."

Con thought of what the whore had in store for the young woman and his blood turned to ice. He glanced at Charlotte. "I'll go and get her back."

"I'm coming with you. She won't trust a man by himself."

"Charlotte, you cannot." Merton glanced from her to Con and shrugged. "Worthington will not allow it."

"I completely agree," Harrington said. What the devil was he still doing here? And who the devil cared for his opinion? "Lady Charlotte, you may not accompany Lord Kenilworth. I forbid it."

"*You.*" Her voice shook with growing anger. "You have no business telling me what to do. Nothing will keep me from going. If need be—"

"Go where?" Worthington asked, striding up, his wife next to him, almost running to keep up.

"Miss Betsy abducted another young woman." Charlotte turned her slender back on Harrington. Her chin had firmed and her normally soft blue eyes flashed with anger. "Kenilworth is going to the inn they are taking her to. I am going with him."

"Kenilworth?" her brother asked.

This was his chance to prove to her he could be trusted. That he would not expect her to be less than she was.

"I'll keep her safe," he promised. Truth be told, he would give his life for her.

The smile she gave him was so brilliant it made him blink. "I'll be right back."

"I object." Harrington started after Charlotte.

Con grabbed his shoulder. "You have no business disagreeing. It is her guardian's decision to make and he has done so."

The man jerked out of Con's grasp. "I see what's going on," he said to Worthington. "You are encouraging Kenilworth's suit over mine."

Her brother turned and stared at Harrington. "This man"—he pointed at Con—"has actually asked to marry my sister, which is more than I can say for you. I suggest you leave, before you are forced to do so."

Con struggled not to laugh or grin. "I'll need to get a message to my mother and my valet."

"I'll see to it after you've gone," Worthington assured him. "Send word if you do not think you'll be able to arrive back this evening. I'll think of something."

Lady Merton pulled her husband away and after a hushed discussion said, "We'll follow them. Merton suggests we stay at the Star and Garter."

She crossed the street into the house, and Merton started issuing orders to his coachman.

"My lord." The footman named Hal cringed. "Jemmy jumped on the back of the coach."

"This is getting to be a habit of his," Con mumbled. And not a good one for a lad who was only six.

Less than five minutes later, he and Charlotte were on their way toward the Richmond Road.

Charlotte held on to the side as Constantine threaded the phaeton through the morning traffic. The moment he had recognized the villain, his expression had hardened into stone.

"Thank you for agreeing I could come."

"If anyone has a right to be there, you do." He glanced at her for a brief moment. "This time we'll catch her and turn her over to the magistrate."

"I hope we get there in time." She could imagine how frightened the young woman was. "Why would she pick a female who was just visiting? How would she even have found out about her?"

Con was quiet for a few minutes as he negotiated the carriage between a milk wagon and a large coach. "It's possible that she is procuring for individuals. She doesn't seem to have a brothel to take them to. Otherwise she'd use that instead of country inns."

She took a large breath. Surely, he could not mean what she thought. "You mean she supplies . . ."

"In a word, yes. Someone has a desire, and she finds the person to fulfill it. In this case, that customer may have wanted Miss Cloverly." He dodged a vegetable cart. "The question I have now is why did she abduct you?"

Charlotte shook her head. "We always thought it was for revenge."

He looked at her again. "Then why not Lady Merton? Her husband was involved. Or your sister Louisa, or Lady Worthington?"

That was a good question. Grace and Dotty had been there when Matt and Merton had ruined the woman's brothel. Why her indeed? "I wish I knew."

"Well, when we find her, we'll ask." The traffic was finally thinning. "Did you bring your basket?"

"Yes, your groom put it under the seat."

"Does it include the kitten this time?"

She could not tell from his tone if he would be upset about her cat coming or not. She pulled a face and nodded. Collette had refused to be left behind. Even Dotty was unable to detach her from Charlotte's pelisse without ruining the fabric. "I'm afraid so. She was adamant that she stay with me. She must have sensed my-my . . . that I was upset."

"It's not a problem. I shall simply have to remember not to stick my hand in the basket without giving her warning first." Constantine's tone was dry, but the corner of his mouth twitched.

She bit back a smile as they turned onto the Richmond Road. The tension in the air was palpable, but it was around them, not between them. She supposed it was because they were a team, acting in concert with each other. And he had trusted her enough to bring her with him. She had been prepared to argue with him and anyone else who tried to stop her from going, but he had made it easy for her brother to agree.

"Look, straight ahead of us past the landau." She pointed, although there was really no need. "That's Jemmy on the back of the coach."

"So it is." A slow smile formed on his lips. The ones that felt so good when they were kissing her. "We'll just stay back here."

Jemmy waved, letting them know he saw them too. "I'm really going to have to have a discussion with him about jumping on carriages," she said more to herself than Constantine. "At least he should have some money with him this time."

"Why do you say that?" Constantine glanced at her again.

"You gave him largess. The amount was significantly more than what he had to pay for the stage coach and hackney."

"He is an enterprising young lad." His tone was thoughtful and she wished she knew what he was thinking.

"Yes, he is. He was going to offer you the amount left over, but I told him you would want him to keep it."

"That turned out to be a good decision." Constantine took the ribbons in one hand and briefly covered her fingers with his. "We'll make sure both he and Miss Cloverly are safe."

The more Charlotte considered it, the more she wanted

Jemmy to come with her when she married, if it wouldn't harm his chances for finding his family, that is. Still, now was not the time for that discussion. First they must rescue poor Miss Cloverly.

As they traveled through Richmond, the landau in front of them turned off at the Star and Garter.

"I believe that is the inn Dotty and Merton are planning to stop at."

Constantine slowed down and surveyed the inn for a moment. "It's certainly grand enough for two marquises. I assume that decision was made when you went to fetch your basket. What did you and she talk about?"

"Dotty will arrange for Miss Cloverly to stay with our maids. She also plans to get a change of clothing from the Wharton housekeeper, and one of their footmen will depart immediately after we return with Miss Cloverly to notify the housekeeper that her niece is safe." Charlotte grinned to herself. "When I left, she had my maid packing a small trunk for me." She glanced at Con. "Dotty is very practical."

"I got that impression from her."

They had passed through Richmond and the roof of a building showed through the trees. "We should be there soon. What is our plan?"

"We walk in and ask for a chamber for you to refresh yourself, and a private parlor." They were betrothed, surely that was allowed.

Her face fell a bit. "I thought . . . well, it doesn't matter. Your idea will work."

He wondered if she had wanted to do something like what he'd done at the Hare and Hound. "Thank you."

The inn came into sight. It was much smaller than he had imagined. More of a tavern than an inn, really. He doubted they had more than one or two bedchambers, and those would be taken by the villains. They would very possibly be turned away and directed to the Star and Garter.

Yet, if it was an emergency . . . Perhaps he could indulge her after all. "How dramatic can you be?"

At once, Charlotte's countenance lit up. "I do quite well in our Christmas theatricals. Do you have in mind something like you did when you rescued me?"

"Indeed." Con was correct. She did like a bit of drama, and when she looked at him like that, he was happy to provide it.

They arrived at a building with a sign with a white dove on it. As expected, the coach turned into the yard. They followed closely behind.

Charlotte grinned, and cried in a carrying voice, "Oh, I can go no further. I must have something to drink. I am so parched. And the weather is far too warm to bear."

"Yes, yes, my dear." He took her fan and began applying it. "You see we are halting here." He motioned to Jemmy, who ran immediately to the horses before anyone noticed he had not arrived with them.

She and Constantine shared a collusory look before the ostler hurried out to them.

"Help my groom with the horses, man, and be quick about it!" he ordered, lifting her down into his arms, and striding into the inn. "I must have a chamber for my lady. Landlord, landlord! Now, if you will."

An older man came from down the corridor. "My lord." The landlord bowed. "Crowe's the name. We're honored by yer presence, but I ain't got the type of lodging ye'd be lookin' for. There be the Star and Garter in Richmond—"

"I must have a chamber now. My lady can go no further." The innkeeper looked as if he would argue, and Constantine lowered his voice. "Please, I merely require a room for my lady to rest, and a private parlor." He had lowered her to her feet and taken out his quizzing glass. "Surely, you can provide such simple accommodations. It is only for an hour or two." He leaned over and in a low voice said, "I shall pay well. I do not want a hysterical female on my hands for the rest of our journey to the duke's residence."

"Whatever ye want, me lord." The landlord motioned to a young woman who'd come up. "Maisy, show his lord and ladyship to the big front room and tell Mrs. Crowe they'll be wantin' tea and whatever she can get together quick-like."

Con swept Charlotte into his arms again, and she had an opportunity to look over his shoulder. Miss Cloverly, looking more angry than frightened, was being escorted by a man Charlotte hadn't seen before.

Thank God for small favors. At least she would not be recognized. She decided it was time to swoon.

"Oh, my dear!" she moaned before going limp in Con's arms.

Maisy opened the door for them and handed Con the key. "There ye be, me lord. I'll send up some tea. Don't think she'd be wantin' ale?"

"Tea will be fine for her ladyship. However, send up a tankard of ale for me, and warm water. She will wish to clean the dust off when she awakens."

"Yes, me lord."

"Oh, and miss"—Con flipped her a half crown—"see that my groom knows where I am and has something to eat, if you will."

"Pleasure, me lord." Through slitted eyelids Charlotte could see the girl grin.

Maisy sauntered off as Constantine set Charlotte's feet on the floor once more. "That part went easily enough," she said. "Now how do we capture Miss Betsy and save Miss Cloverly, who, by the looks of her, is furious?"

He removed his hat and gloves, placing them on a

bureau. "That is going to take some planning. If only we knew when Miss Betsy was arriving."

"Perhaps Jemmy could find out." Charlotte drew out the hat pin from her bonnet and placed it next to his gloves.

"Charlotte, he is a child," Constantine said, clearly unhappy about involving the boy. He, however, did not yet know Jemmy's past.

"Yes, but an extremely enterprising one, and he is clever. He lived on the streets before I found him and knows better than to take stupid risks."

Rubbing the back of his neck, Constantine frowned. "Very well, we'll ask him."

Charlotte gave him an encouraging smile, but Con wasn't at all happy about having a child help them. He'd just as soon send the boy back to Richmond.

Yet when Jemmy arrived a few moments later, he was full of news. "They got Miss Cloverly three doors down near the stairs. How are we going to rescue her?"

Chapter Twenty-Two

"Wait a minute." Con was shocked that Jemmy could have discovered the information so quickly. "How do you know that?"

"Weren't hard." The lad shrugged. "I knocked on the doors, quiet-like, until a woman answered. Then I asked her name."

He dragged his hand over his face. So much for not taking stupid risks. "What if one of the miscreants had answered the door or heard you?"

"They're both down in the taproom." Jemmy gave him a saucy grin.

"Very well." Charlotte was right about the boy. "Now all we have to do is figure out a way to get her out of here."

"Got all night for that. They ain't"—he slid a glance at Charlotte—"I mean they aren't coming for her till morning. I heard them say so."

"I do not want to leave her here all night," Charlotte said. "What if something happens and they come for her earlier? If he knows his accomplice was caught, he might have told Miss Betsy, and she will arrive as soon as she is able."

Jemmy looked around Con to answer his mistress. "I

don't think that'll happen, my lady. The landlady says they always get left overnight to think on their wickedness. I asked what that was, but she told me I was too young to know."

"Wickedness!" Charlotte spat the word. "If Mrs. Crowe only knew how she was helping perpetuate wickedness."

"There is no moon tonight. I doubt the woman would want to make a journey in the dark," Con said, hoping to lessen Charlotte's concerns.

"That may be true, but I shall not have Miss Cloverly frightened more than she is." She glanced at Jemmy, her brows drawn together. "Go back downstairs and try to keep anyone from coming up. And if someone does get near the stairs, make a loud noise."

"Yes, my lady."

"Oh, there is one more thing," Charlotte said. "Maisy will be bringing up the tea and water. Perhaps you can tell her that I'm resting and do not wish to be disturbed."

"I'll do that, my lady."

Con watched the lad grin before he scampered down the stairs. At least someone was having a good time.

When they reached Miss Cloverly's door, Charlotte gave him two of her hair pins, and he began trying to pick the lock.

After what seemed like several minutes, but could really only have been a few moments, she asked, "Are you sure you do not want me to try?"

"You didn't have much luck the last time." He knew his answer sounded surly, but they didn't have all day, and he would make it up to her later. Not only that, but he was more than a little embarrassed that it was taking him so long to accomplish what thieves seem to do so easily.

"I've been practicing. I think I know the trick now." Her

tone was sweet, but he thought he detected a thread of steel beneath the honey.

"I have too." *Bloody hell.* "Why the deuce is this lock so hard?"

Charlotte leaned over his shoulder. "Most likely, they have not oiled the tumblers in a while."

What in the devil *had* she been up to? He eyed her suspiciously. "How do you know that?"

She gave him an exasperated look, as if he'd accused her of doing something untoward. "From my housekeeper. She saw me practicing on one of the attic doors."

That would teach him to question her. He sat back on his haunches. "So how do we solve the problem?"

Charlotte drew out a small copper bird from her pocket.

"I thought ladies didn't have pockets anymore. Is that a peacock?"

"I had them made, and it is an oil horn in the shape of a peacock. I borrowed it from our housekeeper." She stuck the long beak inside the lock. "Now try it."

"No." It was time he stopped acting like a stupid male, as his youngest sister would say. "Please." Con stood and handed the pins to her. "You found the solution. You shall do the honors."

She graced him with a smile so full of joy he blinked and vowed to find ways to make her smile more often. A moment later, the tumblers clicked, and Charlotte swung the door open.

"Oh, no!" She rushed over to the young woman who'd been gagged and tied to a chair. "However were you able to answer Jemmy?" A very feminine noise answered them. The child had gone on the tone of the sounds the young woman had made. "I understand."

While they untied Miss Cloverly, Charlotte kept up a low, steady stream of talk. "I am Lady Charlotte Carpenter.

My family's home is a few houses down from where your aunt works. This is Lord Kenilworth, my betrothed. We've come to save you. Other than being abducted and tied up, have they harmed you?"

This last question came as the gag fell away. "No, my lady, but I'd like to do a deal of harm to them."

"I do not blame you at all. We were able to capture one of the blackguards."

"I'm glad to hear it. The other one thought he got away."

That would give them some much needed time. "He would have if it hadn't been for one of the Great Danes," Con added. "The dog caught him and held him down until the rest of us could get there."

"There." Miss Cloverly rubbed her arms, probably to get the feeling back in them. "I told my aunt they were useful. And sweet too."

"Yes, they are," Charlotte said with feeling. "Daisy, the female, will be having puppies soon. Perhaps you'd like one of them."

"If they didn't eat her out of house and home," Con muttered to himself.

"Come. Let us take you to our room." Charlotte helped the woman up and said to him, "Will you relock the door?"

"Certainly. I'll join you soon."

No sooner had the lock snicked closed, than the sounds of a coach coming into the yard reached him.

Doors opened and shut. Jemmy appeared at the top of the stairs and announced in a loud whisper, "Lord and Lady Merton are here."

They might be of assistance in getting Miss Cloverly out of this place. It would be much easier to deal with the villains and the tavern keeper and his staff with more help. "Tell them to come up."

Jemmy nodded and ran back down the stairs. Not more

than a minute later, Merton and his lady were striding down the narrow corridor toward him.

"Is she safe?" Lady Merton asked, concern writ on her features.

"Yes. Charlotte is with her. We must decide how best to proceed."

Her ladyship swept past him. "We shall, but in the chamber where we'll not be overheard. It is at the end, correct?"

"Yes." With his long strides Con managed to get to the door first. Why that was important, he didn't know. Only that it was. "Charlotte." He tapped on the door. "The Mertons are here."

The bolt drew back, the door opened, and Charlotte and Lady Merton flew into each other's arms.

"Dotty, I thought you were going to remain in Richmond." Charlotte took her friend's hand, leading her into the room.

For a second, Con felt forgotten, then she caught his gaze, her blue eyes sparkling with delight.

"We decided you might need us. There was no knowing how many scoundrels would be here." Lady Merton grinned. "It could be helpful to have two marquises instead of just one."

From the corridor, he heard a gruff laugh before Merton commented, "Intimidation and access are the only uses she has for my title."

Con might say the same about Charlotte. His title meant nothing at all to her. Until he had admitted he'd been wrong about his mistress and had tried to make reparations, she'd had as little as possible to do with him.

He had never wanted a woman who would marry him only for his title, but, until he'd met her, he *had* considered it to be one of his more desirable attributes.

"Cousin, please come in." She stood aside. "Kenilworth reserved a parlor downstairs, but I do not wish to leave Miss Cloverly alone."

"Of course," Merton said, entering the small chamber. "I suppose we must decide how we're going to get her out of here."

"Indeed." His wife pulled a face. "I've looked at the windows, but there is no way for her to climb down without being seen."

"I say we simply take her out," Merton said. "Our outriders and I are armed."

Con brightened. Simple and straightforward. It also might mean he would be able to hit someone, which, after seeing how they had tied Miss Cloverly up and distressed his betrothed, he desperately wanted to do.

"I suppose that would work, my love." The lady glanced at her husband a bit dubiously.

"But, as with spiriting her out of here, that does not net us Miss Betsy," Charlotte said, effectively quashing the idea.

"Or any of her tools," Con said, trying to think of a way to accomplish all their goals even if it meant he wouldn't get to fight anyone.

Charlotte began to pace from one end of the chamber to the other. After a few moments she stopped. "Jemmy." The lad turned, giving her his complete attention. "Did the landlady appear to be concerned about Miss Cloverly's behavior?"

"Yes, my lady."

"They were most likely told the same type of story that was told about me." Charlotte's blue gaze once again held Con's. "Why do we not try to make them our allies? We shall tell them what Miss Betsy is really up to, and recruit their help in arresting the men who brought Miss Cloverly here and capturing Miss Betsy when she arrives."

"That might actually work," he responded. They would require a backup plan. "And if they do not believe us?"

"In that event"—Charlotte gave him a wicked look—"you, Merton, and his servants will simply have to fight our way out."

She was a minx when she wanted to be. Con's life had definitely taken a turn for the better when he had met her. "Jemmy," Con said to the boy, "please ask the landlord and his wife to attend us."

"Yes, my lord."

"And Jemmy," Charlotte said, "make sure Lord Kenilworth's carriage is harnessed, and tell Lord Merton's outriders to go into the taproom and prepare themselves for trouble."

The lad grinned widely. Well, at that age, Con would have thought this was a great deal of fun as well.

Merton lounged against the wall on one side of the door, and Con took the other side. Miss Cloverly was seated on the bed. Lady Merton and Charlotte sat in chairs pulled next to the bed, flanking Miss Cloverly. Both ladies drew out their pistols, placing them in their laps under their reticules.

A few moments later, a knock came on the door. "My lord," the landlord called. "Your lad said you wished to see me and my wife."

He nodded to Merton, who opened the door. Once the innkeeper and his wife were in the room, Con closed it.

"How did she—" The man started, his eyes round as saucers.

Charlotte cut him off. "She was abducted from the park in front of the house where her aunt is employed. I shall tell you everything, but first we must introduce ourselves."

Before she could say another word, such as tell them she was unwed and in a bedchamber with an equally unwed gentleman, Con said, "Mr. and Mrs. Crowe, I am the Marquis of Kenilworth. This"—he pointed to Merton— "is the Marquis of Merton. These"—he motioned to Lady Merton and Charlotte—"are our ladies," he said, carefully skirting Charlotte's marital status. Other than closing her eyes for a moment, she didn't make any indication that he was playing fast and loose with the truth. "As you were told, this young woman was kidnapped. We happened to be in the square with my wife's brothers and sisters when we saw the commotion. Naturally, we followed the coach in the hope that we could rescue her."

Con glanced at Charlotte and she continued the tale. "Our understanding is that a person by the name of Miss Betsy may have told you that Miss Cloverly was running away from either her parents or her husband."

The landlady nodded. "We was told she didn't like the man her parents wanted her to wed."

"That is not true. In fact, she was visiting her aunt."

Miss Cloverly nodded in confirmation. "I'm getting married in two weeks to the son of the man who owns the largest haberdashery in Luton. My family owns the best fabric warehouse in the town, and our parents have planned for us to marry since we were children." A blush rose from her neck to her cheeks. "My Ben is also the handsomest man around. I wouldn't have any reason not to marry him."

The landlord's wife opened and closed her mouth a few times, yet seemed unable to speak.

Lady Merton glanced at Charlotte and shook her head. "My husband and I, as well as Lady Kenilworth's brother"— that threw them from the frying pan into the fire. But Charlotte hadn't even blinked—"destroyed Miss Betsy's brothel in London. Somehow, she escaped the law before reaching Newgate."

By this point, Mrs. Crowe looked close to having

apoplexy. She plopped onto the end of the bed, fanning herself with her apron. "I never thought . . . She looks and acts like such a lady, such a good person."

Leaning over, Charlotte patted the woman's hand. "You are not the only one she has deceived. We need to get this young woman to safety and call the magistrate to arrest the men who brought her here. We must also capture Miss Betsy so that she can no longer prey on other innocents."

Mr. Crowe, who had been silent, finally said, "Just tell us what we can do, me lords. Can't have my inn get a bad reputation."

"The first thing," Con said, "is to contact the magistrate. If you tell us where we may locate him, one of Lord Merton's servants will fetch him. If you have a cellar or if there is a gaol nearby, we can detain the blackguards until then."

"Nearest gaol is Richmond. That's where Sir John, the magistrate, is too. I got a cellar we can lock them in until he gets here."

Charlotte exchanged glances with Dotty before looking at Con. She had been a bit worried that the Crowes would either not believe their tale, or not want to become involved.

This was going much better than expected. Then again, not everything in life should be difficult. "It is a shame we do not know where Miss Betsy lives or her real name."

The landlady cleared her throat. "I might be able to help with that."

All of them turned their eyes to her. This was almost too much to hope for. "How?"

Mrs. Crowe ran a hand over her apron, smoothing it. "Most of the time, one of the men can read and write, and I just give his letter to our stable boy to post. This time, the man who brought—brought . . ." She glanced at Miss Cloverly.

"Miss Cloverly," she supplied.

Mrs. Crowe nodded her thanks. "Who brought Miss Cloverly handed me a letter to be sent to Miss Betsy." By this time they were all, even her husband, leaning toward Mrs. Crowe as if she was telling the most interesting story they'd ever heard. "The name on the letter was Mrs. E. Bottoms, and it was addressed in care of the White Swan in Twickenham."

"Twickenham isn't far at all," Merton said. "Just a few miles." He looked at Con. "We could be there and back in under two hours."

"And have Miss Betsy under lock and key," Con mused.

Chapter Twenty-Three

Before Constantine and Merton were too far into their scheme, Charlotte stopped them. "And how do you plan to prove that Mrs. E. Bottoms is Miss Betsy? For that matter, how do you propose to prove that any woman you have arrested is abducting people against their will? We have been *told* that it is Miss Betsy, but unless we have proof, she will be let go. Especially if she is known as a good citizen of her town."

Merton opened his mouth, but Dotty forestalled him. "Charlotte is correct. We need to catch her in the act, as it were."

Not saying a word, Constantine flattened his lips and tilted his head to one side. The rest of them were quiet as well.

After a few minutes, Miss Cloverly spoke. "If you can protect me, I'll agree to go with her tomorrow. I have a craving to find out just who paid her to have me abducted."

"No." Merton's tone was firm, as if he would brook no objection. "It is not right to use you in such a way."

"I think it would work," Dotty said slowly. "Naturally, we must ensure her safety."

Charlotte quickly reviewed the possible scenarios, and

nodded. "I agree. We would have to have more than one person following the coach, and, mayhap, outriders." She glanced at her friend. "Dotty, how many footmen and grooms do you have with you?"

She gave Charlotte a rueful smile. "At least ten. Is that not right, my love?"

"Twelve," Merton said gruffly, in a somewhat defensive tone. "One never knows when a horse may become lame or a man fall and injure himself. I wished to make sure you were safe. Besides, my love, we need to put to work all the people you rescue."

"Well, that is true," Dotty replied, not at all embarrassed. "The more training they receive the more quickly they will be able to find permanent employment."

"There, you see?" Charlotte grinned at her friend and cousin. "We have plenty of men in the event of trouble." She turned to Miss Cloverly. "It is your decision. Will you feel safe enough?"

They all seemed to focus on the young woman as she considered her options. After a few long moments she gave one decisive nod. "I will, my lady."

Charlotte let out the breath she had been holding. "Thank you. Until then, you shall remain with us. That way if Miss Betsy does come early, you will not be in danger."

"Well then." Constantine pushed himself off the wall. "Let's make certain those blackguards below are secured."

"What will we tell Miss Betsy about her men?" Mr. Crowe asked.

Remembering her own abduction and the one cur who got drunk, Charlotte said, "We can say they went off drinking."

"That might work." Mrs. Crowe nodded. "Except for the one man that isn't here, they do put down the ale."

Raising an eyebrow, Constantine said to Merton, "After you, my lord."

"Just one thing." Mrs. Crowe twisted her hands in her apron. "Try not to make a mess. The midday meal starts soon, and there'll be no time to clean up before service."

Con gave her an elegant bow. "As you wish, madam."

"Indeed," Merton said. "It shall be as quick and clean as possible."

"As long as I get to plant at least one facer, I'll be a happy man," Constantine mumbled.

It didn't appear the landlady had heard him, but Dotty shook her head as Charlotte stifled a chuckle.

She went to the door, and once Merton and the Crowes had left the chamber, Constantine turned to her. "Promise me you will remain safely here."

Placing her hand on his cheek seemed the most normal thing in the world to do as she rose up on her tiptoes and kissed him. "I shall."

She closed and locked the door behind him. "Do you think they'll be long?"

"Not if they are forbidden to make a mess," Dotty said, clearly holding back her laughter. "And you? How do you feel about Kenilworth now?"

Like a bird singing joyfully in a tree. Like I can walk on clouds.

A week ago, Charlotte could not have imagined she would come to like and admire Constantine Kenilworth so much. In fact, after the past few days, she could easily envision a life with him. She didn't know if she loved him yet, but if not, she was very close. So close she had decided to tell him she would marry him. She glanced at Nell Cloverly, who was staring at her, curiosity writ in her eyes.

Charlotte would like to have a complete discussion with her friend, but not with another person present. "Much like you did when Merton kept living up to your expectations, I suppose."

"Except you had none," Dotty pressed.

"Oh, I had plenty of them." Charlotte laughed. "And none of them were good."

Constantine had more than met the challenges she'd given him. Today he had acted like a partner instead of the way most men acted. And when he had introduced her as his wife, even if there had been no choice, she was, at first, astonished that the idea did not bother her at all. In fact, she actually looked forward to telling him.

"But now?" Dotty prompted.

"Everything has changed." Perhaps it was time for more than kisses.

"Well, if you ask me, my lady," Miss Cloverly said, "I would say you are both in love."

Charlotte's cheeks heated and someone started to pound on the door.

"Charlotte," Constantine said. "It's time to go."

When she opened the door he filled the space, looking as if he'd just had a brisk walk.

"I take it all went smoothly."

"Merton had so many men on hand, there was little to do. The scoundrels barely even attempted to fight."

"That must have been a disappointment for you." Although, it would have made the landlady happy. She kissed his cheek. "Has the magistrate been summoned?"

"Yes, along with a message that he can find us at the Star and Garter if he has any questions."

"In that case, we should be on our way."

Her stomach growled, and he grinned at her. "We never did receive our tea."

"No, we did not, and I'm becoming quite peckish." She shook out her skirts.

He held out his arm to her. "That won't do at all."

It was decided that she, Dotty, and Miss Cloverly would

travel in the Merton coach. Merton was on horseback, and Constantine would take Jemmy in his phaeton.

Yet, Miss Cloverly demurred. "Thank you for the offer, but I'd feel more comfortable on the outside seat."

"If you are sure?" Dotty asked, surprised at the woman's decision.

"Yes, my lady. I've been cooped up long enough, and it looks comfortable."

She was right about that, Charlotte thought. There was even a convertible hood on the boot of the coach.

"Very well." Merton helped Dotty into the coach.

One of the footmen assisted Miss Cloverly, and Constantine handed Charlotte into the coach. His green eyes seemed to reflect the leaves of the trees as he searched her face. "I shall see you soon."

"You shall, indeed." Soon. Charlotte decided. She would tell him that she'd be his wife. She took a seat next to her friend. And it was definitely time for more than kisses.

The door closed and he signaled the coachman to start.

"Now then," Dotty said, her eyes sparkling with curiosity. "Have you decided to put the man out of his misery and wed him?"

"Yes." Charlotte couldn't keep from grinning. "I think a week or so will be all the time we shall need." Then a thought occurred to her. "Dotty, I need to know how it is between a man and a woman."

A wicked smile graced her face. "It is glorious."

That was not very helpful. "So I inferred from you and Louisa, but I believe I require a little more information than that."

"Ah, yes." Dotty sat up straighter. "If you are planning what I think you are planning, you do need a bit more information. Has Grace told you anything at all?"

"Other than when you marry a man you love, marital relations are wonderful, nothing at all."

"I see. In that case, perhaps a better understanding is in order."

By the time they arrived at the inn in Richmond, Charlotte was not quite as eager to pursue more-than-kissing as she had been. "It only hurts the once? You are sure?"

"Positive." Dotty punctuated her statement with a sharp nod. "Do not be concerned. I think Kenilworth will make sure you enjoy it."

"If you say so." Charlotte was a little dubious. Then again, he had had a great deal of experience, even if she did not wish to consider that part at all.

In for a penny, in for a pound, as her mother used to say. All she had to do now was to put her scheme in place.

Blast it all! Con had hoped he'd be able to speak with Charlotte before they arrived in Richmond.

Lately, he had seen warmth in her eyes, instead of the ice shards that had been there before. When she had kissed him before he'd gone down to arrest the blackguards, it had shocked him to his toes—not that she had kissed him, they'd done that already, but that she would do it in the presence of Lady Merton and Miss Cloverly.

Merton had immediately decided Con was joining the family and suggested they address each other more informally.

"After what my wife told me, I had my qualms you would be able to change Charlotte's mind," he said. "But you seem to have done a good job of it. Congratulations. I would be honored if you would call me Merton."

"Thank you." Con would be much happier if he was as

certain about Charlotte. "Please feel free to address me as Kenilworth."

He'd thought to use the ride to Richmond to solidify his future with Charlotte. Yet, he could not argue with the decision that she travel in the coach. It would present a more proper appearance. There was no reason to court more talk and every reason not to. Richmond was a well-known refuge from the dirt of Town, and the Star and Garter a popular inn with the *ton*. And one would expect to come across someone either he or she knew.

It was time to ensure she would indeed marry him, and he needed to form a plan as to how he would approach her. But with Jemmy sitting next to Con talking a blue streak during the short drive, and many times not even waiting for an answer before rushing on, Con could not concentrate enough to do anything but answer the lad.

"That was the best facer I ever saw. Will you teach me how to do it?" Jemmy asked. "Thought for a bit he'd give you trouble, but you just took him down all right and tight. Will you teach me how to drive? His lordship said he'd teach Phillip and Walter, but didn't say anything about me."

"If his lordship allows it," Con replied, wondering exactly what Jemmy's place in the Worthington household was.

"That would be beyond anything!" Jemmy bounced on the seat, and Con reached over to keep him from tumbling out of the phaeton.

"Sit. I cannot teach you anything if you fall off and bash your head."

"Mr. Winters isn't going to like that I missed lessons again." That was said a bit glumly.

"Do you like your lessons?" Con asked, wanting to know more about the child.

"I like learning about different things, and his lordship said I need to know as much as Walter and Phillip."

Con was beginning to wonder what Worthington was doing with the lad. That he was educating Jemmy was clear, but to what end? The child, however, didn't have an answer for that.

Not long after, Merton not being at all shy about making an impressive entrance, their group came to a stop in front of the Star and Garter in grand fashion. Of course, that was hardly to be avoided with the number of outriders, most of them in livery, he had flanking the coach.

Jemmy scrambled down from his perch. "I'll see to the horses, my lord."

"Thank you." One thing was clear, the lad was horse mad. Con strolled over to the coach, opened the door and let down the steps. "My lady."

Charlotte's lips tilted up. "My lord, how kind of you."

"It is my pleasure." Once she was on the ground, he pressed his lips to the back of her gloved hand.

While they waited for Merton and his lady, Con led her off to the side, and time seemed to stop as he gazed into her clear blue eyes. Somehow, between the Dove and here, he'd come to the conclusion that he did not merely want her because of his promise and his pride, but he needed her in his life. "Charlotte, I—"

"Come along," Merton said. "I have been informed that my wife must immediately have sustenance."

"I as well." Charlotte placed her hand on Con's arm. "Let us find a time to be private."

That would not happen until much later. "Very well. By the by, did you know Jemmy's tongue runs like a fiddle-stick?"

"He is extremely curious." The corners of her mouth

took a definite downward turn. "I hope you were not bothered by him."

"I am merely interested in what Worthington plans for the boy. I gather he is joining your brothers and sisters for lessons."

"Indeed he is, and doing wonderfully well. When I found him, he could not read or write. Now he is surpassing Phillip and Theo."

"Found him?" How the devil did a gently bred young lady "find" a child from the streets? Then he remembered what her brother had told him.

"Um, yes." She bit her lower lip, and a line appeared between her well-shaped brows. "You know that children are sold to kid kens."

She posed it as a statement, not a question. "Yes."

"We have been able to rescue and find the homes of quite a few of those taken. Jemmy was with another boy." She sighed softly. "We have not yet found his family."

"You believe he is from the gentry?" Con glanced back at the child. It was possible. Jemmy had the regular features of any boy in Mayfair, as well as what looked to be a budding patrician nose. Then again, he might be someone's by-blow.

"Most of the children in that particular group were. He had been there for a long time, and has no clear memory of his parents." They entered the inn and were ushered up a wide staircase. "We are hoping, praying if you must know, that as he becomes older he will resemble someone and be recognized."

Con greatly doubted that would occur. What, after all, were the odds that someone would come across the boy by chance?

As if she had heard him, she said, "It already happened with a little girl. A lady, who turned out to be the child's grandmother, saw her playing in the Park and almost swooned. The girl looked exactly like her mother at that age."

"And the mother?" he asked, although he knew the answer.

"Murdered."

They had reached the apartment Merton had hired. There was a large parlor with two doors on either side of the room. "What will you do if you are unable to find his family?"

"Keep him as one of ours." She smiled a bit sadly. "Eventually, he will become used to living with us. Right now, he feels compelled to work part of the time in the stables. Matt intends to send him to school the year after Phillip goes."

"He may just like horses." Con grinned down at her. "At his age, if I had been given the choice between living in the house and living in the stables, I assure you the stables would have won out."

Charlotte chuckled lightly. "I imagine they would have." She glanced around the room. "My, this is elegant."

It was. Now that they were in the parlor, he could see a balcony beyond a pair of French windows. She strode over to them, drew back the curtains, and stepped out. "Richmond is a lovely little town. I wonder if they have a market."

Standing behind her, he glanced down at the street below. "I will ask."

"Thank you." Once again her smile made him want to drag her into his arms and never let go. "After all, we are in no hurry to return to Town."

Other than to marry. Yet, before then, he must make sure of her and their future. He looked around the parlor again. The door on one side of the parlor was slightly open, and he could hear her cousins talking in low voices. She would most likely be in the chamber on the opposite side of the parlor from the Mertons. He wondered where his room was located, and hoped it would not be too far away. Although, if Merton was as protective as Worthington appeared to be, it could be on the other side of the inn.

"My lord?"

Con turned around. His valet stood just outside the door, but not from the main corridor.

Obviously, he had been paying so much attention to Charlotte he had failed to notice the smaller corridor located before the main door to the parlor. "Cunningham."

He bowed. "Your chamber is this way if you would like to wash before luncheon."

"My dear." Con raised Charlotte's hand, but this time turned her palm up, kissed the center of her palm, and closed her fingers around it. "I shall be back shortly."

Gently, she cupped his cheek with the same hand. "I will be here."

By Jupiter, he hated leaving her. Still, the chances were that he would not be able to find time to be alone with her until after dinner when her friend and cousin retired for the evening.

He followed his valet past two doors and into a large bedchamber with one door on the right and the other on the left. As in many older houses, all the rooms must be connected, so that if one opened all the doors it could make for an easy passage between parlors. The small corridor he had been taken through had to be an addition built when the inn bought the neighboring house.

That meant that Charlotte's bedchamber was one door down from his, with only a dressing room between them. Obviously, he had misjudged Merton's intentions. The man

Chapter Twenty-Four

Burt couldn't believe his luck. There she was. Right in front of him, looking down from that grand inn across the street. He'd stopped in Richmond to get a pint of beer before he finished traveling to the Dirty Duck, a hedge tavern between here and Twickenham. Not wanting to see his chief, he'd decided to leave a note for Miss Betsy at the Duck. Now he wouldn't have to tell her he'd lost Lady Charlotte. He could just bring the mort to Miss Betsy.

He flipped the barmaid a coin. "I'll be needing a room for the night after all."

Reaching under the counter, she took out a key. "That'll be a shilling. Up the stairs on the left. Dinner's included. It's on the street and small, but ye won't have ta share it." She leaned over provocatively. "Unless ye have a mind to."

As she expected, he looked down. Dark pink nipples drew his attention and his cock stood up. It had been a long time since he'd had a woman, and he deserved a reward for finding the rum mort. "Meet me after you finish here."

"Be me pleasure." She smiled and he was glad to see she had most of her teeth.

He picked up his bag. After he put it in his room, he'd scout around and find a good place to snatch Lady Charlotte.

First he had to send a message to Miss Betsy that he'd have the gentry mort by tomorrow. He took out the small traveling desk he used, penned the note, then went back down to the taproom.

"I need someone to carry this to Twickenham."

The same woman who'd served him earlier, signaled to a lad of about twelve. "Eddy here can take it." She strolled over to him, her hips swaying. "Who's it to?"

"Me employer," he said, using the posh word. "I need to tell her I stopped here to pick up a package she wanted."

There wasn't any point in making the woman jealous. Burt was looking forward to tonight.

"In that case, Eddy"—she kept her eyes on Burt as she spoke—"better get going so she won't be expecting you."

He handed the lad the letter and a penny. After the last several days, his life was good again, and he was looking forward to his payment.

It was late afternoon when Betsy Bell strolled into the entrance of the White Swan in Twickenham to collect her post. She stood at the desk for a few minutes before the landlord appeared.

"Good afternoon to ye, Mrs. Bottoms."

She inclined her head slightly, a perfect imitation of what she'd seen real ladies do. "And good morning to you, Mr. Griffen. Will you see if I have any letters, please?"

"Two of them. One just got delivered by hand a few hours ago. If you'll just give me a bit I'll get them for ye."

"Certainly." Betsy glanced around, pleased with what she saw. No one but her would have thought a girl from

St. Giles would end up in a nice village like Twickenham. She'd known she'd make herself a better life, and she had. A snug little house she owned, as well as a maid and a cook who came in three times a week, and a coach and coachman. All her neighbors were gentry. Not the rich kind, but still gentry.

A lot of hard work had gone into getting here, and not only on her back. When her father had sold her to her first nunnery when she was thirteen, she hadn't been able to read or write. She knew enough numbers to make sure she wasn't cheated, and she'd found an old lady to teach her the rest.

Now, sixteen years later, she was being treated like a lady, and pretty soon she'd have enough to retire on. Once the war was over, she thought she might fancy Italy. Some of the gents Betsy had been with said it was warm all the time there and cheap to live in. But she'd miss her house. She could visit and see how she liked it.

No, it wouldn't be long now, and she'd have everything she wanted.

"Here ye be." Mr. Griffen handed her two letters.

"Thank you." As expected, the missive sent from the Dove had her own handwriting on it. That package would bring her a pretty penny. The stupid girl should have accepted what the gent had offered, but then Betsy wouldn't be making so much money off her. And it'd been a quick job. Seems the girl was only in London for a few days.

The other letter was written by Burt. With any luck he'd found Lady Charlotte. She stopped herself from frowning and gave the landlord a polite smile. "I shall see you in a few days, Mr. Griffen."

"Yes, ma'am."

Betsy strode as quickly as was proper to the cottage she'd bought in an area not far from the church. She'd even attended the services a time or two. Smirking, she imagined the looks on the faces of Mrs. Hall and Mrs. Eccles, the ladies living on either side of her, if they knew a common whore had drunk tea with them.

She laughed to herself, but, on second thought, it wouldn't be very funny at all. They'd chase her out of her house and the village. Not only for being a whore, but for acting better than she should.

Her maid opened the door for her. "Shall I bring tea, ma'am?"

"Yes, please." One day she'd have an indoor male servant. The problem now was that they were more expensive and damned government put a tax on them too. "I shall be in my parlor."

The girl bobbed a curtsey. "Yes, ma'am."

Sitting down at her desk, Betsy pulled out a sheet of plain foolscap. Her pen had already been sharpened, and she dipped it into the ink.

> *My dear sir,*
>   *The package you ordered will be delivered tomorrow. Meet me at the Dirty Duck off the main road between Richmond and Twickenham at ten o'clock in the morning.*
>   *Payment must be rendered in coin before you receive the package.*
>   *Yr. Servant*
>   *B.*

She sprinkled sand on the paper and dusted it off before folding it, writing the address, and applying the sealing wax.

Next, she opened the letter from Burt.

Dear Ma'am,
    I found the package. I'll deliver it tomorrow
morning at the Duck.
                    Yr. Servant
                    B.

She could scarcely believe her good fortune.

Once again she wrote a note directing the second gentleman to meet her tomorrow at nine thirty in the morning. That was pushing her luck. It was early for a nob, but it would not do for the two men to meet, and she couldn't take the chance of any of the Duck's regular customers seeing her there. Not only that, but the next young lady should arrive at the Hare and Hound no later than this evening or tomorrow morning.

All in all, this was a good day's work. Once she delivered her ladyship to the gent, and the next package was delivered, she would be able to retire sooner than she'd thought.

She pulled out another piece of pressed paper, and wrote a note to her solicitor asking him how long it would take him to make arrangements for her to travel to Italy, and to lease her house while she was gone. Six months ought to do it.

Dinner was long over when Charlotte cast Dotty a pleading look. Could she not take Merton away and give Charlotte time with Constantine? She wanted their future settled, and that was impossible to do with her cousins present.

Putting her fingers over her mouth, Dotty feigned a yawn. "My love, I require your assistance."

Merton slid her a smoldering glance. "In that case,

we should retire." He rose, holding out his hand to her. "My love."

A moment later their door snicked shut, and Charlotte let out the breath she had been holding. Now she simply needed to be bold and go up to Constantine and kiss him.

The next thing she knew, she was in his arms. So much for having to be bold. "I thought they would never go to bed."

He lowered his mouth to hers and she opened, allowing him access, running her tongue along his as he explored her mouth. He tasted like wine and male, and she had never tasted anything as good as he did at this moment. She hoped this meant that he had the same thoughts as she did. After all, earlier today she'd done her best to let him know that her feelings for him had changed. That she now looked forward to being in his arms and his life.

Throughout the past week and particularly today, she had been amazed at how often their views ran in tandem. She spread her fingers through his hair, enjoying his soft tresses as she explored his mouth as well. Would he be surprised that she had changed her mind about him? No. He couldn't be. Charlotte had given him enough hints. She'd been right not to let him kiss her like this until she was sure she wanted him, because now, she did not wish to stop and she had every intention of making him hers.

Finally, Con was alone with Charlotte for the first time since they'd left the Hare and Hound. He thought the Mertons would never retire and allow him to show her how much he wanted her. Wanted to marry her, make her his marchioness, helpmate, and the mother of his children.

He pulled her into his arms, slightly surprised that she came willingly.

"Charlotte." She tilted her head, deepening their kiss. If

only they could do this all night, but he had to make sure she was not simply overcome by her first experience with lust. He drew back, and wanted to preen when her lips followed. "I think we worked well together today."

"I agree," she said, her voice low, seductive. "We seldom disagreed at all."

Damn. When had she turned from an innocent into a siren? She slid her arms around his neck, pressing her lush breasts against his chest for the first time. His breath hitched and his cock swelled.

This was even more of a statement than she had made earlier when she'd kissed him. He bent his head again, touching his lips to hers. Perhaps talking could wait for a while. Her mouth opened, and he took full advantage, tasting her, drinking as if he'd been stranded in a desert. A soft moan escaped her lips and her tongue touched his, tentatively at first as she learned how to take control, then with more confidence as if she wanted everything he could give her.

She felt so good, so soft and lovely. Slowly, so as not to frighten her, Con cupped one of Charlotte's breasts and feathered her nipple with his thumb. Tilting her head, once again she deepened the kiss and pressed her body tighter against him. This time, he moved his hand to her bottom, pulling it against him. Her fingers tangled with the hair at the nape of his neck, scraping his skull.

Was this her way of telling him she would marry him? Or was it the danger they'd been in while rescuing Miss Cloverly making itself known? He damn well better find out before this went too far.

Charlotte tightened her hold, slipping her body up his as she did. God, she was going to be the death of him. His cock was harder than it had ever been, pressing against her, and damn he wanted her like he had never desired another woman.

He'd wanted her since the first time they'd met, but this . . . this was more. Not merely a seduction. Although, at the moment, he had no idea who was seducing whom. This was the woman he wanted for the rest of his life.

Her grip on his neck loosened, and one of her hands slid beneath his jacket, then down to the small of his back. Her fingers hovered just above his bottom, tantalizingly close to touching him as he touched her.

Con's blood heated as if fires blazed on his skin and in his veins. He wanted his hands on her naked body and her hands on his. Never would he have thought an innocent could make him so hot. He wanted nothing more than to lift her skirts and plunge into her, making her his forever.

Then she'd have to wed him. Or hate him for the rest of their lives. Christ, he didn't even know if she knew what she was doing or the effect she had on him.

And he needed to know.

Now.

If she was not willing to commit to him, to them, this had to stop before it went any further.

He eased back from their kiss, pressing his lips to the corner of her mouth, then over her jaw and down her neck as she sighed.

"Charlotte, my love."

Constantine's lips were pressed against Charlotte's neck, muffling his speech, but still she heard him clearly. She fought down the excitement she felt at being called his love. Did he truly love her, or was that just a term of endearment?

How would she know? "Yes?"

"Does this mean we will marry?" His voice was a low growl. "Soon?"

Opening her eyes, she looked up at him. An anxious look clouded his green eyes. As if he had as many questions as she did, and she smiled. "Yes, it does."

"Thank God!" The words sounded more like a groan, and his mouth came down hard on hers.

She almost laughed when he swept her into his arms. He must love her. Why else would he risk her anger and her family's?

"Your chamber, is it over there?"

"It is." Or perhaps he just wanted her and wasn't in love, and didn't care about what she felt.

He held her close as his long strides ate up the distance to her door. "Your maid?"

"I told her she wouldn't be needed." Charlotte pulled his head down and kissed him. Her friends told her his kiss would tell her what she wanted to know, but she wasn't quite sure. Yet, perhaps it was herself she didn't quite trust. Although, she should. Despite everything, her initial impression of him had been correct. Constantine was kind, and caring, and wanted to help those less fortunate than he. He had simply not understood he was hurting others. And once he had realized his mistake, he did something about it.

She knew she was right. All this questioning herself was just a slight bit of fear at the change she was about to make. And the fact that he had not told her he loved her.

He juggled her as he lifted the latch and opened the door. Once in the room, he carefully lowered her and she could feel every inch of his muscular body slide against hers as her feet touched the carpet.

A ridge as hard as steel—that must be the reason some

referred to it as a sword—rode against her stomach, and she wanted to caress it, but that might be a little too bold at the moment. Instead she rubbed against it, grinning to herself when he groaned again, gathering her into his arms.

This, being with Constantine, felt right. Earlier today was the first time she'd thought she wanted him forever; now she knew she would never let him go.

He lifted his head, breaking the kiss. A smile played around his firm lips, but his eyes were warm with desire. "Are you seducing me, my love?"

There was that word again, *love*. Did he love her? She wanted to ask, but fear stopped her. What would she do if he did not? Yet, she was sure she loved him. But could she love him if he did not love her as well? Wrinkling her nose, she concentrated on the question at hand. "I'm trying to."

"Why?" He gazed down at her with a look so intense she was almost speechless.

"Because we shall be m-married?" She felt like a fool. Surely, this was the moment she should tell him she loved him.

"Is that all?" Constantine's fingers tightened, binding her closer to him. "Charlotte, when this first—drat it. That's not what I want to say. Charlotte, I love you. I cannot imagine a life without you. If you do not feel the same—"

Thank heaven! "I love you too." She pressed her lips to his, more eagerly than before. "I want to spend the rest of my days with you."

He rested his forehead against hers. "Then let's do this properly." He held her shoulders out just enough that they could see each other's faces. "Lady Charlotte, will you do me the honor of being my wife, the mother of our children, and my marchioness? Will you go to bed with me every night and wake up with me each morning? Will you grow old with me? And will you always tell me when I'm being an idiot?"

Tears of joy pricked her eyes and she wanted to laugh at the last part. She had not expected a proposal at all, nevertheless such a lovely one. "I will marry you, Constantine Kenilworth, and spend the rest of my days loving you and our family. And I shall never stop telling you when you are wrong." He took her mouth again, and her gown sagged. "What are you doing?"

"Helping you seduce me," he mumbled against her lips.

Chapter Twenty-Five

"How thoughtful." Charlotte's gown made a whooshing sound as it dropped to the floor.

"I aim to please." Constantine started on her petticoat and stays.

She untied his cravat, tossing it aside, then went to work on his collar, shirt, and waistcoat. Soon they were down to their shoes, which came off easily enough. He unfastened the clasp on her garter, and her stockings slipped to her feet. Constantine lifted her and placed her on the bed before climbing in beside her.

Spreading her hands over his chest, Charlotte twined her fingers in the soft hairs covering his taut skin. "You are so different from me."

Cupping her breasts, he licked one nipple, making her moan with need. "I can't but think that's a good thing."

She held his head against her. "A very good thing."

He spread her arms out to the side, holding them there as he licked and kissed his way over her stomach and down. A strange sort of tension began between her legs and spread through her body. She'd never felt such heat and need. Part of her wanted him to stop, but the other part wanted him to keep on.

More. Oh, please more.

His tongue touched her mons, and she arched into him. "Oh, Heavens. Whatever you're doing, don't stop."

"You taste like spiced honey." Constantine chuckled, and licked again. "Come for me, my love."

His finger filled her, and she thought she'd go out of her mind. How much more could she stand? The coiling tension burst and released. For a moment Charlotte thought she'd died as tremors of pleasure gripped her.

Con's large, strong body covered hers, as he kissed her lips and held her. "Do you know what marital congress is?"

Her limbs were loose and Charlotte had never felt so relaxed in her life. He settled between her legs, his member nudging at her entrance. She rubbed against him, trying to encourage him to take her. "Dotty told me."

"What did she tell you?" His voice was tight. With strain or something else, Charlotte didn't know.

"That at first it would hurt, but then it was glorious."

He pushed into her, slowly filling her. "Trust me and I'll take you to Heaven."

Again. She could not imagine anything could be better than what he'd just done. "I trust you."

Good God, Charlotte was tight. Con had done all he could, all he knew to do to prepare her. He was relieved she knew at least a little of what to expect. This first time would be something she would remember for the rest of her life, and he must make her enjoy it. Especially after his boast. Heaven, indeed. He should have stuck with glorious.

He slipped in and out of her, keeping control over himself when all he wanted to do was plunge into her and bury himself in her body. He'd never had trouble before. He had always made sure his partners had their pleasure as well. But with her, everything was different somehow.

He loved her more than he had thought possible and

prayed she wouldn't feel much pain. "Wrap your legs around me." Charlotte did as he asked, and Con surged forward. She cried out, tensed around him, and he stopped, allowing her pain to recede. "That was the worst of it, my love. Are you all right?"

She was quiet for a few moments, then she gave him a small smile. "I shall be fine."

He moved again, slowly, waiting for a sign that her desire was building again. A soft sigh escaped her lips, swollen with his kisses. Her breathing hitched, and her legs gripped him harder. A moment later she cried his name, and he pumped into her, spilling his seed. Making her his in the most primitive and elemental way possible. She would never leave him now. She could never leave him.

Charlotte was his forever. Thank the Fates this had gone well.

The stress Con had been feeling flowed out of his body. He barely kept himself from collapsing on her instead of falling off to her side. He tugged her close to him, cradling her against his chest, and murmured into her hair, "Charlotte, I love you. I never knew how much love made a difference."

"I love you too, Constantine." She rolled, snuggling her cheek against his chest. "You were right. It was Heaven."

He never wanted to move again, never wanted to leave this bed. Then he remembered she had been a virgin and if he didn't do something soon, everyone in the blasted hotel would know what had occurred. "Stay there. Right where you are. I'll be back."

In three long steps he was at the wash stand. He took a piece of linen and wet it. The water had cooled, but perhaps that was better. He cleaned himself. Even in the relative darkness, he could see her blood. He rinsed the piece of linen and returned to Charlotte, gently wiping her and blotting the sheet.

"What are you doing?"

"Washing us up a bit." He would take care of the water in the morning. "Your maid will have to see to the bed-clothes in the morning."

He threw the cloth toward the basin, and climbed into bed, cuddling next to her again. A contentment he'd never experienced before filled him. "When shall we wed?"

"In the next week or so." She lifted her head and smiled at him. "I do not think we'll be allowed to marry before then. Fortunately for us, Matt wants to get Daisy back to Stanwood before she whelps."

Con tried to imagine a litter of puppies running around Stanwood House and laughed. "Thank the deities for preg-nant dogs."

"Indeed." Charlotte's lips curved into a smile. "I know when we went to pick out Daisy she had ten brothers and sisters."

Con would have to tell Worthington he and Charlotte wanted a puppy. "I'm surprised he decided to breed them while you were all in Town."

"Well, that is not exactly what happened." She began to laugh. "As a matter of fact, he had a pen built for Daisy to keep Duke away from her."

That should have done the trick. At least it had with most of his hunting dogs. "What happened?"

"Mary and Theo." Charlotte chuckled. "It was clear to them that the Danes wanted to be together, and they thought it wouldn't hurt anything if they let Daisy out."

He joined her laughter. "My mother once had a pug dog who developed an infatuation for one of my hunters. Natu-rally, we separated the bitches when it was their time. One day a stable hand found the pug had dug his way under the stall, and the hunting dog was pulling him by his ears out of the tunnel."

Con kissed her as she went into whoops. "I'm sorry. I should remember we cannot be loud."

"Not at the moment. When we are in our own house we shall do as we wish."

Her eyes began to close, but he wanted her attention for a moment longer. "We shall have puppies someday."

Something landed on the bed and began to purr. He had forgotten about the cat.

"And kittens," Charlotte murmured in a sleepy voice.

Con pulled the rest of the covers up over them. A second later, the cat curled up next to Charlotte on his chest. He stroked it, marveling at the dense soft fur. "And kittens."

This is what his life would be like with Charlotte. Dogs, cats, their children, stray children, and other assorted people, and a love that he could never have imagined.

Con couldn't wait for it to begin in earnest. As soon as they returned to Town, he'd procure a special license.

Hours later, light stole through the slit in the curtain, waking him. He lay there listening to Charlotte's soft breathing, marveling that he had her in his life forever.

Mine.

No matter what happened, she would always be with him.

The kitten stretched and patted his chest. Its large, yellow eyes seemed to study his.

"I suppose you need something." He stroked the cat again, and found himself to be inordinately pleased when it began to purr. "We shall break our fast soon."

What he really wanted to do was to make love to Charlotte again, but Con wasn't quite sure what would happen if he made the kitten move. He definitely didn't want to get clawed. She would probably be sore as well. Tonight would be soon enough.

Sounds came from his room, disturbing his peace. *Damn*. Cunningham was already up and about. They had to leave the inn early to return Miss Cloverly, but surely it couldn't be late enough for that.

Con slipped out of bed, gathered his clothing, and opened the door to his bedchamber.

His valet's eyes might have widened, but he couldn't swear to it. "You may wish me happy. Lady Charlotte and I shall wed next week."

"The best of news, my lord. Congratulations." Cunningham finished laying out Con's kit for the day. "Breakfast shall be served soon."

Two doors opened and closed, and he resisted the urge to wipe his brow. A few moments longer, and he would have been found in her bed. Somehow that was infinitely more troubling than his valet knowing he'd slept with her.

About a half hour later, he entered the parlor. Lady Merton, who had told him to call her Dotty, was pouring tea for Merton, and Charlotte was just taking a seat at the table. The kittens were rolling around the floor, not paying attention to anyone else.

Con stepped around them, taking the chair next to Charlotte. "Good morning."

She smiled, a sleepy expression on her beautiful face. "Good morning to you. How do you like your tea?"

"Milk and two lumps of sugar." He noticed a second pot of tea next to her elbow. Taking the cup she handed him, he sipped. "Perfect."

"That is another thing we have in common," she said, fixing her own cup. "I'm going to take Collette for a short walk before we leave. I wasn't able to work with her at all yesterday."

A vague feeling of uneasiness slithered down his spine.

Something akin to the one he had experienced when he'd started this adventure with her.

One of the men who had abducted her was still missing. But he did not dare forbid her to go. She would not take that at all well. Nor could he hover over her. He could, though, watch her from the balcony that overlooked the front of the inn. "Will you do me a favor and remain in the yard?"

She nodded and swallowed the bite of toast she'd been chewing. "I shall stay on the side, out of the way of the carriages and horses."

"Thank you." He covered her hand. Con caught a look from Merton. He was her cousin and had been nominally put in charge of her well-being. She turned her hand in his and held it, as if giving her approval to share their news. "Charlotte and I have decided to marry next week."

"How wonderful!" Dotty came around the table and hugged Charlotte. "I'm so happy for you." She glanced at Con. "And you as well. You will never find a sweeter, kinder person than Charlotte."

Or a stronger woman. "I know how fortunate I am to have won her."

Merton shook Con's hand. "I wish you well."

The four of them chatted for a few minutes as they finished breakfast. Yet it was clear they were thinking more of what would occur once they arrived at the Dove.

Charlotte rose. "I'll meet you in the yard." She glanced around the room. "Collette, *allez.*"

To his utter surprise, the kitten ran to Charlotte and sat at her feet. "I can honestly say I have never heard of a cat doing that before."

A few minutes later, Con stood on the balcony watching Charlotte walk her kitten on the lead. Jemmy stood not far from her, standing watch over her basket. Con's pair, harnessed to his phaeton, was led to the center of the yard, not far from Charlotte.

It was time to go. As he turned from the window, a black coach pulled up next to Charlotte. A man jumped down, grabbed her and threw her into the coach, slamming the door.

Bloody hell! Not again.

"They've got Charlotte!" he shouted as he ran out of the parlor.

"Damnation," Merton swore.

Con reached the yard first, and jumped into his carriage. "Jemmy is on the back of the coach." Something else that would have to cease. "Hand me Charlotte's basket."

"Where is Collette?" Dotty called.

"In the basket," Merton answered, taking the cat out and handing it to her. "She can stay here with Cyrille."

"I'll take her inside."

"Who is that boy?" an older lady demanded in a shrill tone. "The boy on the back of the coach. I demand to know who he is."

A woman a little older than his mother was striding toward him, but he had no time to waste. He had to go after Charlotte. "That's Lord Merton. Ask him."

The coach had been out of sight for several minutes before Con saw Jemmy waving. With any luck, they would turn off at the Dove. Con just prayed the Crowes wouldn't be shocked to see Charlotte brought in and ruin their plan.

He passed the Dove, and his hopes that this would be an easy rescue died. Where the devil was she being taken?

A large stagecoach pulled in front of him. Con tried to overtake the vehicle, but the blasted thing stayed close to the middle of the road and did not give way until they had reached Twickenham.

Hell and damnation! The carriage carrying Charlotte

had disappeared. How the hell was he going to find her before it was too late?

The sound of hooves behind him beat a tattoo, and he pulled over to the side of the road.

"My lord." One of Merton's outriders came up on Con's side. "His lordship sent us to help you."

Thank God. "How many men do you have with you?"

"Four, my lord."

"The coach turned off somewhere between the Dove and here. Search every road and path. She must be found, and soon."

"Yes, my lord."

The riders galloped back down the road. Con turned his phaeton. If only he had taken notice of the lanes and other roads, but he'd been so intent on passing the coach he hadn't paid attention. Fortunately, the outriders would be able to cover more ground than he could on his own.

The saving grace was that it wasn't that far back to the Dove. He dragged a hand over his face. But how many blasted side roads were there? That is what mattered.

He prayed that Charlotte would be safe until he arrived.

Chapter Twenty-Six

Drat, drat, drat. Charlotte pulled herself up from the floor of the coach and tried the handle on the door. Locked, and there didn't seem to be a keyhole.

Well, blast it all!

She drew in a long breath and straightened her bonnet before taking stock of her situation. No pistol, no knife, but at least Collette was secure. She would have climbed into the basket. It was her safe place.

Jemmy knew Charlotte had been abducted again, but he was on the back of the coach. That would not bring help. The question was, did anyone else know?

With luck, Burt—she remembered the villain from the last time she was abducted—would stop at the Dove. Then she would be rescued when Constantine and her cousin arrived.

Glancing out the window, she was just in time to see them pass the inn. So much for that idea.

Blast! She really must learn some better oaths. They would be useful in times like this.

Constantine will find me.

The thought came to her, filling her with calm. He loved her, and he would never allow anything to harm her. Yet, how long would it be before he discovered she had been kidnapped and where she was being taken? Yes, he would be looking for her, but she had better try to help herself as well.

Sometime later, the coach dipped, as if the wheels had gone into a hole, it came to a stop, and the door opened.

"Ye won't get away from me this time, my lady." Burt grabbed her arm, his fingers digging into her flesh, and dragged her roughly out of the coach. "Ain't no fine nobs to help ye here."

Charlotte wanted to tell him that he'd be dead or in prison as soon as her betrothed found her. But there was no point in putting him on his guard. Instead she kept her mouth shut, straightened her shoulders, and gave him her best Lady Bellamny you-are-dirt-under-my-feet look.

"Ye won't be so high and mighty when that gent comes for ye." He sneered.

Bile threatened to choke her, but she refused to allow him to see her fear. Constantine was right. It was not revenge. Someone had paid to have her abducted. But who?

She gave herself an inner shake, not difficult at all considering she was being dragged by a brute into an inn that was sure to have all sorts of vermin in it.

Still, she had the strong feeling that he was not far behind. Maybe if she dug her feet into the ground and made it hard to manhandle her she could gain some time.

She studied her surroundings. They were only about four miles from the Dove. The Richmond Road was visible through the trees. A sign hanging crookedly off the building proclaimed it to be the Dirty Duck. Well, it certainly lived up to its name. The tavern was painted a dingy white. The roof tilted to one side, as if part of the building was sinking.

"Come on." Burt jerked her arm.

Charlotte grabbed her skirts, lifting them to keep them out of the mud puddles that covered the yard. He led her around to the side of the building, drew out a key, opened a door, and pulled her through.

The room was surprisingly well appointed and clean. Almost as if it was part of a different building. A desk stood at one end of the room just off-center of a window. Irrationally, Charlotte wanted to move the furniture so it sat in the center of the wall. There was a square table with four chairs. A sideboard held decanters. One of which had to be brandy, she was sure. There were several sash windows: three were on the same side as the door and two overlooked the yard. Another door looked to be an entrance to the tavern, and a third was at the back of the room.

If he left her alone here, it would not be at all hard to escape. Provided the windows opened, that is.

He yanked her arm again and towed her to the back of the room, shoving her into a small chamber. Complete with a bed. The only window had iron bars on it. This was not good at all.

She whirled around in time to see the door slam shut and hear the lock click.

Well, at least she was alone. Going to the door, she pressed her ear to it. There was no sound at all. Did that mean the blackguard wasn't in the room? She did the same to the wall with the tavern, and faint voices filtered through.

There was only one thing to do: try to open the door. Charlotte drew two pins from her hair, and began to work on the lock. After a few moments, it was clear that the lock hadn't been attended to in a while, and her oil can was in the basket. She would have to think of another means of escape, but what?

A bed took up most of the small space. Pristine linen sheets covered the mattress. Satisfied there were no vermin, she began to sit, but stopped. The sheets were too clean for her comfort. She could not quite put her finger on why that bothered her, yet it did.

She and Constantine had wondered where Miss Betsy delivered her victims. This must be one of the places. Charlotte wiped her suddenly damp hands down her skirts. No matter what happened, she would not allow herself to be frightened.

That blackguard Burt had said a gentleman was coming for her. Did Miss Betsy encourage the men to rape their captives before they left? Did she make sure the sheets were clean because of the gentlemen? Charlotte glanced at the bed again and shivered. It was the only reason she could think of for the presence of a bed. She tried not to shudder again or think about the horrors this room had seen.

As she paced the room—refusing to sit on the bed—she tripped and almost fell over a small wooden stool. It had four legs with wood spokes, or whatever they were called, between the legs. Charlotte lifted it up to get a feel for the balance. Although not large, it was well made and sturdy. She practiced swinging it side to side, then down and back up again. After a few moments, she smiled to herself. The stool would do nicely. No matter how she hit whoever entered the room, she was sure to do some damage. The only question now was who to use it on.

The sound of a pair of horses coming to a halt could be heard from the front. A door opened and banged shut. She clung to the stool, glad she had found a weapon.

A woman's voice floated through the air, yet Charlotte could not understand what the female had said.

"Ma'am," a man answered.

"That is Burt," she murmured to herself. The woman had to be Miss Betsy.

Charlotte put the stool down and stood in front of it, hoping her skirts would hide it.

A door near her, probably to the parlor, opened and closed. "Well done," Miss Betsy said as she opened the door to the bedchamber. "Go to the Dove and collect the other package. Our first customer should be here soon."

"Package? Customer?" Rage coursed through Charlotte as she thought of all the lives this villain had destroyed. "Is that all people are to you? Do you not care who you harm?"

"I provide a service," Miss Betsy replied in a composed voice, then shrugged. "What goes on afterward is none of my concern."

Before Charlotte could grab the stool and bash the miscreant over the head, Miss Betsy closed the door. Soon the jangle of a harness interrupted the silence.

There was the sound of metal clinking, most likely the payment being made, and the door to the bedchamber opened a crack. "When you're done, leave through the side door. No one will see you."

"You think of everything." The man entered the room, and Miss Betsy pulled the door shut. "There is no one to rescue you now, my dear," Lord Ruffington said. "Your brother will have to agree to our marriage."

Good Lord! *Ruffington?* Charlotte barely knew him. In fact, she did not think she had even danced with the man or been introduced to him. He always seemed to be just outside her circle.

Straightening her spine, she raised one brow. "Lord Kenilworth, however, will not."

"Do you truly think he'll want you after I'm done with you?" He looked at the bed. "I was going to wait, but it might be easier to simply take you here."

Ruffington sauntered forward unbuttoning his falls, then stopped and glanced down as if he was having trouble with one. Charlotte lifted the stool and smashed it as hard as she could on his head.

He fell to his knees, hitting his forehead on the bed frame. "Bloody bitch," he roared as he tried to stand. "You'll pay for that."

A wheel hit the rutted road, causing Con to lurch to one side.

Bloody hell! He'd have to slow down. Where the devil was the damn place? Less than a second later a large, grubby building with a sign hanging crookedly from a wooden arm appeared. A coach stood in the yard, horses still hitched.

He had to find Charlotte. Pray God he was in time.

Movement from one side of the inn caught the corner of his eye as a gentleman entered a side door. Stopping his phaeton to one side of the yard, he jumped down and dashed to the side, ducking so that he couldn't be seen from the windows.

"Bloody bitch!" a man roared. "You'll pay for that."

Every muscle and sinew was alive and ready to do battle as he jerked the door on the side of the building open, ran to the door at the end of the room, and kicked it in.

Clutching a stool over her head, Charlotte stood like a Valkyrie. Ruffington—the bloody cur—had blood running from a gash in his head as he rose.

Con grabbed the cur by his cravat. Someone was going to pay dearly, but not his love. "This is for insulting my betrothed," he growled as he drove his fist into Ruffington's nose. The sound of bone crunching made Con grin. Blood flowed down the blackguard's face onto his neckcloth as the man lurched backward. "And this is for even thinking of dishonoring her." Still holding the neckcloth, Con rammed his fist into the villain's jaw. Ruffington slithered to the floor, unconscious. "It's too bad I didn't kill him." Con had wanted to. He reached for Charlotte, pulling her to his side. "Are you all right? I was so afraid I wouldn't arrive before—"

"Yes, yes, I'm fine." She had thrown her arms around his neck, but let go. "I cannot believe he—he—" She reared back and kicked Ruffington hard in his ribs. "I wish you had killed him as well. The scoundrel! What are we going to do about him?"

"I'm not sure yet." Bringing a criminal case against Ruffington in the House of Lords was not an option. That would only serve to ruin Charlotte. "I'll think of some fitting punishment." Con wanted to hold her again, but they had to escape before anyone found them. "We must get him out of here. We do not know when that villainess will arrive with Miss Cloverly."

"She left not long ago," Charlotte said.

Con opened the side door. Merton's men had arrived and were ready to help. He pointed to the bedchamber. "Get the man in there, bind him, and put him in his coach."

Turning to take Charlotte's hand, he almost bumped into her. "Let's go."

"Should we not wait to see it through?"

Naturally, she would not want to leave immediately. He'd been foolish for even thinking she would. "If you wish, but not in here."

"No." She shivered, as if the horror of the morning was catching up to her.

He heaved a sigh. "Better yet, hide his coach and put him over by my phaeton. That way we can keep an eye on him."

"Yes, my lord."

Charlotte and Con stood outside as Ruffington was carried out to the trees, dumped on the ground, tied up, and gagged with his own bloody cravat.

"We've got him trussed all right and tight, my lord," said the same outrider who had found the hedge tavern.

"What is your name?" Con asked.

"Jeffers, my lord." He was a good man. Con was bound to require outriders to protect Charlotte. Perhaps Merton would be willing to let the servant go.

"We have to find some way to keep Miss Cloverly safe," Charlotte said. "Could you go back to the room and stay there until we ensure she is safe?"

Con hesitated. He would much rather remain with Charlotte and keep her safe. For a moment he thought of ordering one of the other servants to man the room, but if one of them struck a peer, or even the son of a peer, they could be in a great deal of trouble.

"We shall take good care of her ladyship," Jeffers said.

"Very well." Con escorted Charlotte to where his phaeton was hidden. "If you are in any danger, do not wait for me. Just go. I'll find my own way back." He glanced around. "Where is Jemmy?"

"Right here, sir." The boy popped up from behind the carriage.

"You stay with Lady Charlotte."

The lad grinned. "I'll protect her, my lord."

Con ruffled the child's hair. "I know you will. By the by, when all this is over, we must have a discussion about you jumping onto the back of coaches." Jemmy opened his mouth, but Con said sternly, "There is no time to talk about it now."

The boy's face fell. "Yes, sir."

Striding back to the tavern, he remembered the woman from this morning.

Blast it all. He'd forgotten to tell Charlotte about the older lady who had been asking about Jemmy. Con hoped the woman would turn out to be Jemmy's relation. Con was growing fond of him, but Charlotte would be glad that the lad had found his family. If that was indeed the case. He couldn't think of another reason the woman would ask about the lad.

Meanwhile, back at the Star and Garter . . .

Matt rode into the yard just ahead of his coach. Several servants in Merton's livery were mounted on horses, ready to go. He had been satisfied to leave this mess to his cousin and Kenilworth, and would have if his unexpected guest had not arrived.

A moment later, Matt spotted Merton being harangued by an older woman. What the deuce was going on?

"Madam, I shall explain everything later," Merton said in a haughty tone Matt hadn't heard him use since he'd married Dotty. "At the moment, I have an urgent task to which I must attend."

"I demand—" The woman started to reach out.

"Come with me." Dotty took the woman by the arm. "I shall explain everything, but my husband must leave immediately."

Merton blew out an audible breath. "Worthington, what are you doing here?"

"Trying to find out what the devil is going on." He'd had a long morning thus far and it wasn't even eight o'clock.

"I wrote you," his cousin said in an offended tone, as if that explained everything.

"I received the letter, but Grace was concerned, and"—Matt pointed to his coach—"Miss Cloverly's betrothed arrived."

Merton swung up onto his horse. "We do not have time for introductions at the moment. I suppose you will want to come along?"

Matt nodded, as if there was any real choice in the matter.

"Then let's go." Merton's coach started forward as they rode out of the yard. "I doubt you'll need your carriage. I have mine."

"I'll explain later," Matt said as Merton urged his roan gelding into a gallop, and Matt could do nothing more than follow. A few moments later, he caught up to his cousin. "Do you know, Dominic," Matt shouted over the sound of the hooves, "you have only yourself to blame for my arrival. The letter you wrote was terse at best and largely uninformative. Grace was not at all happy."

"I can be trusted to take care of this matter," he grumbled, slowing to a canter.

Matt slowed to match Merton's pace. "I'm sure you can be, but she figured out that this was no longer a matter of simply rescuing Miss Cloverly, and she became concerned. Then, early this morning, Ben Mitchell, the young woman's betrothed, arrived with my neighbor, Lord Wharton."

Merton closed his eyes for a second. "I suppose you had to bring him?"

"You know as well as I do there was no choice. Would you remain behind if Dotty was in trouble?"

"No, of course not."

That was exactly what Matt expected his cousin to say. "This man might not be gentry, but he is no less concerned about his betrothed. By the by, where is Kenilworth?" Matt had known Kenilworth for years. It didn't make sense that he wasn't present. "I can't imagine he wouldn't be involved in this."

"Going after Charlotte." His cousin's jaw tightened. "She was abducted this morning while walking her cat. There is nothing to worry about. I sent four men with him."

Bloody hell. "How in Perdition did that happen?"

Before his cousin could respond, a servant in livery, turned his horse to ride next to them. "My lord. I have a message from Lord Kenilworth. He said to tell you all is well and he will remain at the hedge tavern."

Thank the Lord Charlotte was safe. Grace would have murdered him if anything had happened to her sister. But what the devil were they doing at a hedge tavern?

"Good," Dominic said. They had reached the Dove, and his gaze scanned the inn's yard. "We're in time." The Merton coach rolled to the back of the Dove, and, once again, Matt wondered what was happening. His cousin turned to one of his outriders. "Hide our horses and Lord Worthington's coach. Bring Mr. Mitchell in through the back." Dominic glanced at Matt. "As soon as we're in place, I'll explain everything to you and Mitchell."

"Very well." After all, there was no other response. They could not sit around the yard discussing the matter.

His cousin turned to the servant. "Jeffers, come to me when you're done."

"Yes, my lord."

The innkeeper met them at the door. "Everything is ready, me lord. Me wife is taking Miss Cloverly to the room."

"Thank you. Worthington, this is Mr. Crowe. We explained the situation to him and his wife yesterday. They have been very helpful."

"Good morning." Matt inclined his head. "And thank you."

"Good morn to ye, me lord." The innkeeper grimaced.

"Will we have to tie Miss up again? Don't sit right with me rib."

"No," Dominic assured the landlord. "Miss Betsy won't know she was bound."

Mr. Crowe led them to a room at the top of the stairs. "It's not as nice as the one Lord and Lady Kenilworth had yesterday, but I thought it might be better for what we're doin'."

Lord and Lady Kenilworth?

Chapter Twenty-Seven

Someone had a great deal of explaining to do if Charlotte and Kenilworth were going around the country pretending to be married. Matt wondered just how long it would take to discover the entire story. He had half a mind to simply take his sister back to Town and demand Kenilworth marry her immediately.

"Excellent." Merton clasped Mr. Crowe's shoulder. "Her betrothed, Mr. Mitchell, is with us as well. We instructed him to go around to the back of the inn with Lord Worthington's coach. Send him to my chamber as soon as you can. I also imagine he will wish to ascertain that Miss Cloverly is safe."

"I'll tell him, me lord." Crowe bowed to Merton, then to Matt.

"He seems like a good man." Matt watched the innkeeper move swiftly down the corridor.

"He and his wife are both good people," Merton said. "It was Charlotte's idea to recruit them. They were shocked at how they had been duped."

"I imagine they would be." Duped? Matt was confused by his cousin's statement, and it occurred to him that neither he nor Grace had asked Charlotte for all the details surrounding her abduction, and she had not volunteered the information.

Apparently, she had discovered much more about Miss Betsy's operation than she'd let on. Then again, they hadn't asked her exactly what had occurred. Not only that, but Charlotte had been dealing with an unwanted betrothal to Kenilworth at the time.

At least that seemed to have changed. As soon as he returned home, Matt would secure a special license and see the two wed.

A few minutes later, the small room seemed even smaller. Ben Mitchell was a tall, strapping fellow, with brown eyes and blond hair just a shade darker than his intended's.

"I was able to see Miss Cloverly." Mitchell's brows lowered in a slightly menacing fashion. "She just hugged me, told me she'd be fine, and pushed me out the door. Are you sure she'll be all right?"

Dominic nodded. "She will be guarded the entire way." He motioned to Jeffers. "I take it there was more to tell me."

"Yes, my lord. They're at a hedge tavern called the Dirty Duck. Her ladyship managed to hit the blackguard over the head with a stool and his lordship finished him off, so to speak. They—"

"Why did they not return with you or go to the Star and Garter?"

"Worthington," his cousin said in a tone designed to depress questions, "allow him to finish. We don't have much time before the bawd arrives. I shall explain the entire plan when he's done."

"There's another man that needs to be arrested. If you don't mind, my lords, I should get back in case they need any help."

Dominic nodded. Once Jeffers was gone he turned to

Matt. "Yesterday we, all of us including Miss Cloverly, decided that the only way to put an end to Miss Betsy's villainy was to catch her in the act. Merely rescuing the women wouldn't be enough to hang her." Glancing at Mitchell, Dominic continued. "We gave Miss Cloverly the choice of not being involved, but she agreed to help, as long as we could keep her safe. I promise you, she shall come to no harm."

"That doesn't surprise me." Mitchell's mouth tightened. "She's as brave as they come." He shook his head. "What I don't understand is why her?"

"What we have ascertained," Dominic said, "is that the woman, Miss Betsy, is a procuress. In other words, she is hired by men who want a certain female."

Or child. Matt's stomach turned when he remembered what Charlotte had said.

Mitchell's face turned murderous, and Matt couldn't blame the man. "What about the men who hired her?"

"We'll capture them as well." Merton's voice was as grim as Matt had ever heard it. "Naturally, a trial is out of the question. The only thing it would achieve is to give grist to the gossips." *And ruin Charlotte's reputation*, Matt thought. "However, there are other ways to get rid of the scoundrels."

"I don't normally agree with handling crimes outside of the court." Mitchell glanced at Merton and Matt. "But I also don't want Miss Cloverly to have to testify in court. So, you do as you please."

"It will be much easier for everyone if this remains among us." When Matt had agreed to bring Mitchell with him, he'd forgot about the middling class's objections to aristocratic privilege. Matt was about to ask again how Charlotte had been kidnapped, when a knock sounded on the door.

"My lords, sir, a coach is coming into the yard."

A few moments later, a loud male voice boomed from below. "Where are the others?"

"Don't know, sir," the landlord said. "I ain't seen them since last night. Went to another inn drinking, they did."

"Useless. That's what they are. I told her not to keep them on. Where's the woman?"

Heavy steps landed on the stairs. There was the sound of a door being unlocked, and a pair of lighter feet pattered on the treads. As soon as the front door opened, Dominic, Mitchell, and Matt ran down the stairs. By the time Dominic and Matt had remounted, all they could see was the back of a black coach. He could only trust that Mitchell would keep his head about him.

Back at the Dirty Duck

Charlotte watched as Constantine strode back inside the parlor. It seemed that no one was going to relock the door, but as soon as he was in the bedchamber, Miss Betsy strolled by the windows. Well, damnation! He thought she'd left. The bawd must have just gone somewhere else in the inn.

Grabbing her pistol from the basket Constantine had brought, Charlotte climbed down from the carriage and ran as silently as she could to the bedroom window. Standing on her tiptoes she could just barely see inside. Constantine flattened himself against the wall, and the door opened slightly. Miss Betsy stepped in, looked at the bed, and left. Breathing a sigh of relief that the door blocked the window when it was open, Charlotte crept to the nearest parlor window. The villainess was gone, and their scheme was still secure. She returned to the bedchamber window to look in on him again through the open window.

"I appreciate your concern, my love." Con's low, rough voice caused shivers of pleasure to ripple through her. "But you'd better get back to the phaeton before Miss Cloverly arrives."

"I shall." Charlotte kissed her fingers and reached up to touch his hand. "For luck."

"I would be much happier if I could just take you home," he grumbled.

If she had her way, she would be in the room with him. At the moment, he was the one in danger. "As would I, but we must think of the people she has harmed, and those she would harm in the future if we do not stop her."

"I cannot believe I am so fortunate as to be marrying you." His face took on a chagrinned look. "I didn't make it easy."

"I did not help." Despite their horrible beginnings, he was the perfect gentleman for her. He never treated her as if she was less capable or intelligent. "I love you."

"I love you too. Now go."

"My lady," one of the Merton servants said, "a carriage just turned off the main road."

"Thank you." It was time to hide again. Fortunately, the trees weren't far.

She reached the carriage just before the plain black coach drove into the yard. If events proceeded as before, it would not be long before they would have Miss Betsy and her accomplice in hand.

Charlotte heard a muffled groan, and glanced at Ruffington. His eyes were still closed and one of the ropes binding him was also secured to a tree.

"I think he's waking up, my lady." Jemmy had come up next to her. "We could hit him over his head again."

Charlotte considered his suggestion. The man was tied up like a hog, and gagged as well. He really couldn't cause any problems. Still . . . she picked up a thick stick. His eyes opened and the idiot had the gall to leer at her. Any sympathy she might have had for the rogue fled, and she smashed the wood down on his head, knocking him out again. That would teach him to have ladies abducted.

"Charlotte." She jumped and was sure her heart had stopped.

"Matt. What are you doing here?"

He glanced at Ruffington. "Being superfluous, it appears. I'd ask how you're doing, but you seem to have everything in hand."

"Yes." She gave her brother a brief hug before turning her attention back to the side of the tavern.

"What exactly is going on? Merton mentioned a plan, but the events have been unfolding so quickly, I have not yet had the full story."

"Thus far, our plan to capture Miss Betsy is succeeding. Kenilworth is inside. He arrived—in time." She did not dare tell Matt what a close call that had been. "I hit Ruffington over the head, and Kenilworth broke his nose, and then Merton's men carried him out and tied him up."

"I take it that is Ruffington?" Matt asked in an equable tone. "It's hard to tell."

"It is. He hired Miss Betsy to abduct me." Charlotte was surprised her brother was not more upset about her being here.

"Have you decided what you are going to do with him?" Matt seemed almost too calm. Just like Constantine had been, just before he'd grabbed the scoundrel's neckcloth and pummeled him.

"Not yet." Charlotte glanced at the side of the tavern just in time to see Miss Cloverly being taken through the door. "As soon as the man who wants Miss Cloverly arrives, we will capture him as well. The decision will wait until then. Where is Merton?"

"I may have some ideas as to what to do with them." Matt looked at Ruffington once again. "Merton is hiding closer to the front of the tavern. Is it safe to get closer?"

"As soon as the other cur arrives we can listen from under the windows. As you can see they are well above the ground. She took Ruffington through the inn, but I do not know if that is what she always does."

"Charlotte," Matt said in the same calm tone that was beginning to unnerve her, "is there a reason Mr. Crowe referred to you as Lady Kenilworth?"

"Oh, that." Heat began to creep up her neck into her face. She really had not thought she would have to explain that. Then again, she hadn't thought Matt would be here.

"Yes, that." Matt waited wordlessly.

"Well . . . you see . . ." She glanced at him, but his face was like a mask. This was not going to be good. "When . . . um . . . when Constantine, I mean Kenilworth and I arrived at the Dove yesterday, we had to put on an act in order to get to Miss Cloverly." Charlotte's throat was suddenly dry. Maybe if she said the rest quickly, he wouldn't notice it as much. "The inn only had one large room and we took it. Then Dotty and Merton arrived, and we all spoke with Mr. and Mrs. Crowe, and it just happened." Charlotte slid another look at him and his expression hadn't changed. "We shall marry next week." Thankfully, the sound of a carriage reached her. "Ah, the other man has arrived."

"Do not think this has saved you," Matt warned. "We shall finish discussing this later."

She let out a breath. This must have been how Louisa felt after she'd had to admit to Matt the reason she had declared her betrothal to Rothwell. At least Charlotte would have Constantine, Dotty, and Merton on her side.

The door to the inn slammed shut. "Come, we may move closer now."

They reached the windows just as Miss Betsy and the man entered the parlor.

"I shall wish to see her before I pay you." Charlotte did not recognize his voice at all, yet next to her Matt tensed.

"Naturally." As before, the door to the bedchamber opened briefly.

"She is as lovely as I was told," the man said in a pleased voice.

"You mean you have never seen her?" Miss Betsy sounded surprised.

"No, I was told about her and could not resist. Here is your payment."

"You have no more than an hour before the inn's regular customers begin arriving," Miss Betsy said. "I suggest that you use the side door to depart. You would not wish to lose the woman or your purse."

"I shall take your advice. Good day, madam."

"Good day, sir."

The rogue opened the door to the bedchamber. "You are beautiful. I predict we shall have a great deal of fun together."

Miss Cloverly shook her head. "I don't understand. Who are you?"

"The name is Corning. I'm a friend of Gerald Smithton."

"Lord Wharton's nephew?" she asked in an astonished tone. "What has he to do with this?"

"He could not afford you. The procuress's price was too high. You see, once his uncle had a son, his allowance was reduced. When I'm done with you, I'll ask if he is still interested. It seems only fair."

Her complexion paled, and Charlotte was concerned the woman might faint. Instead Miss Cloverly clenched her fists. "You are vile and disgusting. You shall not touch me. Ever."

"Oh, I shall do more than touch you, my dear. I plan to use you very well indeed."

As he sauntered into the room, Constantine kicked the door shut, and his fist plowed into Corning's face.

"That should take care of him for a while," Constantine said, heading to the side door.

A furious female scream came from the front of the inn, as well as the sound of fighting. A second later, a man Charlotte didn't know raced into the parlor.

"That's Miss Cloverly's betrothed," Matt whispered.

"Ben." The handsomest man in Luton. Charlotte grinned to herself.

"Nell?"

"Here! Oh, Ben." Miss Cloverly threw herself into his arms. "I'm so glad you've come. He was horrible. Even though I knew his lordship's men were all around, I was afraid."

Ben stroked her back, calming her. "Everything is fine now, and think of the other women you've saved."

"I know. I couldn't have done otherwise, but I'm so glad it's over."

From the corner of her eye, Charlotte saw Corning begin to rise. "Behind you!"

Ben whirled around and drove his right fist into Corning's stomach first, then his left fist into the man's face. The scoundrel fell to the floor, blood spattered over his face.

Before he could try to rise, Merton grabbed the rogue and took him outside.

Constantine stepped outside and wrapped his arms around Charlotte. "I cannot tell you how happy I am this part is over."

"I am too, but why did you not strike him over the head?"

He barked a laugh. "Jeffers told me Mr. Mitchell was here. I assumed he'd want a chance to avenge his betrothed."

"Right you are, my lord." Ben chuckled as he joined them, his arm possessively around Miss Cloverly's shoulders. "I would have been put out if I had been denied that opportunity." He drew her closer to him. "It's time we returned to Luton, right, my love? Lord Worthington has offered us the use of his coach and driver."

She had a misty smile on her face. "I cannot wait to be home again." She glanced at Charlotte. "You will rescue the other woman you heard about, my lady?"

"Yes, we will. Mr. and Mrs. Crowe are not expecting anyone else, but I believe I know where she will be taken." As long as Matt didn't attempt to stop her, she'd be right there with Constantine, seeing that this ended. Yet considering that the Hare and Hound's innkeeper and his wife might have bad memories of them, they had better take Dotty and Merton as well.

Once Miss Cloverly and her betrothed headed to the coach, Matt turned to Constantine and Charlotte. "As soon as we return to Richmond, we are going to have a talk about the way in which the two of you have been presenting yourselves."

"Of course," he replied, not acting at all intimidated by her brother.

Matt strode off toward one of the outriders, and Constantine glanced at her. "What was that about? He looked as if he'd like to string me up."

"He found out that we allowed the Crowes to believe we were already married."

He was silent for a few moments, then shrugged. "We shall be wed as soon as he likes."

Charlotte's heart filled with love and joy. She could not imagine being any happier than she was right now. Matt had managed to daunt Louisa's Rothwell, and to some extent Merton before he and Dotty wed, but Constantine seemed immune to her brother's wrath. Charlotte could do nothing other than be as sure of herself and their love as he was of himself.

Chapter Twenty-Eight

Charlotte and Constantine were halfway to his phaeton when a shot rang out.

"What the devil?" He lifted her into his arms, carrying her to his carriage.

"It's from the front of the inn," she said. "I hope it isn't Merton."

"You two stay there," Matt called to them. Lengthening his stride, he headed to the road. "I'll find out what's going on."

A few moments later, Jemmy came running full tilt from the front of the inn. "My lord, that woman is dead and the man that kidnapped Lady Charlotte disappeared."

"What happened?" Charlotte asked, trying not to fall onto the bench seat.

"Somehow she got a gun. One of the outriders was trying to take it away from her, and it went off. Right into her chest. There was blood everywhere, and Lord Worthington said she were dead."

"Oh, my God." Charlotte felt a little faint. She was very glad Matt had ordered them to stay with the phaeton. "I suppose she knew she wouldn't get away this time."

Constantine picked Jemmy up and put him on the back

of the carriage before climbing in himself. "Jemmy, how much did you see?"

"Not much. The footmen wouldn't let me look, they just told me what happened."

"Thank God for that." Constantine closed his eyes for a moment. "We're going back to Richmond. Merton and Worthington can handle the rest of this. I want you and Jemmy out of here before anyone sees you."

Charlotte slipped her arm around Constantine. "We should stop at the Dove and tell the Crowes the matter is settled."

He glanced back at the boy, who was still trying to get a look at what was going on, and whispered, "When I left Richmond this morning, a lady was asking about him."

Her heart began to beat a little faster. "Do you think . . . ?"

"I believe it is a decided possibility, but we won't know until we can get the two of them together."

She sent a fervent prayer to the Deity that Jemmy had found his family. "What will happen to the gentlemen?" Using the term with regard to the scoundrels who had paid Miss Betsy left a bad taste in Charlotte's mouth, even if they did deserve the title by birth.

Before they could start off, Matt signaled to Constantine. He handed her the ribbons. "I'll be right back. Keep Jemmy here." A few moments later her betrothed returned. "Worthington knows a sea captain who will ensure the curs are occupied for a very long time."

"Good. After what they did, I hope they never return."

"If they know what's good for them, they'll never grace England's shores again."

It appeared that almost everything was settled, except for . . . "What happened to the money she was paid?"

"Lord Merton has it, my lady," Jemmy said. "He said it will be used to help her victims. Does that mean the people she hurt?"

"That's exactly what it means." Wanting the solid feel of Constantine, Charlotte leaned against him until they reached the main road. "Jemmy, when we get back to the Star and Garter, I want you to go straight up to May and tell her you need a bath and clean clothes."

"Do I have to? I took a bath the other day." Charlotte tried not to grin. She would never understand why young boys did not like to bathe. "Be that as it may, yes, you have to."

They stopped at the Dove. As soon as they drew up into the yard, Mr. and Mrs. Crowe came out to greet them.

Constantine told them what had occurred, including the deaths.

"It's hard to believe I was so taken in," Mrs. Crowe said. "She was so pretty and refined."

"I think it is always hard to believe the worst of people." Charlotte patted the woman's shoulder. "From what I understand, you were not the only ones she deceived."

"All's well that ends well. That's what I say." Mr. Crowe stepped away from the carriage. "Thank you for what ye done, me lord and lady. Ain't many as would do what ye did."

"And thank you for your help," Constantine replied.

Less than twenty minutes later they pulled into the yard of the Star and Garter. Jemmy jumped down and ran inside.

"Despite what he said, he looked eager for a bath."

"I do think he enjoys it more than he lets on." Charlotte laughed. "My brothers are the same."

"My mother will tell you that young boys are heathens, and she only had me." An ostler came out to take the horses. "Well, my lady, let's find out if Jemmy has a new family."

"Yes, let's." She smiled as he came around to her side of the carriage.

Constantine lifted her down from the phaeton, lowering her slowly to the ground. "I have a feeling Worthington will try to make you return to Town with him."

"I won't, even if he orders me. We are to be married next week at the latest. He can be very intimidating. Yet, for good or ill, he doesn't have the same type of power over me that he did over Louisa. If he pushes me, he will discover just how determined Carpenter ladies can be." Constantine raised a dubious brow. "Aside from that, he wants this marriage. Dotty and Merton must accompany us in any event. I do not think either the innkeeper of the Hare and Hound or his wife will remember us fondly."

"Not after the way we tied up their daughter," Con mumbled.

"Precisely why we need them with us." Charlotte tried to suppress a giggle and couldn't. "Merton is so very good at being a marquis."

Her betrothed turned an outraged face to her. "Are you saying that I do not present the proper countenance for a marquis? I will have you know, my lady, that my title is older than his by at least fifty years."

She went off into a peal of laughter. "Oh, no, my love. It's just that he used to be so pretentious. Did you not know him then?"

"Not well," he grumbled. "I do recall something about him being stuffy."

"He was so puffed up in his own consequence that the younger children, Theo especially, used to call him His Marquisship."

"That *is* bad." Constantine's face was still all lean, hard planes, but his eyes twinkled and the corner of one lip trembled. "I see your point."

She tucked her hand in the crook of his arm. "I can't wait to hear what Dotty has to say about Jemmy. And I am sure she will have the whole story out of us before my cousin returns."

Con left Charlotte at the door to the parlor, and he went

to his chambers to wash his face and hands, and get one small item he had not yet given her.

Once he had washed and changed his cravat, he called for his valet.

"My lord?"

"Bring me my jewel box." His mother had given him three rings before they'd left Hillstone Manor. At the time, neither of them knew Charlotte well enough to guess what her tastes were. Now he knew that he would let her pick her own ring.

Cunningham placed the box on the dresser and opened it. "Which of them will you give to Lady Charlotte, my lord?"

"She shall decide." Con picked out the rings. Each one had different stones and were from different centuries. The newest being scarcely a hundred years old.

"A wise decision, my lord." His valet closed the box and took it away.

Holding the rings in his hand, he knocked before opening the door between their chambers. "Charlotte?"

Her maid finished tying a green ribbon in her mistress's hair, and giggled. Charlotte had changed from her carriage gown into a frothy confection of yellow muslin trimmed with green grosgrain ribbon.

She met his eyes in the mirror and smiled. "You may go, May."

The servant bobbed a curtsey, and disappeared through a door Con hadn't noticed before.

"Forgive me, my love. I did not even think of your maid being present. Will she make problems for you?" he asked, thinking the girl might tell Worthington that he'd come into her bedchamber. Worthington was already unhappy with them.

"No, she has been with me for years. I told her we are

going to marry, and she is ecstatic." Con stood behind Charlotte, his hands resting on her shoulders. He didn't dare touch more of her for fear he would not be able to stop before she looked thoroughly kissed. Her slim hand came up and covered one of his. "Not to mention that ever since Dotty and Merton married, my maid has wished for me to wed as well."

Con didn't understand. His friends' weddings had not prompted a desire in his valet for him to join their new state. "Why is that?"

Charlotte laughed. "Dotty's maid and my maid, May, are best of friends, but also rivals in a way. Now May will also be lady's maid to a marchioness."

"Ah, I understand." Affecting a calm he did not feel, he leaned over, opened his hand, and spilled the rings onto her dressing table. "Speaking of marriages. My mother gave me these. Rather than choosing one for you, I decided you should pick the one you like best."

She cast him the most brilliant smile he had seen yet. "They are all beautiful." Her index finger fluttered over the jewels as she studied each ring. Finally, her finger hovered over a figured gold band set with a large emerald and flanked on each side by opals. "This one I believe. Green is my favorite color and my birthday is in October."

Picking up the other two rings, he placed them in his waistcoat pocket. He took the one she had selected and held her hand as he slipped the ring on her hand. "It's perfect on you."

Forgetting his resolve, Con lowered his mouth to hers, slipping his tongue along the seam of her deep-pink lips. Charlotte opened, touching her tongue to his, as he tilted his head, wanting more, wanting to be closer to her. "I want to be with you more than I can say."

His hands started to trail down her shoulders and arms, and her fingers roamed his back.

"Where is Charlotte?" Worthington's deep voice seemed to bounce off the walls.

"Go." She pushed Con through the door to his room. "I shall meet you in the parlor. Jemmy should be there soon. May said he was with Merton's valet, dressing.

"I'll be out in a moment, Matt." Charlotte blew Con a kiss as he strode through the door.

A minute or so later when he strolled into the parlor, Dotty was there along with Worthington, Charlotte, and Jemmy.

Worthington met Con's gaze. "I have told Charlotte that I want her to go back to Town with me. She has refused."

"She told me she would." He glanced at his betrothed and held her eyes with his. The warmth and love in her gaze told him everything he needed to know. Not bothering to look at his friend and future brother-in-law, he said, "If you would like, before we travel to the Hare and Hound, where she was held, we will stop by Doctors' Commons, where I shall obtain a marriage license. I am positive Lord and Lady Merton will agree to witness our vows."

"Only if you're attempting to get me murdered," Worthington scoffed. "Grace and the children, not to mention her aunt and uncle, would have my head if they were not present at Charlotte's wedding." Rising, he paced the room for a few moments. "Charlotte, does this mean that much to you?"

She kept her eyes on Con, but nodded. "Yes. I must see this through."

"Matt," Dotty said, "no one can object to all of us traveling together. And they are betrothed. If you go home and tell Grace to begin planning the wedding, she will ensure the entire *ton* knows about it."

"Lady Bellamny and Kenilworth's mother will be happy to help," Charlotte added. "Even those who traveled to Belgium will know before a week is out that we are marrying soon."

Worthington's gaze flicked from Charlotte to her friend as he appeared to consider their argument. "Very well." He took Charlotte's hand. "You are not as easy to intimidate as Louisa was. Then again, I had eighteen years to work on her." Charlotte flashed him a smile. "I shall have to trust that you know what you're doing."

She rose up on her toes and bussed his cheek. "You have been the best guardian a lady could ask for, and I thank you. But I shall take it from here." She smiled at him. "Grace will understand. I promise you."

"She had better," he muttered. "I do not like being in my wife's black book."

"Give her my love, and I'll see you soon."

Not more than five minutes after he left, a knock came on the door.

"Come," Dotty called.

A footman opened the door and a middle-aged lady dressed in dark gray bombazine sailed into the room.

"Lady Merton." The woman inclined her head.

That was interesting. She was either of the same rank as Dotty, or a higher rank. Con studied her carefully from her light brown hair, still free of gray, to her sharp blue-gray eyes that reminded him of . . . "Jemmy?"

"Yes, my lord." The lad stood from behind a sofa, and immediately went to Charlotte. What the devil had he been doing back there?

The older woman gasped, her hand going to her throat.

"My lady," Dotty said, "may I introduce Lady Charlotte Carpenter and her betrothed, the Marquis of Kenilworth. Lady Charlotte, Kenilworth, the Marchioness of Litchfield."

"Lady Merton told me how this child came to be with you. I commend you, Lady Charlotte, for rescuing him." Her lips formed a thin line. "There is only one way to know the truth. The boy must remove his clothing."

Jemmy grabbed Charlotte's hand. "I already had a bath."

She glanced down at him. "Yes, I know, sweetie." Addressing Lady Litchfield, she asked, "For what purpose?"

"If he is who I think he is"—oh good, they were all dancing around the issue—"he will have two birthmarks, one on his shoulder and the other on his thigh. They are both a brownish color."

"Rather than making Jemmy shed his clothing for a stranger—" She arched a regal brow. Lord, she'd make an excellent duchess, but Con wasn't giving her up, so she'd have to settle for being a mere marchioness. "—I suggest we call in my lady's maid. She has been in charge of his grooming and will be able to tell you if he has the birthmarks."

"A lady's maid?" Lady Litchfield said, doubtfully.

"Yes," Charlotte stated firmly. "She has a number of younger brothers and sisters, and has a way with children."

"Very well, call her in."

"Will you have a seat, my lady?" Dotty asked, ushering the woman to the sofa as she spoke.

After their visitor was seated, Dotty yanked the bell pull and one of Merton's numerous footmen appeared. "Tea, please."

He bowed, and was leaving the parlor as Charlotte's maid entered.

"You wanted me, my lady?" She bobbed a curtsey.

"I do. May, can you tell me if Jemmy has birthmarks? One on his shoulder and another on his thigh?"

"Yes, my lady. I mean he does. Brown they are, and in odd shapes. One looks like a horseshoe and the other like a bird's nest."

Charlotte glanced at Lady Litchfield. "Does that answer your question?"

"It does." She rose and looked at Charlotte. "I am sorry to have imposed upon you."

She and Dotty shared a crestfallen glance. It was a deuced good thing none of them had said anything to Jemmy.

"Can I change into my regular clothes now?" he asked.

"Charlotte gave him a quick hug. "Yes, you may."

The child ran out of the parlor, and Con wrapped his arms around her. "I'm sorry."

"As am I. With two birthmarks, I thought surely we had found his family." She blinked back tears, determined not to allow them to fall.

"Yes, indeed." Dotty stood next to her, and Charlotte hugged her friend. "It is their loss."

"He has a family. Us." Con's voice seemed gruffer even to him. It must be because he had come to care for the lad. "Forever or for as long as he needs us."

He would do his best to find the boy's family, but if he could not, he would raise the child with the ones he and Charlotte would have. Someone had to teach him not to jump on the back of carriages.

Chapter Twenty-Nine

An hour later, Merton finally arrived. "I saw Jemmy in the stables."

"The lady who stopped you thought he was related to her." Charlotte shook her head. "Apparently, she was mistaken."

Yet Constantine had been wonderful. She was so happy to know he wanted Jemmy with them.

"Well then." Merton cleared his throat. "I suggest we decide how we will handle the rest of this mess with that Betsy woman."

"Are the blackguards that hired Miss Betsy gone?" Con asked.

"Indeed. They were stripped of anything that could identify them and shipped off to the London docks. Apparently, Addison knows several ship captains and gave the names to Worthington. We need not worry about them again."

Dotty laid a hand on her husband's arm. "Are you sure, Dominic? What if they escape and return?"

His wicked grin surprised Charlotte. "I made it exceedingly clear to them that if Kenilworth, Worthington, or I ever saw them again, they were dead men."

"But if they disappear," Charlotte said, "will not someone start looking for them?"

"I did allow them to write letters to their men of business saying they would be out of the country for a time. That should take care of any problems. I understand that neither of them are what one would call well thought of."

"Ruffington is under the hatches," Constantine added. "It wouldn't surprise me if his creditors are after him."

"What about Miss Betsy? What does the magistrate intend to do about notifying her family, if she had any?"

"At the moment, it appears we are the only ones, other than Mr. and Mrs. Crowe, who know where she receives her mail," Merton said. "Once we have the information we're looking for, we shall notify the magistrate. The only miscreant missing is the one who got away."

The one who had abducted her twice, Charlotte thought. As to the others, it was really the only thing they could have done short of murdering the men outright. "I know it has already been a long day, but I propose we go to the White Swan in Twickenham after luncheon and ask for Mrs. Bottoms's direction. I can pretend to be an old friend of hers." She looked at Constantine for support. "At some point Sir John will remember that the Crowes were involved and ask for any information they have. I would rather use the information we have to find the other person Miss Betsy had kidnapped."

"I agree with Charlotte. According to Miss Betsy, there is another victim. If the woman is at the Hare and Hound, Sir John won't have jurisdiction, and we need to get her out of the way before the magistrate becomes involved," Constantine said. "The sooner we finish this, the better. Aside from that"—he grinned—"I have a wedding to attend."

"I agree," Dotty said.

"As you wish. I appropriated the key to her house,"

Merton said. "As well as the money that was exchanged today. We shall use anything of value we find to help her victims."

"We need to find them before we can rescue them," Constantine added in a grim tone.

Shortly after they dined, they drove the short distance to Twickenham.

The landlord of the White Swan believed Charlotte's story of being friends with Mrs. Bottoms and not only gave Charlotte the direction of the woman's house, but a letter for her as well.

Minutes later they found the small house. A red climbing rose draped gracefully over the front entrance that was covered by a porch with a peaked roof. The trim, painted white, was well maintained. On each side of the entrance was one window.

Merton knocked, as if expecting the house to be occupied. When no one answered, he used the key and opened the door. "Talk as if there is someone here. I do not wish to have to explain to her neighbors or the local watch, if there is one, why we are entering an empty house."

After he closed the door Charlotte took in the neat front hall, flanked by doors. Another door covered with green baize stood in a corner across from the entrance and off to the side. A staircase leading to a second level was situated directly across from the front door. Next to the stairs was a narrow corridor. The house was deeper than it appeared from the outside.

"I'll look for her desk," Dotty said, starting down the corridor.

Charlotte opened the letter the innkeeper had given her. "I was right. The next victim is already at the Hare and Hound." She glanced at Constantine. "Do you have any idea how far that is from here?"

"Unfortunately, I don't. I'm sure the Star and Garter will have a map we can look at."

"I found a pocketbook with entries dating back three months," Dotty said as she came bustling from the back of the house.

"That would be before we closed her brothel," Merton said.

"Indeed." Dotty's lips thinned. "She went from one business subjecting people, straight to another."

"May I see it?" Charlotte took the book from her friend. "Did you find ledgers or anything else that might help?"

"There are several ledgers as well as other documents. We should take them all."

"Yes, but how are we going to get them out of here?" Con pointed out, frowning. "It will appear strange if we stroll back to the coach carrying account books."

"She must have a bandbox or something we can use." Charlotte headed up the stairs with Con following close behind.

There were three rooms, all with their doors closed. She looked in them one by one. Two were devoid of furniture, but the third chamber contained a bed and clothes press. On top of the clothes press were several boxes.

"Allow me." Con plucked one of the bandboxes off the top. "This should be large enough."

She opened the box and took out a bonnet, placing it on the bed.

By the time they returned to the hall, Dotty and Merton had the ledgers ready to be packed. Less than fifteen minutes after they had arrived, they strolled out of the door, all of them pretending to wish the imaginary person in the house farewell.

"That was an interesting bit of playacting," Constantine

commented when they reached the coach. "One would think you had done it before."

Charlotte caught Dotty's eye and laughed.

"Pantomimes," they said at the same time.

Constantine's jaw dropped. "Christmas pantomimes?" Charlotte nodded. "I was never able to join in them," he said, "first, I was too young, and when I got older, my sisters were all out of the house."

"I've never even seen one," Merton groused.

"You shall this year," Dotty assured him.

"You as well," Charlotte said to Constantine. "It really is unfair that you were left out. In my family, the children joined in as soon as they could toddle around."

Charlotte linked her arm with Con's and he was glad to have her by his side. Christmas was only one of many changes about to take place in his life. He had a feeling the holidays would be spent with the Worthington family whenever possible.

Mentally, he counted up the number of people who would most likely be present, and decided to ask his steward if any of his properties were near her family's main estate. He thought there might be one. Still, Christmas was months away, and he had a young woman to rescue, and a wedding to get through first. Everything else would come later.

"May I look at the pocketbook?"

"Of course." Charlotte handed it to him.

He spent the rest of the ride back to Richmond reading over the entries. Almost immediately, he realized he knew several of the men who had tried to buy women. Worthington was right. Before Con met Charlotte, he'd been keeping low company. He must find a map and figure out the best way to travel to the Hare and Hound.

When they arrived back at the Star and Garter, a message from the magistrate awaited them.

Merton opened it up and read it, and growled. "Rubbishing commoner!"

"What does it say?" Charlotte asked.

Con plucked the paper from Merton's fingers and read it. "The long and short of it is that Sir John is of the opinion that the man who abducted Miss Cloverly and the coachman should be tried in London. He is having them moved to Newgate. Drat. I had hoped to have it finished here. It would have been much faster." Con read down a little further. "He is sending with them the statements Merton and I wrote."

"That is something, I suppose." Charlotte's nose wrinkled as it did when she was displeased. Con thought it was adorable. "Well, there is nothing we can do about that. I do have an idea for rescuing the last victim." He nodded. "I think Dotty and Merton should go in without us."

Her suggestion surprised him. It was true that, using her plan, there would be no need to explain Charlotte and Con's presence to the innkeeper, his wife, and their daughter. However, it also meant Dotty and Merton would have a more difficult time convincing the landlord that Miss Betsy had been a scoundrel. "My love, I loath saying this, but I find myself in disagreement with you. Who better to convince Mr. Wick and his family that Miss Betsy used them to perpetuate prostitution at best and slavery at worst, than you, who were abducted, and I, who rescued you?"

Charlotte's brows drew down and she pulled her bottom lip between her teeth. "Well, when you put it like that, I suppose you are right. It would not be fair to place the entire burden on Dotty and Merton."

"There's my brave lady," Con whispered in her ear.

"I still feel bad about tying the maid up."

"Ah, well, needs must. We did not have any choice that I could see."

On the way to their apartments, he had borrowed the landlord's map of Surrey and Kent. Rolling it out on the table, he pinned down the edges with candlesticks. He followed the route leaving London that the villains had used. *Blast and damnation*. He had missed a minor road leading to the post road to London.

"That's how I became disoriented," he murmured to himself.

"What is it?" Merton asked.

"Nothing. The inn is only about ten miles on the other side of Twickenham."

If he had known where he was, Con could easily have had Charlotte back in Mayfair shortly after dawn. Well, he damned sure wasn't going to tell her that now. Maybe in four or five years, after they had children and she might think it was a funny story. He just hoped she wouldn't figure it out for herself.

"That close?" his beloved exclaimed. "I would never have known. It took us hours to get there."

"It makes sense though," Dotty mused. "Miss Betsy would not have to travel far, but there is enough distance between the Crowes and the Wicks that they would not know each other."

Merton glanced at the maps and raised his brow.

Con quickly rolled them back up again. There was no point in tempting the Fates. "We could return here, or go to Hilltop Manor. That's a bit farther, but none of the servants would ask questions."

"There is no reason why we cannot bring the woman here," Merton said. "Once we discover where she lives, we can more easily return her from a busy town than from a country estate."

"If we depart early tomorrow morning, we can be on our way back to Town by tomorrow afternoon," Dotty added.

Charlotte looked up from the papers she had been reading. "We will want to return to Town as soon as possible in any event. It appears that Miss Betsy has a daughter. Her solicitor's direction is in these documents, along with her will. The girl is being raised by a couple in Shrewsbury and does not know they are not her true parents. Everything has been left to her."

That might have been the only selfless thing she ever did. "Tomorrow morning it is then."

Chapter Thirty

Later that evening, Con entered Charlotte's bedchamber. She was sitting at the dressing table, already in her nightgown. Her golden hair spilled over her shoulders, glinting in the candlelight, and curling down to her waist. He sucked in a breath, unable to believe how lucky he was. For the rest of his life the most beautiful woman in the world would be the last person he saw before he slept and the first person he saw when he awakened. He could not imagine ever wanting anyone else.

For years he had run from marriage, unable to believe that an innocent could stir his blood. That he could be content with one woman. That conjugal relations could be more than a business arrangement. He had cursed himself for stopping to help her, and cursed the Fates for placing him in a position where he was the only man who could help her.

Yet no whore, widow, or other woman had given herself to him as freely as Charlotte had. Nor had he ever given his heart, mind, and soul to another woman as he had with her. His mother was right when she'd said if he could convince Charlotte to marry him, it would be the making of him. In the short time they had been together he *had* changed, and for the better.

"Constantine?" Her soft blue eyes warmed as she looked at him. "A penny for your thoughts."

"I was thinking"—he strolled to her, taking her in his arms—"that I have never been happier than I am with you."

A light pink colored her neck and face. He hoped that years from now he could still make her blush. "I feel the same. I watched my sisters, cousin, and friend fall in love, and I wondered if I would find the right man for me." She wrapped her arms around his neck. "And I have. Imagine what would have happened if you hadn't got lost."

He groaned. "You knew?"

"I *am* able to read a map, and you talked to yourself about it in the carriage." Her eyes danced and her lips tilted up. "I am delighted it happened. If not, we would not be together. And your mistress would still be stuck in a life she did not want."

"I'm usually quite good with directions. I must have been distracted."

"Constantine, are you upset that you did not realize how close to London we were?"

Bending his head, he nibbled her jaw, fluttering kisses down her graceful neck. "Now? Not at all. Had I discovered my mistake earlier, I would have been. Still, there was something about you that drew me to you." His hands cupped her breasts, the nipples already furled, waiting for his touch. "Even when I thought you were being stubborn for no reason, I was thinking of ways to make you agree to wed me."

Her breath hitched as she leaned into his palm. "I know what you mean. Something about you called to my heart."

"I wish your brother had taken me up on my offer to marry you immediately." He moved his hands lower. Someday he would be able to spend hours making love with her.

Someday when he had her at home, and they didn't have to rise early to attend to a kidnapped woman.

"No, you do not." Charlotte laughed, a light tinkling sound. "The revenge my sisters would exact would not be worth it."

He thought of the twelve-year-olds and their huge bonnets and the two younger girls who were so earnest in their interrogation of him. "You're probably right." He took one rosy pink nipple in his mouth and sucked. "We should make use of the time we have before we're separated."

That was not something she was going to think of at the moment. Charlotte's breath became ragged, and she rubbed her body against his erection. "The feelings . . . I do not know what else to call them, are stronger than they were last night."

He slid his hand over the swell of her hips, brushing his fingers against her mons. His lips curved against her full breasts. "There?"

"Yes." His deep, seductive voice increased her desire. "As if everything coalesces right there."

She grabbed his face, pressing kisses along his lips, demanding he open to her. Her tongue tangled with his, and she moaned as he raised her gown, and slid his finger back and forth, dipping it into her sheath. "As if you'll die if you don't get relief."

"I need you."

He lifted her up and carried her to the bed. "You are not the only one who is going to die."

Drawing her nightgown over her head, he released the fastenings on his banyan and shrugged it off.

"I love your chest." Abandoning his mouth, she kissed her way down his throat, down to his chest, and licked one of his nipples. "You like that. I can tell."

Con groaned. "If I don't get inside you right now, I'm going to spill."

"In that case"—he could feel her lips curve against his chest—"what are you waiting for?"

They barely made it on the mattress before Charlotte wrapped her legs around Constantine, urging him to take her. He thrust deep, deeper than he had last night, filling her, taking her. She reveled in their joining.

The sharp feeling of need spun tighter and soon her tension broke and she found Heaven again. A moment later, he plunged even deeper, and cried her name. She held him to her for a long minute before he fell off to her side, and drew her against him. For the rest of her life, this was where she belonged. She prayed that they would have a very long life together. She knew how easily it could be cut short.

Charlotte drew patterns on his chest, simply to play in the soft hair covering it. "Will we sleep together after we are wed?"

His breath stopped for a second. "If I have my way."

"Good." That was exactly what she wanted him to say. "I enjoyed waking up with you this morning. As far as I know, my parents always slept together. At least, they were in the same bed when I had bad dreams."

"As we shall be for our children." He nuzzled her hair, and her already loose bones threatened to melt.

If only this could last forever. She stroked lower down his chest, over his hard stomach, and allowed her fingers to delve down the line of hair to his member. At first it was soft, then it grew hard in her hand.

"Lord, Charlotte, what you do to me."

He rolled her over onto her back, and covered her, entering gently. This time their lovemaking was slower, not so frenzied. She came quickly, bringing him with her to completion.

He kissed her forehead, and eyelids, and lips before pulling her back against his chest. "We need to go to sleep."

She closed her eyes, then a thought came to her, causing them to pop open again. "I'm going to hate going back to Town."

"Let's not worry about that now." Constantine's voice was low, sleepy. "We'll manage something. Preferably a quick wedding."

They woke just as the sun showed through the slit in the curtains. Collette was curled up next to Charlotte, purring.

His hand stroked her breast and desire filled her again. She wanted him. "I'll move the kitten."

"No need." His chest rumbled against her back as if he was chuckling. "I'll show you a new position."

An hour later they were in the parlor with Dotty and Merton, breaking their fast. Constantine handed Charlotte a piece of toast that had already been spread with jam, just the way she liked it. "Thank you. I didn't know you paid attention."

"There is nothing I do not notice about you." His look made her heart flutter as if butterflies had taken up residence. "How could I not when you fix my tea so perfectly."

Charlotte wondered if this was simply part of new love, or if it would last throughout their marriage. Her stomach growled, disrupting her thoughts. She was more ravenous than she had been in years, and for a few minutes hadn't noticed no one else was making conversation.

After she had finished, she set her cup down and sighed. "I do not know when I have eaten so much."

"I know what you mean," Dotty replied. "Ever since I married, my appetite has increased."

Merton flashed Constantine a sly grin Charlotte didn't understand. "You *are* eating for two, my love."

"I suppose you are right." Dotty started to push her chair back, but her husband jumped up to assist her. "Thank you, sweetheart."

"The coach will be ready in a half hour," Merton said over his shoulder as he followed Dotty to their chamber.

"We shall be ready." Charlotte poured another cup of tea and watched Constantine finish his breakfast.

His movements were neat and efficient but graceful, in the same way he drove his carriage, rode a horse, and moved. She stifled a chuckle. And undressed her. Heat rushed into her neck and face.

"Do I dare guess what you are thinking of, my love?" He cast her a wicked grin as he set down his silverware. "If only we had more time."

"Yes." An idea occurred to her. "I have something I must do before we depart."

He rose when she did, drawing her into his arms. "At the very least we have one more night."

And, if she had her way, many more nights in the very near future. Rising on her tiptoes, she pressed her lips to him. "I love you."

She spun out of his arms. "I shall see you soon."

Charlotte strode into her chamber and over to a small writing desk in the corner of the room. She took out a piece of paper, made sure the pen did not require mending, and dipped it into the ink.

My dearest Grace,
    I shall assume that by now Matt has told you Kenilworth and I wish to marry and soon. I would like to add my plea that it be shortly after we return to Town. Now that I have found the man I wish to spend my life with, I see no reason to wait. It would

please me a great deal if Matt could procure a special license, and contact the clergyman (I cannot for the life of me remember his name) who performed the other services, and arrange a date for four days hence. That should give us sufficient time to settle matters here and return.

In the event Matt asks, Kenilworth knows nothing about this, and I wish to keep it that way.

> *With much love,*
> *Your devoted sister,*
> *Charlotte*

She sprinkled sand on the paper, let the ink dry, then addressed it, pressing the ring she wore on her little finger into the soft wax.

Grabbing her bonnet, gloves, and pelisse, she walked quickly back into the parlor, knocked on Dotty's door, and called out, "I have a letter I wish a messenger to deliver for me. I'll be back in a moment."

Making her way out of the apartment and into the corridor, she summoned the floor steward. "I would like this sent by messenger." She handed him a letter and a coin. Giving servants vails almost always ensured a task was accomplished quickly. "It must arrive today. There is no need to wait for an answer."

"Yes, my lady." The man strode to the stairs and signaled someone else. In a scant moment, a younger man appeared. "Have this taken to London immediately."

By the time she regained the parlor, Constantine was pacing the room. "Where did you go?" Worry lines marred his forehead. "Not even your maid knew."

"I'm sorry. I just stepped into the corridor for a moment. I had a task I wished the steward to perform." She brushed a lock of hair that had fallen across his brow back in place. "I did not mean to concern you."

"It is not your fault." His hands settled on her waist. "I merely reacted to what happened yesterday. I do not want you to think I will smother you, but I do want you to be safe."

Part of her was concerned about his reaction. After all, she had only been in the corridor for a short time. Then again, the last few days had been stressful, and she had been abducted, again. And he did recognize it was his problem to resolve. "I understand."

Dotty and Merton joined them a few moments later, and they left the inn, headed to the Hare and Hound. She and Charlotte rode in the coach, while the gentlemen decided to ride accompanied by at least ten of Merton's outriders.

She hoped that Constantine would not insist on so many servants to protect her. Then again, Matt was always adamant that she keep a footman with her when she left the house. He had done the same with Dotty and Louisa before their marriages. Mayhap that was what a dependable gentleman did to keep his family safe.

Charlotte turned her mind to the letter she had written to Grace. The one thing Charlotte had forgotten to consider was whether Louisa could receive notice of Charlotte's marriage and travel to Town in time. She supposed she could put off the wedding for a day or so if need be. On the other hand—she grinned to herself—the new duchess was a force of nature. Once Louisa knew about Charlotte's wedding, her sister would move heaven and earth to be there.

Chapter Thirty-One

Con had a bit of a problem convincing Jemmy he could not accompany them. However, in the end, Jemmy finally agreed to remain at the hotel if Charlotte's maid would find him an ice. The kittens were put in Charlotte's bedchamber until they departed. It was almost strange to be traveling without the boy and the cat.

Their party arrived at the Hare and Hound shortly after ten that morning. Con had spent the journey considering how he and Charlotte should approach the landlord and his wife. He agreed with her that the pair would not be at all happy to see them again. How difficult would it be to convince the couple that they had been cozened by Miss Betsy? He also wondered if Charlotte had brought the letter that had been sent to the procuress. Perhaps he should have mentioned it to her.

Con moved his horse closer to Merton. "I suggest we take several of your men into the inn. Based on my previous experience with the bawd's tools, they will be in the common room." Merton nodded. "One or two should be in the stable in the event anyone attempts to escape or send a message. We still do not know what her arrangements for her customer were."

"Would you like me to enter first? From what Charlotte said, the innkeeper and his wife might attempt to attack you for spiriting her away."

"If they plan on harming us," Con said ruefully, "it will be because we tied their daughter to a bed and gagged her."

"There is that. I definitely think I should go in first with a few of my servants. Yesterday I thought we had them all. I hope today proves me correct." Merton called Jeffers to him. "I expect there might be trouble either from the innkeeper and his people or from the blackguards who worked for that woman. Please have some of the men go into the common room. I shall want three of them with me before Lord Kenilworth enters the inn."

"Yes, my lord."

The man started to leave, but Con stopped him. "I do not want Lady Charlotte to leave the coach until we know the inn is safe."

"We'll make sure both ladies are safe, my lords." Jeffers touched his hat, and trotted off.

He and Merton slowed their horses and rode into the yard. They waited for the outriders to take their places before dismounting. "We shall soon know what we are dealing with."

A few of the servants who were dressed in everyday clothing entered the inn. Three others who were in Merton's livery stood to the side of the door. Merton entered and Con followed.

"Innkeeper!" Merton called.

Mr. Wick hurried out from a room on the right of the hall. "My lord." He looked past Merton and the man's eyes widened, then narrowed in anger. "We don't want your kind here. Take yourself off right away."

Ignoring the landlord, Con took out one of his cards. "We have not been properly introduced. I am the Marquis of Kenilworth. My companion is the Marquis of Merton. I was here the last time for the same purpose I am here today, to rescue the person who was brought here under the instruction of a woman called Miss Betsy."

Mr. Wick's mouth gaped. "Rescue?"

As the man did not continue, Con went on. "Indeed. The woman is a flesh-dealer. The lady I rescued was abducted for the purpose of selling her to the man who requested the kidnapping."

"I don't believe you." The innkeeper's chin pushed out belligerently. "What proof do you got?"

"I am proof," Merton said. "My cousin, the lady's guardian, and I destroyed Miss Betsy's brothel. She forced the women there into prostitution."

Wick stuck out his chin belligerently. "So you says."

"Perhaps a letter would help." Charlotte spoke from behind Con. "This is from Miss Betsy to the man who paid her to abduct me." She held the missive out so that the landlord could read it. After a few moments she said, "Now do you believe us?"

"We know what she told you." Dotty stood next to Charlotte. "She said the same thing to another innkeeper and his wife. I am sorry to have to tell you that you have been taken in by a villainess who sells women and children."

Mr. Wick opened his mouth, then shook his head and handed Con a key. "She's in the same room as the last time."

"Where are her men and how many are there?" Con asked.

"The coachman is in the stable," the landlord replied, his Adam's apple working furiously. "One of them is in the tap-room, and the other is two doors down from the lady. They're expecting Miss Betsy anytime."

"You do not have to worry about seeing her again," Merton said before glancing at Jeffers. "Take care of the coachman."

Con signaled for the other two outriders to remain in the hall. "I'll be back in a few minutes."

When he entered the taproom, one of Merton's servants was talking to a medium-sized man dressed in dark brown clothing sitting at a table near the bar. The man looked at Con, obviously decided he was not a threat, and turned back to his ale.

Strolling up to the table, Con waived the servant away. "I hear you work for Miss Betsy?"

The miscreant glanced up from his mug and stared at him. "Name's Smith. Be you wantin' to get a message to her?"

"That would be a bit difficult." He smiled humorlessly. "She is dead. As you will be if you do not tell me what I wish to know."

Right on cue, the blackguard lunged at Con. He struck out, slamming his fist into Smith's jaw. The cur fell back, then came at Con again. He rammed his fist into the man's gut, grabbed him by the hair, and planted the blackguard a facer. Blood and spittle flew over the table.

Grabbing Smith by his scarf, Con lifted him and shook hard. "There's more home brew where that came from if you wish to continue, or we can have a conversation."

"I ain't talkin'."

"In that case, you shall hang." Con motioned to the outriders. "Tie him up. I shall find out who the magistrate is for the area. If Mr. Smith is lucky, his case will be heard here; if not, he'll be taken to Newgate." Con slid a glance to the man. "That is what the magistrate in Richmond decided to do, as the abduction took place in London."

At the mention of Newgate, the man paled. "I just pick 'em up. I don't know nothin' else."

Con raised a brow. "That is a pity. If you had more knowledge, you might be sentenced to transportation instead of hanging."

"Wait, I might know somethin'."

"Indeed?" The man nodded. Clearly this was not one of the bullies of St. Giles. He wondered briefly where Miss Betsy had found him. "Very well. What do you know?"

"She, Miss Susan, was right chatty. She was happy when we picked her up. Said someone called Sir Reginald was comin' fer her, and they was goin' to get leg-shackled."

Sir Reginald? The only man Con knew by that name was not only at a standstill but wasn't fit company for a young lady. As far as he knew, the man was not received in Polite Society.

"Do you happen to know where Miss Betsy was to meet him?"

"A hedge tavern not far from here. Called the Gray Horse."

"You have been helpful. I'll have more questions for you later." A loud crash sounded from above them. "Please excuse me. There is something I must see to."

He strode out of the room in time to see a big bruiser come tumbling down the stairs with Jeffers running after him, shouting, "Don't let him get away!"

The blackguard landed at Merton's feet and tried to get up, but Merton held a pistol to the side of the man's head. "I wouldn't if I were you. in general, I object to using violence around ladies. However, I will make an exception for you."

The next thing he knew, a woman was screaming. "Sam! Did he hurt you?"

The woman bustled forward, and Charlotte whispered in Con's ear, "Mrs. Wick."

"This seems to be a family affair." The landlady looked as if she was going to jump on Merton. Before she could act, Con drawled, "I wouldn't do that if I were you. Unless you want Sam dead?"

"You!" Her eyes narrowed. "I'll get the magistrate on you."

"Please do call him. I believe he will be extremely interested in the part you and your family have played in a flesh-selling scheme."

"Flesh-selling?" Mrs. Wick's hands fisted at her hips. "I'll have you know I'm a good Christian woman."

Charlotte took in the vignette. Merton still had his pistol pointed at Sam's head. Jeffers seemed to be frozen on the first stair tread. Mrs. Wick still looked as if she would like to fly at someone, but could not decide who. Two outriders stood in the doorway to what Charlotte assumed was the common room, holding a man whose hands were tied, and Constantine was surveying the scene through his quizzing glass. She could only think he was attempting to intimidate the landlady.

Standing to the side, Mr. Wick looked like a scared rabbit—although, hare might be more appropriate—ready to spring.

She decided to deal with the landlady first. "Mrs. Wick." The woman's eyes rounded as she finally noticed Charlotte. "The truth of the matter is that Miss Betsy was a procuress. She did not rescue women and children. She took orders from men just as you might order a bonnet, and sold them." The older woman's mouth dropped open. "I—none of us"—Charlotte waved her hand at Dotty, Constantine, and Merton—"believe that you were aware of her activities. As a matter of fact, based on the short conversation I had with your daughter, I am quite sure you did not know what Miss Betsy was doing."

Mrs. Wick shook her head. "No, my lady. I didn't." She pointed her finger at Sam. "But I'll wager my last penny if that blackguard didn't know." She speared him with a furious look. "And didn't say a word to me."

Sam, apparently, had the good sense to keep his mouth shut as he said not a thing.

"Well, then," Charlotte continued, "my cousins and my betrothed came here to rescue the young lady Miss Betsy was to have collected."

"She'll make ye pay for interferin', Peg," Sam said.

Not so sensible after all. "She died yesterday," Charlotte replied. Sam seemed smaller all of a sudden. "What we would like to know is how many times she brought women and children here, and if you can tell me anything about them."

Mrs. Wick straightened and nodded slowly. "I'll write it all down for you."

"Thank you. We appreciate all the help you can give us. Your daughter might be able to help you."

Constantine had lowered his quizzing glass sometime after Charlotte had begun to speak. "Nicely done, my lady. What made you decide to intervene?"

"The look on her face when you accused her of being in league with Miss Betsy. She was so furious I did not think she would listen to anything else you had to say."

He drew out the room key. "I should tell you that the young lady may not believe she requires rescuing. Apparently she has been deceived by Sir Reginald Stanley. What I don't understand is how he got anywhere near her."

"Who is Sir Reginald? I've never heard of him." Charlotte waited while Jeffers and another outrider removed Sam from in front of the stairs.

"Your brother would have put a bullet into him if he had come within a half mile of you or your sisters. A year or two ago, dear Sir Reggie tried to make off with an heiress who did not appreciate his efforts. Suffice it to say he is shunned. Not only that, but he's been barred from his clubs for not paying his gambling debts." Constantine held his arm out for her. "Come to think of it, I haven't seen him around Town lately."

"If he was able to deceive her, he must be very charming and handsome."

"I suppose some women would think so." He sounded disgusted. "He looks rather like Byron, but blond instead of dark."

That was all that was needed. "Oh, dear. We may have a problem with her." They climbed the stairs. "I suggest we not disagree with her about Sir Reggie. She may try to run away from us."

"Her name is Miss Susan." Constantine opened the door, standing back for Charlotte to enter the room.

A young lady whirled around from the window, a wide smile on her face. As soon as she saw them, the smile faded. She had dark brown hair and blue eyes. Her skin was clear for the most part, with only one spot on her wide forehead. Charlotte sucked in a breath. Miss Susan could be no more than sixteen at the most.

"Are you Miss Betsy?" she asked, remaining near the window.

"No. I am Lady Charlotte Carpenter." Charlotte stepped into the room, a little at a loss as to how to explain that neither Miss Betsy nor Sir Reginald would be coming.

The girl brightened. "Oh, I dare say Sir Reginald asked you to come for me. I was a little surprised that he has not arrived."

Constantine touched Charlotte's elbow and left the room.

Charlotte drew her brows together slightly, trying to place the young lady's tone. It was not quite as cultured as her sisters' . . . Suddenly everything fell into place. Miss Susan's family was not gentry, but most likely wealthy merchants of some sort. That would explain how Sir Reginald had managed to make her acquaintance, and the reason he wanted to do so. "Yes, that is it. Sir Reginald has some business to which he must attend. Miss Betsy had an unfortunate accident yesterday and is unable to come at all." Charlotte studied the girl's expression, hoping that she believed her story. At that age, the young woman was perfectly capable of making just the type of scene that would sink them all when they arrived at the Star and Garter. "We, my cousins and my betrothed, are visiting not far from here and have come to fetch you." She leaned forward and lowered her voice. "I must confess, my betrothed has a lamentable memory, and as Sir Reginald mostly referred to you as Miss Susan, I do not know your surname."

"Merryville." She smiled. "Miss Susan Merryville. My eldest sister is Miss Merryville."

Charlotte would wager her high-perched phaeton that Miss Susan was not out yet and would not be for a few years yet. "It is very nice to meet you, Miss Susan Merryville."

She curtseyed. "It is very nice to meet you as well, my lady. I suppose that when Sir Reginald and I are married I will meet many ladies."

Charlotte doubted the girl was even old enough to wed in Scotland, and wondered what the rogue's game was. But for the moment, that would have to wait. She must discover where the girl lived and decide upon the most expeditious way to take her home.

She smiled encouragingly at Miss Susan. "Tell me, how

did you meet Sir Reginald? I have not seen him in Town of late."

"Oh, we did not meet in Town, but in Bath, where my grandmother lives. I was visiting her and met Sir Reginald while I was running an errand for my grandmamma."

Not only young, but confiding as well. "I am sure your grandmamma must have adored him, he is so handsome and charming."

"She did at first." Miss Susan took on a mulish look that reminded Charlotte strongly of her sister, Theo. "But she thinks he is too old for me."

Charlotte tapped one gloved finger on her cheek. "I am not certain that I know how old he is, but surely not over two-and-thirty."

"Nine-and-thirty." Miss Susan's voice was scarcely a whisper. "He thinks I am very mature for my age, and I dare say age does not matter when one is in love."

"Oh, indeed. Love cures all sorts of difficulties." If Sir Reginald was in love with this child, Charlotte would eat her bonnet. "But surely you did not come all the way from Bath?"

"Not at all." Miss Susan giggled at the idea of being abducted from Bath. "I was at Gunter's."

"My love." Constantine came up behind Charlotte. "We are ready to depart."

"Thank you, my love." She linked her arm with the girl. "I adore Gunter's. Let us continue our conversation in the coach."

Chapter Thirty-Two

Somehow Charlotte must convince Miss Susan she had made a terrible mistake in trusting the cur. She hoped her friend had some ideas. A footman assisted the girl into the Mertons' large traveling coach. Dotty was talking to her husband, and Con stood next to Charlotte.

"Do you know her last name yet?"

"Merryville. She is very trusting. By the time we reach Richmond, I shall know her life history."

"I'll leave it to you, then." Raising her hands to his lips, Con kissed them. "If you can figure out a way to return her to her home, I'd be thankful."

She climbed the steps into the coach. "I shall do my best."

Charlotte made a point of sitting next to the girl in the coach as they waited for Dotty.

For the first time the girl showed signs that she might not be as ready to trust Charlotte as she'd thought. "Will Sir Reginald know where I have gone? Perhaps I should remain here."

"No, no, we must depart immediately," Dotty said, taking her seat across from Charlotte and Susan. "Merton has ordered luncheon and does not wish to be late." She cast her eyes to the roof of the coach and sighed. "He is an absolute bear if his meals are late. We simply cannot delay our return." After settling her skirts, Dotty directed her attention to Susan. "Lady Charlotte, who do we have here?"

"I would like to introduce you to Miss Susan Merryville. Miss Susan, I shall make you known to my dearest friend, the Marchioness of Merton."

"I am pleased to meet you." Dotty smiled graciously at Susan.

The girl's jaw dropped. "I-I never dreamed I would meet a marchioness. I mean, I know Sir Reginald is part of the *ton*, but I did not know he had *such* friends."

Charlotte's gaze met her friend's and she grimaced. "Susan—may I call you Susan?"

"Oh, yes, my lady."

"Thank you. As I was saying, Susan has been telling me how she met her beloved. It is a most romantic story. We have just got to the point that her grandmamma does not approve of his age, and how she did not come directly from Bath, but from Gunter's." Charlotte glanced at the girl. "How did you decide to do something so daring?"

"Oh, wait," Dotty said, thankfully picking up on Charlotte's pose. "Do not tell me that your grandmamma poisoned your lover to your parents? That would be too bad."

"That is exactly what she did." Susan nodded. "When I tried to tell Mama and Papa about him, they refused to even receive him. We had to use my maid and his valet to exchange letters."

Dotty clapped her hands together. "Ah, *billets doux*. How romantic!"

Susan glanced at Charlotte, confused. "It is French for love letters," Charlotte explained. The girl nodded. "But where is your maid? Would she not have wanted to come with you?"

"She did not dare. My mama would have turned her off without a reference. Once the men put me into the coach, and we started to leave, she began to scream so that no one would blame her."

Dotty leaned forward a little. "Lady Charlotte lives on Berkeley Square. Is that where you live as well?"

"No, I live on Russell Square. We used to live in Cheapside, but my parents decided it was time to move. That is the reason I was at my grandmamma's."

"Russell Square is quite lovely," Charlotte said, "and a much better neighborhood than Cheapside. Although, there is nothing wrong with the area."

"My best friend is still in Cheapside." Susan's tone was glum and her mouth drooped. "I miss her a lot."

Charlotte wondered if her friend's counsel would have kept Susan from making such a disastrous mistake.

Dotty's eyes widened. "I am sure that you do, but I must know, who is this man of which we speak?"

"Sir Reginald Stanley." The girl practically breathed his name. "Do you know him, my lady?"

"Sir Reginald." She tapped her cheek and after a few moments smiled. "Why, yes. I was introduced to him. After I married, of course, and very much by accident. He is not received in Polite Society, you know."

Susan's face fell, and Charlotte could see all the girl's dreams of moving in the *ton* start to wobble. "N-not received?"

"He has a reputation of being a rake and an inveterate gambler. That is not the type of gentleman ladies want around their daughters."

"But rakes can reform." The girl rallied. "Once they are wed, of course."

"Yes, indeed they can. In fact, some claim that reformed

rakes make the best husbands, but first he must marry."
Dotty's brows drew together. "My dear, how thoughtless of
me. You are planning to marry him?"

The girl's countenance brightened again. "Yes, my lady.
We are to travel to Scotland."

"Well, naturally, if you are to wed, that would change
everything." She glanced at Susan again. "How old did you
say you are, my dear?"

"Fifteen," Susan pronounced as if it was a great age.

"Fifteen?" Dotty asked, her voice full of doubt. The girl
nodded. "No. That will not do at all. One must be sixteen
to marry in Scotland. Unless you have your parents' permission, that is." She let the silence stretch for a few moments.
"But you do not."

Susan clasped her hands together in her lap and stared
at them. "N-no, my lady."

"Lady Merton," Charlotte said, "are you quite sure it is
sixteen?"

"Indeed I am. Do you not remember the couple who
eloped earlier this Season?" She did, but she was equally
sure that was not to whom her friend was referring, but she
nodded anyway. "She was not even out. They reached the
border two months before her sixteenth birthday and were
turned away. Naturally, she will never be allowed a Season,
and she is ruined forever."

Charlotte covered her mouth and gasped. "Oh, yes. I
remember now. How horrible it was!" She slid a look at
Susan, whose eyes were wide with horror. "My dear Susan,
how fortunate you did not go to Scotland."

The girl promptly burst into tears. Charlotte wrapped
her arms around the child and took out her handkerchief,
pressing it into the girl's hands. "There, there. We are here
to help you."

"I doubt Sir Reginald could afford the journey to Scotland," Dotty mused. "He does not have a feather to fly with."

Well, that ought to clinch the matter.

Susan began to sob even harder. "W-what will become of m-m-me?"

Charlotte and Dotty shared a glance. Whatever the answer to the girl's question, the result was likely to be much better than what Miss Betsy and Sir Reginald had planned for poor Susan. Thank God they had been able to rescue her. The question was how to find the man and see him punished before he could harm another girl.

Con rode next to Merton, discussing what they were going to do with the young lady. Neither of them were experts on the subject, but agreed that she could not be out yet.

"I'll be interested to hear what Charlotte and Dotty say," Con said.

"Augusta seems older, or at least more mature," Merton replied, referring to Charlotte's fifteen-year-old sister.

"And more sensible." They fell silent for several minutes, before Con said, "I had wanted to remain at the Star and Garter tonight, but I am of the opinion that we should return to Town."

"You're probably correct. The question is what to do with the girl."

"I have every confidence our ladies will have an address for her parents by the time we sit down to luncheon. I overheard some of the conversation Charlotte was having with her, and apparently, she has decided to play the compassionate lady. I was told specifically not to speak badly of Sir Reggie."

"That won't be hard for me," Merton said. "I'd never heard of the man before you told me about him."

"No, you wouldn't have. He's run with a fast crowd for years," Con said. "Miss Susan must be an heiress."

"Do you know her surname?"

"Merryville." He had never heard of the family and hoped Merton had.

"There is a Merryville in the City who is involved in trade and shipping. I recently invested in a project where his name was mentioned."

"If they are Cits, they wouldn't have heard about Sir Reggie. That would be the reason her parents didn't have her under lock and key. I wonder if extortion and not marriage is his game."

"We may never discover what it is if the man can't show his face in Town."

Con thought that might be the best resolution to the problem. "With Miss Betsy gone, he won't know where the girl is. He might even think that she was not abducted."

"And she will believe he never came for her," Merton mused.

"She will be heartbroken, but only for a short while, not for a lifetime." Marriage to a bounder like Sir Reggie would be hell, if that was all he had planned for her.

Merton urged his horse faster. "The sooner we return her to her family, the better."

Con agreed wholeheartedly.

When they arrived at the Star and Garter, Charlotte whispered to him that luncheon must be ordered without Miss Susan's knowing it had not already been done. "It is the excuse Dotty used for our leaving as soon as we did. She had started having doubts about going with us. We have won the girl's confidence, but if she catches us in the least little lie, we run the risk of losing it."

"I'll take care of it," Con said as the Mertons led Miss

Susan into the inn. "We have decided to return to Town today."

"That is for the best. We will not have more time alone together, but we must get her home. I imagine her parents are beside themselves."

"How old is she?"

"Fifteen. That cur told her they would marry in Scotland, but does she not have to be sixteen?"

Con nodded. "For a runaway marriage, yes."

"And why meet her east of London and not somewhere on the Great North Road?"

"That may have been Miss Betsy's doing. Unless she has a house north of Town as well."

"I do not believe he intended to wed her at all." Concern echoed in Charlotte's voice. "I think they had something much more nefarious planned. I wish I knew what it was. Selling the girl into prostitution would not provide him the money he needs."

No, but an auction would, and that was not something he was going to mention to her. "I do not think we need to worry about that now."

"You are probably right. Although, I wish we could find that blackguard and punish him. There is also Burt. The miscreant that got away." She rubbed her forehead. "We still have a great deal of work to do rescuing the other victims."

"I agree, but we do not have to do it all ourselves." Con was relieved she had changed the subject. "I have not yet introduced you to my excellent secretary. He will be happy to have a project that will challenge him."

She tucked her hand into the crook of his arm. "I'm feeling peckish."

"We can't have that," he said in a dramatic tone.

"You think you are funny." She scowled. "I assure you that I am not at all nice to be around when I'm hungry."

"If that's all I have to do to keep you happy, my life will be pure bliss."

Charlotte lowered her lids. "Well, there might be one or two other things."

May had taken charge of Susan Merryville, and when she joined them in the parlor her good humor had been restored. She talked the whole way through luncheon. By the time they had finished eating, and were getting ready to depart, Con knew everything he had wanted to know and much more. The chit had no discretion at all. No wonder she had been such an easy target for Sir Reggie.

Jemmy had joined them, and more than once, Con had found himself in complete sympathy with the boy, but obliged to chastise him for criticizing the girl. Not only that, but he had a feeling the lad was just a little jealous of Miss Susan spending time with his heroine.

When they rose from the table, he pulled Charlotte aside. "Sweetheart, will you ride back to Town with me? It will be our last chance to be alone for several days."

She glanced at Miss Susan, who was playing with Cyrille, Collette having had the good sense to hide in her basket. "I'd love to. Even if Dotty tires of the girl, Cyrille will keep her occupied." Charlotte gazed up at him, a line marring her lovely brow. "I detest lying to her, yet I do think the story Dotty came up with did the trick. She is much too trusting. I only hope her parents will try to understand how she could have fallen under the cur's spell."

"I knew you wouldn't like this pretense. Still, telling her a faradiddle was the best thing you could have done. If it makes you feel any better, Merton has heard of her father and sent a note to your brother to find the Merryvilles."

"Thank you for telling me." The news made Charlotte feel much better. "She is very young. In many ways, much younger than Augusta."

Even the twins and Madeline had more sense than their charge. "I cannot see any of your sisters doing anything as ill-advised as this."

"I agree, but we should not discuss it here." Charlotte already had the feeling that Susan knew the gentlemen were not as much in sympathy with her as Charlotte and Dotty were. "I'll get my bonnet."

They were halfway to Mayfair when Constantine suggested there must be something wrong with his phaeton, necessitating an overnight stop at an inn he knew was just up the road.

Charlotte was trying not to laugh, when Jemmy piped up, "I don't see anything."

After that she went into whoops. "He has you there. Sweetheart, we will be married soon."

"But how soon? When my sisters wed, it seemed as if the poor chaps had to wait for an age."

She almost told him that in four days they would be saying their vows, but, wanting it to be a surprise, she held her tongue. "At least gentlemen do not have to buy new clothing."

"No." He slid a look at her before returning his attention to the horses. "Tell me why young ladies have to dress in pastels? Wouldn't it be easier to allow them to wear what they want?"

"You mean the colors that suit them best. It would. It would also be considered fast, and the ladies who rule Almack's would refuse to give them vouchers, and other ladies would refuse to invite them to entertainments. All in all, it is less expensive to play by the rules."

"You always look lovely."

"I am fortunate that I can wear some pastels well. However, many ladies cannot."

"Once we have wed, you may shop for whatever you like." He sounded so magnanimous. She wanted to go into whoops again.

"Thank you, I shall." This was another secret she was keeping from him. Encouraged by Grace and Lady Kenilworth, Charlotte had already ordered a new wardrobe. Her conscience gave her a twinge about her mendacity. All she could do was pray it would all turn out well in the end.

Chapter Thirty-Three

It was late afternoon by the time Constantine's carriage rolled into Berkeley Square. Merton's coach would not be far behind. No sooner had Constantine lifted her down from the phaeton, than small arms grabbed onto her legs.

"We missed you," Mary said.

Surprisingly, Theo merely nodded.

"Please, my lady, come into the house." Royston held the door open, and a footman held Daisy.

"Yes, of course." Charlotte stepped across the threshold, Constantine and Jemmy close behind her, and the butler shut the door. "Good afternoon, Daisy. I missed you as well."

The Dane wrapped herself around Charlotte. A chirp sounded from the basket, and Collette jumped out, rubbing herself around Daisy's legs.

"I am not sure we are going to actually get all the way into the house," Constantine commented.

"It just takes a bit sometimes," Jemmy said.

Gradually, Charlotte pushed her way farther into the hall. "Dotty and Merton will be here soon. Let's go to the morning room. Have you had tea yet?"

"Hours ago," Theo said. "Dinner will be soon."

"Goodness, is it that late already?"

Mary nodded. "You have enough time to wash up and change. That's what Matt and Grace are doing. We saw you come down the street."

That answered that question, Charlotte thought. She had wondered where everyone else was.

"If his lordship is joining us, I shall escort him to a chamber," Royston volunteered.

"Thank you." Constantine grinned at her. "I'll meet you in the drawing room."

She shook dog hair from her skirt. "Until then."

As soon as she got to her room, May began unlacing her gown. "The house was at sixes and sevens when I got here."

"How so?" Charlotte stepped into the warm bath water May had waiting for her. "This feels good."

"Lady Worthington got your letter and sent a message to the modiste. Lord Worthington dashed off to the church and had just got back when I arrived." Charlotte washed quickly and stood for May to rinse her. "He had the special license and you are to wed at nine in the morning. But he said the day you wanted was full, so you're getting married in three days instead of four." That was even better than Charlotte had hoped. "They told me in her ladyship's study so the children wouldn't hear."

"That was clever." If any of the younger children knew about Charlotte's wedding, they would be bound to let it slip and Constantine would know.

"Lord Worthington said he never knew you were as managing as Lady Louisa, I mean her grace, and Lady Worthington just laughed and told him he hadn't been paying attention."

"I think it is just that Louisa has a different way." Charlotte grinned. "Has he never noticed how my sister manages everything?"

"That's men for you, my lady. My mother says they can't

see what's in front of their faces unless you hit them in the nose."

She laughed at that. "I have a feeling my mother might have said the same thing at times." She thought about how quiet Theo had been earlier. "Can you talk to one of the nursery maids and find out how Lady Theo has been doing? I am a bit concerned. She was very subdued when I arrived home."

"I'll do it after the little ones go to bed, my lady."

"Thank you." Charlotte recalled how Louisa's maid was concerned about being a duchess's dresser. "How are you doing? Are you looking forward to the changes that are about to happen?"

"Couldn't be happier, my lady." May's grin was as broad as Charlotte had ever seen it. "I had a good talk with Polly, I should say Miss Franks, and she told me when she went to Merton House, she made her place right away, and I should do the same. So I did. His lordship's valet calls me Miss Walker, as will the other servants. Truth to tell, when we got here Bolton took me in hand. That was a great help."

By this time Charlotte was dressed and her maid was closing the clasp on a strand of pearls around Charlotte's neck. She would have to refer to her maid as Walker, as well. It would not do for Charlotte to show a lack of respect for her personal servant.

"I'm glad you had someone to show you the way."

"Yes, my lady." Walker stood back. "I'll try to have something about Lady Theo when you return."

"Thank you, again." Charlotte stood as her maid placed her silk shawl around her shoulders. "I am lucky to have you, Walker."

May glowed with pride. "I'm lucky to have a mistress as fine as you, my lady."

A knock came on the door and Charlotte answered, "Come."

Grace floated into the bedchamber. Someday, Charlotte vowed, she would learn to do that. Her sister hugged her tightly. "You must realize you are driving Matt absolutely mad."

"Actually, I didn't consider him at all." She gazed into her sister's eyes. "I suppose I should have. I just want to be married."

"I know." Grace chuckled lightly. "I have to tell you that I let Lady Kenilworth in on the secret. It would not have been fair not to."

Charlotte could understand that. "I suppose I am having a wedding breakfast."

"Naturally. However, none of the invitations will state that it is a wedding breakfast." Her sister chuckled. "We are calling it an End-of-Season breakfast."

"What a brilliant idea." She had not expected a wedding breakfast at all.

"Lady Kenilworth thought of it." Grace grinned like she had when she had planned surprises for their parents.

"So Kenilworth will not know what is going on until Matt takes him to the church?" The more Charlotte thought of surprising him, the more excited she became.

"We shall keep our fingers crossed." Grace hugged Charlotte again. "I am so glad you found your love."

She blinked as tears of joy threatened to fill her eyes. "As am I."

When Charlotte entered the drawing room that evening, Constantine was waiting for her. He handed her a glass of sherry. "I didn't expect to see you so soon."

"I had no idea I would be the first, but I'm very glad I am." She pressed her lips against his. "I have a surprise for you, but I cannot tell you yet."

His arms went around her, tugging her to him. "That, my lady, is not fair."

"Oh, I believe you will enjoy it a great deal when you find out what it is."

"Minx." His mouth came down on hers, and she opened to him, tangling her tongue with his.

Charlotte drew back. The children she would hear come down the stairs, but Matt could move quietly when he wanted to. Despite knowing she and Constantine would be married in three days, she did not want to risk her brother being upset with them, especially after all he was doing. "I shall miss sleeping with you, and spending my days with you."

Con's fingers tightened. "I am meeting with your brother tomorrow about the settlement agreements. I shall press for an early marriage."

Feet pounded on the stairs, the door opened, and the children rushed into the room. "Charlotte, you're home!" The twins and Madeline threw their arms around Charlotte's waist and she returned their hugs. "We missed you."

"I missed you too. Mind your manners and say good evening to Lord Kenilworth."

The three girls curtseyed. "Good evening, Lord Kenilworth."

He bowed, then rubbed his chin. "I believe that under the circumstances, you should call me Constantine, and I like hugs as well."

The girls stared at him for a moment before embracing him. "We like you the best."

"You do?" His eyes widened. "Why is that?"

"We have to call Louisa's husband Rothwell," Madeline said. "Because he's a duke."

"And Dotty's husband, Merton," Eleanor added. "Because he's a bit stuffy."

"We like Constantine," Alice said. "When are you and Charlotte getting married?"

"As soon as I can convince your brother to let me." He practically growled and she hid a smile.

Grace and Matt strolled in at that moment. "About that," Matt said. "I shall meet with you tomorrow morning to discuss the settlement agreements."

"I'll see you at nine if that is not too early."

Matt poured glasses of sherry for himself and Grace. "Not at all."

A few minutes later, the Mertons arrived with Susan and joined the pandemonium in the drawing room. Con wanted to find out if anyone had been able to contact the girl's family, but there was no way to have a private word. A few minutes later, the butler announced dinner.

He placed Charlotte's hand on his arm. "I promise you, I will make your brother agree to let us marry next week."

"I am positive you will succeed." Her countenance was too serene. Did she not care how soon they wed? Or was she certain he would prevail?

Dinner was as lively as he thought it would be, and it occurred to him how lonely he had been as the last child. He glanced at Mary and wondered how she would feel when her brothers and sisters were gone. Then he remembered that Grace—she had asked him to call her that before dinner—was expecting a child in late December. Next to him, Charlotte was talking to her brother Walter, and Con marveled at how easily they got along. Of course, he got on well with his sister Annis, but it was nothing like Charlotte's family.

The sound of a door opening and closing filtered through the air. A few seconds later, a young man with the Carpenter coloring entered the room. "Is there a place for me?"

Chairs scraped back, and the children rushed forward en masse.

"Charlie!" someone called.

"You're home!" a few others said.

"We missed you." Con recognized Theo's voice.

Worthington rose. "You made good time."

"Half-term began today. I was eager to be here." He finished hugging the younger children and was halfway to Charlotte's chair when she rose. "I hear you are getting married."

Her eyes filled with tears, and she smiled at him. "I am." She took his hand. "Come and meet him."

Con pushed his chair back and stood, waiting.

"Constantine, this is my brother Charlie, Earl of Stanwood. Charlie, the Marquis of Kenilworth."

The young man had what Con thought of as the Carpenter look, and it was clear by the way he held himself that he cared deeply about his sisters and brothers, even his new sisters. His throat tightened. Soon he would join this family who loved each other so fiercely. "Stanwood."

"Kenilworth." The younger man clasped his hand. "Welcome to the family."

"You can call him Constantine," Phillip called out.

"And you can call him Charlie," Alice said.

A place was set, and everyone went back to their seats. Charlie glanced around the table and greeted Dotty and Merton. Then his gaze stopped on Miss Susan. "I believe someone forgot to introduce us."

"Miss Susan," Dotty said, casting a sparkling look at Charlotte, "may I introduce, my brother, the Earl of Stanwood? Charlie, this is Miss Susan Merryville. She is visiting me for the nonce."

He bowed. "My pleasure, Miss Susan. I hope you are enjoying your visit."

The minute Charlie had looked at her, Susan's eyes had rounded, her lips formed an O, and Con was sure she had forgotten all about Sir Reginald. "I am, my lord. Very much."

Charlie sat next to Grace, and for the rest of the meal conducted a low-toned conversation with her. He glanced at Charlotte once or twice and Worthington another time.

Charlotte leaned closer to Con. "Grace is telling him what has been going on. After dinner or tomorrow, he will spend most of the day with Matt. When the children have finished their lessons, he'll be with them."

"How old did you say he was?"

"Sixteen. He takes his responsibilities seriously."

"I can see that." Charlie's attitude, his whole bearing almost made Con feel as if he was lacking. Or had somehow neglected his duties. That was ridiculous, of course. He always took care of his land and dependents. "He will be a force to be reckoned with some day."

Under the table, Charlotte slipped her hand in his. "As you are now."

As he would damn well make sure he was. "Have you noticed how Miss Susan looks at him?"

She grinned and nodded. "An infatuation with a younger man might be just what she needs. And Charlie is safe. He will be kind, but treat her as he would one of us."

"Do you know if Worthington was able to contact her parents?"

Charlotte shook her head. "No one has said anything. I do hope they come soon."

An hour later, Grace rose from her chair. "Let us leave the gentlemen."

The gentlemen and footmen assisted the other ladies. Charlotte squeezed Con's hand. "I'll see you soon."

The door closed behind his beloved, and the males all

moved to the head of the table. Footmen brought lemonade, brandy, and port. The younger boys and Charlie had lemonade, Con and Worthington selected brandy, Merton chose port. The talk turned to sports and, at an elementary level, politics. Yet all Con wanted to do was join the ladies and spend time with Charlotte.

The clock struck eight, and Worthington stood. "Gentlemen, shall we join the ladies? Walter and Phillip, it's time for bed."

Con was surprised at how quickly the boys left the room. Yet once the door closed behind them, Charlie said, "I heard you rescued Char not once but twice. I owe you my thanks."

"I can assure you, it was my pleasure. To be completely honest, she had rescued herself the first time. All I did was provide the carriage. The second time, I can take some credit for."

Charlie grinned. "I hope you decide to have the ceremony before I go back to school."

Con glanced at Worthington. "That will be discussed in the morning. Shall we join the ladies?"

A half hour later, the butler entered the drawing room and spoke in a low tone to Worthington. He motioned to Con and Charlotte.

"I think the Merryvilles might be here."

"I hope that's what it means. I cannot think of anything else." She placed her hand on his arm. "We shall find out soon."

Merton caught Con's eye as they followed Worthington out of the room. Con shrugged and the other man nodded.

They crossed the square to Worthington House. "How

did your family come to be living in two houses?" Con asked Charlotte.

"As you know, Stanwood House belongs to Charlie. Before Matt and Grace married, he, his step-mother, and his sisters lived with him in Worthington House. When he and Grace married she suggested they live at Stanwood House as well, but Matt would not even consider taking Charlie's bedchambers and none of the other beds fit him. But Worthington House was too small for all of us, and Dotty came to us for the Season." By God! Con could not imagine having eleven children, one's step-mother, and an extra young lady in a town house. "There was a great deal of discussion, but in the end, Matt and Grace decided that they would sleep at Worthington House, and everyone else, including his step-mother would live at Stanwood House. It gives them more privacy than they would have with all the children about." Con had no doubt that was Worthington's idea. "They are renovating Worthington House, and next Season, Charlie will lease this house to Matt's step-mother and her new husband. That was part of the arrangement when they wed."

"Who did Lady Worthington marry?"

"Viscount Wolverton. They were childhood sweethearts. I don't know why they didn't wed when she came out."

Con found he'd had to listen carefully to keep all the parts of what Charlotte had said from getting muddled. "You have a complicated family."

"I have a large family with many different needs." She slid him a look as they walked up the steps to Worthington House. "Will that be a problem for you?"

Con tugged her closer to him. "Absolutely not. I am coming to care deeply for your family, and I hope our children will be close to their aunts, uncles, and cousins."

Charlotte relaxed against him. "I'm glad."

Charlotte entered a parlor on the right side of the hall
first, followed by Matt and her betrothed. Her brows rose.
"I didn't even know this room was completed."

The parlor held two sofas. A low table stood between
them. Two wide cane-backed chairs were positioned at the
end of the long table between the sofas. The walls were
lined with yellow silk printed with small violet flowers and
green leaves, and botanical paintings hung on the walls.
The effect was bright but soothing, and a brightly colored
carpet covered most of the floor.

It was a comfortable room, but impersonal. One where
people who were not friends or family would be shown.

A man and a woman, who could only be the Merryvilles,
stood when they entered. They were well dressed in the current mode. The man was tall and loose-limbed. His hair a
dark blond. The woman was an older version of Susan.
Currently, their faces were lined with worry.

Charlotte stepped forward. "Mr. and Mrs. Merryville?"
The man inclined his head. "I am Lady Charlotte Carpenter." She motioned toward Worthington. "This is my
brother, Lord Worthington, and my betrothed, the Marquis
of Kenilworth. Lord Kenilworth was with me when we
rescued Susan."

Chapter Thirty-Four

Mr. Merryville bowed, and his wife curtseyed. Charlotte took a seat on the opposite sofa, Con sat next to her, and her brother sat on a chair.

"May we ask how our daughter is doing?" Mrs. Merryville asked. She clutched the handkerchief with which she had dabbed her red-rimmed eyes.

"Let me assure you that Susan is safe and unharmed." Charlotte gave the woman a reassuring smile. "She was quite forthcoming regarding her behavior."

Mrs. Merryville let out a breath. "I am afraid she is a bit of a chatterbox." She twisted the handkerchief in her hands. "I—we had no idea she would do anything like this."

"It is beyond the pale," Merryville said. Of the two he was clearly the angrier.

"It will probably not make you feel better," Con said, focusing on the girl's father, "but Sir Reginald is an accomplished rake. I do not believe any young girl would have the experience to counter him."

"It did not help matters that her grandmother accepted him at first, then rejected him without giving Susan a reason," Charlotte added. "She is at that age, after all."

"He can be very charming," Con said. "However, he is

deeply in debt, as you most likely already know, and not received by Polite Society."

Charlotte watched the girl's father as his lips thinned and his countenance hardened. That did not bode well for poor Susan. "You cannot blame her. While in Bath, she was given freedom to go off on errands for her grandmother, alone or with only a young maid. Although the town is not London, it is still not safe for a young girl to walk around alone. It would not surprise me at all if Sir Reginald saw her and made inquiries about her. I understand he is quite desperate."

"He'd have to be if he went to Bath," Constantine said under his breath. Charlotte resisted the urge to cast her eyes to the ceiling.

"We only sent her there because my mother begged for one of her granddaughters to visit," Mr. Merryville said. "I had no idea she'd be so lax. Then again, we keep more of a watch over our children than was kept over us."

"It is unfortunate that she did not take better care of Susan." Charlotte sympathized with the couple.

"She is not even fifteen!" Mrs. Merryville cried and broke in to tears. Her husband put his arm around her shoulders. "How could he do what he did?"

For a moment Charlotte was distracted by the woman saying Susan was not yet fifteen, then she understood what actually concerned Mrs. Merryville. "Excuse me, ma'am, but when I said she was well, I meant that she had not been touched."

The woman lowered her handkerchief from her eyes. Mr. Merryville stared at Charlotte. "Are you certain, my lady?"

"I am quite certain. She also understands what a horrible mistake she made in trusting him." She softened her tone.

"I think you will find that she very much wishes to be forgiven."

"If I may make a suggestion," Matt said. "I do not allow my sisters out of the house without at least one experienced, older footman with them."

"I have found them more useful than my maid," Charlotte added. "Particularly, when I am shopping."

"Have you received any correspondence from Sir Reginald?" Constantine asked.

"Nothing at all." Mrs. Merryville frowned. "We had no idea where she might be or who would have taken her until we received the note from his lordship."

Her husband's jaw had developed a tick. "You are not surprised by that."

Constantine's gaze focused on the other man. "How great of an heiress is Susan?"

"My father started the business. I have built upon it and we are well off. However, I have four daughters. The eldest will come out next year. Not, of course, in Polite Society, but the expenses are significant. Their dowries are sufficient. And, although I do not aim to marry any of them into the aristocracy, I wish them to marry well." Mr. Merryville stood. "Thank you for your assistance. I know where the fault lies, and it will not happen again." He looked at Matt. "I will take your advice regarding the footmen. We would like to take our daughter home."

"Naturally." Charlotte rose. "She is across the street at Stanwood House."

The Merryvilles decided to remain in the hall while Susan was sent for. She glanced at her parents and began to weep. Her parents immediately hugged her and spoke in reassuring tones.

Constantine slid Charlotte an amused look. "That is probably the best thing she could have done."

"It appears so."

She took his hand and they were about to slip away when Mr. Merryville approached them. "I cannot thank you enough for finding and protecting Susan. If there is anything I can do to repay you, please let me know."

"Her safety was our main concern," Charlotte said. "We are glad she is back with you."

He bowed and ushered his wife and daughter out the door. When it shut, Matt turned a horrified look at Grace, who had entered the hall. "Have I told you how much I appreciate the fact that you do not enact me Cheltenham tragedies? The weeping would drive me to distraction."

"As opposed to merely fainting," his wife replied. Before they had married, Grace would faint whenever she was surprised. Fortunately, that did not include the times Charlotte and her brothers and sisters acquired frequent cuts, scrapes, and broken bones.

"Swooning is much better. Once I learned it is not unusual." He slid an arm around Grace's waist. "Have you noticed that you have not fainted once since we wed?"

She appeared to consider the matter for a moment. "I do believe you are correct. Then again, I am not now living in fear the children will be taken away from me."

"There is a story behind that exchange," Constantine whispered in Charlotte's ear, causing pleasurable shivers to flit around her neck.

She found she was still holding his hand as they headed to the drawing room. "One day I shall tell you all I know. Yet, I have a feeling even that is not the whole story."

Waking early the next morning, Con decided to surprise Charlotte. He might not be able to wake up next to her, but he could break his fast with her. Not to mention that he had an appointment to discuss the settlement agreements with her brother.

Afterward they could take a ride in his phaeton, where he would find some little-used paths in the Park where they could be alone.

He yanked the bell pull, and a few moments later his valet appeared.

"Good morning, is everything in order, my lord?"

"Couldn't be better. I shall be joining Lady Charlotte's family for breakfast."

Hot water appeared as if by magic, and in less time than he would have imagined, he was dressed and on his way down to the hall. How had he never noticed how efficient his staff was?

"My lord," his butler, Webster, said when Con reached the hall. "Mrs. Henley would like to know if Lady Charlotte will be inspecting the house soon."

That stopped him in his tracks. Naturally, Charlotte would wish to inspect the house. Whatever that entailed. He did not know what, exactly, the protocol was for a change in mistresses. Should his mother be in charge of her visit? Clearly, he would have to ask for advice. The problem was determining who should advise him. "I am sure she will wish to do so at some point." If he had his way, it would be after their wedding. "I shall have to find out when she wishes to meet with Mrs. Henley."

"Very good, my lord." His butler opened the door. "Will you return for luncheon? Cook wishes to be informed."

Con stopped and speared Webster with a look. "I do not recall ever being asked by my cook when I shall be here to dine."

"No, my lord. However, you never spent much time at home before."

That took Con aback. Still, his butler was right. Since

moving out of his rooms into the house, he had had a series of mistresses and had spent most of his time with them, or at his club, or elsewhere. Come to think of it, he had spent more time here since he'd met Charlotte, than in the past four years together. "I shall have luncheon here, and tell her ladyship I would like her to join me."

"Thank you, my lord."

Luncheon would be the perfect time to tell his mother that his wedding had been moved from sometime in the summer, or the autumn, or never—to next week. He could also ask Mama when it would be appropriate for Charlotte to meet with his housekeeper.

He walked down the steps and lengthened his stride, entering Stanwood House about ten minutes later. His arrival barely caused a moment of silent surprise in the din he'd heard from the hall.

"Good morning." He entered the breakfast room and strolled to Charlotte. "I thought we could at least have breakfast together."

"I am glad you are here." She gave him one of her sunny smiles, and he basked in the warmth.

Worthington nodded, and his wife grinned.

Phillip jumped up from his seat. "Good morning, you may have my chair. I'm finished."

A footman cleared the remains of the boy's breakfast, and reset the place. After Con filled his plate at the sideboard, he sat next to Charlotte. "What are your plans for today?"

"Do you mean after we meet with Matt about the settlement agreements?"

We? Con had assumed her brother would handle everything. "Yes. Before we left, I'd sent my information to him." He was about to go through all the details with her, but stopped. He had not received the contract from his solicitor, and he and Charlotte would have enough time for that later.

"He mentioned it to me." She handed him a cup of tea, and he spread jam on her toast. "I understand it is the same agreement that was used for Dotty and Louisa. Albeit with my information." Charlotte munched on her toast. He even liked the sound she made when she ate. "You might as well know that there will be a provision for my property to be held in trust for my use only."

He froze. His cup halfway to his mouth. "Did Merton and Rothwell agree to that stipulation?"

Her eyes began to dance. "Merton was not at all happy, but he wanted to marry Dotty, and that was the only way Matt would agree to the wedding. You must understand that he was not well liked at the time. Rothwell was having some financial difficulties, most of which have been re-solved, and insisted Louisa not only retain her property but not use it to benefit the dukedom."

"And now there is me." He took a sip of his tea, wishing it was something stronger.

Charlotte's sky-blue gaze was steady. "And now there is you."

His family had always gained wealth through marriage. Con had given no consideration to Charlotte's portion. It simply did not matter to him. But if he had, based on the number of brothers and sisters she possessed on the Car-penter side of her family, he would have thought her dowry was no more than respectable. Still, a little voice suggested that might not be the case. It was entirely possible that Wor-thington, clever man that he was, was more devious than Con had previously thought. Her friend and sister had got married within a matter of weeks of meeting their be-trotheds. That was quick even by the standards of the *ton*.

Ergo, by the time the agreements were presented, a man

in love would never oppose them. To do so would be to risk losing the only woman he needed. "I shall not disagree to that provision."

Con thought he heard her let out a breath, but he could not be sure. He knew in his bones that if he did not agree, Charlotte would never be his, and her presence in his life was more important than increasing his family's wealth.

As the children left, the breakfast room gradually quieted. Soon they were alone with Matt and Grace, who were seated at the other end of the table, their heads together, speaking quietly.

A clock struck the quarter hour and Worthington pushed back his chair and rose. "I shall see you in fifteen minutes."

Con leaned closer to Charlotte. "I did not know he was such a stickler for timeliness."

"He is very busy at the moment." Her tone was airy, yet her answer struck him as somewhat evasive, and he didn't know why. "There is a great deal to do before this house is closed and the construction schedule on the other house is finalized, and the journey to the country is made."

That sounded right, but the niggling feeling that he was missing something returned. Con just wished he knew what it was.

The meeting across the square at Worthington House was brief. The settlement agreement was presented to him *fait accompli*. Considering Charlotte's portion was much larger than Con had thought, the contract might have bothered him if it had not been so fair. The primary part dealt with her well-being in the event anything happened to him before an heir had been born.

"This came about," Worthington explained, "because I did not trust my putative heir to take care of my wife in the manner I wished her to be cared for. I have heard of too many widows who have been left impoverished."

Con had heard the same stories. Some of the women had taken protectors, and that was not what he wanted for Charlotte. Not that her family would allow it in any event. And he barely knew the cousin who would inherit his title if he should die without issue. He took the pen in Worthington's hand and signed the documents.

As soon as Constantine left, Grace called the town coach. "Madam Lisette is ready to attend us as soon as we arrive. I cannot tell you how glad I am that you already ordered your bride clothes."

What had been an exercise in shopping to convince Polite Society Charlotte was betrothed, had turned out to have been a wonderful decision. "Do you think Louisa will be able to travel here in time?"

"I hope she will." Grace shrugged. "We shall have to see."

Charlotte and Grace spent the next three hours at Madam Lisette's shop making final fittings. They left with a list of other items Charlotte would need.

When she and her sister entered the morning room for tea, they found not only Matt and the children, but Constantine, his mother, and another lady who shared the same green eyes, conversing with the twins and Madeline.

"Charlotte." In three long steps he was with her. "My sister Annis arrived, and my mother wanted you to meet her." He looked as if he had lost control of his life, and she was hard pressed not to laugh. "I did not know how to stop them from coming."

Charlotte was certain he'd had no hope of achieving that goal. "Your sister seems to be making friends." She took his hand. "Please introduce us."

Shortly after meeting Annis, Lady Kendrick, Charlotte was happy the lady would be her new sister.

"If you have things to which you must attend," Charlotte said to Constantine, "your mother and sister may return home in our coach."

"Yes, my dear," Lady Kenilworth agreed. "Please go about your business."

As soon as the door closed behind him and his steps could be heard going down the corridor, Annis said, "Mama told me you have planned a surprise wedding. What a charming idea. Other than keep it a secret, you must tell me what I can do to help."

"I have enlisted my cousin Merton's help in keeping Constantine busy, but if you could also keep him occupied enough that he does not guess what is going on, that would be wonderful." Charlotte wrinkled her nose. "I sometimes have the feeling that he is suspicious."

"Hmm, let me give that some thought." The lady's lips quirked up. "I am much better at keeping my mother engaged. All I need do is mention shopping. However, I am positive I can think of something."

Charlotte hoped so. Although she loved spending time with her betrothed, she had a wedding to plan and very little time in which to do it.

Chapter Thirty-Five

The next morning, Constantine once more joined Charlotte and her family for breakfast. They had discussed the need for her to meet with his housekeeper, but, unbeknownst to her betrothed, the meeting would have to wait until after their wedding.

"I wish I could accompany you." He glanced at the clock and frowned. "But Merton sent me a note asking me to give him advice on a horse he had heard was coming up for sale at Tattersalls. Unless you wish to put this off, I will not have time to do both."

She sent up a prayer of thanks for helpful cousins. "Not at all. You will have much more fun looking at horses. You might even see if you can find a matched pair for me. Matt bought Louisa and me a pair, but I assume he will wish to keep them."

Constantine's countenance cleared. "That is an excellent idea."

Shortly after they finished eating, Charlotte and Grace were off to the Bond Street Bazaar to finish shopping for stockings and other necessities.

Charlotte returned home in time for tea and found Louisa had arrived with Rothwell in tow.

She pulled Charlotte aside, suppressed excitement infusing her tone. "The letter I received was that the wedding was a surprise, and that I could not tell Gideon."

"The fact of the wedding is not a surprise, just the date," Charlotte explained. "Other than Matt and Charlie, I was concerned that the gentlemen would let the secret out. The children do not know either. Merton is being a dear, keeping Constantine occupied."

"Charlotte, do give over," Louisa whispered. "What has happened? A month ago, you did not even know him."

"I shall tell you everything, but not here." She glanced around the room. "Meet me in the Young Ladies' Parlor before dinner."

Louisa looked as if she wanted to roll her eyes. "Very well, but I want all the details."

"And you shall have them. At the moment, I need to speak with Grace."

Con had a better time at Tattersalls than he had thought he would. He and Merton had ridden together in Con's carriage. There were other men present he had known at school and had not kept up with. The Earl of Huntley and Viscount Wively greeted Con. Marcus Evesham was out of town as his wife was due to give birth shortly. Rutherford was present as well, but getting ready to leave for the country. Their discussion of horses was intermixed with politics and family issues. Huntley and Wively still eschewed marriage, but had not cut themselves out of Polite Society as Con had.

What was I thinking, to ignore my friends for the company of other men not nearly as worthy or interesting?

Where the hell had that thought come from? Or perhaps it was the truth. Worthington had warned him about the low

company Con had been keeping. And now that he considered
it, he had never gone out of his way to make plans with those
gentlemen. He would not have, for example, dined with them
at Brooks's.

"If you are looking for a pair for Lady Charlotte's carriage," Wively said as he inspected a roan mare, "you'll
want grays."

"Grays?" Con had never even seen her high-perched
phaeton. Yet he was most likely the only gentleman who
had never seen her drive it.

Wively nodded. "Her carriage is green, and the grays
Worthington bought for it set the rig off to perfection."

Perhaps Con should try to buy the pair from his soon-
to-be brother-in-law. He meandered over to Merton, who
was looking at a matched pair of Cleveland Bays.

"What do you think of them?" Merton asked.

They had deep chests. A groom led the horses around,
showing off their high-stepping action. "Their points are
excellent."

"Of course they are." He looked at Con as if he were mad
to have questioned Merton's judgment. "I'm referring to
the color. My wife's carriage is red with gold trim."

Con would have laughed if his friend hadn't looked so
concerned. "I think they will do."

He strolled over to Huntley. "Is this what marriage does
to a man?"

"You will find out soon enough." Huntley shook his
head. "The sad thing is that Lady Merton doesn't care if her
horses are perfectly matched. But it's good to see him go
out of his way for her. I never thought I'd see it."

Con would approach Worthington when he joined them
for tea this afternoon. Not so much to see Charlotte cut a
dash, but because she had most likely grown attached to
the horses.

Once the purchase was made, they went to Brooks's fo
luncheon.

"Have you and Lady Charlotte set a date yet?" Huntley
asked.

"Not yet." That was another issue Con would discus
with Worthington. "I must visit Doctors' Commons for th
special license."

"After the End-of-Season breakfast, then." Wively cu
another piece of his beef.

End-of-Season breakfast? Why hadn't Con heard abou
the entertainment? He was receiving all the invitations now
"When is this to be?"

"The day after tomorrow, if I am not mistaken." Huntley
looked up at Con. "You must have received an invitation."

"My mother might have it." And he had not seen much
of her lately. She had been too busy with his sister.

"That accounts for it," Merton said. "You will have to
ask her."

Still, it was strange that Charlotte hadn't mentioned it
but it might have been planned while they had been running around the country. "I shall make a point to do so."

He'd ask her this afternoon at tea. Even though he had
not been invited, he was sure he would not be turned away
After all, the children liked him.

"Has anyone seen Ruffington around lately?" The query
came from a gentleman at the next table. "He owes me a
pony."

"No chance you'll get it," another man said. "I heard he
left the country."

That was one way of putting it, Con thought, pleased
their ruse had worked after all.

A few hours later he was admitted to Stanwood House
by the under-butler. "The family is having tea in the morning room, my lord."

"Thank you." He and Charlotte had only been apart for few hours, yet he was impatient to see her.

Yet when he entered the room, the only people present vere Worthington and a gentleman Con recognized as .othwell. Sounds of the children playing came from the arden. "Are the ladies outside?"

Rothwell raised his goblet in a salute. "In a manner of peaking. They are shopping." His discontent was clear rom his tone. "We had not been here for twenty minutes vhen my wife, your betrothed, and Grace deserted us."

Con wondered if Rothwell was concerned about money. They cannot accomplish too much in the amount of time hey have. It is only another two hours until dinner, and they vill wish to change."

"You obviously do not know how efficient they can be," Vorthington mumbled.

He poured Con a glass of claret.

"Come to think of it," Rothwell continued, taking a large lrink of his wine, "when I came to Town to be inducted nto the Lords, Louisa had renovated the kitchen and redec->rated several rooms by the time I returned." He frowned nto his wine. "I was only gone for two weeks. I still do not :now how she managed it."

Even if Con could not spend time with his beloved, he :ould find out about the party. "I understand there is to >e a large breakfast event in two days."

"Grace wanted to do something before we left for the :ountry. She had planned a ball for our sisters and Dotty, >ut weddings kept interfering." Worthington took a sip of vine. "We agreed that an evening entertainment would be :oo much work with your marriage coming up, and decided >n a breakfast." Worthington glanced out the window and vatched the children for a moment. "Your mother has 'our invitation."

Again, that made perfect sense. Still, Con had the feelin
that he was missing something. "I'll look forward to it. It
too bad we could not have combined my wedding breakfa
with your entertainment."

Worthington paused for a long moment before replyin;
"Yes, indeed."

"Speaking of my marriage, I would like to set a date a
well as purchase from you the pair of grays Charlotte :
using for her carriage."

"The horses can be arranged. As to the other, I am sti
waiting for my wife to give me a date for the wedding."

Just then the children ran into the morning room, fo
lowed at a slower pace by the Great Danes.

Worthington heaved a sigh. "I really must get Daisy t
the country before she drops that litter."

The children began to surround them, but he directe
them to the schoolroom. "I shall invite Kenilworth to din
with us."

As they left the parlor, the children chattered happily
debating who was to sit next to him.

Rothwell looked confused. "What about me?"

"I am their favorite brother-in-law." Con couldn't sto
himself from smirking.

"What the devil did you do?" the duke groused. "The
liked me perfectly well the last time I saw them."

Knowing he had the advantage, he puffed out his ches
"I allow them to call me by my first name."

"Those children do nothing for my consequence." Roth
well snorted. "I never feel less like a duke than I do aroun
this family."

Worthington raised his glass. "And that is exactly how
intend it to remain."

"You could allow them to call you 'Gid,'" Con said

Rothwell scowled and Con forced his lips together so he wouldn't laugh. "They would like that."

"I am sure they would. While they're at it, they can call you Connie."

"No, they can't," he retorted. "That's what we call my sister Cornelia." A circumstance he had always been thankful for. "Aside from that, Barton—you remember him—is called Connie. We'd confuse everyone."

"Don't feel too bad." Worthington poured more wine in Rothwell's glass. "Merton thought Dotty would never find a use for his title."

Con recalled him saying something to that effect in the inn. "I for one would rather be wanted for the person I am rather than my title." Even if he had never expected that would be the case.

Or expected to be rejected despite his title and wealth.

The next afternoon, Louisa, Dotty, and Charlotte were ensconced in the Young Ladies' Parlor discussing Charlotte's wedding.

"Are your wedding clothes finished?" Louisa asked. She had taken out a sheet of paper and had a pen poised over it.

"Every last item has been delivered." Charlotte had been amazed at that. Then again, Madam Lisette was no fool, and she knew she would have years of orders from them. "May—or rather, Walker—is packing as we speak."

"Where will you go on your honeymoon?" Louisa frowned. "Will you make a wedding trip?"

"We shall. Where depends on what happens on the Continent. If it is still unsafe, we shall go to the Lake District. I hear it is beautiful."

"The wedding breakfast is planned," Dotty pointed out. "You can add that to your list."

Louisa scribbled on the foolscap. "Special license?"

"Matt has it," Charlotte said.

"Wedding present?"

"I had an emerald tie pin made for him. It almost matches his eyes and my ring."

Louisa's lips formed a moue. "He will not have anything for you."

"It doesn't matter." Charlotte shrugged. "I am sure he will make up for it later."

"I for one am amazed you have been able to keep this a secret," Dotty said. "Dominic figured it out but promised not to tell anyone. I believe he thinks it is slightly roguish."

"Poor Constantine hasn't had much time to think about it." Charlotte was relieved her cousin had agreed to keep her betrothed busy. "With you and Louisa spending so much time with me, Rothwell and Merton are spending time with him."

"By this time tomorrow you will be married." Louisa blinked rapidly. "When I wed, I was worried that you were the last one left and would be lonely. I am so happy you have found a man to love."

Charlotte's eyes misted, but she was determined not to cry. It would set them all off. "As am I."

Louisa put her pocketbook in her reticule and rose. "We may as well use the hour or so we have left to finish your shopping." A knock came on the door and Louisa sat back down again. "I hope it's not our gentlemen. We have too much to do."

"We shall find out soon enough," Charlotte said. "Come."

"My lady." Royston handed her a card.

She did not recognize the name at all. "Did she say what she wanted?"

"No, my lady."

Shopping would have to wait. "Very well. Send her up."

Her friends glanced at her. "A lady I have never heard of wishes to see me."

"I hope it is not bad news," Louisa muttered.

"I am positive it's not." Dotty leaned over to see the card. "Royston would not have allowed her past the door if there was anything smoky about her."

Chapter Thirty-Six

A lady Charlotte judged to be in her mid-twenties was ushered into the parlor. She was dressed in a blue silk walking gown, and had light brown hair and blue-gray eyes that held a slightly concerned look.

"Lady Pierrepont," Royston intoned.

Charlotte still held the card Royston had given to her. She set it down and stepped forward to welcome her unexpected guest. "Good afternoon, I am Lady Charlotte Carpenter. This"—she motioned to Louisa—"is my sister, the Duchess of Rothwell, and my cousin, the Marchioness of Merton."

Lady Pierrepont curtseyed. "Your grace, my ladies."

Louisa and Dotty smiled politely and inclined their heads. "Please," Charlotte said, "join us." She motioned to a chair next to the small sofa she shared with Dotty. "The tea tray will be here shortly."

"Thank you." The woman focused on Charlotte. "I should like to get straight to the point, if I may. You met my mother, Lady Litchfield, in Richmond a week or so ago."

Dotty and Louisa straightened, their complete attention now focused on the lady. "Is this about Jemmy?"

"Yes." She opened her reticule and drew out a small book.

'Almost everyone in the Mooring family has birthmarks.
Most of us have two. As my sisters and brothers and I had
children, I made drawings of the marks." Lady Pierrepont
opened the book to a page marked with a blue ribbon and
handed it to Charlotte. "I must know if the boy—if Jemmy's
birthmarks look like these."

Dotty shook her head as if unable to believe what the
lady was saying. "But your mother was positive that Jemmy
could not be the child she thought he was."

"Yes, well"—Lady Pierrepont pressed her lips together
and sighed—"Mama is always very certain. Though I seriously doubt if she has seen any of us or her grandchildren
without their clothing, not to mention being able to keep
all the markings straight. There are eight of us, and we all
have at least one child." Charlotte looked at the drawing
and handed the book to Dotty. "Please, if you could take
that and compare the marks, I would greatly appreciate it.
I spoke to my eldest brother and we agreed that we must
know if he is a Mooring."

Charlotte strode to the bell pull and tugged twice. "My
maid should be here in a moment. She will be able to tell
you if they are the same. Although"—looking over her
friend's shoulder she studied the drawing again—"they
appear to match the description my maid gave of them."

Walker arrived, followed by a footman carrying the tea
tray. After he placed the tray down on the low table between
the two sofas, she set out the cups and straightened. "Yes,
my lady?"

"Do these look like Jemmy's birthmarks?"

Charlotte held her breath and it seemed as if the rest of
them did as well until Walker nodded. "They do, almost
exactly."

Charlotte's breath rushed out of her. "Oh, thank the Lord."

"You could not have received a better wedding present."

Dotty had tears in her eyes, and Louisa hugged them both
"I'll pour while you talk."

"No, I do not believe I could have." Charlotte took ou
her handkerchief and dabbed the corners of her eyes. "Lad
Pierrepont, would you like to meet him?"

"Thank you. I would love to meet him," she said an
promptly broke into tears. Louisa handed the lady he
handkerchief. "Thank you, Your Grace. I do not know wha
came over me. We had almost given up hope of ever find
ing James."

"Will your mother accept him?" Charlotte asked. Lad
Litchfield had been so convinced when she had rejected th
child.

"Yes, she will. If you must know, I abused her roundl
for not bringing me with her." Lady Pierrepont blew he
nose. "But my youngest sister had just given birth, and m
mother would not wait." She gave a watery chuckle. "Thi
will teach her." The lady wiped her eyes. "When will we b
able to take him home?"

"Let us take one step at a time, shall we?" Charlotte said
Lady Pierrepont's face fell.

Charlotte did not wish to hurt the woman, but Jemmy
must feel comfortable about his new family. "My wedding
is in the morning, and I know he will wish to be presen
for that."

"Please do not mention the wedding to anyone," Louisa
said. "It is somewhat of a surprise."

"You have my word," Lady Pierrepont said. "All I am
interested in is the child."

"I'll go fetch him, shall I?" Walker asked.

"Yes, if you would." Charlotte took the cup of tea her
sister handed her. "We will have a better idea after you've

poken to him. Perhaps you can tell him about his parents nd the rest of your family."

"Yes, of course." The woman accepted a cup and plate f biscuits from Louisa.

"You should know," Dotty said, "Charlotte found him in vhat is called a 'kid ken,' a place where young children are rained to be thieves."

The woman's hand went to her throat just like her nother's had. "How long ago?"

"Only about three months." Charlotte's throat tightened nd she sipped her tea. "He has been taking lessons with ny brothers and sisters, and learning quickly." She sought o reassure Jemmy's aunt. It would not do for the family to eject him. "He has one of the best hearts I've seen in a erson."

"Thank-thank"—Lady Pierrepont's voice broke as she lotted her eyes with the linen—"thank you for rescuing im. I cannot imagine how horrible that must have been."

A knock came on the door, and Walker entered, holding Jemmy's hand. He was chattering and grinning. Mary, Theo, and Phillip trailed in behind them.

"He is the image of my brother." Lady Pierrepont gasped. "Jemmy, will you come here, please?"

He glanced at Walker, who nodded.

He moved slowly to her as if he was a little afraid. Once he reached her, he made his bow. "Good afternoon."

"Who is she?" Theo asked in a loud whisper.

Louisa pulled Theo to the sofa and whispered something Charlotte couldn't hear.

Lady Pierrepont started to reach out to Jemmy but must have thought better of it and placed her hands in her lap. "I am Amelia Pierrepont, your aunt. I believe Jemmy is short for James. You would have been about four when you went missing. Do you remember anything about your parents at all?"

He shook his head. "No, ma'am."

She took out a locket and opened it. "This gentleman and lady are your parents. They died two years ago. You look just like your father did at your age."

Jemmy took the locket and sat on the floor, staring at it. Finally he looked up at his aunt. "Are you going to take me away?"

"If you will let me," she said gently. "You have a very large family who have been looking for you for a very long time." She took a miniature out of her reticule. "This was made when your father was about six years old."

Mary, Theo, and Phillip crowded around him, looking from Jemmy to the portrait and back again.

"He does look like you," Mary commented.

"If you want him to live with you," Theo said, "you have to love him as much as we do."

"And promise to be nice to him," Phillip added.

Lady Pierrepont crossed her heart. "I am true blue and will never stain. I promise we will all love him and no one will ever harm him."

Mary placed her hand on Jemmy's shoulder. "You could try it for a little while, I suppose."

"We'll come get you if you don't like it." Theo glanced over her shoulder at Louisa. "Isn't that right?"

"Yes, sweetie, it is."

The door opened, and Constantine, Merton, and Rothwell strode into the parlor, making the room seem much smaller than before.

Constantine put his arm around Charlotte, then glanced at Lady Pierrepont. "What is this I hear about Jemmy's family finding him?"

"I'll tell you how it came about later, but yes," she whispered. "Lady Pierrepont is Lady Litchfield's daughter, and Jemmy's aunt. His family name is Mooring. She would like to take him to meet his aunts, uncles, and cousins."

Constantine studied Jemmy for a few moments. "You know, I always thought there was something familiar about him. I went to school with a Lord James Mooring."

"He is apparently Jemmy's father."

Mary tugged on Con's jacket. "They want to take him to meet his family."

Recalling her manners, Charlotte said, "My lady, allow me to introduce you to my betrothed, the Marquis of Kenilworth. The gentleman next to her grace is my brother, the Duke of Rothwell, and the other gentleman is my cousin, the Marquis of Merton."

Jemmy's aunt curtseyed as the gentlemen bowed.

"I know you ladies are busy," Constantine said. "But we are at loose ends for the moment. Why don't we accompany Lady Pierrepont and Jemmy to meet his family?" Merton and Rothwell inclined their heads. "If you do not mind, of course."

Charlotte would have liked to be present when the meeting took place, but Constantine was right. It should be done sooner rather than later, and tomorrow was their wedding, even if he did not know about that part. And, after all, she could trust him to ensure Jemmy wasn't forced to do anything he didn't like.

She looked at Dotty and Louisa. Both of them gave almost imperceptible nods. "That is an excellent idea."

"Lady Pierrepont?" Constantine asked.

"I have no objection to anything that will make the meeting easier." The lady set her cup down and rose.

"In that case." He picked Jemmy up from the floor. "Let's be off."

"May we go as well?" Phillip asked.

For a moment, Constantine seemed at a loss for words, then said, "If Grace and Worthington agree, you may accompany us. I'm sure Jemmy will feel better having you there."

Con opened the door for Lady Pierrepont, and the rest of them followed behind.

"Well," Louisa said once the door shut behind them, "Kenilworth has certainly made himself part of the family."

"He has, rather." Charlotte smiled to herself, thinking of their less than auspicious beginning. "All of our husbands, or, in my case, soon-to-be husband, have joined our family." She slid a wicked look at Dotty. "Even Merton."

"Stop it. Even Louisa must admit that he has changed a great deal since he first came to Town," Dotty retorted.

"Indeed, I do admit it." Louisa stepped over to the bell pull and tugged it. A moment later Hal entered the room and addressed Charlotte. "My lady?"

"Champagne, if you please," Louisa said.

He bowed. "Right away, Your Grace."

"I think a celebration is called for." She glanced around the room, as if memorizing it. "To think, this will be the last time we shall be able to call this parlor ours."

"Think of all the discussions we've had here," Charlotte mused. "I suppose it will now be Augusta's."

"Until she weds," Dotty agreed. "Let's not become maudlin. We have a great deal for which to be thankful. I, for one, am thrilled that our husbands, or"—she grinned at Charlotte—"soon-to-be husbands, get on so well."

"Let us agree to visit each other frequently," Louisa added. "I shall make a list." She ducked as Charlotte threw pillow at her, and laughed. "Someone has to keep track of plans."

The door opened. Hal entered with two bottles and four glasses, opened one bottle and began to pour. "Miss Turley is on her way up."

"Another person who has become a good friend, despite our first impressions," Charlotte said.

The evening Dotty and Merton became engaged, they thought Elizabeth had attempted to trap him into marrying her. Yet, since then they had become very close.

"Elizabeth," Charlotte greeted the other lady, bussing her on the cheek. "How are you?"

"I'm doing well. I would ask you, but you look as if you are walking on clouds."

"That is one way to put it." She really had never been happier.

Once her sister and friend greeted their guest, they passed around the glasses of wine and arranged themselves on the sofas.

Elizabeth's eyes sparkled as she glanced at Louisa, Dotty, and Charlotte. "I did wonder if your original plan to wait until summer to marry would last."

Heat bloomed in Charlotte's cheeks. "I discovered I was as unable to wait as the rest of my family." Wanting to change the subject, she asked, "Do you have any prospects? There are still a few weeks left in the Season."

"I have had my eye on one gentleman," Elizabeth said cautiously. "As you are no longer on the market, he is looking in my direction."

"Harrington?" Charlotte had thought from what Elizabeth said a few weeks ago that she might be interested in the gentleman. "You must put him through his paces before you agree to wed him. He is entirely too sure of himself."

"I quite agree. At least, he used to be. He had a bit of

a shock when he realized you were going to marry an other gentleman."

"I hope you're right." As far as Charlotte was concerned Harrington needed to be taken down a notch or two.

Then again, if he had remained in Town, she never would have met Constantine and would not be as blissfully happy as she was now.

Elizabeth remained another fifteen minutes, before rising "I'll see you tomorrow at your breakfast. I just wanted to stop by and wish you happy." She hugged Charlotte. "I could not be more pleased for you."

And that was exactly how Charlotte felt. Everything was perfect.

Chapter Thirty-Seven

Charlotte, Louisa, and Dotty were contemplating a fresh bottle of champagne when Merton, Rothwell, and Constantine strode into the parlor. Con and Rothwell perched on the sofa arms next to Charlotte and Louisa. Merton sat on the sofa next to Dotty.

A moment later, Hal entered carrying more champagne and glasses. He poured the remainder of the first bottle into the ladies' goblets, opened the new bottle, and filled the glasses he'd just brought.

"What are we celebrating?" Con asked.

"Our family and friendship."

Con raised Charlotte's hand and kissed the palm. He wanted to take her into his arms, but even in this company, he would not.

"How did the meeting between Jemmy and his family go?" Charlotte asked.

"Quite well." Con took a sip of wine. "He met his grandmother, Lady Litchfield, who was more than a little distraught that she had misidentified his birthmarks. He has a number of cousins all within a few years of him." He set his glass down, twining his fingers with hers. "Naturally, Theo, Mary, and Phillip were extremely protective at first. Yet,

even they agreed that his family seemed to care a great dea
about Jemmy."

"Where is he now?"

"He agreed to remain for dinner," Con said. "Afte
which, he'll return here until after our wedding. Which
hope will not be much longer."

"Then what is the plan?" Charlotte tightened her finger
around Con's.

"As you know, Worthington is taking the family t
Stanwood as soon as he can after our wedding." If he kep
repeating that they were to marry, he might get a date. "H
would have done it sooner, but I understand your sister tol
him he could make the arrangements if he thought movin
the family was that easy." Thinking of the boy, Con sobere
again. "Jemmy will go to the Moorings' after our weddin
breakfast, with the knowledge that your family is not far i
he needs them."

"So all's well that ends well?" Charlotte asked.

"It appears so." He kissed her lightly on her head. "H
will miss all of you, but he does seem happy. We would no
have left him there otherwise. Once he goes to live wit
them, he has orders to write every week."

Tears of joy pricked her eyes. "I'm so, so glad he foun
his family."

"As am I, my love. As am I." He resolved to make Worthington agree to a date. The last Con had been told, his futur
brother-in-law had to speak to someone at St. George's.

"I propose a toast before all the ladies begin to cry,'
Rothwell said, pouring more champagne into everyone's
glasses. "To new families and to my newest brother."

"And," Merton said, standing, "to our families always
remaining close."

They raised their glasses. "Hear, hear."

"We have something else to celebrate." Louisa blushed

osily. "Rothwell and I are expecting an interesting event at
the end of February."

"Oh, Louisa, that's wonderful!" Charlotte leaned over
and hugged her sister.

Dotty hurried over and embraced Louisa as well. The
men slapped Rothwell on the back, congratulating him.

Con drew his arm around Charlotte, and whispered,
"We'll be next."

Even now she could be carrying his child. What he did
not understand was why the devil her brother would not
make his wife set the damn date.

Con woke early the next morning as had become his
habit recently. Last evening the Worthington table had been
expanded to accommodate the Mertons and Rothwells.

Most of the talk had centered around Jemmy and the up-
coming party to which all the children were going to be
allowed to attend. There was so much energy infusing the
room, he thought the children would resist going to bed. Yet
he was wrong. The mere threat of being deprived of the
treat made them docile.

Con had been able to sneak a few moments alone with
Charlotte, but since they all had to be up early, their party
broke up shortly after nine. Still, the evening had been successful. Worthington had agreed to tell Con this morning
when he could marry.

A noise came from his dressing room, and Cunningham
came out carrying his black silk breeches.

"I thought I would wear pantaloons this morning," Con
said.

"Not to the breakfast, my lord." His valet appeared
shocked.

"No, but until then. I still have several hours to go."

"You received a message from Lord Worthington that h
wishes you to attend him at eight-thirty."

Perhaps this was it. Con would find out when he wa
marrying Charlotte and they could announce it at the break
fast. "What time is it now?"

"Just on seven, my lord. Your bath is ready."

He was tying his cravat when Cunningham answered a
knock at the door. He came back carrying a small velve
bag. "This is for you, my lord."

"In just a minute." Con lowered his chin, making sur
the creases in his neckcloth were perfect. "Now you may
give it to me."

His valet pulled out a folded piece of paper and a tie pin
Con opened the paper.

For my beloved,
  I shall see you soon.
              With all my love,
              Charlotte

"It reminds me of the ring you gave her ladyship."

A flawless emerald winked at him from a bed of small
pearls. "It does at that. I shall have to visit Rundell and
Bridge after the breakfast today."

Perhaps he would take Charlotte and they could find a
piece together.

"Your sister said she would meet you in the breakfast
room." His valet helped him with his jacket. "There you
are, my lord."

A pot of tea was being set on the table when he entered
the breakfast room. Annis was already there, dressed for the
day instead of in her customary morning gown.

"Where are you going?" Con asked, taking a piece of

toast and placing it on his plate. Slices of ham and a baked egg followed.

"I'm going visiting." She set down her cup. "Mama said to give you this. It is for Charlotte." His sister handed him a large velvet pouch. "It is to go with the ring she chose."

He took out a necklace. Opals were interspersed with emeralds set into the same figured gold pattern as her ring. "She will love it. She sent me this tie pin this morning. I think I shall send this over to her. She may wear it at the breakfast."

Annis raised her cup, hiding her expression. "That is a lovely idea."

Con ate quickly, then went to his study. He pulled out a piece of pressed paper and tried to think of something romantic to write, but he was no poet.

My darling Charlotte,
   This is for you with all my love.
   I shall see you soon.
                    C.

"Webster, have this delivered to Lady Charlotte."

His butler bowed and Con thought he saw the man's lips twitch. His eyes must be playing tricks on him. Just the idea was shocking.

Charlotte was dressed in a silk gown of Pomona green. Her maid was putting pearl-tipped pins in her hair when the door opened and Mary and Theo ran in.

"Grace just told us you are getting married this morning and that is what the party is for." The words rushed out of Mary's mouth before Theo could get a word in edgewise. "Why didn't you tell us?"

Taking their hands, Charlotte drew the little girls to her. "Because it is a surprise for Constantine. He does not know he is being wed this morning."

"Does Merton know?" Theo asked a bit belligerently.

"He does, but only because he had to keep Constantine busy." Charlotte hoped Theo would understand. "But Rothwell, Cousin Jane, Cousin Hector, and almost everyone else do not know. Dotty and Louisa had to be told because I needed their help. And Lady Kendrick and her mother know for the same reason."

"Then I don't feel bad." Mary hugged Charlotte carefully.

"I don't either." Theo kissed Charlotte on the cheek. "You look beautiful, but we don't have anything for you."

"Let's not be so hasty." Grace strolled into the bedchamber holding a posy of pink roses with blue nigella blooms. "What do you think of this?"

Eyes shining, the girls nodded. "That's the best posy we've ever given anyone."

"We have accomplished something blue." Grace shot Charlotte a grin. "I am afraid Madeline and the twins are slightly put out as well."

As if they had been summoned, the three girls entered the room. They each held a handkerchief embroidered in white work. "You would have had more," Alice said, "if we had been told."

"These are beautiful. Please forgive me, but I truly want to surprise Constantine."

"Almost no one knew," Theo said. "Only Dotty, Louisa, Grace, Merton, and Matt."

"And Constantine's mama and sister, because Charlotte needed them to keep the secret," Mary added.

"We forgive you," the older girls said as one.

"My lady." Walker turned from the door. "This came for you."

Charlotte put the bag on her dressing table and took out the most beautiful necklace she had ever seen. Setting it down on her dressing table, she read the note. "It's from Constantine. Do you think he knows?"

"Not at all," Grace said. "Annis remembered a necklace went with the ring, and she gave it to him this morning."

"Are we late?" Dotty strolled into the room. "I see you have new handkerchiefs, blue flowers, and an old necklace. You may borrow my butterfly pin."

"I have earbobs for you." Louisa spilled out a pair of earrings of emeralds and opals into her hand.

"Thank you both." Fighting the tears that threatened to fill her eyes, Charlotte hugged her friends. "These are perfect."

"Don't forget me." Augusta rushed into the bedchamber and handed Charlotte an opal bracelet. "Grace said I could buy one with emeralds, but I thought you might want something you could wear more often."

"That is very thoughtful." Charlotte kissed her sister on the cheek. "I shall wear it often."

"Char." Charlie tapped on the open door. "It's time to go. Matt has Kenilworth in his study so we can leave from the front."

"Are we going to walk this time?" Mary asked.

"No, sweetheart," Grace said. "We don't want Constantine to see you. He will arrive at the church last."

"So now everyone knows but him?" Theo asked.

Charlotte nodded. "Yes."

When they arrived at the church, Mr. Peterson, the young clergyman who had performed all the Worthington marriage services, had a grin on his face.

He greeted Charlotte. "My lady, I have never heard of the bride planning a surprise wedding, but I understand from your brother the gentleman is happy to be marrying you."

"He has been trying for the past several days to convince my brother to agree to a date."

"Well then." Mr. Peterson chuckled. "As Lord Worthington is bringing the groom, who will give away the bride?"

"I shall." Charlie stepped up next to her.

"My brother, the Earl of Stanwood."

Mr. Peterson glanced around the church. "Will your other brothers attend?"

"Yes," Louisa, standing next to Dotty, said. "They are coming with our husbands."

Annis slipped into a pew with her mother and gave a little wave.

The girls had just settled down when Walter, Phillip, Jemmy, Rothwell, and Merton arrived.

The boys had wide smiles on their faces. "We had to tell the coachmen to bring us," Walter said.

"I have never heard of a surprise wedding." Rothwell strolled up to Louisa. "And you knew all about it."

Dotty tucked her hand in the crook of Merton's arm. "Thank you for helping to keep the secret."

"Anything for my family." He bent and kissed her cheek.

"They are coming," Hal called from the door at the side of the church.

The children settled down. Dotty and Louisa stood next to Charlotte with Charlie, and Merton and Rothwell stood on the other side where Constantine would be.

Charlotte caught Constantine's eye as he strode in with her brother. "Isn't he handsome?"

"Are your insides fluttering as if birds had taken up residence?" Dotty asked.

"I had trouble breathing. It was as if my breath had been taken away," Louisa added.

"All that and more." Charlotte's smile grew as Constantine's grin broadened.

When he finally reached her, he took her hands. "You had me completely flummoxed. But now that I think about it, I can see the hints our families accidentally dropped."

"You are happy?" She did not even know why she asked. His eyes told her everything she needed to know.

"Can you doubt it?"

"No, never." She glanced at the clergyman. "We are ready to begin."

Charlotte had heard the words so often of late; still, she was almost surprised to hear herself repeating them. She wanted to laugh out loud when Constantine's gaze heated as he promised to worship her body.

When the vicar pronounced them man and wife, he shocked everyone by kissing her at the altar. "Finally."

"Yes," she whispered. "Finally."

Constantine turned to leave and she tugged them to the side. "We have to sign the register."

"I forgot it as well," Rothwell said.

"Something about wanting to be alone with one's bride," Merton added.

"Now that that's done," Constantine said, "we have an End-of-Season wedding breakfast to attend. Did you plan our wedding trip as well?"

Charlotte widened her eyes. "Of course not. That would have been much too forward, my lord."

He chuckled. "What do you think of the Lake District? I hear it is lovely this time of year."

"What a wonderful idea." She shot a suppressive look at Dotty, who had gone into whoops.

"I am glad you agree. I might even have a lovely little house near Lake Windermere. With very few servants."

Charlotte slid him a sultry smile. "Even better."

Epilogue

Eight months later

Charlotte ambled into Con's newly decorated study and lowered herself into one of the two leather-covered chairs in front of his desk. How she remained so graceful, as heavy with their child as she was, he had no idea.

"This came for you." She held out a letter. "It's from France."

The only one he knew in France was Aimée, and he had certainly never expected to hear from her. "Open it."

After neatly popping off the seal, Charlotte spread the paper on his desk. And read, "*Mon ami*." She looked up at him. "Did she always call you her friend?"

"Yes." Now that he considered it, that was a rather strange form of address. Many mistresses referred to their protectors more intimately. "That or Kenilworth."

"Never Constantine or Con?" Charlotte had a curious expression on her face, and he wondered if he would do well to tread carefully.

"No. She was never that informal. I always thought it was something to do with her being French, but after that last conversation with her, I believe it was her way of keeping a distance."

His wife nodded as if she understood, and went back to the missive. "'You may end the account you set up for me. I have married and have no further need of your funds. Trust me when I tell you I have never been happier. I wish for you the same. Aimée.'"

"I'm glad," he said as Charlotte refolded the paper. "She deserved to find happiness."

"Yes, she and so many others." She slid the note across the desk to him. "Are you surprised that she will no longer accept your largess?"

Con put his hand over hers, stopping the motion. "No. She would still see it as payment for what she did in her former life. It would not shock me if she somehow found a way to return all the money." He glanced down at their hands, and up at his wife. "This belongs in the fire."

Incinerated. Reduced to ashes, as was Aimée's past life. Con would not keep anything that could connect her to that past.

Charlotte gazed at him for a long moment, her head tilted to one side. Then she gave an almost imperceptible nod, took the letter to the fireplace, and tossed it in. A few moments later she returned to the chair. "What shall you do with the money if she returns it?"

"Donate it to your charity. It should continue to help others in need." He reveled in the bright smile she gave him. It had never occurred to him that he could be this happy.

Suddenly, Charlotte's expression changed to a grimace and her hand went to her stomach. "They are getting closer together and stronger."

"*What!*" He jumped up, knocking his heavy leather chair over, and ran around to her. "You're in labor?" It was too early. She should not give birth for a few weeks. He lifted her out of the chair. "You should be in bed." Reaching out, he yanked the bell pull, and the door opened. His butler bowed. "Call the midwife and the doctor."

"The midwife has been called, my lord. She arrived several minutes ago."

Con put his arm around Charlotte, supporting her as he walked slowly toward the corridor. "What about the doctor?"

"Attending another birth, my lord." Webster frowned. "He sent a message saying he'd be here as soon as he could."

"Constantine," Charlotte said, laughing. "Cease. I'm fine, and I refuse to be cooped up in my bedchamber until these children come."

His mind went blank for a second. "Children?"

"Yes." She grinned at him. "Mrs. Connor thinks she felt two babies the last time she examined me." Charlotte patted his cheek. "They typically come a little early, but I'll be fine. Both the little ones and I are healthy and have stayed active."

"I am sure you are supposed to be in bed." He tried to infuse his tone with authority, but was truly at a loss. He had never felt so helpless in his life.

"Even though I was a child for the births of some of my brothers and sisters, I watched my mother go through them. She never went to her chamber until she was sure her time was near."

His butler hovered, and he didn't know how to respond. "But-but—"

"The worst that can happen is the babies are born in some other room than my bedchamber. If you wish to be helpful, stroll with me."

"If you're sure." Her poor husband sounded like a warrior facing a battle without a sword.

"I am quite sure." She began to walk slowly toward the door.

Grace had written Charlotte shortly after giving birth to her son, Gideon, Viscount Vivers, telling her what to expect. She had also received a letter from Dotty a month later after Dotty had given birth to her daughter, little Lady Vivienne, and one from Louisa after the birth of Matthew, Marquis of Langton. So, despite having never given birth before, Charlotte felt amazingly confident and knowledgeable.

Her sister's missive had been the most important. Grace had attended their mother when the twins and the younger children were born, and had also been the recipient of their mother's story of when Mama had carried Grace. The advice to walk and take light nourishment for as long as possible was exactly what Charlotte intended to do. It was fortunate that the midwife agreed. The doctor, however, was another matter entirely, and a problem she hoped not to have to deal with. She really wished their butler had not taken it upon himself to summon the man.

After an hour of Charlotte ambling and eating, Constantine and the rest of the household quickly realized what she was doing. Footmen with worried expressions hovered nearby with trays of light delicacies from Cook. Nourishing broths were added to small pieces of toast topped with chicken, cheeses, and fruits from their succession houses.

Collette hovered around Charlotte, staying close to her skirts but never getting in the way.

Every now and then, Mrs. Connor would come up to ask questions, place experienced hands on Charlotte's stomach, and nod. After the first such examination, Constantine began looking at his watch each time she cried out with a contraction.

After five hours, the midwife pronounced, "I believe it's about time."

Part of the way up the stairs, Charlotte felt an urge to push. "Oh, God. Hurry. I think the babies are coming."

Constantine swung her up in his arms, and even as heavy as she was, carried her as if she weighed no more than the cat.

May was in the bedchamber, ready to remove Charlotte's clothing when Constantine started to leave.

"Do not go." She reached out and touched his arm. "I want you to be here. My father stayed with my mother."

The strong planes of his face tightened, but he inclined his head. "If you wish."

Maids brought in hot water, linens, and ice chips piled in a silver bowl.

Mrs. Connor pulled the birthing chair from the corner of the room. In the meantime, May quickly stripped Charlotte to her chemise.

"My lord," the midwife said, "please help her ladyship into the chair."

Constantine cocked Charlotte a look. "Grace sent it," Charlotte explained.

She had barely been lowered onto the chair when the urge to push came again.

"Now then, my lady. Let's see how much progress you've made." Getting on her knees, the midwife lifted the hem of her shift. "Not long now. Once or twice more."

"What in the name of heaven?" The Dowager Lady Kenilworth strode into the chamber. "Charlotte, get in bed. Kenilworth, leave this room immediately, where is the—"

"Mother, be quiet. Or leave." Constantine's tone was more commanding than she had ever heard it.

Eyes wide, the Dowager Marchioness of Kenilworth snapped her mouth shut.

Constantine winced as Charlotte squeezed his hand again and pushed. She felt the first baby slide out of her body. One of the older maids rushed forward with a wet cloth.

"A fine boy, my lady," Mrs. Connor announced. "Let's see what else you've got."

Seconds later the second child appeared. "A girl. Now once more and we'll get you cleaned up."

In what seemed to be a very short period of time, Charlotte had been washed, dressed in her nightgown, and put in bed, where she nursed the babies.

Constantine kissed her softly on her forehead and took one of the infants from her. "I never want to go through that again."

"It will be easier the next time." She was exhausted, but had never been more content. "At least we'll be able to tell them apart. We had to mark the bottom of Alice's and Eleanor's feet."

"And you have an heir, Constantine," his mother said. The first time she had spoken since he'd told her to be quiet. "But I do not understand. What is that chair?"

"A birthing chair, my lady," the midwife replied. "Doctors don't hold with them, but they make birthing a babe much easier."

"My sister sent it to me," Charlotte added. "She had it made for me. The one my mother used is at Worthington Place."

"What happened to the doctor?" her mother-in-law asked, apparently still confused.

"Unable to be here, fortunately." As far as she was concerned, he need never arrive. She had a feeling he would cause problems. He had also not agreed with the midwife that Charlotte would have twins. "I'm sure he would have argued with me and Mrs. Connor."

"Well, you certainly had a much easier time than I did." Lady Kenilworth reached for the baby Charlotte was holding. "Have you hired a wet-nurse yet?"

"No. The one the doctor sent smelled of ale, and we decided not to use her." Constantine kissed the baby and cuddled her. "If you insist on going through this again, we shall ensure he is not invited. Especially if he is going to make this process more difficult for you."

Charlotte gazed up at Constantine. His support and his willingness to always listen to her continued to amaze her. "I am the luckiest woman in the world, and I love you."

"And I am the luckiest man. I love you."

Mrs. Connor curtseyed. "No relations for two months."

Constantine swore under his breath, and Charlotte couldn't suppress her giggle. "Yes, Mrs. Connor. Thank you for your help."

Author's Note

Once again, I touched on the underbelly of Regency England. Kid kens were real—think of *Oliver Twist*—and often the children had been abandoned or orphaned. The kens took in children at very young ages. The bosses of the kens fed, clothed, and housed their charges as the children were taught to pick pockets, break into houses, and to commit numerous other crimes. Why use children? They were able to climb into small spaces, between bars, down chimneys, and through cellar windows. They were also less likely to be hanged or transported than an adult.

Abduction was common as well. Kidnappers ranged from fortune hunters to those wanting ransom. The results of abductions were often tragic. In the case of young ladies, they were made to marry their abductor or rapist. In fact, in the United States until the 1970s, a rapist could have the criminal charges dropped if he married his victim, and I'm not referring to statutory rape. You can imagine how much pressure would have been placed on a Regency lady who had spent time alone with an abductor. Remaining single would ruin her reputation.

As strange as it may seem, there was no police force in England at the time. Bow Street runners were confined to one section of London. Various magistrates were in charge of discrete areas of cities and counties. They frequently did not wish to be bothered, and would move a crime to another jurisdiction if they could. Victims of crimes were responsible for prosecuting the transgressions against them, which meant paying for the solicitor and barrister. Peers and peeresses charged with offenses could only be tried in the House of Lords. Justice for the middling classes and the poor was swift and brutal. Stealing almost anything was a hanging offense. If one was lucky, one was transported to what was to become Australia. However, if a lady was abducted, the case would never go to trial. It would have ruined her reputation. Those matters were always handled privately. Punishment of the offender was either death, forced transportation, or the agreement of the miscreant to leave the country permanently. You may have noticed that Miss Cloverly was not subject to the same rules or concerns as Lady Charlotte. That is because, right or wrong, they were treated differently than a gently bred lady.

You will also have noted that, most of the time, I refer to Matt as Charlotte's brother, Louisa as her sister and so on. Under the law at the time, once Matt married Grace (*Three Weeks to Wed*) he became her brother. In fact, it was illegal for a man to marry his sister-in-law. Because of that, and the close relationship all the children have with each other (not to mention how boring it is to constantly write brother or sister-in-law all the time), I refer to them as sisters and brothers. In case you're wondering, the word "siblings" did not exist in the context of brothers and sisters until 1903.

Before I end, I'd like to touch on Chartreux cats. They are an old French breed known for their blue fur and yellow eyes. They were hunted for their fur and food (they have an extremely diverse diet) during the Middle Ages. I was fortunate to live with one for many years and can attest to their love of travel. Raphaella was the only cat we've ever had who would happily climb in her carrier rather than be left at home.

I pride myself on getting my facts correct, but I'm only human, and there will probably be some mistakes.

If you ever have any questions, please contact me on my website, www.ellaquinnauthor.com. I am always happy to answer questions, and I love hearing from my readers.

Now, I'm on to the next book!

Ella